MOVING ON UP

Sue Welfare is the author of *A Few Little Lies*, *Just Desserts*, *Off the Record* and several erotic novels. Born and raised and still living on the edge of the Fens, she is perfectly placed to write about the vagaries of life in East Anglia. She was runner-up in the *Mail on Sunday* novel competition in 1995, and winner of the Wyrd Short Story prize in the same year. Her comedy 'Write Back Home' was part of the 1999 Channel 4 Sitcom Festival. *Moving On Up* is her fourth mainstream novel.

D0809853

SUE WELFARE

Moving On Up

HarperCollins*Publishers*

This novel is entirely a work of fiction. The names, characters and incidents portrayed in it are the work of the author's imagination. Any resemblance to actual persons, living or dead, events or localities is entirely coincidental.

HarperCollins*Publishers*
77–85 Fulham Palace Road,
Hammersmith, London W6 8JB

www.fireandwater.com

A Paperback Original 2000
5 7 9 8 6 4

A catalogue record for this book
is available from the British Library

ISBN 0 00 651350 6

Set in Sabon by
Rowland Phototypesetting Ltd,
Bury St Edmunds, Suffolk

Printed and bound in Great Britain by
Clays Ltd, St Ives plc

To Tracy, Claire, Suey Newey, Heather, Sarah, Moira, Sam, Mary, Sylvie, Chuck & Kate, little Sam & Joe, James & Ben – all magical and very special people who I am proud to call friends

'I've learned that it takes years to build up trust, and only suspicion, not proof, to destroy it.'

'Things I have learned' attrib: G.F. Dec 1999

Chapter 1

'Sarah? Have you seen the thing with a handle?'

Sarah Colebrook was sitting in the bathroom with the door locked.

'The thing? What thing?'

'Triangular. Like a stop sign, you know what I mean. It's sharp, for smoothing plaster with.'

'You opened the lager bottles with it when we had the barbecue?' she called back through the door.

'That's the one. Have you seen it anywhere on your travels?'

'Can't this wait until I come out, Chris?'

'No, the polyfilla's setting even as we speak. I have to have the thing with the handle. Have you got any idea where it is?'

Sarah groaned. 'You could try the sand-pit? Or Charlie's toy box?'

Outside the bathroom door her husband's voice was joined by a high pitched wailing.

'Mummmeeeeee.'

'What do you want, Charlie?' Sarah asked calmly.

'I need a wee.' Sarah glanced up at the handle dangling from the toilet cistern; pulling it would be tantamount to surrender. 'Why don't you use the downstairs loo while Daddy looks for the thing with the handle.'

There was a growl of complaint from Chris. 'Stay exactly where you are, Charlie,' he barked, and then to Sarah, 'He'll pee all over the polyfilla.'

'But I can't wait,' Charlie strained on an outward breath.

The desperation in his voice was so intense that Sarah instantly developed X-ray vision and saw him on the landing, hopping from foot to foot, clutching the front of his shorts.

'Two more seconds, Charlie. Hang on, love.'

Chris leant closer to the door. 'Just have a quick look in the cardboard box under the sink while you're in there, will you?'

But Sarah was already on her feet and cut off any further requests by pulling the flush, although a straightforward tug didn't work at all, it was more a matter of teasing a constant trickle into a monsoon flood.

As she opened the door Charlie belted past her so fast he blurred around the edges and slammed the door shut. Chris was waiting on the landing, hands on hips, jeans and T-shirt splattered with what looked like pigeon droppings. 'Well, was it there?'

'I didn't get a chance to look.'

He rolled his eyes heavenwards. 'I told you it was in the box under the sink.'

Sarah nodded. 'Right, well Charlie shouldn't be long.' She glanced down at her watch. 'Then I'm going to have a quick shower and I'll be off.'

Chris screwed up his nose. 'Off?'

'That's right. I'm going out. I told you this morning when we were in the garage looking for the polyfilla. I'm going early because I'm taking Jack to his friend, Peter Beck's over at Harehill. Then tonight Peter's mum will bring him back at around nine. Don't worry, it's all arranged.'

Chris looked at her quizzically as if she was speaking Esperanto. 'So, what time do you think you'll be back?'

'I'm not sure, eleven, maybe a bit later.' There was a little pause when they both looked at each other. Chris's expression remained deliberately uncomprehending. Sarah shook her head. 'Don't pretend you don't know anything about it, Chris. I've been talking about this party for weeks. You told me you didn't want to go.'

He sniffed.

'So, what's happening with Charlie?'

Sarah didn't flinch. 'I'll check the notice board.'

'That's not what I meant. What's Charlie going to be doing while you're out gallivanting?'

'Staying here with you.'

Chris shook his head. 'Uh-uh. I'm going to get that filling done and then I'm going over to Barry's. I promised I'd give him a hand with his concreting –' He flicked his wrist over and peered myopically at his watch. 'Shit, look I need the thing with the handle. Your palette knife came to bits, but it'll be all right, just needs another screw. It'll be fine.'

'My palette knife?'

'Don't go on about it. It won't take more than a couple of minutes to fix.'

Sarah watched him hurrying down the stairs; two minutes to fix if you didn't count the five years it would spend in the drawer waiting to get done.

'What about Charlie –' she called to his retreating back.

Chris didn't even break his stride. 'You can take him with you. I mean, this party's no big deal, is it?'

Before she could launch her indignation their middle son, Jack, ambled out of his bedroom in his boxer shorts. At thirteen and a half, part of his body was fighting to stay a boy while the other louder, pushier, muscly half was struggling to spring fully-fledged into manhood. He was at the eerie stage when he looked as if he was constructed from an amalgam of elbows and knees.

'Seen my new T-shirt and Bermudas?'

'Did you put them out for a wash?'

He wrinkled up his face and peered at her as if she were totally mad. 'What?'

3

Why was it the whole family seemed to think she spoke some obscure ancient language. 'Because if you did then they're probably in the linen basket in the kitchen. I ironed a whole pile last night while the video was on.'

He tucked his chin tight up against his chest as if to get a better look at her. 'Were my things in there then?'

'Haven't got a clue, I was watching Mel Gibson, I could have been ironing live baby seal cubs and not noticed. Just go and have a look will you, and don't pull everything all over the kitchen floor.'

He glanced back over his shoulder as he padded across the landing, giving her the, 'and exactly what do you think I am?' look that children perfect sometime between the moment of birth and their first feed.

Her husband Chris's head appeared in the stairwell below. 'Was it under the sink?'

'Charlie isn't out of the bathroom yet.' She knocked on the door. 'Come on love, are you going to be much longer?'

'There's a dead earwig in the toilet.' Charlie's voice crept out from under the door.

'Don't worry, just hurry up.'

'Does wee kill earwigs?'

'Charlie, will you please hurry up.'

'. . . only, if it does, then people could spray it on their gardens and stuff.'

'Charlie!'

The door opened very slowly and he grinned at her, still struggling to pull his shorts up over his perfect slim hips. He was toffee brown, with streaky blond and mouse coloured curls; four and a half and nearly edible. She couldn't resist touching him. He was on the change too, losing the plump patina of babyhood. Lean, boy's limbs showed through the glowing smooth flesh. She stroked his hair back off his face.

4

'You know, you're my last little baby,' she purred, relishing his puppy-ish smell.

He pulled a face. 'I am not a baby, I'm a big boy,' he growled indignantly. 'You know you could use wee for all sorts of things if you thought about it.'

Sarah nodded. 'Save thinking about it until later. And no practical experiments. Can you go and . . .' she paused, and what? 'Why don't you go and see if Daddy needs any help?'

'I heard that,' Chris snapped from somewhere downstairs. 'Have you found the . . .'

Quickly Sarah pressed the bathroom door closed, slid the bolt across and turned on the shower, deciding as she shed summer hot clothes, that it was time to check the small print on their marriage certificate. There had to be some sort of money-back guarantee.

Sarah had soap in her eyes when she discovered that somebody had taken all the towels and was drying herself on her discarded blouse when Jack announced, through the door, that his T-shirt was most definitely not in the ironing basket. And he'd found his shorts under the bed. The indignation in his tone implied she had put them there on purpose. Charlie appeared to have used the last of the loo roll.

'This party thing is at Monica's new house, isn't it?' Chris was making a pot of tea when Sarah teetered downstairs in her new sandals. He was talking over his shoulder into the ether. She often wondered if he actually talked all the time and just didn't realise she wasn't there listening.

'That's right, she's bought a place over at Barton.'

'Well, there's no problem then,' he said, stuffing a Rich Tea into his mouth. 'You can take Charlie with you. Monica won't mind. She's good with kids. I'm going to Barry's when I've had this.'

Sarah tried hard not to feel resentment, fury, murderous rage and said in her most reasonable voice, 'I'm sorry, Chris, I can't. Why can't you take him with you?'

Chris moved along the work surfaces scattering tea leaves and biscuit crumbs, and carried on talking if she hadn't said a word. 'Oh, and there's something in that fridge that's off. Smells bloody horrible.' He turned round, mug in hand. 'Jesus, you're not going out in that, are you? What is it, the annual old tarts' convention? What on earth have you done to your hair?'

Sarah flushed crimson. Usually she chose very conservative clothes but there had been this little black dress on sale in Petermond's in the High Street, half price because the hem was down. It had only taken a couple of minutes to tack it back up. The dress was very simple, very chic, bias cut, reaching to just above the knee, long sleeves, with a round neck. She'd pushed her shoulder length dark hair up into a soft curly heap.

She had been so uncertain about buying the dress, even when the sales assistant – who looked like something out of a fashion magazine, all crumpled linen and expensive bridge work – said it looked as if it had been made for her. Suited her colouring and her new summer tan and everyone but everyone should have at least *one* little black dress in their wardrobe. She could wear it anywhere. And then Sarah had done a twirl in front of the shop mirrors, feeling grown up and glamorous and not in the least bit mumsy.

The girl had studied her thoughtfully. 'All you need is some really nice jewellery, something simple – sandals and lipstick. You need to wear a really stunning lipstick with a black dress.'

Across the kitchen Chris was still staring at her. Sarah could feel tears welling up behind her eyes and was furious with herself for being so hurt.

'It's just that Monica is so, so – sophisticated.' Amongst the debris in the kitchen it sounded ridiculous.

'Oh, c'mon, Sarah, it was a joke. Where's your sense of humour? Anyway, you ought to be yourself. You look a lot better in jeans and a T-shirt, you look daft in that –' He waved his mug in her direction, while, with his spare hand he scratched his belly where it hung over his belt. 'Well, not daft exactly, just a bit overdone. And there's cat's hairs on the car seats, they'll get all over that.'

'I asked you to hoover it out yesterday,' she said, still trying to swallow back the tears that still threatened to ruin her make-up.

'Tell me, Sarah, when have I had the time?' he said, looking wounded. 'Oh, and you'll need to get some petrol.

'Do you want to have a quick look at the plastering before you go?'

Sarah shook her head as Jack wandered into the kitchen. She didn't trust herself to speak.

'So, are we going now?' His Bermudas looked as if somebody had died in them and hadn't been found for some time, and the oversized T-shirt top had a large crisp gingery stain down the front.

'You're not going to go out wearing those are you?' she asked incredulously.

'It isn't my fault you didn't wash them,' he said, picking at the stain.

Charlie came in behind them all, wearing an outsized baseball cap back to front, and carrying a large plastic bag full of comics, toy cars and felt-tip pens. 'Dad said I'm going to a party for fat boring old women,' he said cheerfully and jiggled his bottom up onto one of the stools. 'So, when are we going then?'

'Right, now you be good at Grandma's,' Sarah said over her shoulder as she drove down the main road with one eye on the petrol gauge. Surely that wasn't all you got for ten pounds. Maybe the needle had stuck.

Charlie, cradling his bag of treasures, looked at her thoughtfully in the rear-view mirror and chewed his lip. 'But I really wanted to see all the fat old ladies.'

'Well, you can't,' she snapped. 'I've told Grandma that Daddy will be coming over in the van to pick you up when he's finished work at Barry's but if it's late you're going to stay the night. All right?'

Sarah's mother's house was twenty miles out of her way and five miles, in the wrong direction, from Burdetts garage where Chris insisted that they buy their petrol because it was 2p a litre cheaper.

She hadn't changed her dress – on principle – but now she wasn't so sure. Was it too over the top for Monica's housewarming party? What if everyone else turned up in flowing Indian cotton and Laura Ashley frocks. Or what if it was a barbecue and they were all in shorts and ecologically sound T-shirts? Sarah pulled the hem down over her thighs as she negotiated the roundabout at the bottom of the High Street. Besides which by the time she'd found something else it would have been too late, though too late for what exactly was difficult to tell.

All sorts of thoughts about Monica's party had wormed their way through her mind since she received the invitation, most of which had been excuses not to go at all.

Jack, who was sitting in the passenger seat beside her, started to fiddle with the CD player, while strapped in, in the back seat, Charlie was sulking hard.

'And you,' she said, slapping Jack's fingers away from the controls, 'you behave yourself at Peter's mum's and don't forget to say thank you. And don't go giving her a list of things you don't eat. All right? You've got Barry's number if you have any problems. If Dad's not at Barry's he'll either be at home or at Gran's.'

8

Sometimes family life struck Sarah Colebrook as being not unlike organising a military campaign. A couple of toddler-hardened mothers could have quite easily organised the D-Day landings over a pot of tea – and ensured everyone arrived on time with their wellingtons, sandwiches and something to amuse them on the journey.

Jack nodded. 'Yeh, all right, don't keep on. I am house trained, you know.' He was practising looking bored and seriously hard done by. She sighed and flipped the indicator to turn left into the village where his friend Peter lived.

Jenny Beck was in the garden. She looked Sarah up and down as she got out of the car and smiled sympathetically. 'Girls' night out?'

Sarah nodded. 'Yes,' she said guardedly. 'Can you still take Jack home?'

Peter's mother was wearing a dusty-pink tracksuit and had extremely lank hair. 'That's just how I started,' she said darkly, tucking a stray tendril back behind her ear.

'I'm sorry?'

Peter's mum crossed her arms across her generous chest and nodded over her shoulder towards the house. 'My old man started going out on his own and I thought to myself, what's sauce for the goose – you know. So, me and few friends from work started to go down the Lamb on a Thursday. They've got live music, Country and Western, line dancing and everything. You know how it is.'

Sarah said nothing, sensing a baited trap, instead she nodded in what she hoped was an open ended, cheerful, supportive, comprehending way.

Jenny made a dark gurgling sound somewhere in the back of her throat. 'Monday it was darts and dommies; six months later and he clears off with the girl out of Weigh and Save. Twenty-one she is. A trophy wife.'

Sarah felt her mouth fall open. 'A trophy wife?'

Peter's mum nodded sagely. 'Oh yes, that's what they call them, you know. I saw a programme on daytime telly about it. That's my Tony, I thought. Successful man, you see. It's the power thing. Women just can't resist it. The men use us when they're on their way up and then when they've made it . . .' she shrugged, lifting her hands to encompass the futility of it all. 'Once they get to the top they want a status symbol. He had the best years of my life, that man, the best years.'

Sarah felt extremely uncomfortable. Until now she had only ever nodded to Jenny. Behind them the two boys were already banging a football around in the unkempt front garden.

'I'm really sorry,' Sarah said lamely, trying to work out how she could end the conversation without causing offence. 'What does your husband do?'

'Mr Whelk.'

'I'm sorry?'

'That's his trade name. He has it on the side of his vans. He does wet fish, shellfish, fish sticks, scampi. Whole range of fish products. Though my sister says he's diversified into dried goods now. His new girlfriend's probably got connections, sort of Weigh and Save on wheels.' Jenny Beck looked heavenwards. 'So I understand what you're going through,' she said. 'I'll have Jack home about nine, all right?'

Sarah was relieved to get back into the car. In her absence Charlie had busied himself picking the stuffing out of the split in the back seat and breaking into a packet of custard creams.

'Is Granddad still dead?'

'Yes, love. As far as I am aware death is permanent.'

'What about Grandma? Is she dead?'

Sarah checked her rear-view mirror and pulled into the

offside lane to turn right. 'No, no, I think she's just fine, Charlie, or at least she was when I spoke to her half an hour ago.'

Sarah often wondered about the female mind. Every woman she knew had an uncanny ability to be doing one thing, while thinking about another, and still find enough spare mental capacity to explain celestial truths to small children. She remembered her mother doing the same but couldn't remember when it had happened to her, maybe it was one of the many unseen things that sneak up on you at puberty.

Beside her in the passenger footwell lay her handbag, a clothes brush, a roll of brown parcel tape – which she hoped would remove any cat's hairs that the towel she'd laid over the car seat failed to block – and alongside them Monica's party invitation with instructions on how to get there. She glanced at the car clock. She was running late and the dusty red Astra van in front of her was obviously looking for somewhere, creeping along at half the speed limit, touching his brakes and/or indicators every few yards. The road was a snake's tail of winding blind bends, with cars parked on both sides – overtaking was impossible.

'What if she's died since you rang her up?' asked Charlie.

'Then we'll ring Daddy up and he can come and collect you both in the van. Grandma can lie in the back and I'll probably – Oh for Christ's sake!'

The Astra came to a dramatic and very sudden halt. 'Oh, you bloody moron,' she screamed. 'Why can't you just sodding well pull over and walk to find the bloody address. You – you –'

The driver climbed out. He was in his late twenties, maybe early thirties with a dramatic tangle of straw-blond hair hanging down his broad suntanned shoulders. He was wearing denim dungarees, no shirt, and had very long legs.

He grinned when he saw her car sitting three feet from the Astra's rear bumper. Stuffing his hands into his pockets he wandered back towards her. He was also stunningly, astoundingly good looking. Sarah lowered the window and turned down the CD player.

'I'm so sorry,' he said in a cultured dark brown voice. 'I'm totally and utterly lost. You don't happen to know where Kersley Road is, do you?'

Sarah swallowed hard as he rested one hand against the car roof in a chummy sort of way. He smelt gorgeous, all sun and wind with a soft hint of something musky and vanillary. She could feel him looking at her legs.

'My mum said you are a bloody moron,' said Charlie, right on cue from behind the driver's seat.

Sarah coughed loudly. 'Kersley Road? I don't know this area very well but I think it's down the bottom of the hill, after the mini-roundabout.'

He winked. 'That's great, spot on, thanks,' he paused, holding her gaze. 'I'm really sorry about messing you around.' His eyes moved slowly down over her little black dress. 'You've been a real help. See you around.'

Sarah puffed out her cheeks after he'd driven away.

'Wow,' she said, closing the window. 'Now wasn't he drop dead gorgeous?' speaking mainly to herself.

'Who?' said Charlie, peering out expectantly from between the seats. 'Who's dropped dead?'

Sarah's mother was in the shed in the back garden potting on her cacti collection.

She glanced up at Sarah without really seeing her. 'So, what is this then? Some sort of party?'

Why do I always feel so defensive, thought Sarah, as she steered Charlie and his bag of bits inside. 'That's right. At Monica's new house.'

Her mother lifted her bifocals and took another look.

'You've done something to your hair, haven't you?' She considered for a second. 'Monica? Not Monica Carlisle? I thought she'd moved abroad somewhere. Didn't she marry a foreigner?'

'He was a carpet salesman from Liverpool.'

'Thought so.' And dropping her glasses back on to her nose, she tapped out another pin cushion on to a sheet of newspaper. 'You know I prefer a little bit more notice.' She nodded towards Charlie. 'Not that I mind having the boys, but I might have been planning to go out.'

Sarah took a deep breath; this from a woman who barely ventured beyond her front gate. 'Sorry, it was a bit of an emergency. Chris was . . .'

'Of course,' her mother continued, overriding her, 'your sister, Alice, and Robert always let me know at least a fortnight in advance. She and Robert are having a long weekend away with some friends of theirs, in the Lakes. They've taken the children this time, or I wouldn't have been able to have Charlie for you. I never thought in my wildest dreams it would be Alice who would grow up to be the sensible one. So organised now. She was always such a scatterbrain. Who'd have thought she'd end up married to Robert?'

Sarah bit her lip. Who indeed? Her little sister, Alice, had married Robert – the celestial all powerful wealthy one – who had a job that demanded he wore a good suit and travelled to work by train. As far as her mother was concerned neither Alice nor Robert could do any wrong, an illusion greatly enhanced by the fact that they rarely came within spitting distance of each other. Their mutual admiration was mostly conducted by phone on a Sunday evening after *Songs of Praise*.

Alice's children, Simone and Quentin, had stayed with their grandma only once. Occasionally the Celestial Robert and the holy family would appear for tea on Sunday but never stayed more than two hours. During that time the children were so unnaturally well behaved that Sarah wondered if Alice had drugged them.

Her mother peered at her again. 'Shouldn't there be trousers with that outfit?'

Chapter 2

Chris Colebrook pushed back a tuft of damp hair off his forehead and leant on his shovel. 'So, what do you reckon then, Barry? Couple more loads be enough?'

Behind him the cement mixture gulped and snorted and churned as Barry got up from tamping the surface of the drive into an ocean of ripples. He looked thoughtfully at the sticky waves and remaining patches of bare brick rubble and metal re-enforcing. 'Yeh, two more should do it. Not going too bad though, is it? I'll just nip round the back and grab another scaffold board.'

Chris puffed out his cheeks. It was hot and his back and shoulders ached from shovelling gravel, sand and cement into the gaping maw of the mixer Barry had hired. Even though they had taken turns it was far from easy. His T-shirt clung and sucked at every inch of his skin.

'Fancy a can?' said Barry, as he high-wired his way across the crisscross of boards they'd arranged over the newly laid concrete.

'Too bloody right. I think I could drain a brewery single handed.'

'What? Lager?'

Chris nodded. He and Barry had worked in sales together before Chris decided that it was time to do something he really wanted to do. He'd been running his own landscape gardening business for what – five years now. That wasn't easy either, Sarah and the kids had had to make sacrifices, no holidays, no luxuries, that sort of thing, but it was worth it. Definitely.

Barry leant in through the kitchen window and fished two cans out of the sink. 'I thought you were going to bring Sarah over with you –' He bowled the wet glistening can to Chris. The tab popping was like the voice of an angel. The lager tasted like ambrosia. 'We could have had a barbie or something later then.'

Chris wiped a bow wave of froth off his lips with the back of his hand and belched. 'Yeh. I did think about it but she's got this thing on tonight over at Barton. Where's Lisa?'

Barry waved towards the bungalow. 'Staying well out of the way.'

Lisa appeared in the open kitchen window and grinned, 'I'm not daft. I can't be doing with all this macho boy sweat and beer stuff.'

Barry threw out his chest. 'Man's stuff,' he growled play-fully and drained the can in one, climaxing the feat with a dramatic and resonant belch.

Lisa – who worked as a secretary at the same school as Sarah, and was blonde with a penchant for heavy gold bracelets and tight fitting sleeveless black tops – looked heavenwards. 'And who started the mixer?'

Barry snorted. 'So, I didn't see that poxy little button. In my day it was down to pure muscle power –' He aped jerking a starting handle.

'And ordered the sand, the cement, the gravel?'

Barry pulled a face. 'Women, eh? Who'd have 'em.'

As he spoke Lisa was continuing the list, counting the items off on her fingers, 'Found the trowel, emptied the wheel barrow, borrowed the scaffold boards from next door, laid the beer in.'

Barry gave her a withering look. 'All right, all right, no need to go on, we get the general idea. Mild mannered secretary by day, superwoman nights and weekends.'

'I saw Sarah when I was getting the petrol for the mixer.

She looks great in that black dress. Is that the one she got from Petermond's?' asked Lisa.

Chris sniffed. He'd got no idea where she'd got it, and certainly hadn't considered that she'd bought it, let alone bought it specially.

Lisa helped herself to a can. 'Going somewhere really special I thought. I was surprised when you showed up here this afternoon. I assumed you pair had got a romantic little dinner *à deux* planned somewhere.'

Chris tightened his grip on the icy beer can. 'Really?'

Lisa giggled. 'Shipping the kids out for the evening and going in for some good old-fashioned romance . . .'

Chris could feel his colour deepening.

'. . . should have known better though. What man can resist the call of the concrete and the smell of the spirit level?'

When he looked up Lisa had vanished back into the shadows. Barry sniffed. 'Two more loads then, mate. So what's this do Sarah's going to then?'

Chris looked thoughtfully at the stormy grey sea of concrete. Sarah had definitely looked different and she'd been very insistent that Charlie couldn't go with her. He chewed his lip thoughtfully.

'I dunno. Some sort of girls' get-together, I think. A housewarming party. Did you ever meet Monica Carlisle?'

Barry rolled his eyes. 'Oh my God, not the "I've gotta go over and see an old friend," gag, Chris? You didn't fall for that one, did you?'

Chris went very, very still. 'What?'

Barry laughed and leant in through the window to fill a glass with water. 'Only kidding. Christ, it's bloody hot out here, isn't it?'

Sarah slowed up by the grass verge and leant across to undo the passenger side window. 'Excuse me, I wonder

17

whether you can help me? I'm looking for a house called The Orchards?'

She had already driven through Barton twice. The last person she had stopped had been a Swedish tourist on a walking holiday.

The elderly man who she'd rounded up with the nose of her car, nodded and reined in his Jack Russell. 'First on the left, along that avenue of trees. Of course in my day –'

Sarah thanked him quickly and drove off. She was already late and flustered and beginning to think it might be easier to have a quick drink and then head home. Her head ached and the more she looked down at the dress the more she thought it was a mistake.

First on the left she pulled up under the shadow of the horse chestnut trees and re-read Monica's instructions. This had to be the place but it looked far too big. Monica and Sarah had first met when she and Chris had moved in together into a tiny flat behind the hospital in Norwich. Monica had lived opposite in a huge rented Victorian semi.

Sitting under the cool puddle of darkness beneath the trees Sarah tried to remember how it was that she and Monica had become friends but the exact memory was lost somewhere. One minute they'd been people who nodded on the street and the next they'd been giggling over bottles of cheap wine and going round to each other's houses for supper and a good gossip.

Sarah had been working in a bookshop then, and Monica, who was quite a bit older than Sarah, though she didn't know exactly by how much, maybe ten years, maybe more, had been living the life of Riley without any apparent means of support. But then again Monica kept lots of things secret, her age being one of them.

Chris had immediately been suspicious of Monica in the way men always are of close relationships between women. Sarah and Monica had kept in touch over the years, with

Christmas cards, the odd letter, photos. Monica had eventually married Terry, a carpet salesman from Liverpool and gone to live in Spain.

Except that none of that fitted with any of the things she was looking at now. Between the trees Sarah could pick out the regular elegant lines of a large Georgian house. On the light breeze came the distinctive call of a peacock. Sarah read the note again. Maybe Monica had rented a cottage or something in the grounds. Dropping the car into gear she crept up the drive praying that no one would stop her for trespassing.

She was under dressed.

Monica Carlisle swept out through the front door before Sarah's ageing Golf had puttered to a halt. Monica looked like Gloria Swanson in *Sunset Boulevard*. Her dress was a gold lamé sheath, her hair caught up in an ornate twist of matching fabric.

'Sarah! Oh God, I'm so glad you could come, darling. I thought maybe you'd changed your mind. Let me look at you.' Monica held Sarah at arm's length and looked her up and down.

Sarah grinned. 'Never mind that. Let me look at you, you look amazing.'

Monica did a pirouette. 'What, this old rag? I thought I'd dress down, it's only a casual do for a few friends. I usually do the dustbins in this.'

Sarah giggled.

'Come into the house and meet everyone. Fredo will park your car, just leave the keys in.'

'Wait,' said Sarah, as Monica slipped her arm through hers. 'Fredo? What the hell is going on here, Mo? What happened, did you and Terry come up on the lottery?'

Monica stopped mid-stride. 'Terry? Who's . . . Oh, you mean Terry Braithewaite. God, no, we've been divorced for years.'

'And you remarried?'

Monica threw back her head and roared with laughter. 'Oh shit, yes. God knows how many times. I must have written and told you all about it surely?'

Sarah shook her head as Monica steered her into a large hallway where an elegant stairway curved up into galleried shadows.

'This is some house –' said Sarah, looking round in astonishment. 'How the hell did you end up here?'

'The Orchards? When I was in Spain I met this dinky little German industrialist, Kurt – he must have been eighty if he was a day – the kinkiest old bastard you've ever clapped eyes on. The things we didn't . . . Anyway, he had rented this big villa for the summer and I'd go up there every afternoon to teach him Spanish.'

'You speak Spanish?'

Monica shook her head. 'No, but his wife didn't know that. To cut a long story short when the old boy died he left me a little something to remember him by. Quite an enormous amount of something actually. I'm sure I must have told you?'

'Trust me, I would have remembered – your Christmas cards always say the same things. "Hope you and the boys are well, weather is lovely, I'm fine, lots of love Monica." You're a real dark horse.'

Monica pretended to be outraged. 'Who me? Good God, no, I just hate writing letters.'

'So, what happened to this man's wife?'

Monica shrugged. 'Not a peep, not a word, whether he divorced her, whether she was dead – I've got no idea, maybe he had so much that she'd got no reason to complain. Anyway, I decided to come back home to Blighty and settle down. I saw this place in a magazine at the dentist's.'

They were now standing outside an open set of double doors. Monica grinned. 'But I want to hear what you've been doing. Why don't you come through and I'll introduce you to some people.'

'I thought you said you were just inviting a few friends?' said Sarah in disbelief as Monica steered her out into a conservatory full of elegant people, all laughing, talking and drinking. Along one wall was a buffet table that stretched the whole length of the room.

A waiter with a tray of drinks circled them and Monica handed her a glass.

'There are only about fifty or sixty. When I was with Morden we used to do regular dinners for two hundred. God, that was such a drag –'

'Morden? Who was . . .' Sarah began, but Monica was already guiding her towards a group of people in full evening dress standing around the end of the buffet.

'Georgio, Leana? I'd like to introduce you to an old and very dear friend of mine, Sarah Colebrook, this is –'

Sarah felt nervousness grab her stomach in a strangle hold. She managed to smile and say polite inane things while not really focusing on the faces or catching any of the names.

'Actually,' said a low even voice, 'I think we've already met.'

Sarah's attention snapped back and she looked up into the dark brown eyes of Mr Red Astra.

'Hi,' he said pleasantly, 'I didn't expect to see you again so soon. I'm Mac. Mac Filby.' He extended an elegant lightly tanned hand.

Sarah was so surprised she nearly dropped her glass. 'You?' she began.

Monica smiled. 'Maybe Mac, you'd introduce Sarah around for me? You don't mind do you, Sarah? Only I've got to go and see what's happened to the band.'

There was a splintery uneasy pause while Monica glided off amongst the sea of expensive frocks.

'I was the guy playing silly buggers in the red Astra, remember?' Mac said pleasantly.

As if she could forget. His leonine mane had been subdued into a sleek ponytail. Oh yes, thought Sarah, I remember and you still smell wonderful and that dinner jacket makes you look like a box of very expensive chocolates. Rather than trust herself to speak she decided nodding would be a better option.

'You know, you really saved my life,' he was saying. 'Mo sent me to pick up the lobsters. She'd have murdered me if I'd come back without them.'

'The lobsters?'

Maybe her children were right, Sarah thought, maybe she didn't understand English.

'That's right. For the buffet. By the way, have you eaten yet?' Mac said.

'Er, no,' said Sarah.

Mac slipped his arm through hers. 'No time like the present. I'm totally and utterly famished.' He nodded towards French windows. 'Mo's put out tables and chairs on the terrace, it'll be cooler out there.'

Sarah followed wordlessly and wondered how long it would be before she woke up.

'The Wheeeeeels on the bus-s-s-s go round and round, round and round, round and –'

'Charlie, will you please be quiet,' snapped Chris Colebrook as he drove out of the avenue of bungalows where Sarah's mum lived. 'When we get home you can have a bath and then it's straight upstairs to bed. All right?'

Charlie pulled a miserable face. 'This seat belt cuts right through into my body,' he whined, tugging it off his chest. 'And I don't need this stupid baby cushion thing.' He wriggled his bottom back and forth on the booster seat. 'I'm a big boy now – I'm . . .'

'Leave those straps alone and shut up,' said Chris crossly.

Charlie stared at him with big hurt blue eyes and set his lips into a narrow disapproving line. Chris sighed. He'd been thinking a lot about Sarah since he'd left Barry and Lisa's place.

She'd definitely been acting oddly. Microscopic cells of doubt were beginning to reproduce themselves at a terrifying rate somewhere in the back of his head. He sniffed and told himself not to be ridiculous. He and Sarah had been together for years. He just couldn't quite remember how many. He still thought she was nice looking, sexy – maybe he should tell her more often, mention it in passing.

All right, so he didn't always buy her the right kind of thing for her birthday or necessarily get the right date, but realistically how important was that in the great scheme of things? The thought was there – Christmas was a different matter obviously; he'd really never understood what all the fuss was about. The thing was that Sarah didn't always appreciate the same things as he did.

Some women would have thought a steam iron was a perfect gift, and he had never fully understood why Sarah had got so upset about the leggings. All that fuss about being a couple of sizes too big? He hadn't meant to suggest she was that size, he was playing safe and anyway, he'd kept the receipt. Chris stretched; he'd clean the garage out for her tomorrow if he got the chance. Wash her car maybe. Put things right, back on an even keel.

He swung the van into the outside lane to overtake an open-top sports car. Inside two middle-aged men and two girls were giggling. One of the girls in the back was wearing a little black dress. As Chris watched she turned round and kissed the man beside her, his fingers were resting lightly on an acre of exposed thigh. It was one of those kisses, a sort of teasing jokey kiss but it made Chris shudder, it was an explicit invitation. A hundred yards later the sports car turned off towards the river. Chris dropped the Transit van down a gear and roared towards home.

Charlie pressed his fingers against the van window. 'We saw someone drop dead down there today,' he said conversationally.

Chris glanced across at him. 'No, you didn't. Don't make up stories, Charlie. I've told you about that before. No one dropped dead.'

Charlie swung round and glared at him indignantly. 'Oh yes, they did, Mummy said so. She told me.'

Chris sighed. 'No, she didn't, Charlie.'

Charlie glanced back out of the window as if to fix the truth in his mind. 'Yes, she did. She said that man who stopped his car to talk to her had dropped dead.'

Chris stared at Charlie. 'What man?'

Charlie sighed as if his father was a complete idiot. 'The man in the red car that we followed down here. He stopped to talk to Mummy. She said he'd got something.'

Chris could feel the doubt cells in his brain multiply. 'What did he have, Charlie?' he said with studied disinterest.

'Gorge-us,' said Charlie carefully. 'She said he'd dropped dead with gorge-us.'

It was all Chris could do to stop himself from turning the van around and going to track Sarah down in Barton, instead his internal organs performed a funny tight little dance that started somewhere up in the back of his throat.

'And what else did Mummy say?' he heard himself saying softly.

Charlie looked at the traffic thoughtfully. 'She didn't say anything else. But the man said he'd see her around.'

'Oh, he did, did he?' growled Chris, gunning the engine.

* * *

Chris didn't bother about Charlie having a bath. He scurried him upstairs, whipped the curtains closed, slapped *The Jungle Book* story tape into the cassette player and kissed him a hasty, distracted goodnight.

Charlie rolled out his bottom lip and slunk miserably beneath his duvet while Chris ran back down to the kitchen and picked up the phone. It was answered on the second ring. 'Directory Enquiries, what name please?'

Chris cradled the phone under his chin. 'Carlisle, Monica Carlisle.'

'And have you got an address for that, caller?'

Chris bit his lip. 'Yes, Barton.'

'Thank you.'

'It's a new number,' he said quickly into the yawning silence. On the end of the phone line the girl made a little noise to acknowledge she'd heard him and then there was nothing. A split second later an electronic voice told him there was no such listing. Chris hung on for more help and looked around the kitchen, trying to focus on something other than the funny feeling he had in his stomach.

'No. No, I'm afraid we've got nothing listed for a Monica Carlisle at Barton. Are you spelling that LISLE?'

'Yes,' said Chris hastily.

'No, I'm really sorry, caller, but we've got nothing at all under Carlisle at that address. I've got an M Carlisle, ironmongers, at Cuthbert St Andrew –'

Chris had no sooner laid the phone back in its cradle than it rang.

'Hello. Is that you, Sarah?' he said way too quickly, trying to keep the emotional edge out of his voice.

'No, Dad. It's me, Matthew. Isn't Mum still there?'

'No, she isn't –' Chris had completely forgotten about their eldest son.

'I rung up to check what time she's going to come round to pick me up.'

Chris glanced up at the kitchen clock. 'What time did she say she'd be there?'

Matthew made a series of teenage thinking noises. ''Bout eleven, I wondered if she could make it closer to midnight, only me and Hannah wanted to watch this film on 4 . . .'

'Did she say she'd ring you?'

Matthew snorted. 'No. What is this anyway, the Spanish Inquisition?' Chris heard someone close in the background say, 'Nobody expects the Spanish Inquisition,' and then giggle madly.

Chris was suddenly filled with a white hot impotent rage that made him want to break something. 'You spend too much time over there with Hannah,' he snapped furiously. 'You expect us to run around after you like some bloody taxi service. When I was seventeen I didn't expect to be out gallivanting all over the place, I can tell you. I was –'

'Whoa, whoa,' interrupted Matthew, in a calm, terribly reasonable voice. 'I'm sorry. If it makes it difficult then eleven'll be fine. I was just asking that's all.'

Chris ran his fingers through his hair. 'All right. I get the idea. If your mother rings I'll get her to call you.'

Before Matthew had a chance to reply Chris hung up and stared unseeing at the chaos in the kitchen. He sat down at the table and tried to back-track to find out how the dark little trolls in his head had started to multiply. Part of him – the rational sane part – that sounded uncannily like Sarah, asked him why on earth he was being so hysterical. A new dress, a new hair style and a night out with the girls does not mean that your wife is hopping into bed with somebody else, said the voice calmly and firmly.

Charlie's voice was next, explaining all about Sarah spending the afternoon chasing good looking men in cars. And then there was his own voice; a small nervous voice that sounded as if it just might be afraid of the dark.

'When was the last time you told her she looked good

without wanting to get her into bed, or wheedle her into doing something that you didn't want to do, eh? When was the last time you bought her flowers or took her out for a meal? Took her out anywhere at all?'

The same little voice whined with all sorts of excuses about why he hadn't been able to find the time or the money, but none of them sounded very plausible. Chris sighed and felt a disturbing flood tide of guilt lifting in his gut.

On the kitchen table, beside the teapot, was an old tin box where, in theory, Chris kept his tools. He'd brought it in while sorting out the downstairs loo. The chisels were blunt, there were two screwdrivers missing out of the set that Sarah had bought him one year for Christmas, and one of those that was there had the equivalent of a club foot where he'd used it to prise up paving slabs.

Once, when he and Sarah had been having a row, she had got the tool box out and set it on the table in front of him like a reliquary.

'There you are,' she'd said, pointing dramatically, furious and in full flow. 'See that? You treat me like you treat your bloody tools. You neglect them. You use them for all the wrong jobs, leave them lying about all over the place to rust and then – all of a sudden, when you want to do something, you assume they'll all still be there. Waiting for you. You think that you can pick them up and off you go, with no harm done.' At the time he had thought she was quite mad.

And then tonight, when she'd been all dressed up to go out what had he said? Chris winced.

'Jesus, you're not going out like that are you? What is it, the annual old tarts' convention? What on earth have you done to your hair?'

Chris groaned unhappily and covered his face with his hands. What had he done? And perhaps more to the point, what was Sarah doing? She must know he cared; after all, he changed the light bulbs on the landing because she hated heights, ran the kids to school when she was too busy, took out the rubbish for her on a Wednesday. Well, most Wednesdays.

'I mean,' said the voice inside his head, 'isn't that the true measure of real love? The everyday practical solid things that we do for people. Things you can count and measure. That should be enough for anybody –' Even before the inner voice said it, Chris knew it *wasn't* enough.

He only touched her when he thought there was a ninety percent chance he'd get his leg over. He'd thought she was safe and tame and . . . and . . . Chris couldn't bring his mind to think it. Out loud his mouth said the words, '. . . Mine. I was so certain Sarah belonged to me.'

And now she had gone off in a tarty black party dress and if she'd run away with some gorgeous caring sensitive romantic man, who in God's name could really blame her?

Hot on the heels of his admission of neglect an internal Neanderthal voice growled in his defence, 'You can. She should be grateful, you don't beat her, you let her drive a car. Good God, you even let her work . . .'

Chris groaned and prayed that Sarah would be home soon.

There was a light breeze out on the terrace at The Orchards. The garden rolled away towards a small babbling river. Evening was coming and the air was heavy with the scent of wallflowers, honeysuckle and old English roses. In the distance the bells of Barton church pealed away the day to reveal the soft gold tones of evening. Mac had found them a sheltered table under the lee of the wall and from the house Sarah could hear the band playing a smoky blue jazz standard, something timeless and deeply deeply moving.

'So, you work with children. Do you teach?'

Sarah jumped. Part of her was still expecting to wake up, while another was relishing the scenery and the soft mischievous tingle of the wine in her veins.

'Oh, I'm sorry. I was just taking all this in.' She lifted her arms to try and encompass some of the things she felt.

He grinned at her, a sort of soft teasing lazy grin. She wondered what it would be like to wake up to his face in the morning. As the phantom thought vanished, she flushed crimson, grabbed hold of her mind and shook it back under control.

'Actually, I'm a classroom assistant,' she said briskly and sitting up straight. 'It's a bit like being a teacher, without the hassle. I help with the art and design, and some of the technology syllabus. I'm responsible for the art displays in school – it fits in well with my family. Although I've been looking out for something that stretches me a little bit more –'

He nodded, tipping his head so that it appeared as if he wanted to catch every word. 'So, are you secretly a frustrated artist?'

She took another sip of wine. 'Maybe. I married young. I'd have liked to have gone to art college but –' she shrugged. 'It never happened. Anyway, when I was that age I wasn't sure what it was I wanted to do. No good dwelling too long over the might have beens.'

Mac refilled her glass. 'Oh come on. You've got plenty of time. You could go back now. I finished my degree last year.'

'Yes, but you *are* young. I've got three kids, a home, a husband, I'm rushing headlong towards forty . . .' she stopped suddenly, alarmed that she might sound deadly dull.

'I'm not that young. I'll be thirty in November. If you're motivated enough you can do anything. Anything at all . . .'

When he spoke his eyes glittered, and his lips lifted at the corners so that even though he wasn't smiling it seemed as if he might. 'You should give it a go. Seriously.'

She drank her wine, it was crystal clear and icy cold. Out on the lawn a peacock silently spread his tail feathers, sunlight glittering in his petrol blue plumage. She suddenly had this feeling as she watched the bird strut around the urns of tumbling green creepers that Mac was right: anything truly was possible if only she was brave enough to try.

Mac touched her arm, the sensation made her shiver.

'I've hidden the best lobster. What do you say we share it and drink to a brave new future?'

Sarah held out her wine glass. 'You must have read my mind. It sounds like the most marvellous idea. I've never eaten lobster before.'

Mac grinned. 'No time like the present.'

'Is there anything you want me to do? I could get plates –' she said to his retreating back, aware as she spoke that she sounded like nothing so much as a natural-born mother.

He turned, toasting her with their empty glasses. 'Just sit there and look beautiful,' he purred. She blushed and wondered how it was he managed to say something so totally ridiculous without it sounding corny.

'God, this is wonderful,' she giggled a while later with her mouth full, a rivulet of lobster juice trickled down her chin.

Mac handed her another napkin. 'And unashamedly messy. Here.' He dabbed at her chin. It was a gesture so intimate and unnerving that Sarah blushed furiously. All sorts of defensive alarms went off inside her head.

'I'm married,' she spluttered indignantly, pulling away from him.

He laughed and topped up her glass. 'For Christ's sake, we're only eating bloody lobster.'

She threw back her head and laughed with a genuine sense of relief. 'You're right. I'm so sorry. Are you going to tell me about you and Monica. I mean, are you her friend, her lover –'

He dropped his napkin on to the table. 'Not exactly. Would you like to go for a walk? There is this beautiful place by the river.' He pointed to the line of lush summer trees at the bottom of the garden. 'There's this fantastic old summerhouse.'

Sarah hesitated long enough for him to laugh.

'Don't panic,' he said, holding up his hands in surrender. 'You're a married woman with three kids and a husband. I haven't forgotten. Honest, and I won't forget. I promise. Cross my heart.'

Sarah took his out-stretched hand. 'As long as you remember that,' she said softly.

As long as I remember that, Sarah thought, as she got unsteadily to her feet and felt his long fingers close around hers.

Chapter 3

Back at home in the kitchen Chris Colebrook had poured himself a very large scotch and was on his second very large scotch when the phone rang again.

'Dad?'

'Hello, Matthew? Has your mother rung you yet?'

'No, that's why I'm ringing. Hannah's mum said I can stay the night if I want to. I thought I'd better call and ask if it was all right.'

'Right, so you haven't heard from your mother yet, then?' His words were slightly slurred and he felt as if he were hearing them from a very long way off.

'No. Are you all right, Dad?'

'Oh yes. I'm fine, son. Just fine.' Chris peered through the bull's-eye dimple at the bottom of his glass. He was trying to drown a few of those little doubting multiplying brain cells. They'd used whisky in the trenches as anaesthetic, hadn't they? It had a proven track record in field hospitals throughout history. He belched miserably.

'Are you sure you're all right? You sound weird. I can come home with Mum, or Hannah's mum will run me back if you like.'

'No, no, son, you're fine, just fine,' he said with forced joviality. 'Can you ask your mother to give me a ring if you ever see her again, will you?'

'Sorry?' Matthew sounded anxious.

'I mean, when she gets there. Get her to ring me when she gets there so I'll know when to expect her back. You can stay, stay and enjoy yourself, why not?'

Chris had got hiccups now and said his goodbyes without letting Matthew get another word in. He stared at the phone. Bloody woman. It was nearly ... he struggled to focus on the kitchen clock; nearly half past eight. What the hell did Sarah think she was playing at?

The path down beneath the trees by the river was cool and fragrant and picked out by a string of tiny silver lights in the chiffon evening light. Here and there the bank had little inlets upholstered with thick moss and trimmed with wild irises and a fringe of reeds.

Sarah felt as if she'd walked on to some stunning romantic Merchant Ivory film set. She was walking barefoot, swinging spiky heeled sandals. Mac was carrying a wicker basket from which peeped a bottle of chilled champagne. She watched the black liquid-silk water swirling hypnotically around a fallen tree stump, relishing the sensation of the moss and wood bark beneath her feet – a couple of glasses of white wine and it felt almost as soft as thick pile carpet.

Get a grip girl, she whispered to herself, while ahead of her Mac bent down to skim a stone across the shimmering water.

'So,' she began conversationally to Mac's broad back. 'You were going to tell me all about you and Monica.'

He half turned, his handsome profile accentuated by the inky water. 'Was I?'

She nodded.

'Actually I came with the house,' he said, getting up to slip his arm through hers.

'I'm not with you.'

'I rented the gardener's cottage from the last owners. When Monica moved in she let me stay on. The other guy let me use the garden, Monica does too.'

'And do odd jobs, like fetching lobsters?'

'Anything to help the balance of payments. Lovely here, isn't it?'

Ahead of them an octagonal summerhouse nestled amongst a stand of mature horse chestnuts, dappled evening light pooled on the immaculate lawn in front of it, leading the eye down a narrow path to the riverside. The French windows were open and wooden sun loungers had been arranged outside around a low table set with a storm lantern. The whole thing could have come straight out of a double page spread in *Homes & Gardens*.

Sarah couldn't remember a time when her husband, Chris, had ever said anything was lovely.

Mac grinned and spun round to face her. His eyes had darkened down to something stormy, and for an instant Sarah experienced a poignant little kick in the pit of her stomach that she recognised as desire. It hadn't been used for a long time but that didn't stop it firing into life. Sarah looked away just in case Mac spotted it.

He was still speaking although she had to reach back and re-assemble the words to make any sense of what he was saying. 'Seats, lights – seems like Monica is one jump ahead of us as usual. That woman thinks of everything. Come on.'

He caught hold of her hand and Sarah hurried to keep up with him. The breeze carried the sound of the music from the house down between the trees. At the edge of the clearing Sarah stopped for a second to store the images away in her memory. If I had to die young, she thought, looking around at the trees and the all engulfing heart-lifting scenery, let it be somewhere like this. I'd go now if I could just die here.

Mac looked back at her and smiled softly. 'Well?' he asked.

'It's beautiful.'

'You poor misguided little soul,' said a familiar voice from the shadows of the summerhouse.

'Monica?' Sarah said incredulously.

'Too bloody right,' said her friend, teetering out through the French windows with a joint in one hand and a glass of something alcoholic in the other. 'The company was getting terribly dull. Come and sit in here and tell me what you've been doing since we last saw each other. I've got some brilliant grass, shame to smoke it all on my own.' She passed the reefer to Sarah and then peered at Mac.

'And you, open that champagne you've got secreted in that basket and pour us all a glassful. I noticed you took the best lobster. Again.' She ruffled his hair playfully. 'Talk about taking liberties.' She glanced at the basket he was carrying. 'You didn't bring the lobster with you by any chance?'

Mac shook his head. 'Afraid not, we've already eaten it.'

'You thieving little bastard. Tenants these days. Never mind, I've got loads of stuff in here, come in and share. I've got the most devastating case of the munchies.'

'Coo-eee, anyone in? It's only me. I've brought Jack home.'

Chris Colebrook registered a woman's voice somewhere far off in a distant and quite foggy corner of his mind. He peered up from the kitchen table where his head seemed to have fallen when he wasn't looking. He couldn't remember it falling so far and it felt as if it might be too heavy to lift back up.

'Sorry we're late,' said the same cheery voice.

Chris closed one eye and peered at the plump pink apparition bustling towards him. 'Who-the-fuck-are-you?' he said, except that it came out as a sort of slurry jumbly mess. Like sick only it was words. In his delirium he was vomiting words.

Peter's mother, still dressed in her dusty-pink tracksuit, looked down at Chris thoughtfully. 'I'm Peter's mum. You ought to shut these windows, the place is full of moths and those little biting things. I'll put the kettle on, shall I?' She peered at him thoughtfully.

Chris swallowed hard and licked his lips, watching the woman potter around his kitchen. Maybe he had inadvertently woken up inside someone else's life.

'You know, drinking really doesn't help,' she said as she unscrewed the coffee jar. 'I've found aerobics very useful myself and my friend, Lorraine, found Jesus when her Kevin started carrying on.'

Chris screwed up his nose. 'Jesus?'

Peter's mother nodded. 'Helps spread the word outside Boots on a Saturday now.' She considered for a moment, frozen with the coffee jar in one hand and the lid in the other. 'She looks ever so well on it. But, trust me, booze definitely isn't the answer.'

Chris licked his lips. It felt as if he had borrowed someone else's tongue and it didn't quite fit. 'What the hell are you talking about?' he said.

'Infidelity,' she said, spooning coffee into the mugs. 'Let me tell you, your wife's already guessed what you've been up to. I saw her this afternoon all done up to the nines with her hunting gear on. Believe me, she knows all about you and whatever it is you've done. If you want my advice, stop now, before it's too late – get a hobby instead. I should have said that to my Tony. I should have said get a hobby. Koi carp. My sister's husband's got Koi carp and he never so much as looks at another woman. He's out in his shed tinkering with his filters. Happy as Larry. If my Tony had only got a hobby instead of going after that little bitch in Weigh and Save I'd never have gone down to the Lamb on a Thursday and then we'd still be together.'

Chris stared up at her. 'Do you come from this planet?' he said slowly.

'Ooh yes,' she said, sliding a coffee mug in front of him. 'But I used to live in Basildon.'

Sarah, Mac and Monica were lying on their backs amongst the warm summer grass and watching the stars come up and the night slowly darken from dove grey to darkest navy, passing a joint and a glass of champagne between the three of them.

Monica rolled over on to her side and peered at Sarah in the growing darkness, her eyes glittered mischievously. 'So you're still married to Chris, then?'

Sarah took a long pull on the joint and passed it over to Mac. 'I am.' She stared at the glowing end of the reefer. 'It's years since I've done anything like this.'

'And what's he like, your Chris? Is he still the same?'

Sarah shrugged, feeling the movement ripple through every bone, every muscle, every single bright shiny cell. 'Chris? He's – well – he's okay.' It worried her a little that she couldn't find a better, more positive adjective.

Monica snorted derisively. 'I always knew he would be. I knew it. I took one look at him when you moved into that place behind the hospital. He looks the type.'

Sarah pulled herself unsteadily up on to her elbows. 'You make it sound as if okay is a bad thing to be.'

'Play nicely girls,' said Mac, from somewhere in the gloom. 'Marijuana is supposed to make you mellow not bitchy.'

'Who said anything about being bitchy, I was only pointing out that Chris is true to type. Just like you, Mac,' Monica said.

He made a soft noise of surprise. 'What do you mean, like me?'

Monica shifted in the darkness. 'Oh, I can see right

through you, golden bollocks,' she said with a hint of admiration. 'You were going to bring my sexy little friend down here, get her pissed and then screw her senseless in my summerhouse. All caring, loving and oh, so, sensitive, Mr New Man.

Mac made a wounded little sound somewhere deep in his throat. The end of the reefer glowed red, illuminating his profile.

Monica laughed. 'Go on then, Mac,' she said, rolling back on to her belly. 'Tell me that I'm wrong.'

He said nothing.

Sarah tried to focus on his face in the dark. 'Is that true,' she said. 'Is Monica right?'

Monica giggled. 'Of course I'm right, darling. But don't be hurt or upset, you ought to be flattered. Shouldn't she, Mac?'

Mac groaned and pulled himself up so that he was sitting. 'You know Monica, you can be a perfect cow sometimes.'

Chris hasn't closed the bedroom curtains, Sarah thought. The sunlight streaming into the bedroom was waking her up and she was cold, the duvet must have slipped on to the floor again. She opened her eyes, and then blinked.

'Oh my God,' her mind said, and then her mouth said it too, 'Oh my God, oh *my God*, oh . . .' She pulled herself upright.

The sunlight was just breaking through the trees surrounding Monica's summerhouse. Some time during the night she, Mac and Monica had hauled themselves off the grass and on to the sun loungers. Monica was still asleep, wrapped in a white linen tablecloth, and Sarah had Mac's dinner jacket draped over her shoulders. Mac, in his shirt sleeves, his body picked in what looked like dew, was snoring softly.

'Oh, my God,' Sarah whimpered and struggled off the sun lounger, grabbing at Mac's wrist. Oblivious to the constraints of his anatomy she twisted it round to look at his watch. 'Shit, shit, shit.'

Monica wrinkled up her face and opened one eye. 'Morning, people. What the hell's going on?'

Sarah's mind was busy doing back flips. Chris would go ballistic, Chris would – and then there was Matthew, she was supposed to have picked him up at eleven – Sarah felt sick to the pit of her stomach. Waves of panic exploded under her solar plexus like a series of grenades going off. She pulled on her high heels.

'I've got to go – I've got to go. It's half past five. It's half-past-bloody-five.' Her mouth seemed hell bent on repeating itself.

Her hysteria had woken Mac who pulled himself up on to his elbows. 'Are you okay?' he said thickly, rubbing his eyes.

'No, I'm not,' she said, desperately fighting with the buckles on her sandals. 'It's half-past-bloody-five.'

Mac screwed up his nose and then flipped up his wrist to look at his watch. 'Oh yeh. You're right. Would you like me to drive you home?' he asked pleasantly.

Sarah stared at him. 'Are you totally and utterly mad?' she snapped. With her sandals half on and half off she struck off across the lawn. After a few ungainly steps she kicked them off as the heels sunk into the soft damp turf. 'Oh shit.' She scooped them up and ran headlong towards the house.

Inside the house it looked like something out of *Sleeping Beauty*. People, still in full evening dress, seemed to be asleep everywhere. Some looked as if they had just dropped where they'd been standing in some kind of magical trance.

'It's half past five,' Sarah gasped as she hurried in

through the French windows. Those must have been the magic words because as she hared frantically through the house people started to stir and stretch.

At the double doors into the hall she ran full tilt into a tall balding man in an immaculate dinner suit. 'We'll be cooking breakfast later,' he said in a very pleasant voice. 'Would you like some orange juice? Or maybe we can rustle up a little Buck's Fizz.'

Sarah waved his hospitality away. 'Where's my car?' she gasped breathlessly. 'I've really got to get home.'

Unfazed he nodded. 'Of course. What sort of car do you drive?'

'A Golf,' she managed to hiss. 'A black Golf with a child seat in the back.'

'It's parked near the stables. Would you like me to drive it round for you?'

Sarah collapsed down on to the stairs and prayed he would hurry. She didn't dare think much further than getting into the car. The territory beyond sliding behind the steering wheel was untamed, untouched, unfriendly, mine strewn country.

Still languishing by the summerhouse, Monica Carlisle stretched luxuriously and scratched her head. 'Ummm, I slept really well. Maybe we should sleep out here more often. Have you got anything exciting for breakfast over at the cottage?' Sitting up she slipped on her shoes.

Mac considered for a few seconds. 'I've got a couple of really nice kippers in the fridge. By the way your roots are showing.'

'Why do you think I was wearing that thing on my head?' Monica tipped her head forward and gave her scalp a wild dog scratch, exploding her flattened bleached blonde bob into a haystack. 'Kippers sound rather good, can I have a poached egg with mine?'

Mac nodded and then looked towards the main house. 'What about the rest of the guests?'

Monica was climbing stiffly to her feet. 'Fredo will look after them.' Amongst the morning mist and stillness there was the sound of a car engine revving hard. 'That'll be Sarah going home.'

Mac picked up his dinner jacket and slipped it on. 'I didn't realise you'd be down here last night,' he said with affected casualness.

'I rather guessed that. I couldn't have you seducing my friend, Mac, she's not wired up to cope with flash buggers like you. She's spent twenty years with an okay sort of man. It would hardly have been a fair contest.'

Mac sniffed. 'She would have enjoyed it though.'

Monica laughed. 'I have absolutely no doubt about that but you would have broken her warm little heart, you shameless cad.'

Maybe I can tell Chris I was in an accident, thought Sarah, as she roared down through Barton frightening dozy pigeons into flight. If I drive any faster I might still be in time to have one.

The trees, at speed, joined together into a green and grey sunlit bunting. When she got on to the bypass, Sarah slowed down. Christ, what the hell am I hurrying back for?

Slowing to a funereal thirty her mind continued to work overtime: What am I going to say, what can I say? her mind asked again and again, punctuated by a string of profanities. She glanced up into the rear-view mirror.

'I'm nearly thirty-nine,' she said very reasonably to her dishevelled reflection. 'What am I worried about? I've done absolutely nothing wrong. Chris doesn't own me. I'm a responsible grown up, a woman, a mother – I'll just tell him the truth. I got so totally stoned and so completely pissed that I passed out on the lawn with a strange man who was hoping to seduce me and Monica Carlisle, who, by the way, said that she knew you would turn out to be okay –'

Sarah winced and screwed up her face. No, the whole truth wouldn't do at all and it was only a couple of miles to home. She slowed down to twenty then pulled into a lay-by to do her hair and suck on a Polo mint.

Monica Carlisle licked her fingers and then guided the remains of the kipper off her plate with a chunk of bread. 'Is there any more Assam or are we reduced to the Earl Grey?'

Mac snorted. 'What you ought to be is on the phone ringing Sarah's husband.'

'Since when did the lady of the manor take orders from one of her serfs?' Monica dabbed at her mouth with a seersucker napkin and then threw it on to the table along-side the wreckage of breakfast. 'I'll ring later and pour oil on troubled waters. Maybe I ought to invite her and her husband and her kids over for a meal.'

Mac shook his head. 'Why did you invite her in the first place? I wouldn't have thought she was your type at all.'

'What are you, my husband? We were friends years ago and she was – oh I don't know – funny, good company, all bright and shiny and new with ideas and possibilities. She'd just moved in with her husband then. Young love can be so refreshing. Anyway, I like her, she's my friend. It seemed like high time we met up again –'

Gravel cannot be silenced. Sarah eased the Golf up next to Chris's battered Transit van and wondered optimistically whether perhaps he might still be asleep. Maybe she could creep upstairs and swear blind she'd been in bed for hours.

42

As she picked her way across the weedy gravel the back door opened with a savage burst.

'Where the fuck have you been?' bellowed Chris, framed like a marauding Viking in the open doorway.

Sarah took an instinctive step back, while behind him a strangely familiar figure, dressed in a faded dusty-pink tracksuit, appeared.

'We've been really worried about you,' said Peter's mother.

Sarah stared at them both in astonishment. 'What the hell is going on?' she stammered, 'and what are you doing here?' she asked a very dishevelled looking Jenny Beck.

Jenny pouted. 'I fell asleep on the settee. Couldn't very well leave Chris on his own, could I? He was very upset.'

Sarah shook her head to clear it. 'Why? I don't understand,' she began, but Chris was too quick for her.

'Don't try and turn this one around, Sarah. Where have you been all night?'

She took a deep breath, someone needed to keep a clear head. 'At Monica Carlisle's, you knew that, Chris –' she began again.

His face deepened a shade to heart attack crimson. 'There is no one called Monica Carlisle living at Barton. I've been on to Directory Enquiries, they'd never heard of her. You said eleven, half past – you said –'

'He's right,' interrupted Peter's mother. 'I rang again just to check.' She stopped and flicked a lank strand of hair off her face. 'There is no such person as Monica Carlisle in Barton. They'd never heard of her.'

Sarah stared at her. 'What is this, some sort of Greek chorus? I want to know exactly what are you doing in my house at, at – whatever time this is?'

Peter's mother huffed and folded her arms over her pink tufted bosom. 'I brought Jack home and then I was telling

43

your husband the hidden costs of being unfaithful. We used to get all the plaice off-cuts, you know, prawns –'

'Wonderful,' snapped Sarah. 'Tales from the life and times of Mr Whelk.'

Chris frowned. 'Who?'

Peter's mum touched Chris's arm in a friendly intimate way. 'Don't worry about it, why don't you come back inside and I'll make us all a nice pot of tea.'

Totally bemused Sarah felt she had no option but to follow them both inside.

On the kitchen table was an empty bottle of scotch, a single glass and several dirty mugs. Chris stationed himself by the fridge and leant heavily against its reassuring bulk.

'I've been really worried,' he whined. 'I can't believe that you stayed out all night. What the hell happened?' He'd gone white now and his lip was quivering. 'If it hadn't been for Peter's mum I don't know what I would have done.'

Sarah dropped her handbag on to the table. 'Gone to bed and slept it off I should think,' she said under her breath.

Chris glanced up at her. 'So where on earth were you?'

Sarah sighed as Peter's mother busied herself with the washing up and tea making.

'I went to Monica Carlisle's party,' she said quietly and evenly. Before Chris could protest she held up her hand to silence him. 'I have no idea why she isn't in the telephone directory. I had a lovely time. She lives in this huge house, there were loads of other people there, a band – it was fabulous. I drank lots of champagne. I ate lobster for the first time in my life and to cut a very long story short I ended up getting drunk and thought it would be safer for all concerned if I stayed the night. I really am sorry, Chris, I didn't mean to worry you, it was just one of those stupid things. And I do know that it was a stupid thing to do.'

Chris nodded. She could see he was still quite drunk himself, and hoped that from a distance it sounded fairly reasonable. The fact that it was also the truth didn't seem to be of any consolation whatsoever.

Peter's mother turned around very slowly, brandishing a tea towel. 'So why didn't you ring and let us know where you were?' she asked triumphantly.

Sarah sat down. 'What? What the hell is this "us" business. And what are you still doing here anyway?'

But it was too late to pull the indignation card. Chris glared at Sarah with red rimmed eyes. 'She's right, why didn't you ring me?'

Peter's mother nodded. 'Anything could have happened. Anything at all.'

Now Chris nodded. They looked for all the world like two little plastic birds dipping their heads into glasses of water.

Sarah exhaled thoughtfully. 'I didn't think about it. Look, up until now I've never done an irresponsible thing in my life. Anyway, you said yourself she's not on the phone. I couldn't have rung.'

Peter's mother lifted her eyebrows. 'Really,' she said suspiciously. 'So what about the man Charlie saw you talking to who dropped dead?'

Chris leant forward pointing a finger aggressively at Sarah, 'Exactly, what have you got to say about that?'

The phone, which was hanging on the wall, rang once, twice. Chris eyed it with a bemused expression – as if it was taking him a while to work out exactly where the sound was coming from – and then finally picked up the receiver. After saying hello he listened in complete silence and then turned to Sarah, his tone was icy.

'It's for you. Some man who wants to know if you got home all right. He says he's ringing from Monica Carlisle's place.'

Sarah swallowed hard, brain cells arcing like lightning in a thunder storm as she took the receiver out of Chris's fingers. Realistically there was only one person who could be ringing her.

'Hello,' she said with exaggerated politeness. 'Hello?'

'I was worried about you, you seemed so upset this morning,' said Mac.

Sarah bit her lip. 'How very nice of you to call, Reverend.'

'Reverend?' snorted Mac. 'What the hell's going on there? Are you all right? I was worried what your husband might say.'

Sarah looked up into two pairs of accusing eyes which were fixed on her like guns' sights. 'You're not the only one,' she said and then added hastily, '– I had a lovely time too.'

'Monica was planning to ring and explain to your husband, pour oil on troubled waters if needs be and all that sort of thing,' said Mac, 'but she's busy and I know she's desperate to get to bed. It might be midnight before she gets round to it, if she remembers at all.'

Sarah tipped her head on one side. 'It's a shame it wasn't her,' she said carefully. 'I wonder whether you could let me have Monica's telephone number. My husband was trying to contact me last night and couldn't seem to get it from Directory Enquiries.'

'It's not going very well there, is it?'

'No, no, not at all,' Sarah said as lightly as she could. 'So it's – ?'

Mac read off the number and she wrote it down with the piece of paper and pencil that Peter's mother provided her with.

'The number is listed under Mrs Monica Dunbar,' said Mac. 'Shall I give you mine as well?'

'No, thank you,' she said firmly. 'This is the number for

the main house, isn't it?' Sarah scribbled Monica's name alongside the number. 'Thank you for your concern, it was really nice to have met you last night.' Her voice was so stiff and formal that she sounded as if she'd got lock-jaw.

Mac chuckled. 'You know, I'd really like to see you again. Monica said she might invite you and the rest of your family over for a meal.'

'That would be very nice,' said Sarah.

'Nice wasn't really what I had in mind,' Mac purred mischievously. 'Maybe we could meet up for lunch some time, just you and me.'

Sarah could feel her colour rising. 'Thank you so much for ringing, Reverend. No, no, really I'm fine now, I was explaining to my husband about drinking too much – yes, I certainly will know better next time. Yes, it was a lovely party, wasn't it? I'll ring Monica later,' she said in answer to a flurry of imaginary questions.

On the other end of the phone line Mac chuckled. 'Think about it, I'll ring you soon,' he said softly and hung up.

Sarah lay the phone back on the hook and picked up her tea. 'Now,' she said, 'where was I exactly?'

'The man who dropped dead,' said Peter's mum. 'The man who you followed and who Charlie saw you talking to.'

Sarah hesitated for a split second before launching into the story about going down the road with Charlie and the red Astra van, driven by a man looking for the fishmongers in Kersley Road. And yes, he was drop dead gorgeous and no, there was no harm in window shopping, was there – and – and Sarah didn't say a single word about Mr Red Astra also being the imaginary Reverend.

What was it that made it so difficult? That for once in her life she had thrown caution to the wind and embraced recklessness and irresponsibility? Chris wouldn't think twice about turning up in the wee small hours or even not coming home at all if the occasion demanded.

He looked across at her with drink glazed eyes. She couldn't tell whether he believed her or not, and felt ridiculously contrite even though she had done nothing to be ashamed of. So why the terrible feelings of guilt? She didn't really have to ask that question; she already knew the answer.

If Monica hadn't been in the summerhouse it might just be that all Chris's deepest darkest fears would have materialised. Even though it wasn't likely Sarah felt she was guilty of adultery by imagination – and if her imagination was anything to go by it had been one of the greatest sexual encounters in history. Across the kitchen, Chris sniffed and Peter's mum, who had listened to the whole account with her arms folded across her chest, and did not look convinced, sighed heavily.

Sarah took a deep breath. 'Any more tea in the pot,' she said, holding out her mug.

'I'll make us fresh,' said Peter's mum.

When Sarah woke again it was ten o'clock and for one brief beautiful moment she thought it had all been a dreadful dream, until she saw Peter's mum standing at the foot of their bed. Chris was on his back, red faced, arms flung over the edge of the bed, snoring and hacking like an elephant seal.

Sarah held up her hand in greeting. 'Hang on, I'll be there in just a minute,' she said, dragging on her dressing gown.

Downstairs Peter's mother had made a good job of clearing up the kitchen. 'I thought I'd just wake you to let you know I'm off home now. I've given Charlie his breakfast. He's in the sitting room watching cartoons. Jack's gone up the shop because you're almost out of milk. Matthew rang to say he'll be home about eleven this morning and he hoped everything was all right now. Oh and I've just made a pot of tea, there should be just about enough milk left for you –'

Sarah looked at her in open mouthed astonishment. 'I cannot believe that you're still here,' she muttered.

Peter's mum didn't appear to have heard her and sucked her teeth. 'So me and Peter will be off home now. We'll be back later. Unless of course it would be easier to pick us up on the way.'

Sarah blinked. 'What?'

Peter's mum nodded. 'Chris's invited me and Peter to go to the barbecue with you all at Cuthbert St Andrew.' She wrinkled up her nose and then glanced over her shoulder as if there was some remote chance that they might be overheard. 'To say thank you for all I've done,' she said in a loud whisper. 'You know he's okay, your Chris.'

Sarah just stared at her.

Chapter 4

Peter's mum drove her aging Ford Escort on to the forecourt of the cut-price petrol station, Burdetts, that Sarah and Chris always used and rubbed her aching eyes. Peter was busy playing with a computer game in the back seat and appeared oblivious to everything other than the peculiar blips and growls emanating from the tiny green screen. She yawned and slid out of the seat, and then very carefully eased four pounds eighty-six pence worth of petrol out of the pump, which was exactly what she'd got in her purse.

In the pay booth her friend, who worked the early shift, lifted a hand in recognition as Peter's mother pulled her handbag out of the footwell.

'Nice morning,' said her bleached-blonde friend from behind the plexi-glass screen. 'So, how's life been treating you then, Jenny?'

Peter's mother smiled. 'So, so. Mustn't grumble.' Carefully she counted out the money on to the counter.

The blonde woman looked her up and down. 'You're up and about early this morning.'

She grinned. 'Haven't been home yet.'

Her friend feigned shock. 'Oh God, not that bloke from the shoe shop with the ginger wig? I thought you told me it was all over with him.'

Jenny rolled her eyes heavenwards. 'Oh for God's sake, no, not him. Do you know Chris Colebrook?'

The woman pulled an appreciative face. 'The landscape gardener bloke from Hevedon? Used to be a salesman or something – got really nice hands.'

Jenny nodded slyly and snapped her purse shut. 'The very same.'

Her friend was leaning forward on her elbows now, serving the next customer without taking her eyes off Jenny's face.

'You have got to be kidding? He's absolutely gorgeous. His wife was in here yesterday all dolled up to the nines –'

Jenny – who had always had a quick mind and an even quicker tongue and was never afraid to use either – winked salaciously. 'Don't say anything to anybody, but she's got a fancy man. She didn't come home last night. I know because I took my Peter and their son, Jack, back to his around nine.' Jenny tapped the side of her nose. She had the woman's undivided attention.

'It was all arranged. If you get my drift.' Jenny didn't think it worth mentioning that it had been Sarah who had been doing the arranging, instead she left a delicate open silence at the end of the sentence that her friend was only too eager to fill. Without any more effort on her part the lie was already gathering its own momentum.

'My God, you didn't. Not with Chris Colebrook?'

Jenny shrugged.

Her friend hastily joined the dots. 'Oh my God,' she hissed again. 'You sly little cow. You never let on. Not a word, not a peep. I'd got no idea. I'm impressed.'

Jenny preened a little, and then the lie dropped down a gear and accelerated away so fast that Jenny could barely keep up with it. 'We've had to be very discreet. After all he's got his business to consider and then there's the children, of course. But it's all out in the open now. It's a relief for all concerned to be perfectly honest. We're going out to the barbecue tonight.'

Her friend's eyes widened. 'Not that do over at Cuthbert St Andrew?'

Jenny nodded.

'Who's having Peter for you?'

Jenny smiled a thin but confident smile. 'No one. Chris thought we ought to take Peter with us.'

Her friend's jaw dropped. 'Bloody hell. Everyone's going to be there.' She broke off to serve a man with cigarettes and then turned her attention back to Jenny. 'So, it's over with him and his missus then, is it?'

Jenny, still lying on the hoof, said, 'They've only been staying together for the sake of the kids. You know how these things go. She's been going out with some vicar over at Barton for ages.'

Her friend's eyes were so wide now that the whites showed all the way around the pupil. 'No! I don't believe you. My God, he christened my sister's baby in March. Fancy him carrying on with a married woman – God.'

Jenny shrugged. 'There's just no telling about some people, is there? Gotta go.' She yawned theatrically. 'Some of us have got to catch up on our beauty sleep, you know.'

'I don't suppose you'll be down the Lamb now then?'

Jenny smiled. 'Depends on what Chris has got planned.'

She pulled back her shoulders and stuck her nose in the air as she walked back to the car. When she looked back her friend nodded and waved, but Jenny knew that the very instant she drove out of the forecourt she would be on the phone. And eventually – in a day or two, maybe even before that – Mr Tony-bloody-Whelk would hear all about it. The miserable conniving cheating little bastard. She'd teach him to leave her with six industrial freezers, forty pounds of tuna in garlic butter and no sodding money. She sincerely hoped his new girlfriend gave him a dose of something seriously anti-social.

When Chris Colebrook woke up again it was almost lunch time and some bastard had given him flu. It had to be flu, you always get flu when you get a headache as bad as –

He stopped and stretched out his hand to feel Sarah's side of the bed, it wasn't even warm. Recollections, jumbled memories, the previous night's furies and fears and fantasies came flooding back to him in a torrent of cold hard consciousness. He threw back the duvet and rolled very gingerly out of bed.

'Sarah?' he shouted at the top of his voice and immediately regretted it as each letter of her name detonated a land mine somewhere down deep under something wet and unpleasant in his skull.

The whisky may have stemmed the flow of doubts the night before, but now in the daylight they started all over again. He could feel them exploding as bright pinpricks of light amongst the pile of sluggish grey matter – like firecrackers in unset concrete. On the landing lay a pair of seriously sexy black sandals that he couldn't remember seeing before, each heel delicately ringed with a little halo of turf. He closed his eyes, and felt his way towards the bathroom.

A few minutes later, Chris made his way downstairs and into the kitchen. Stepping across the threshold he stared at Sarah, she looked up at him and almost instantly the air thickened up until you could have cut it into bite sized chunks. He suddenly saw her with new eyes. She was dressed in a long grey T-shirt and black leggings which – until now – he had always thought – and occasionally told her – made her look like a female Max Wall. This morning he could pick out every curve of her hips, flat stomach, nice perky little breasts . . . He shivered, best not to think about perky little breasts if he wanted to get anywhere near the truth.

Charlie, Jack and Matthew had been eating toasted sandwiches around the kitchen table and chatting brightly until he walked in.

Sarah tried out a smile on him. Chris had already decided

in the bathroom and on the long slow climb downstairs that whatever Sarah did it wasn't going to work. He frowned. It hurt the muscles in his face so much that God alone knew what havoc a smile might wreak.

'Would you like a cup of tea?' she asked pleasantly, lifting the pot.

He shook his head with some care. 'No, I don't want tea. I think we need to talk.' He glared at the boys and seconds later they vanished, taking their sandwiches with them.

Sarah swallowed hard and pulled out a stool. 'Sure,' she said lightly. 'What do you want to talk about exactly?'

He noticed with a disproportionate sense of pleasure that she had gone quite pale. 'What the hell do you think I want to talk about? Us, Sarah, I want to talk about what's happening to us,' he said, with as much dramatic emphasis as he could muster. 'I want to talk about why my wife stayed out all night. That's what I want to talk about *exactly.*'

Sarah sat down and wrapped her fingers round a mug of tea. 'Chris love, I don't honestly think that we've got anything to talk about. I'm really incredibly sorry about last night. I just got drunk, that's all – I've got no sordid confessions to make or terrible things I have to own up to. You know I'm no good with booze. But I should have rung. I'm sorry.'

He stared at her; she'd done something different to her hair. Last night's heap of curls was back again, soft tendrils framed her face and made her look unbelievably sexy. He took a deep ragged breath. It was as if she was deliberately trying to throw him off the scent; women could be so bloody clever.

'Then why did you tell me Monica Carlisle hadn't got a phone?'

Sarah lifted her hands. 'For God's sake, Chris, this is

crazy. It was *you* who told *me* that she hadn't got a phone. I was so bloody drunk that I –' she stopped, immediately flushing scarlet.

Chris sniffed and leant closer, feeling as if he'd found the plump maggot he was both looking for and at the same time dreaded finding in his ripe red juicy apple. 'You were so drunk that what?' he asked very quietly.

Sarah ran her fingers through her heap of hair, unfurling another tendril. 'That I more or less passed out,' she said, in a voice barely above a whisper.

Chris rocked back and threw out his chest. 'Oh, right,' he said in a loud overly aggressive voice. 'Well, that is really bloody wonderful, isn't it? Jesus, Sarah what in God's name were you thinking of? You're a married woman, three children – who else was there? What the hell were you playing at? Anything could have happened. Anything at all.'

Sarah had tears in her eyes when she looked up. 'But nothing did happen. How come you're acting like this, Chris? Since we've been married you must have had a couple of dozen unplanned nights out. I've seen you in some real states. If I hadn't been there to drive you home then you'd have had to stay. How come that's all right and this isn't? What about when you and Barry went to that stag do in Norwich? When you turned up here at half past three the next afternoon, still wearing a party hat with the car half full of crazy foam. I didn't bawl you out,' she paused and gathered herself together.

'That was completely different,' said Chris, with a nasty self-righteous edge to his voice.

She stared at him. 'What? Why? Why is it different, Chris? Because you're a man and I'm not? All the times you've worked away, all those little cash jobs you've done for lonely wives, merry widows – I've never once accused you of – of . . .' she stopped again.

'What?' said Chris, feeling a little glow of triumph. He was driving her up this alley of words and he was determined to corner her sooner or later.

'Sleeping with any of them,' she said quietly.

'I haven't said that's what you did,' said Chris very slowly, pretending to be reasonable.

'But I know that's what you're thinking. That's the implication, isn't it?'

Chris gathered up his mouth into a little *moue* indicating deep thought. 'I never said that. Is this your guilty conscience speaking, I ask myself?'

Sarah looked at him as if he had just grown three heads and a tail. He could see she was planning to launch a broadside and braced himself in preparation when Charlie scuttled in. 'Are you two going to the divorce shop?' he said cheerfully, hefting himself up on to one of the stools.

An enormous tear rolled down Sarah's face and plopped on to the table alongside her mug. Charlie looked from face to face. 'Will we have two houses? Oliver Stanton in my class has got two houses and in the summer he gets two holidays – he went to see the Disneys in France.'

It was just after half past three when the vicar of Barton's friend arrived in his sexy little black 4 × 4 jeep for a spot of afternoon tea. It was the vicar's housekeeper's weekend off. The Reverend Leo Banning opened the front door of the vicarage and smiled. 'Hi, Harry, how's it going?'

Harry Fox grinned. 'Oh God, Leo, it's so good to see you, you've got no idea.' Once inside he leant forward and kissed Leo gently on the cheek. 'Whoa, you smell good enough to eat. What is that?'

Leo smiled, 'Something my flower ladies gave me for Christmas.'

Harry giggled. 'Very nice. You know I really wish you'd come back to London. We all miss you. I always get so twitchy coming down here. Brookie and Pip send their love. They've just opened this great new bar, I've brought you an invite for the official opening – it's all Edwardian green leather and brass studs, very understated, you'd absolutely adore it –'

Leo indicated that they should go through into the elegant sitting room that overlooked the gardens. 'But I adore it here. I've got a dozen charming middle-aged women fawning over me, all trying to marry me off to their daughters. Fag-hags for Jesus.' He smiled and then poured them both a glass of Pimms.

Harry folded his long lean body into one of the leather armchairs. 'I read in the papers that your bishop is jumping on the bandwagon, a welcome return to true family values – all very anti.'

Leo rolled his eyes heavenwards. 'All right for him with all those lovely purple frocks.'

Harry laughed into his sherry. 'Seriously, Leo. I do worry about you being cut off here in the back of beyond. I read his comment column in the nationals last Sunday. He sounds as if he's planning a really tough disciplinary crack down.'

Leo leaned forward and stroked his friend's smooth newly shaved chin. 'Sounds like my sort of evening. Which reminds me, we're off out tonight. I've been invited to the barn dance and barbecue over at Cuthbert St Andrew.'

Harry lit up a cigarette and grinned. 'Damn me and I left my gingham dirndl back in Hampstead. I suppose I've got to masquerade as your hunky cousin up from the Smoke.'

Leo moved closer and took a drag from Harry's cigarette. 'I'd be much obliged.'

The Reverend Leo Banning's housekeeper, Mrs Vine, was not a gossip, she didn't like gossip and she didn't mind who knew it. So when her sister rang her at home during her weekend off she told her she had no intention of gossiping about anyone. No, really.

'Not even your precious Reverend Leo?' her sister said peevishly.

'What about him?' asked Mrs Vine defensively. She had her own ideas about how the Reverend Leo Banning spent his spare time but wild choristers wouldn't have dragged it out of her.

'Well,' said her sister. 'I've just been down to the corner shop to get the twins some ice-cream.'

'And?' asked Mrs Vine cautiously.

At the far end of the phone line her sister sniffed. 'To be honest I thought you might have said something before now. It was dreadful having to find out these sort of things from that horrible common little woman in the garage.'

Mrs Vine braced herself for the worst. Did she light the blue touch paper and ask what had been said or did she ring the vicar now and tell him people were talking? Everyone must have seen that thing in the Sunday papers. They'd reproduced it in the local rag too.

'What did she say?' she said, with her fingers mentally crossed.

Her sister took a long steadying breath. 'Sarah Colebrook.'

The reverend's housekeeper waited for a few seconds to see if there was any more. She should have known better, her sister was a tight lipped bitch.

Finally the silence was too much for her sister to bear.

'The landscape gardener's wife? The woman from the garage says that your dear Reverend Leo has been having an affair with her for ages. Apparently it's common knowledge. All over the village. So how is it I've got a sister working in the vicarage and I'm the very last to hear?'

Mrs Vine covered the receiver in case her sister might be able to hear her smiling.

'Really,' she said very curtly. 'You should realise by now that I've got to be very careful what I say in my position. What if it could be traced back to me?'

At the far end of the line her sister gasped. 'So it is true then?' she said happily.

Leo's housekeeper took a deep breath and prayed that God might find time in his busy schedule to forgive her.

'What can I say, dear?' she said softly. 'He's only human after all.'

Saturday was proving to be a long and very trying day for Sarah Colebrook. The adrenaline that had carried her home from Monica's and on through the first sorties with Chris had finally lost its battle against the small peevish needly hangover that crouched between her eyes.

In the external world Chris wandered around the house like a dark, terribly wounded wraith, his expression alternating between stony grey and very hard done by. Finally he installed himself on the sofa in front of the TV with a pint glass of water and an aura of brooding calm.

Sarah fought every temptation to pour oil on troubled waters, to apologise again or to justify what she'd done or to try and make up or to just grovel. From his demeanour she knew that Chris was waiting for that moment when she caved in.

The boys were subdued and finally headed en masse to the playing field to play football. They even took Charlie, who was really much more interested in cartoons and observing his parents in this chilly state of impasse. But the promise of a three goal advantage and ice-cream to follow was enough to change his mind. As Sarah pressed a handful of change into Matthew's hot sticky palm she tried to suppress all thoughts of rats and sinking ships.

And then they were alone. Chris and Sarah. Not talking except for a series of bright, staccato and unnaturally cheery everything-is-all-right type remarks and questions from Sarah, which Chris answered with an angry grunt or not at all. The whole house was suffused with a tense silence that hung like a dull grey blanket over everything and made Sarah feel sick right down to the pit of her stomach.

Just as she was contemplating whether to join the kids up at the playing field the phone rang, the sound ripping through the silence like a sabre. Sarah hesitated. Maybe it wasn't such a good idea to answer it. What if it was Mac again? Could she get away with ignoring it? Perhaps nipping outside so that she could pretend she hadn't heard it was a good idea, but then what if he left a message? Asked her out to lunch, left a cheeky flirtatious dangerous drop-her-right-in-it kind of a message, which she suspected he was more than capable of doing. The decision was taken away from her by Chris lurching in through the hall doorway.

His face wore a 'so, do I have to do everything?' look.

'Chris Colebrook,' he snapped into the mouthpiece although an instant later his expression softened. 'Jenny? Oh hello, how are you?'

Sarah turned her attention away, back to anger and guilt and all things domestic. It didn't take a genius to work out that Jenny Beck was as mad as a badger.

'Oh no, everything is absolutely fine here now,' Chris was saying, punctuating the sentence with a terrible false laugh. 'What time?' He looked round the kitchen as if the answer might be lying around somewhere. He avoided Sarah's eyes. '...We should get to you at about seven, seven thirty. Is that okay?' There was another little pause and then Chris added, 'And thanks again for everything. I don't know what I'd have done without you last night.'

Before Sarah could say anything or so much as show a flicker of emotion Chris beaded her with an angry stare. 'See you later, Jenny,' he said and settled the phone almost reverently back into its cradle.

Noisily, not avoiding the rocky rasping rims of ice Sarah dragged a bag of oven chips and packet of chicken kievs out of the freezer, feeling much in need of uncomplicated instant comfort food.

'What was all that about?'

Chris straightened his shoulders. 'Jenny Beck checking on what time she should be ready.'

'Be ready? Be ready for what?'

'The barbecue at Cuthbert St Andrew. I thought she told you.'

'You weren't serious about taking her, were you?'

Chris's expression clouded over. 'And why shouldn't I be? God only knows what I would have done without her last night. She was really supportive – really calm . . .'

Sarah couldn't help herself. She laughed. 'Oh come on Chris, don't be so bloody melodramatic. We're not talking about bomb disposal here. I was out. You were drunk.'

Chris's eyes narrowed down to glittering reptilian slits. 'Yes, I was drunk, Sarah, but at least I was here. At home. Not pissed out of my head, making a complete fool of myself in front of total strangers at some party somewhere.'

Feeling her anger rising, Sarah slammed the kievs down on to the top of the kitchen unit. 'You can't leave it alone, can you, Chris? I didn't make a fool of myself. I made a mistake, an error of judgement, that's all. I've already said that I'm sorry. Several times. What more do you want? What more is there that I can say to get you off my back?'

But part of her already knew that Chris wouldn't rest until he had heard every last detail, picked over every juicy little morsel, tripping her up and tricking her along the way, torturing them both until she felt even more wretched than she did now. He had always had a way of making her pay a drop at a time for whatever crime he had convinced himself she was guilty of.

Maybe a night out with Jenny Beck was another part of the punishment.

'And I hate those bloody chicken kievs,' Chris said, before stalking back into the sitting room. Sarah fought the compulsion to throw them at him and switched the oven on instead. It was nearly five, another couple of hours and Mrs Whelk would be giving them both the benefit of her great wisdom. Sarah groaned and lay her forehead on the bag of chips.

It was such a shame it wasn't a gas stove.

In one of the new non-estate bungalows on the edge of Cuthbert St Andrew, Mrs Margaret Tuck, stalwart fund-raiser and flower lady over at the church was delighted by the sudden last minute rush for tickets for the barn dance and barbecue that evening. She'd nipped out to drop a couple of punnets of raspberries off at her daughter's down the road, and by the time she got back the tape on her answering machine was chock-a-block with messages.

She'd barely had time to get her cardigan off before the phone started ringing again. It was rather gratifying, obviously somebody had been spreading the word. At this rate the church would be able to felt the porch roof in no time.

While she was pretty certain that there would be plenty of food for everyone Mrs Tuck planned to leave a few minutes early so she could nip out and pick up a few extra packets of baps and some more sausages from the supermarket on the way. Just in case. They could always freeze them later if there wasn't the call for them. And then she rang Audrey Ball to up the coleslaw.

Before she left for the village hall Mrs Tuck took a minute or two to say a little word of thanks to the Almighty. The Reverend Leo would be so pleased with the turn out.

Chapter 5

'And then, after the left hand star, we break, skip back to where we started and do-si-do our partners,' jollied the caller through his head mike, pacing out the steps, hand in hand with a plump red-faced girl, who looked terribly embarrassed at having been singled out as an example to all. It was barely eight o'clock and the crowd at the Cuthbert St Andrew barn dance was still a long way from warmed up and co-operative.

The caller was a cheery little soul, thin as a whippet, dressed in pied piper stripes, with greying shoulder length hair streaming out behind him as he pranced and grinned and do-si-ed and do-ed. Around him everyone else gingerly felt their way forward through the combination of dance steps moving as cautiously as skaters on untried ice.

'And now swing with your partner on the spot,' he shouted with glee, whizzing the plump girl so fast that it looked as if she might take off.

Over by the refreshments the Reverend Leo Banning handed his friend Harry a glass of fruit punch and winked. The hall was already more than half full. Around the trestle tables peelings of families, grannies, pregnant women and small children were sitting the dance out, while down the centre of the hall the remainder formed two long straggling rows. Above them brightly coloured bunting fluttered to and fro in the heat. There were people of all shapes and sizes, all holding hands, counting off the beats and stepping out, around and back as instructed.

In a spotlight, up on the stage the band's violinist busied

himself teasing the main theme out of a folk tune, playing it very slowly as if laying down a trail of musical bread-crumbs that would tempt the dancers to follow him, lead-ing them in and through the maze of steps.

Harry unfastened another button on his Ben Sherman shirt and took a long pull on the glass before wiping the beads of sweat from his forehead. He was grinning, breath-ing hard, having just finished a reel in the arms of one of Leo's more robust flower ladies.

'You know that was really good fun,' he gasped, bend-ing forward a little to catch his breath. 'Used to do it at school. Years since I've done any dancing other than disco stuff.'

Leo pushed the little mauve umbrella to one side of his glass and took a pull on the straw. 'Don't worry *mon brave*. It'll all come back to you like a bad dream. My verger firmly believes it's the most fun you can have with your clothes on.'

Harry snorted, still far too breathless to come up with any kind of smart answer.

'Wait till you see them strip the willow,' Leo continued, smile broadening out a notch, 'it'll bring tears to your eyes.'

'Wonderful turn out, Vicar, don't you think?' said Mrs Tuck, sailing past them, bearing another enormous jug of fruit punch.

Leo nodded. 'And we owe it all to your organisational skills.' He lifted his glass in a toast. 'You've done an abso-lutely splendid job, Mrs Tuck.' His voice and the compli-ment hooked her and slowed her to a standstill. 'The hall looks magnificent. Who have you got outside manning the barbecue tonight? You've put Harry and I down for a stint, haven't you?'

Margaret Tuck blushed furiously. 'Well, actually I hadn't Vicar, no. My husband and the verger are out there at the moment, but I'm sure they'd be very glad of a hand later on, when things get busy. My husband gets awfully flummoxed when he's under pressure.'

At the far end of the hall the double doors were wedged open to encourage a through draught. On the slight breath of summer breeze came a rich waft of fried onions and behind it, like the base notes in a strong perfume were the softer woody mouth-watering smells of barbecuing food.

Harry glanced down ruefully at his pale cream shirt and pulled a face.

Mrs Tuck patted his arm solicitously. 'Don't worry, Harry, I'm sure we'll be able to find you a pinny from somewhere.'

Behind her, Leo laughed.

'You know, to be perfectly honest I've never understood why people want to barbecue food at all really,' sniffed Jenny Beck, pulling the shawl a little tighter around her shoulders. 'Not in this country anyway. It's different when you're abroad. I mean what's the point of cooking outside in our weather when you can just stick it under the grill? Or microwave it. Even getting the charcoal going in the first place is a pain. I used to say that to my Tony, for God's sake stop buggering about out there under that umbrella, and come in and I'll stick the oven on. Makes no sense at all if you think about it.'

Jenny was busy holding court in the front seat of Chris's Transit van, strapped in between Chris and Sarah Colebrook. In the back, the four boys – Matthew, Jack and Charlie, and Jenny's son Peter were wedged in between bags of compost. No one else had spoken since they got into the van although Jenny was apparently oblivious to the tense silence that lay just beneath the surface of her unbroken monologue.

She took a much needed breath and then busied herself adjusting the straps of her summer dress. Sarah hadn't

66

meant to watch but it was very difficult not to. The shawl was a black, open weave, wispy little number while the dress beneath was purple, and made from something very shiny and very stretchy. It seemed to be a couple of sizes too small, giving Jenny Beck's body the appearance of a wet, ecclesiastical chipolata. It was not flattering but it was certainly very difficult to overlook.

What finally drew Sarah's attention away was the van lumbering down into a rut in the playing field which was being used as a temporary car park. Chris swore as the van bottomed out and then quickly excused himself – to Jenny, Sarah noticed wryly. Having been directed into a parking space he gallantly leapt out of the van and hurried round to open the door and help both women out. Sarah in faded jeans, trainers and a T-shirt got the most perfunctory of elbow holds whereas Mrs Purple Whelk got the whole nine yards, the elbow hold, the solicitous murmurings of 'All right? okay?' as Chris's hand settled on her ample waist to guide her down.

Sarah sighed. He was really laying it on thick. When Jenny took the moment to look up at him adoringly Sarah found herself having to suppress a snort of derision. Should she say something or ignore the pair of them? Before she could make up her mind Chris caught her gaze and bristled.

'Just going to lock up, there's no need for you to hang around. I'll be over in a minute or two.'

Jenny smiled and then scurried across to catch Sarah up. The way Jenny's high heel sandals jammed down into soft summer grass gave Sarah an unpleasant sense of *déjà vu*. Tottering unsteadily beside her, Jenny looked almost jubilant.

'It's ages since I've been out to a proper do, you know a dance or something, not down the pub with the girls. My Tony wasn't much of a socialiser, or at least he didn't used to be when I was with him.' She paused thoughtfully and sucked something troublesome out of her teeth. 'I don't think you know what you've got there, Sarah,' she said, nodding back in Chris's general direction, while having another stab at rearranging the expanse of creamy white flesh contained by the dress.

Sarah looked over towards the van, resisting the temptation to tell her. Chris was checking his hair in the wing mirror. Normally he wouldn't have been seen dead at a barn dance, or in that plaid shirt which she'd put in the back of the wardrobe – Sarah knew instinctively that this show of things familial was for Jenny Beck and also to underline the state of play for Sarah's benefit. Chris wanted to prove what a good and very hard done by man he was. Obviously he was married to a raging, hard drinking, amoral martinette, while he was as blameless and as sensitive as the day was long. There had been an awful lot of false bonhomie and jolly smiles while getting the boys into the van. Sarah paused and looked back towards the van; now that Jenny had gone he waved the kids out with a perfunctory nod of the head.

'Mind the bloody compost, will you,' he snapped as Charlie scrambled over the top in a wild break for freedom.

The older boys loped across the grass towards the main doors, Charlie trotted along behind them clutching a dog-eared book of nursery rhymes, a packet of felttips and a plastic ray gun. Sarah smiled, now there was a boy with all eventualities covered.

Outside the hall other families moved to and fro like bright birds between the wooden tables and benches that had been carried out on to the paved area around the entrance and the barbecue and a little outcrop of stalls.

When she caught Chris's eye he frowned, ensuring that she got the full brunt of his continuing disapproval. The message was unequivocal: they might be out, he might be being sociable but she was still the bad one. Sarah took a long slow breath and decided to ignore the game Chris was playing with Jenny Beck and get on with the evening.

Already it felt as if Monica's party was a life time ago and that she had done guilt and sorry to death. It was time to move on to something more uplifting. Beside her, Jenny, as if engaged in some kind of royal progress, was waving to all the people she knew.

'You know it might be nice to sit outside,' Jenny said, indicating an empty table. 'It's a lovely evening. Get down wind of the smoke.'

Sarah pretended not to hear. She had no intention of spending the whole evening wedged between Jenny Beck and Chris if there was any possible way to avoid it.

As they reached the hall a bright skein of a tune tumbled out of the double doors and scuttled off into the evening. It was the closing bars from a dance tune that Sarah knew well; it was comforting. After she'd paid and given her eyes a few seconds to adjust to the gloom her tension began to ease.

Clustered around the fringes of the hall were their friends, neighbours and acquaintances. Lots of faces she knew well, and people called and waved hello. It was going to be okay after all. Whatever Chris thought, however badly he behaved, whatever Jenny Beck was up to, and however misguided Sarah had been, she suddenly remembered that she was innocent of whatever crime she stood accused of. They couldn't hang you for being silly – Mac's sun-kissed features momentarily flashed through her mind, as bright as a comet – Sarah grinned, or for being attracted to someone else. She'd suffered enough and straightened up.

On the other side of the hall Matthew had already found the tab end of a table close to friends who he went to school with. Lisa and Barry waved too, they'd got a table

near the band. Spoilt for choice Sarah nodded in acknowledgement and waved to them both.

Lisa mouthed, 'Hello. All right?'

Sarah pulled a face.

'Right, so what do you ladies want to drink?' said Chris
cheerily, interrupting Sarah's train of thought. He was
directing them towards the makeshift bar.

Jenny Beck didn't take long to make up her mind. 'Gin
and bitter lemon would be good, please.' She turned and
continued conversationally to Sarah, 'We used to drink
that when we were in Ibiza you know, they drink a lot of
it out there. In a long glass with ice and a slice of lime.
We went there the year before last, to this really nice hotel.
Although of course, with hindsight Tony was acting a bit
odd even then . . .'

'I'm afraid we aren't serving any alcohol,' said the
woman behind the counter. 'We don't have a licence. Saves
a lot of trouble with the teenagers, but there are soft drinks
and fruit cup included in the ticket price.' She pulled three
tumblers towards her. 'Or you could have brought your
own, of course. A lot of people bring a bottle of wine along
to have with the barbecue supper.'

Chris scowled. 'Bring your own? What about beer?'

The woman shook her head and shrugged. 'No. Sorry.'

Chris swung round to glare at Sarah. 'They haven't even
got beer for God's sake. You might have said something
before we left home.'

'I didn't think about it. I hardly ever drink, Chris, you
know that.'

His face darkened. 'You bloody well drank last night.'

Sarah flinched and wished him gone.

'Why don't we nip down to the offie in Barton,' suggested Jenny helpfully. Sarah noticed that she settled a hand
on Chris's arm. This was all getting a bit too cosy for
comfort. 'It's only five minutes down the road. Not that I

mind fruit cup or anything. I'm not much of a drinker me, but it is nice to have a little drink now and then, especially when you haven't got to drive.'

Before either Chris or Sarah had chance to reply, the pied piper tripped past and said, 'We just need three more couples for this one.'

Sarah glanced at him. He grinned. She had seen him at a lot of the local dances. They were on good terms without ever having exchanged more than half a dozen words.

'C'mon,' he cajoled in an undertone, holding a hand out towards her, and, desperate to be away from Chris and Jenny, Sarah took a step forwards. Leo Banning, their local vicar who was part of the next group along at the bar, looked up at the same time and for an instant their gaze met. Sarah smiled in acknowledgement. He'd been in to the school where she worked several times and always seemed like a very pleasant man. In his late forties he had unruly curly white hair, shot through with tones of grey and one of those classically handsome, open English faces that suggested he was a good sort; the kind of man who would be terribly useful if you ever found yourself ship-wrecked on a desert island.

At her elbow Jenny Beck said, 'There you go, Sarah. The vicar will dance with you, won't you, Vicar?'

Leo Banning smiled warmly. 'Why not? It would be my pleasure. How are you Sarah? It is Sarah, isn't it?' He offered his arm. 'You work at Whitefriars School, don't you?'

Sarah nodded and accepted it. 'That's right, you came in to judge the art competition I helped to organise earlier this year.'

'Oh yes of course, I remember now – you're the artist,' he said warmly. 'You did that wonderful undersea collage with the children. All along the corridor, I seem to remember. Coral and things?'

And as he spoke Sarah sensed him relaxing as he slotted her into context.

The whole exchange took perhaps thirty seconds maybe less.

In a distant corner of her mind Sarah noticed Jenny moving a fraction closer to Chris, something she said in an undertone had made him laugh. Sarah sighed and stepped in amongst the melee of dancers. No fool like an old fool.

Beside her the vicar was still talking. Hastily Sarah shifted her attention back.

'Can you do this one?' he was asking, as they joined the nearest short set.

Sarah laughed. 'I've got absolutely no idea, but trust me it'll be all right, Vicar.'

'Please, call me Leo.'

The pied piper grinned again and skilfully wheeled them into their proper positions. 'This one's called Drops of Brandy, it's a strip the willow, Leo,' he said. 'And you're going to absolutely adore it. We've never lost a dancer yet.' And with that he lifted his hand for the band to begin. The top couple in each set took a slow turn through the music and through the steps, weaving in and out, guided by the caller, and then a moment or two later the tune kicked in and they were away.

Round by round the dance began to gain its own momentum. It was exhilarating. Leo Banning was surprisingly nimble and fast and uninhibited for a man of the cloth, Sarah thought, turning round to catch hold of her partner's hand. As the music got faster and faster Sarah felt it was as if the dancers were being pulled deep inside the melody, on and on through a rich tribal landscape. It was impossible to stay still. Between twists and turns Sarah clapped and tapped and stamped, aware that part of the pleasure was the relief of not being in the company of either Chris or Jenny Beck.

As Leo Banning swung her left and right, spinning her up and down the line of dancers she caught brief glimpses of the boys settled around the table with Lisa and Barry.

Matthew was talking to his girlfriend, leaning in close, his arm casually draped around her shoulders, beside them Charlie was kneeling up, crayoning and sipping something bright orange up through a straw. Peter and Jack were nowhere in sight, probably outside, but were of an age when that was the place where they were happiest.

The dance was wild and invigorating. It was hard to do anything but grin while each of the dancers spun past the other. Leo Banning clapped out the beat as they moved on and on through the music. When Sarah saw the pied piper lift his hand to indicate the wind down she felt a genuine sense of disappointment. Finally as the last chord faded Sarah was very happy to let Leo Banning catch hold of her hand, press a chaste kiss to her cheek and murmur his thanks. It had been a glorious dance.

'Wonderful, wasn't it?' said Leo as they made their way back towards the bar, both still breathing hard. And then he continued more earnestly, 'Actually, you know, I'm glad we've met. You might be the very person I need. I'm involved in a project locally that might be of interest to you.'

Sarah glanced around. There was no sign of either Chris or Jenny.

A good looking man handed them each a glass of punch. 'This is my friend, Harry Fox,' said Leo Banning, by way of an introduction. 'Harry, Sarah Colebrook.' He paused and took a sip of his drink. 'She strips a jolly fine willow and is a local artist. Very talented in both areas.'

Harry laughed. 'I'm very impressed.'

Sarah flushed and extended her hand. 'I work as a classroom assistant at the local school.'

Leo waved away any false modesty. 'But I've seen some

of your work there, you're very good. The thing is there are plans to open up St Bartholomew's church in Taverstock Road as a community arts centre. Do you know about it? It was deconsecrated a couple of years ago by the Diocese. Lovely old Gothic pile. I've been appointed as one of the trustees for my sins – press-ganged actually but I am terribly excited to be involved. We've been awarded lottery money and all sorts of grants and what have you – you must have read about it in the local paper? The thing is, to be honest we've got quite enough chiefs and had far too many committee meetings, what we need now are a few doers, people with drive and enthusiasm. There's still time to get into the project on the ground floor. There'll be studio space, performance space – that's one of the reasons Harry is down here at the moment. Theatre management is his particular forte. But there are plans for a gallery, a crèche, a café.' He raised his glass to emphasise the point. 'I really think you ought to get involved. You're just the sort of person we're looking for. You could teach a few classes and develop your own work – I know that they're about to go on a bear hunt for part-time staff, people prepared to get their hands dirty. Why don't you come along and have a look around? I'd be very happy to recommend you to the powers that be.'

Sarah laughed. 'That's a fairly persuasive sales pitch.'

Harry topped up her glass. 'Leo always was one of life's natural enthusiasts. But he's right. We went over this afternoon to see what they've been doing. The whole place has got so much potential. Wonderful space, excellent light, and the conversion plans are really quite adventurous. They've opened up a huge section of the back of the building and glazed it.'

Sarah nodded. 'Okay, I'll certainly go and take a look round. Shall I tell whoever's there that you sent me?'

Leo laughed. 'Why not. The chap in charge of the project

is called Adam Gregory. Nice guy. As far as I know he's on site there most days. Just pop in.'

Sarah smiled, thanked him, letting her concentration and her gaze wander around the hall in search of Chris. He was nowhere in sight but the boys were still gathered around the table. Lisa and Barry were talking to people at the next table. As Sarah made her way across towards them, one of the mums from the school stepped up and caught hold of her arm. The gesture was so unexpected that it made Sarah jump.

'Hello. How are you?' said Sarah quickly, subtly trying to extricate herself from the woman's grasp.

The woman grinned salaciously. 'You know you just don't look the type. Then again they always say it's the quiet ones you've got to watch, don't they? You're a real dark horse, Sarah Colebrook.'

Sarah frowned. 'I'm sorry, I'm not with you?'

The woman laughed. 'God, and cool as a cucumber with it. I wouldn't be sorry if I were you. He's absolutely bloody gorgeous. I'd got no idea he was on the look out.'

Sarah's face must have revealed her non-comprehension. And then her stomach tightened. Was it possible that the woman had been at Monica's party and seen her go off into the night with Mac and a bottle of champagne? She didn't look like the sort of person Monica would invite but maybe she was another old friend. Sarah reddened a shade. She couldn't remember seeing the woman there but what did that mean? There had been at least fifty people at the party, there was no way she could have committed all of them to memory.

And, said a mischievous little voice somewhere in the back of her head, she had been far too busy flirting with Mac to take much notice of anyone else. Sarah's colour intensified a shade or two.

The woman moved a little closer, her voice lowering to

a conspiratorial whisper. 'I think I ought to warn you though that the cat is well and truly out of the bag.'

Sarah decided to bluff it out, after all what cat? What bag? How many people knew she had stayed out all night? She took a deep breath.

'I'm really not with you.'

'No, of course not.' The woman winked. 'Front it out. I'd do just the same if I were in your shoes.'

Sarah nodded, in a way she hoped would set her free from this peculiar conversation, maybe make her appear clued up, maybe suggest she knew exactly what the woman was talking about. She smiled benignly

'It's nice to see you again but I've got to go – the boys –' she motioned in the general direction of the tables. Across the hall Lisa grinned and pulled out a chair in anticipation of her arrival

The woman laughed. 'God, you are such a cool customer.'

Feeling far from cool, Sarah hurried over to Charlie, Matthew and Peter, very aware that several people were looking at her. It was not an easy feeling.

'Have you seen your dad?' she said.

Matthew waved towards the door. 'He went to the offie with Peter's mum to buy some drinks. They said they wouldn't be very long.'

Charlie looked up from his picture. 'He said he's going to bring me sweets back and a bag of crisps if I'm good. I am being good, aren't I?'

Sarah caught sight of the woman from school, now sitting amongst her cronies on the far side of the hall. As she noticed Sarah looking in her direction she winked and then waved. Sarah flushed crimson.

'So come on then, spill the beans, how did the party go last night?' Lisa said. 'Did I miss much?'

Sarah struggled to bring her attention back to the table.

She could still feel the woman looking at her. 'Just the end of the world as we know it,' she said, dropping into the chair beside Lisa. 'Would you mind very much if I have a glass of your wine?'

Lisa laughed and pulled a plastic cup off a stack on the table. 'God, you really must be feeling rough. What's this? Hair of the dog?'

Sarah took a mouthful. The wine tasted bitter and dank and made her shiver. 'You have no idea,' she said and closed her eyes. Somewhere out of the periphery of her consciousness, out beyond the beginnings of the new dance and the murmur of conversations Sarah heard the low rumble of Chris's voice, followed an instant later by a high-pitched giggle. Jenny Beck's high-pitched giggle. It seemed that they were back from the off-licence.

Chapter 6

Chris had never danced at barn dances and neither, apparently, did Jenny Beck. Sarah danced in almost every set throughout the evening, in part because she always did, but also as a gesture of defiance to the disapproving huddle of two who sat on the sidelines and watched her every move. Her mood swung between hurt and anger and total bemusement. Lisa eyed her and the rest of her family with increasing curiosity.

'What on earth is the matter with you tonight?' she asked as they launched into yet another gallop down the hall.

'Later,' Sarah mouthed as they dashed in towards the middle of the set.

'It had better be worth waiting for,' Lisa said, grin widening. Over on the table, between Sarah's self-appointed judge and jury, stood a bottle of Gordon's gin, a large bottle of bitter lemon, several cans of beer and coke, and a pile of crisp packets. Barry had joined them to share a few cans of beer. Sarah tried to spend as little time at her table as possible. Instead she danced with Lisa and other people she knew from work and from the village.

Leo Banning partnered her for two or three more sets, and as he was keen to talk about the arts centre – a neutral middle ground that suited both of them, and the conversation inevitably extended beyond the dance – she spent very little time talking to either Chris or Jenny. Leo's dancing seemed to have set a precedent, which meant she also danced a round or two with his friend Harry as well.

If it weren't for Chris and Jenny watching her with

increasing disapproval and the little gaggle of mothers on the other side of the hall who waved and giggled from time to time, it would have been a really great evening out.

'So, who did you say that woman is who's talking to Chris?' asked Lisa as they made their way across to the barbecue accompanied by the kids. 'Her face seems ever so familiar.'

'You mean the divine Madam Whelk also known as Jenny Beck?'

Lisa's face registered a flash of comprehension. 'Oh God, of course that's it. She used to come round on the fish van, with some awful oily little man.'

'That would be the divine Mr Whelk. Her husband or at least he was her husband until he ran away with Miss Weigh and Save.'

'I feel that I'm missing something here.'

Sarah snorted. 'You and me both,' she said without a flicker of humour.

And so, while cooling off, eating a buffet barbecue supper sitting outside the main doors on the grass, in the soft light of a fine summer evening Sarah told Lisa the bare bones of the last twenty-four hours, including all the glorious details about meeting Mac at Monica's party and the delights of being fancied by a wicked golden boy and drinking champagne and getting stoned under a starlit sky.

Lisa paused for a minute to dip a sausage into one of the pots of relish they had been handing out at the buffet table. 'Jesus-H-Christ. No wonder Chris is so pissed off with you. Barry would probably have spontaneously combusted,' she said with her mouth full.

'Angry would be fine, I could handle angry. I understand angry and why he is angry with me, and hurt come to that, but little Mrs Whelk is something else altogether. She is way too keen to stoke the fire under my sins for my liking. She's making Chris ten times worse, shaking him up like a jam jar full of wasps. I'm worried how Chris will react if I tell her where to get off, but she really is pushing it. If she hadn't stayed at our house last night he would probably have just got drunk and crawled off to bed, probably wouldn't even have realised I was gone.' Sarah wrestled a lump of french bread off the piece on her plate and stuffed it into her mouth. 'I might have got away with it if he'd done that. But even if I hadn't, without Mrs-bloody-Whelk hanging around all night he would have cooled off a bit by now.' She paused, letting the idea run through her mind.

'And I can't believe she stayed all night, it makes about as much sense as Chris inviting her to come out with us tonight. He was only coming under sufferance because he knew Barry was going to be here. She had to have suggested it. Without her around fanning the flames he'd just bring Monica's party up as a chorus when we were having a row, you know, "that time you stayed out all night, Sarah, that time I forgave you even though you quite obviously didn't deserve it."'

Lisa laughed. 'Know it? I thought my old man wrote the script.'

Charlie appeared from amongst the ruck and maul of the buffet scrum, cradling an enormous hot dog swaddled in a generous layette of paper napkins.

'The man said did I want onions? Do I want onions?'

'No love.'

Charlie nodded and elbowed his way back into the huddle around the table.

'Excuse me?'

Sarah looked up from tracking Charlie's progress back into the melee straight into Leo Banning's large brown eyes. 'Sorry to disturb you, Sarah, but are you married to that big dark haired chap in a sort of maroon lumberjack shirt – he was sitting at your table I think?' Leo mimed Chris.

Sarah felt an odd tightening sensation somewhere deep inside.

'I don't like to be a wet blanket but he's a little bit the worse for wear. Your friend, the lady in the purple dress, said she doesn't think he's used to gin. She asked me if I'd come and find you.'

Bloody Jenny Beck. Sarah got to her feet. 'Right,' she said, hurriedly fixing on a smile to disguise her embarrassment. 'Thank you, Leo. I'm terribly sorry about this.'

Leo waved the words away. 'I wouldn't say anything except that he was rather rude to one of the flower ladies. He seems rather belligerent I'm afraid. Drink can do strange things to a person. Your friend seems terribly worried about him.'

Sarah sighed, while Lisa made a gallant effort to swallow down a grin.

God alone knows how much gin Chris had put away while he'd been sitting with Jenny. He was on his feet, by the kitchen door, swaying dramatically but otherwise fairly calm by the time Sarah got to him. Barry was trying to placate him but it was quite obvious he wasn't that far behind him in terms of consumption. When Sarah and Lisa appeared he burped and sat down heavily.

'Chris doesn't normally drink very much at all,' she said apologetically to the small crowd that had gathered, while trying to work out how best to tackle six foot of unstable, unfocused potentially dangerous landscape gardener.

'Well, he's certainly made up for that tonight,' said Leo ruefully. 'Here –'

Leo Banning and Harry Fox helped her and Lisa half lead, half carry Chris out to the van and then, after Sarah had wrestled the keys off him, manhandle his unwieldy frame in through the back doors.

After a lot of dark murmurings, some wailing and a few minutes of barely coherent obscenity Chris finally passed out amongst the piles of tools and bags of compost. Feeling hot, angry and self-conscious Sarah was very tempted to go back to the dance and just leave him there to sleep it off; he looked unjustly comfortable. Leo and Harry left almost as soon as Chris was settled.

Lisa sighed as they battled to get the back doors of the van closed. 'So where's the purple Whelk-woman got to?'

'Talk of the devil,' said Sarah, nodding towards the hall.

Caught in one of the floodlights Jenny Beck was teetering out from the hall towards them, carrying what remained of the gin in one hand and the bottle of bitter lemon in the other. She looked confused rather than drunk.

'Oh thank God, I didn't know where you'd all got to, I couldn't get any sense at all out of that Barry,' she said in a high pitched, edgy voice, looking around anxiously as if it were possible that Sarah and the van might still vanish into the ether. 'Your Chris has been so good to me, you know. So understanding. So kind.' The words, soaked with sentiment and an awful lot of alcohol faded into a long soft moan. 'It's been so lonely since my Tony left, you know, you've just got no idea. So lonely.' It was impossible to miss the promise of tears and hysterical sobbing locked in her voice.

As Jenny's shoulders started to heave, Sarah said hastily, 'Why don't I go and round the boys up and then I'll run you home? It shouldn't take more than a few minutes. You can wait in the van if you like.'

Jenny nodded, sat down heavily on the passenger's side step and promptly burst into tears.

Sarah beckoned to Lisa. 'Quick, let's make a break for it, while we still can.' Without a backward glance the two women practically ran back to the hall. Neither spoke; there wasn't that much to say.

By the time Sarah had said her goodbyes to everyone, including Lisa and Barry, and Leo and Harry and arrived at the van with Matthew, Charlie, Peter and Jack, Jenny Beck had made her way into the back and was curled up alongside Chris. They both appeared to be sound asleep.

Sarah clambered into the driving seat and turned on the ignition. As the Transit slowly lumbered across the playing field back towards Harehill and Hevedon and home, the sound of their snores and snuffling was a steady counterpoint to the low drone of the diesel engine.

Nobody said much on the way back about the evening, although Charlie sang a bit. Poor Peter kept apologising profusely for the way his mum had behaved but Sarah shook her head. 'Really there's no need, Chris is just as bad. There's no point apologising for something that's not your fault.'

'This is all your fault,' hissed Chris, nipping the bridge of his nose tightly between his finger and thumb. Sarah handed him another mug of tea and kept her own counsel. It was Sunday morning, a little before nine. Upstairs Jack was in the shower and Matthew and Charlie were in the sitting room watching cartoons and eating toast and chocolate spread. Chris had been up for about fifteen difficult minutes and was still wearing the clothes that he had gone to the barn dance in; the clothes he had slept in.

'I promised Barry I'd go over and help him finish off the drive first thing this morning. You knew that. On site by seven I said, get the heavy work out of the way before it gets too hot.' He paused to make sure she fully understood the gravity of the situation. 'I'll be bloody lucky if I make it by lunch time now, the way I feel.'

Still Sarah said nothing.

'And why did you leave me in the van? I suppose that was your idea of a joke was it? Or were you getting your own back?'

She'd had enough. 'How the hell was I supposed to get

you out, Chris? Anyway you came to bed eventually.'

'No thanks to you. This is all your fault.'

From across the breakfast table Chris peered at her through one rheumy eye, the other one still firmly screwed shut against the citrus yellow sunlight. There was most definitely a hint of accusation in the way he was looking at her.

Sarah slid the biscuit tin towards him. 'You cannot be serious, Chris.'

Still his gaze did not falter.

'You're saying that your hangover is my fault? You spend the whole evening in the corner with Whelk-Woman pouring gin and bitter lemon down your neck like it was going out of style and somehow that is my fault?'

There was another brief but very weighty silence and then Chris sniffed. 'I'm terribly depressed and I think we both know who is responsible for that state of affairs.' Both eyes were open now. 'You.'

Sarah looked heavenwards. 'For God's sake, Chris. This would be funny if it wasn't so bloody pathetic.'

'At least you haven't got the front to deny it. And I'm glad you can see the humour in this because I damn well can't. I was talking to Jenny last night and she said . . .'

It was more than Sarah could bear. She felt a small white flare of fury ignite in her belly. Bloody man, bloody sodding woman. 'Jenny? What exactly did Jenny say then, Chris?' Sarah snapped. 'What iridescent pearls of wisdom did the fabulous Madam Whelk dispense as she was topping up your glass? Eh?'

Chris's face contorted with anger. 'You can be such a bitch at times. Jenny told me that you . . .'

Sarah suddenly realised that she couldn't bear to hang around to hear whatever it was that Jenny-bloody-Beck had told him.

*   *   *

Storming out into the bright sharp morning; the dramatic gesture was exactly what she had in mind, an exclamation mark stamped on the events of the weekend, but once outside Sarah didn't know what to follow it up with.

If she took the car then the kids would be left with Chris which, while not being exactly disastrous, would underline her fecklessness – and if she was going to be feckless then it sure as hell was going to be over something more spectacular than the state of Barry's new drive and childcare. She stood on the drive and kicked the gravel around for a bit. If they'd a dog she could have taken it for a brisk walk down to the common. It would have been a gesture.

Henry, the family cat, black as a Cossack's hat, was curled up on the bonnet of her Golf, absorbing the heat of the morning sun. As she approached he unfurled, stretched to reveal his snowy white belly, all fur, all claws, and then dropped onto the gravel alongside her. Taking the cat for a walk was apparently an option she had overlooked. He wound himself around her calves and ankles and purred a salutation.

By the time Sarah got back from walking Henry around the block Chris had gone out in the van. Presumably to Barry's, although the kitchen looked as if he had just vanished, melted away, abducted by aliens perhaps, despite there being no obvious signs of a struggle. It was one of those *Marie Celeste* moments Sarah realised she was really glad of.

Holmes-like, Henry jumped on to the kitchen table to inspect the mug of tea she'd given Chris. It was still warm, almost full, next to it stood a glass of water and a half eaten digestive biscuit. Sarah cleared the contents of the table into the sink in an effort to exorcise the ghost of Chris's bad tempered hangover with a mass of hot water and bubbles.

Matthew peered around the door. 'Oh sorry, I thought it was Dad coming back.'

Sarah smiled. Of course the sound of washing up would make him assume it was Chris, Chris whose idea of helping around the house was to point out which bit of the carpet hadn't been hoovered and to record with almost carbon 14 accuracy the long slow decay of leftovers in the fridge. She wiped the table with a brisk business-like swish of the dishcloth.

'He was running a bit late this morning. He'd promised Barry he'd give him a hand.'

Matthew nodded. 'Yeh, I know, I was gonna go with him.'

'So what stopped you?'

'He got a phone call.' Mat screwed up his face. 'Weren't you here?'

Sarah shook her head. 'I was out walking the cat.'

Mat grimaced. 'What is going on with you two?'

Sarah wrung the cloth out with a lot more vigour than she intended. The fabric ripped like tissue under her fingertips. 'Nothing much. Just one of those parental rows that you can blame all life's later disappointments on. Something to tell your shrink about.'

Matthew lifted an eyebrow. 'Well, he was incredibly snotty when I asked him if he could give me a lift into town to see Hannah. I told him I'd do the work at Barry's first and he said too bloody right I would. Anyway if he doesn't take me I can always go in on my bike. He said he'd pick me up if he was going to go to Barry's later.' Matthew paused and stared at Sarah.

'What?' she said, feeling she was being asked to pass comment, or judgement.

'That means I'm stuck here all day until he shows up, doesn't it?' Matthew managed to sound affronted and oppressed and imply that somehow it was her fault.

Sarah thought about it for a few seconds and then made an executive decision, knowing full well that whatever she did it would be wrong. 'Tell you what, hang around here until lunch time and if Dad hasn't come back by then you can go. All right? Any idea where he went?'

Matthew shook his head.

Sarah pressed 1471 to check on who had called last. What if it had been Mac who'd rung? She closed her eyes imagining the sound of his flirty, jokey voice while weighing the possibilities and then stopped as the pre-recorded voice picked out the digits.

It wasn't as if this would be the first time that Chris had rushed off to rescue someone or price up a job first thing on a Sunday morning. Sarah jotted down the number. It sounded familiar but wasn't instantly recognisable.

Pinned to the notice board above the phone was a list of numbers Sarah had left for Chris in case he had any problems the night she had gone to Monica's party. Sarah wasn't altogether surprised to see that the number she had just written down belonged to Mrs Jenny Whelk.

When the phone rang Sarah was so far away that it didn't register for a few seconds.

'Mum?'

Sarah looked up, her mind on Jenny Beck. Chris had gone haring off to rescue Jenny-bloody-Beck. This really had gone quite far enough. 'Sorry?'

Matthew was pointing. 'Phone.'

Sarah blinked, finally letting her mind register the ring and picked up the receiver still retaining an odd sense of detachment. 'Hello?'

'Hi,' said Monica with a deep throaty chuckle, 'so how are you?'

Sarah suppressed a sigh. What sort of question was that for anyone to answer? 'Fine thanks, how about you?'

'Glorious, darling. I was ringing to check that everything

was all right, I meant to ring yesterday but I was so tired, maybe pour oil on troubled waters, that sort of thing.'

Sarah laughed without humour. Too late for that.

'And also to ask if you and . . . er, what's-his-name and the boys would like to come over for Sunday lunch next week. I was thinking that we could do the whole business, you know, roast beef, Yorkshire pudding, piles of over-cooked veggies and one of those sponge puddings so heavy that it renders you totally incapable of leaving the table. Treacle or raspberry jam with custard. What do you think?'

Sarah nodded. It was time Chris saw that Monica was mad and kind and rich and eccentric and not just some wild figment of Sarah's imagination. 'That sounds lovely. What time would you like us to get there?'

'Um, let me see – if you turned up about say eleven then the boys could explore, we could have a sherry and then have lunch around one?'

'I'm sure that will be fine – but can I let you know for definite? It all sounds very civilised.'

Monica laughed. 'I wouldn't go that far. Mac wants to come too but I'll try and dissuade him. I'm sorry I didn't ring before. How did it go when you got home the other morning?'

Sarah looked around the kitchen. It was very difficult to know what to say, and screaming down the telephone was probably too graphic and far too rude even if it was an old friend who was mad and kind and rich on the other end of the line.

Chapter 7

'Would you mind handing me the penguins while you're there?' Sarah asked from the top of the stepladder. Lisa, who was taking a short cut through the hall on her way back to the school office set a pile of registers down on a bench and handed up a stack of painted cut outs.

'I dunno, the things you get asked to do in this job. So how's it going this morning?'

Sarah sighed. 'Not so bad. I've got this last panel to finish off and then I'm going to make a start in the main foyer. The infants' show stopper. We've got a full scale circus, big top, animals, clowns, high wire the whole shooting match to get on the walls by . . .' she peered down at her watch, 'Damn, is that the time already? I wanted to try and hit Tesco's and get to St Barts before I go and pick Charlie up. Bugger.'

It was Monday morning, the sun was shining and there was the first hint of lunch permeating the air, doing battle with the miasma of old plimsolls and floor polish. If Sarah stretched up a little she could see out through the top windows on to the playing field. Beyond the green and grey metallic rustle of the silver birch trees the whole school was busy practising for sports day. Putting up the new display her thoughts were punctuated by a series of enthusiastic shrieks and whoops and roars.

'That wasn't what I meant, and you know it,' said Lisa, rifling through another pile which comprised mostly of seal pups and polar bears. 'I was going to ring you yesterday to see how things were going but then Chris turned up at ours and seemed right as nine pence. So how is he?'

Sarah groaned. 'Alive, angry, giving me the big freeze at the moment. I don't think I really want to talk about it.'

'Okay, okay – denial is good. So tell me, what's this all about then?' Lisa turned slowly through three hundred and sixty degrees to admire the almost completed panorama. The art work in the main hall was the culmination of a whole school's term efforts and an awful lot of planning. It was all set to be a high spot on the grand tour during parents' evening.

'Around the world in eighty days?'

Sarah stretched, arching her back to ease the dull ache that seemed to have settled in for the duration. 'Uh uh, close. Actually I thought I'd tender for the make-over of the Sistine chapel next year if they'll have me. It'll be a complete doddle after this.' She drew a hand through the air to set the scene. 'I thought maybe barley white with a dado rail, and one of those nice pale beech block wood floors, what do you reckon?'

'You're getting punch drunk on penguins. Do you fancy some coffee? I'm just making a fresh pot.'

Sarah nodded and then added as an after thought, 'What time did Chris get to yours?'

Lisa pulled a face. 'I'm not sure really, we were all busy – it was before lunch anyway.'

Under a spotlight in the far corner was a collage of the earth done in blue and green and white tissue paper by year six. From this focal point, unwinding in both directions around the hall the display encompassed oceanic, temperate, tropical and desert climates until finally on the far side of the room were the polar regions, specifically the Antarctic where Sarah was currently balanced on top of the stepladder loaned, reluctantly, by Mr Anderson from care-taking services.

Sarah picked up a penguin. The first one off the pile was

fat with nasty beady little eyes and a peculiar lopsided, slightly shifty expression that reminded her of the way Chris looked when he arrived home on Sunday evening. Viciously she staple-gunned it through the head on to a passing sugar paper ice flow.

Chris had arrived home at around seven, putting a very brave face on any residual fragility. He'd announced he was hungry and tired. He smelt of beer. He'd had a shower, and then eaten his dinner while making polite noises about how very tasty the warmed-over quiche and salad were and how the boys really ought to eat theirs up. There were an awful lot of children in the world who would be grateful to have a nice slice of mushroom quiche. Sarah sniffed and handed him the dish of new potatoes wondering whether his conciliatory approach had been provoked by a guilty conscience or not having the stomach for a prolonged skirmish.

To the uninformed observer, watching the Colebrook household gathered around the kitchen table, dinner would have appeared a well-mannered and considerate affair. There were lots of thank yous, lots of no, no after you, please take the last new potato, I really don't want it, no really, type of conversations.

Sarah held a neutral expression for so long that it felt as if she was being slowly strangled by her face and neck muscles. Such was the power of détente, the skilled art of the measured impassive, the un-inflammatory at work. Without a word being spoken by either party an uneasy truce had been declared. Neither Sarah nor Chris asked how the other's day had gone, and when Chris suggested that he was going up for an early night no one protested. There was not a single mention of the phone call from Jenny Beck or what Chris had done between leaving home and arriving at Barry and Lisa's.

Sarah had spent a lot of time re-running the events of

the whole weekend, back to back, end to end, including every possible permutation her busy little mind could crochet together.

On Sunday, after he left their house the likelihood was that Chris had gone straight to Mrs Whelk's house and from there to work on finishing Barry's driveway, although she had no way of knowing how long he had been at Jenny Beck's house or come to that what time he had arrived at Barry's. She certainly had no intention of asking him. He hadn't driven back to the house to pick Matthew up, nor had he rung to ask him to bike over, which might or might not be of major significance. Somewhere in the back of her skull a small overworked neurone fired the information backwards and forwards from positive to negative seeing what it looked like and where it fitted the best.

Chris hadn't phoned home either, which was in itself pretty unusual. In the course of a normal day he could ring anything up to half a dozen times whether she was there or not. Sometimes it was just to say what time he would be home, to check up on phone messages or just to announce that he'd left something vitally important in the shed, on the kitchen table or occasionally on a garage forecourt, and could Sarah bring it over.

It had also occurred to Sarah that perhaps she was overreacting. Maybe he hadn't gone to Jenny's house at all. Maybe Jenny had rung to talk to her or maybe to apologise or thank them both for a really lovely evening or arrange for Peter to come round for tea. Something innocent, and then Chris would think she was totally barking mad to have rung 1471 and assumed that was where he was.

Whatever it was, Sarah wasn't going to give Chris the opportunity to deny going to Jenny Beck's house or worse still look at her as if she *was* barking mad and say in the voice he reserved for just such moments of self-righteous indignation, 'What, go there after last night's little fiasco at the dance? For Christ's sake, Sarah, are you totally and utterly crazy? She rang up to ask if Jack could go round after school next week, swimming or something. I said she'd have to ring and talk to you.'

Sarah picked up another painted penguin from the pile on the top step. The penguin looked as if it had been hit on the head with a shovel. Sarah knew exactly how it felt.

Over at her cottage in Harehill Jenny Beck pressed her lips together on a fold of apricot coloured toilet paper and then pouted, checking the effect of Enigmatic Dawn in the mirror. It had been free on the front of a magazine she'd bought in the supermarket. One that promised feng shui could help kick start your sex life Jenny seemed to remember.

She looked at the hall clock. It was almost half past ten; it was a long time since she'd felt moved to wear lipstick this early on a Monday morning. Chris Colebrook had said he'd drop by around half past, if she was going to be in, and if she didn't mind.

Jenny added a tiny dab of duty free cologne behind each ear from the bottle she'd found in Tony's hand luggage the day they arrived back from Ibiza.

She took a long deep breath to catch the first high notes of the fragrance. It smelt expensive. Even Tony hadn't got enough front to tell her that he'd bought it for someone else. A little surprise he'd said, thinking on his feet, skin turning to the colour of putty despite his new tan, it was something special that he had planned to, to . . . Jenny had moved a little closer, so close that she could see the beads of sweat lifting along Tony's hair line . . . put away for her birthday, he'd stammered. Yes, that was it. Her birthday. Thinking ahead. Barefaced liar.

Jenny grinned. The perfume was called Linger but for Jenny it represented the sweet smell of revenge. She tipped the bottle up on to the end of her finger and ran it down over the warm flesh between her breasts. Bastard, she'd show him that he couldn't treat her like a disposable lighter.

It had taken Jenny a while to think of a good reason to call Chris first thing on a Sunday morning and a lot of physical effort to drag the washing machine out from under the work surface and wrench the hose off the back.

Well, that had been the plan until she realised it might ruin the thread on the water inlet into the washing machine and what she really wanted was something small and spectacular not something overwhelming, expensive and difficult to deal with. After all, plumbing might not be Chris Colebrook's forte, and then where would she be?

In the end Jenny had settled for stabbing the cold water hose with a kitchen knife on a bit that looked as if it was pretty well perished anyway, but appearances can be deceptive. It had taken her ages to get the knife in. Who said British craftsmanship was dead?

In the effort she'd broken a nail and had a moment of complete panic as the water suddenly gushed like an ornamental fountain all over the kitchen floor and straight up the tiled wall. What if Chris wasn't at home or Sarah answered the phone?

But then again she reasoned, drying her hands and picking up the phone, what was the worst thing that could happen? It would take her ten seconds to switch off the cold supply to the machine, ten minutes to mop the kitchen floor, no time at all to call out an emergency plumber and even less to send the bill to Mr Tony-bloody-Whelk. She had nothing to lose really.

Before her attempts at damage-it-yourself Jenny had taken the precaution of giving Peter a fiver to go out and amuse himself, and once she knew Chris was on his way had turned the water off at the mains until she heard his van pulling up outside. No need to go to biblical extremes with the flooding, the smell of stale water was awful. Although, with hindsight perhaps if Chris had had to wade across the kitchen to rescue her, Jenny could have offered to dry his trousers off. Ah well, you live and learn.

Jenny pouted again before smudging some more brown kohl around her eyes, darkening the subtle fog of colour she had applied a few minutes earlier. Not that she wanted to be too obvious but a lot of people had told her her eyes were her best feature.

She was wearing a little turquoise sleeveless ribbed top from New Look and a pair of cream linen shorts that Tony kept telling her were too tight. Mutton dressed as lamb he'd said last time they met in the pub and she had been wearing them. Well, nuts to Mr Tony-bloody-Whelk. What did he know about good taste anyway? Look at the state of Miss Weigh and Save, all black sparkly lycra, high heeled sandals and sun bed tan.

Jenny pulled the top down a bit. Since Tony left she had put on a few pounds – she'd be the last one to deny it – but now, admiring herself in the hall mirror Jenny decided that it just made her curvier, more womanly. Sexier. She pushed out her chest ably assisted by the sterling efforts of a new black mesh wonderbra. In the diffused sunlight of the hall she bore more than a passing resemblance to a young Marilyn Monroe. Maybe there was an upside to comfort eating after all.

And as it turned out, it hadn't taken Chris very long at all to sort things out, isolate the cold supply to the washing machine, switch it off. He'd blushed furiously when she had called him her hero and kissed him on the cheek. It was an unexpected bonus when he'd offered to come back on Monday morning to fit a new hose.

Jenny took another quick look in the mirror. Seducing or actively pursuing Chris Colebrook hadn't really been part of her master plan. What she wanted was to kick start a little game of jealousy and retribution, but Chris seemed quite eager and it was tempting and flattering to see just how far she could go. It felt nice to be the centre of attention for once. There was no escaping the fact that Chris Colebrook was very good looking and good company. Sarah really didn't know what she'd got there. Mrs Stuck Up, thinks she's better than the rest of us, Sarah Colebrook.

Jenny ran her tongue over her lips and blew a big wet kiss at her reflection.

Seconds later there was the sound of a van pulling up outside, a door slamming, footsteps on gravel. Jenny watched Chris's silhouette take shape through the obscure glass, and waited for him to knock at the front door.

She checked her hair and took an extra strong mint out of a packet in her handbag. It didn't do to appear too eager. While crunching the sweet into tiny pieces she fluffed and puffed a little and pulled the top straight.

Chris Colebrook knocked again and this time Jenny sashayed very slowly up the hall to greet him.

'Oh it's you Chris, hello,' she said in a warm but slightly vague way as if she was surprised to see him. 'I was just out doing the garden. I'd forgotten you were coming over. You'd better come in.'

He looked a little nonplussed so she beckoned him inside before he could change his mind and was gratified to notice that before crossing the threshold Chris looked her up and down, taking a few seconds to admire the view.

'I'm sorry. Am I disturbing you?' he said apologetically, colouring up a shade or two. 'I could come back another time if you like. I've brought a new hose over for the washing machine.' He held the large plastic packet out in front of him like a bus ticket, as if there was some chance she might have forgotten the flood on Sunday.

Jenny smiled. 'You are a love, Chris.' She stood to one side. 'Why don't you come through. I'm sure you could use a coffee while you fix it, couldn't you?'

Chris looked uneasy as if he was uncertain exactly what was on offer. 'Actually, I was on my way to the bank,' he said. 'I can't stop for very long.' He held the hose out again, this time a moral shield in case there was some chance she might misinterpret his motives.

Jenny nodded. 'Course you can't. Kettle's just boiled, it won't take a minute. I won't bite you know.'

Without another word Chris followed her inside. The hall smelt of perfume.

'I'm sorry but you can't come in. We're not open to the public yet,' said a man in a yellow hard hat and very battered waxed jacket. His tone was clipped, not rude but a long, long way from welcoming. As he spoke he stepped out from behind a rood screen of debris netting and opaque polythene, blocking Sarah's way up the front steps of the old St Bartholomew's church.

It wasn't funny. It had started to rain. Hard summer rain, serious rain that because of the heat seemed wetter than usual. The church steps were marked with an archipelago of lichens and damp builder's sand, delicate bright little islands picked out amongst a backwash of rotten leaves and debris from the leaky guttering.

Sarah dragged her cardigan up around her ears and suppressed a shiver. The hem of her summer dress was as blue as litmus where it had been drinking from puddles on the short walk from the car park over to the old church. Everyone else had got there first and the only parking space left felt closer to Wales than the town centre and that was before she realised she hadn't brought a coat.

It was not a day to stand around in the rain arguing. Sarah felt the man looking her up and down in an unguarded appraisal, while trying to work out just who she might be, and it made her angry.

'I'm not the public,' she snapped, sounding sharper than was reasonable.

The man did not look convinced nor intimidated. 'I'm sorry, but visitors are only admitted by prior arrangement,' he said and made as if to turn away.

Sarah felt the moment slipping through her fingers. 'Leo Banning, the vicar, said that I could drop in and have a look round,' and then in an attempt to redeem herself, added, 'but if it's a bad time . . .' Her voice faded as she looked around.

A lot of the building's façade was wrapped in a surgical corset of scaffolding. An orange ready-mix lorry, its livery brightened by the steady downpour, was backed up close to one of the outside walls and men were busy barrowing concrete up over scaffold boards and in through a gaping open hole in the masonry. Orange and white exclusion tape fluttered like bunting on the light breeze. The whole place had a look of frantic up-against-the-ropes industry.

'It is a bad time, isn't it?'

The man nodded. For a moment it looked as if he might smile but thought better of it. Sarah wished now that she hadn't been so prickly. He was in his early forties, maybe a little older, with the kind of face that time had folded in a very warm and interesting way.

'Is there any other sort of time? This place is a logistical nightmare, no access and a lot of restrictions – physical and fiscal,' he continued ruefully. 'What was it you wanted to see exactly?'

Sarah pulled a face. 'I don't really know. Leo just said . . .' she paused feeling foolish, rain dripping off her fringe. 'Shall I come back when things are calmer.'

This time the man laughed; it was warmer than she expected, and a lot warmer than she deserved but still formal. 'If you've got any idea when that's going to be I'll arrange to take the day off. You might as well come in now and take a look around while you're here. It isn't likely to improve in the foreseeable future and the man himself is here today –' He caught Sarah's wary expression. 'Honestly. It's fine.' He held out a hand. 'I'm Adam Gregory. Project manager. In theory I'm the guy in charge or at least my desk is where what's left of the buck stops.'

'Sarah Colebrook.'

His handshake was comfortable and strong and for some unfathomable reason his touch made her shiver again. She coloured, embarrassed that he might have noticed, and then worried that he probably thought she was rude and pushy; but he seemed oblivious, his concentration sliding away towards the crocodile of labourers manoeuvring wheelbarrows up over damp boards.

'How long before the centre opens?' Sarah's voice trapped his attention and turned it back towards her.

'Officially September. The end of September, but it's a phased project – some of it should be ready by the end of July.' He waved her in under the lee of the porch and into the cool inky gloom beyond. Noises of construction and men's voices echoed around the vast hollow shell. 'On paper we're bang on schedule. Although we're hanging on to the completion date by the skin of our teeth. It's been –' he paused as if searching around for a suitable adjective.

'A complete and utter pig,' said a familiar voice from somewhere inside.

As Sarah's eyes adjusted to the light she could make out Leo Banning standing by one of the pillars drinking coffee from a plastic beaker. Leo was wearing his clerical shirt and dog collar under a light brown cotton jacket, which was soaked to ginger across the shoulders. It clung to him like some sort of drowned animal.

'I'm delighted you took my invitation seriously, just a

pity you couldn't have picked a better day for it. Although we do have some of the ladies from the steering committee in this morning as well, so it might be a good time to put a word in. We've been discussing the next fundraiser.' He grinned. 'Perhaps as I've whetted your appetite we could persuade you to lend a hand? By the way, how was your husband after the barn dance on Saturday?'

Sarah felt horribly self-conscious but wasn't quite sure of all the reasons why. 'Fine, thank you,' she mumbled.

Next to her, Adam Gregory said, 'I need to go and see what's happening in the crypt . . .'

Before he finished speaking there was an enormous crash, its origins impossible to track down as it reverberated around the interior of the building.

Leo nodded. 'Absolutely, Adam.' He extended an arm towards her. 'Perhaps we could start by getting a cup of coffee and then I'll take you on the grand tour.'

It was over an hour later that Sarah was heading back across the road towards the car park. It was still raining, maybe not so hard and certainly not hard enough to cool the sense of well being she'd developed during Leo's ad hoc tour. There were a couple of the women on the steering committee that she knew from working at school, and a third who seemed terribly familiar. Sarah glanced back over her shoulder to see if Leo was still on the steps waving. Her mind was full, turned inward to consider a bubbling great mass of thoughts that divided themselves between the possibility of working at St Bartholomew's – it looked like it might be a really exciting opportunity – what a genuinely nice man Leo Banning was, what to cook for supper, what sort of mood Chris would be in when he arrived home, if there was still time to get to the supermarket before picking Charlie up, and the way touching Adam Gregory had made her feel and that it mattered that he might think she was bad tempered and rude, all this and trying to keep the leaflets and forms Leo Banning had given her dry or at least if not dry then salvageable. So, brain buzzing, as she leant over to unlock the door of her car the last thing Sarah expected was to feel a hand dropping squarely onto her shoulder.

She leapt back and shrieked in sheer astonishment.

'Well, fancy meeting you here.'

Sarah spun round in amazement. Mac was no more than a breath behind her, sheltering under a large black umbrella so close that he practically had her pinned up against the side of the car. She couldn't believe she hadn't heard him coming up behind her. He was grinning, and was, if anything, unfortunately even more gorgeous than she remembered him.

'I waved but you were miles away. What are you planning? A bank robbery. Total world domination? Or maybe a little illicit assignation?' His voice broke the word up into sensual syllables and lingered over the possibility, his smile widening a little. Now that he had her undivided attention he ran his fingers back through his thick blond hair. Annoyingly Sarah felt herself blush. He made as if to grab the papers she was carrying and in doing so fleetingly pressed his lips against hers. She inhaled so hard she thought her heart might stop.

'Sorry. I didn't mean to make you jump. It's really good to see you again. What are you up to?'

Sarah jerked the car door undone, heart fluttering, the surge of heat she felt in her belly rubbishing every sensible thought in her head.

'I've been to see about a job,' she said, stunned to find herself struggling to get her imagination under control, dropping the fliers on to the driving seat before they were totally ruined. 'Well, maybe. Possibly. I've been to look at the new arts centre.' She motioned towards the old church encouraging Mac to look too, which would give her the chance to step away from him.

But he didn't move, instead, without a shred of embarrassment he leant forward a fraction more and sniffed her hair. 'You smell of schools,' he said, knowledgeably. 'Floor polish and summer rain, it's a really nice combination, someone should think about marketing it.'

Sarah laughed, struggling desperately to regain some sense of composure. 'What exactly are you playing at, Mac?'

He aped offence. 'God, nothing. I was only going to ask if you'd like to come and have coffee and a bun with me. I brought Monica's car in for a service this morning and it won't be finished for another hour or so. I was heading into town.' He nodded towards the high street. 'What do you reckon? Worth the risk? I promise not to sniff you again.'

Right on cue Sarah's stomach rumbled, one of those unmissable, pathetic feed-me-now rumbles.

Mac laughed. 'How about Gina's Pantry near the library? They do great florentines, made with really good Belgian chocolate, trust me – and the most excellent baguettes. Great coffee too.'

Sarah hesitated. Wasn't there something in the regulations about going for coffee with other men?

Mac looked at her and upped the twinkle factor a degree or two.

Sarah looked him up and down as if considering. Chris would be absolutely furious if he ever found out, as if sharing a cappuccino was all the evidence any reasonable man needed to assume infidelity. Although of course there was also the little matter of her having spent the night with Mac, which with the best will in the world, didn't sound innocent whichever way you said it.

Sarah wondered if Mac's flirtatious expression was meant to unnerve her, and with that as her best guess she made a real effort to front it out and meet his gaze without flinching. Mac tipped the umbrella, an invitation for her to join him under it.

Sarah sighed. Was there any point fighting it? Chris was already furious with her anyway. 'Okay, but you're paying.'

Mac held up a hand in protest as if there was some chance that he had meant to wriggle out of it.

'So, tell me what you're going to do at the arts centre. Didn't I read some big thing about it in the *Advertiser* a few weeks back?'

Sarah fell into step beside Mac and started to tell him about Leo's guided tour. The little dynamic electric pulse that Mac fired in her direction gave the conversation a delightful animal edge – although Sarah was wise enough to guess that Mac used this lure indiscriminately whenever it suited him. Fun though, it had been a long time since anyone had flirted with her.

Gina's Pantry stood on the corner of Bethel Street and Park Road, close to the library, the last establishment in an arty little row of shops that sold pottery and herbs, prints and handmade furniture and clothes. It was a popular place on fine days. There were wooden tables and rattan chairs outside, and tubs of box clipped into pyramids set either side of the door, all shaded by a navy blue and white awning and trees in the little park next door. The unexpected downpour added an extra attraction. By the time Mac and Sarah got there the café was packed with warm steaming bodies. Even so they didn't have to wait too long for a table. It was in the window, right in the middle of the window. The big plate glass was fogged, but not so much that they couldn't watch the world go by for a while – and not so fogged that the world couldn't watch them.

Chapter 8

While Sarah was settling herself at a table with Mac and running a finger down the menu of Gina's Pantry, Chris Colebrook was arriving home. The house felt very empty. The only signs of life were the cat, Henry, fast asleep on the top of the clean laundry in the basket and the red blinking Cyclops eye of the answer machine in the kitchen. Chris was not best pleased. He'd told Sarah he was going to be home.

Outside the day had dampened down to the colour of wood ash and every few minutes rain beat against the kitchen windows as if they were being hosed down by someone with a personal grudge. Chris had forgotten to take a jacket with him that morning and was soaked through to the skin. Annoyed, skirting the ragged edge of anger, he knew it wouldn't take very much to push him over – and Sarah wasn't at home. Unless of course she was hiding somewhere. The way things had been going between them over the last few days he wouldn't be altogether surprised if she was. But he was still annoyed.

He pulled off his T-shirt and dropped it on to the floor alongside the trainers and socks that he'd prised off with cold, white water-logged toes. In a placating gesture meant to indicate some appreciation of tidiness and consideration he pushed the wet, muddy bundle in the general direction of the washing machine with one foot and looked around for some sign of comfort.

From outside came a great bellicose roll of thunder, followed by a crackle of lightning. Feeling cold and wet and horribly hard done by Chris pulled a clean, fluffy white towel out from under the cat and dried himself off. Henry, bitter at being disturbed, uncurled like a bull whip and sprang on to the draining board with a demonic hiss.

With the towel around his shoulders Chris rifled through the pile to find something to wear. Halfway down was his favourite grey sweat shirt. It wasn't easy to get it out and one or two things slipped on to the floor in retrieving it, but then again if Sarah didn't stack the ironing in such ridiculously high piles to begin with she wouldn't have to keep moaning about the state they got into. She ought to put the washing away. Really.

It wasn't his fault that the towel and a few other things dropped into the mud that he'd walked in from the driveway. He'd tell Sarah it was Henry, and anyway it wasn't hygienic letting the bloody cat sleep in the kitchen, he must have told Sarah that hundreds of times, more. From the safety of the draining board Henry looked at him with an expression that suggested he could read minds. Chris was the first one to look away.

Monday was proving far too difficult. At the bank the queue for the only cashier on duty over the lunch hour was glacially slow. The woman in front of Chris wanted to do something obscure with traveller's cheques which took the best part of ten minutes, and then, when she'd finished shuffling them backwards and forwards under the security grille, and Chris had assumed she was finished and had taken a step closer to the window, she'd glared at him, had a sudden change of heart and started asking difficult questions.

Nine people behind her in the queue and she wanted to know if she'd be able to spend American dollars in Tierra-bloody-del-Fuego. And what about sterling? No shame some people. The cashier had had to go out the back to find a book and a leaflet. And then when Chris finally did make it to the front the girl was surly. Very surly. She had been courtesy itself to Mrs Blue-Rinse-I'm-Off-Around-the-World with all her complicated, involved and deeply difficult questions but give the silly little cow a paying-in book with the slip correctly filled in, two cheques and a Barclaycard bill and suddenly she had all the charm of Vlad the Impaler.

And Sarah wasn't home, and he'd told her he would probably drop in for lunch. Chris sniffed, feeling hurt and ill used. It wasn't that she was supposed to be there but he would really have appreciated the gesture. That and a little bit of understanding about just how difficult the day had been. There was nothing to eat in the fridge, two crusts left in the bread bin face to face inside a crumpled polythene bag and the milk smelt as if it was on the turn; fate was most definitely conspiring against him.

He'd been rained off on the big job over on the outskirts of Norwich, the van still wasn't running properly, despite all the money they spent on the last service, Barry had been on the mobile about the state of his drive and whining about his mortgage which had made Chris think about the outcome of a couple of jobs that he'd priced up but hadn't heard from. He'd get Sarah to chase those up . . . and then of course there was Jenny Beck and her washing machine.

Chris froze as if there was some possibility that he might have been seen, strangling the idea before it had a chance to take another breath. Standing very still in case the thought spilt out all over the floor and left a recognisable stain on the carpet, Chris tucked the image of Jenny Beck back down deep inside his mind. There was no way he wanted to discuss or even mention Jenny Beck to Sarah. Although of course it was all completely innocent. It must be extremely difficult for a woman like Jenny to manage on her own. Chris smiled. Jenny wasn't at all what you'd expect really, under the brittle exterior she had a kind of soft, warm air of vulnerability, and womanliness that made him feel wanted. Needed. Appreciated. It felt good.

As he was leaving her house Jenny had touched his arm and smiled up at him. 'You know, Chris,' she'd said, moving just a fraction closer, 'your Sarah doesn't know how lucky she is having a man like you around the place.' And then she had hugged him and pecked him gently on the cheek. There was nothing sexual, nothing obviously flirtatious, just a little gesture of genuine gratitude that had made him feel really good. It looked as if she was struggling to hold back the tears.

Of course there was no need for Sarah to know about his little act of domestic heroism. She'd misunderstand, but then again Sarah had totally misjudged Jenny Beck right from the start. They were like chalk and cheese, different sorts of women. Sarah was his wife, and Jenny . . . She wasn't his type at all really, no, she was too big, too rounded too – Chris paused for a second or two, while his imagination conjured up an image of the way Jenny Beck's breasts looked, straining against that little blue top she was wearing, and he took a very deep breath, wrestling with a series of increasingly erotic possibilities. But Sarah was his wife and Jenny Beck was someone else's, snapped his conscience. Chris blushed, making an effort to clear his mind.

To help him regain a sense of equilibrium Chris switched on the kettle, shooed the cat out of the sink and then pressed play on the answering machine.

The first message was about work, which meant that Sarah need only chase up one quote now. After a lot of procrastination, umming and ahhing, it seemed that someone had offered to do the work at a better price. A lot cheaper the man said after an eternity, not quite able to disguise the sound of triumph. Cheaper maybe, but not as good. This really wasn't helping his mood at all. He pressed the button again.

'Hi,' said a slightly aristocratic female voice, just as Chris was considering whether to ring the customer back and match whatever price they had been offered by Rent-a-Spade. 'Sarah, darling, I wondered whether you've made your mind up about coming over for lunch on Sunday. It would be lovely to see you and the rest of the family, the boys – and . . . er . . . and . . . Chris.'

That tiny pause, that feigned struggle to remember his name were like fingernails being dragged across a blackboard. Chris would recognise Monica Carlisle's distinctive tone anywhere.

'Anyway, if you could give me a ring so I'll know whether to defrost the fatted calf or not. Whatever. Talk to you soon, darling. Oh and by the way . . .'

Chris switched Monica off while she was in full flow and felt all the better for doing it. He hadn't liked her from the moment they first met. Monica had invited them to supper when he and Sarah were first married and living in a flat the size of a doll's house. Monica had met him at the door of her enormous town house, paid for – apparently – by some poor misguided old sod, who Monica told everyone, was her husband although Chris thought it was more likely someone else's husband.

He couldn't remember exactly why he'd arrived alone, clutching a bottle of Blue Nun and a potted plant that Sarah had insisted he take . . . maybe he was late in from work – but as the door swung open there was Monica leaning against the frame, dressed in a melodramatic hippy ensemble, all indigo velvet and ostrich feathers that covered her from head to heels.

She had looked Chris up and down and then smiled

before shaking his hand. He could still remember exactly what she said, 'Ah, so you're the infamous Chris Colebrook. I've heard so much about you.'

Although it was not exactly Oscar Wilde for some reason Chris felt as if in those few words and those few seconds he had been weighed in the balance and found wanting. From that moment he always believed that Monica Carlisle knew far too much about him and the life he and Sarah led, and although it was irrational he blamed Monica for knowing, not Sarah for telling her.

He had been genuinely annoyed when Sarah received a card with Monica's change of address on it. Of all the houses in all the countries in all the world Monica had to move in to one less than fifteen minutes' drive away from theirs; the snooty self-serving bitch.

Chris scalded his finger fishing the tea bag out of the mug because he was too idle to get a teaspoon out of the drawer. The milk was most definitely on the turn and Sarah still hadn't arrived home.

Meanwhile over in town, in the warm damp fug of Gina's Pantry, Mac leant across the table and wiped a drizzle of butter off Sarah's chin, his eyes alight with mischief.

'You know, you missed out on a really worthwhile experience at Monica's party. I've got great references. Testimonials. Did you know there's a waiting list for my body?'

Sarah laughed. 'You've got such a bloody nerve, Mac. Anyway I've already told you, I'm married. What I'd really like at the moment is a crack at the job at St Bartholomew's arts centre. They're looking for part-time people to multi-task – a bit of teaching, helping to co-ordinate the exhibitions and events. I'd love that. I feel as if I'm ready for a change. A challenge.' Sarah paused, her mind filling up with possibilities, aware that she was thinking aloud rather than expecting Mac to say anything or offer advice or answers. 'They've got plans for a restaurant and –'

Mac lifted a hand to silence her. 'To be perfectly honest although I'd probably be able to handle coming second fiddle to another man, some successful guy with a Porsche. An oil magnate maybe, who's hung like a donkey, an old church, four walls, vegetarian quiche and finger painting is way too hurtful.' Sarah was about to protest but Mac was hell bent on subversion. 'Did anyone ever tell you that you are gorgeous.'

Sarah laughed – funny, that was what she'd said to Charlie about Mac – blushing furiously and totally thrown off balance even though she knew that was his intention. 'Not for a very long time,' she said with feigned lightness, although as she spoke Sarah realised that Chris had never said anything even remotely close to it, and felt a peculiar little stab of grief and regret.

She wasn't even certain that Chris saw her as a woman at all any more. At least not in the sense of being desirable. Monica's party, the black dress and high heeled sandals had more or less confirmed it. It was as if over the years she had been reduced to the role of a companionable old soul, something comfortable and safe, and tame – little more than a series of domestic functions. Gorgeous had never really come into the equation. To her surprise Sarah felt tears prickling up behind her eyes and she very quickly turned her attention and thoughts back to St Bartholomew's and the possibility of a new career.

Mac looked her over, chewing on the parsley garnish from lunch, but saying nothing, an unexpected sensitivity for which she was extremely grateful.

Mac leant across the table and touched her hand. 'Fancy another coffee?'

Sarah nodded not yet feeling confident enough to speak

in case her voice betrayed the splinter of pain that he'd rubbed.

Mac grinned. 'No chance that you could lend me a tenner, is there?'

Outside in Bethel Street, sheltering under the trees, two young mothers with pushchairs, who were waiting to share a taxi home, looked at each other knowingly. They couldn't quite make out who Sarah Colebrook's companion was in Gina's Pantry, the glass was just a little too steamy to see his face. Sarah's husband? That most definitely wasn't him, they were both agreed on that and they could both recognise gossip when they saw it.

They could hardly believe their good fortune, the perfect opportunity to confirm the rumours that had been rife at the school gates when they'd dropped the older kiddies off at school that morning. As Sarah Colebrook had swung her Golf into the car park reserved for staff and teachers, her progress had been observed and noted by at least a dozen pairs of eyes, and before the engine was cold her life had been unpicked, re-shaped and re-sewn into something else entirely.

Sarah Colebrook and her little bit on the side. Fancy that. She didn't look the type. Fancy seeing them out together, although it was common knowledge apparently, or at least if it wasn't, it very soon would be. Sarah had walked across the playground head up, shoulders back, relishing the warmth of the sun on her face, oblivious that the watchers had seen it as a gesture of defiance.

Under the trees in Bethel street one of the women lit a cigarette off her own and handed it to her companion.

'Vicars and teachers,' said the first young woman, casting a glance back towards the café. Fortunately both toddlers had gone to sleep, lulled by the constant drone of wheels on pavements and voices ploughing the same furrow.

'They're all the bleeding same, like to think they're better than the rest of us, but you know, when it comes right down to it they aren't, at all. Worse if anything, Sunday papers are always full of it. I love my Kevin but he wouldn't stand for me carrying on like that. Mind you, now that we've got our Jade I can't see me or him running off with anyone else.'

A bauble of summer rain trickled down over her face. She sniffed and they both looked back towards the café. They thought they saw a hand drop on to Sarah's and even if they hadn't it wouldn't have mattered, they could easily have imagined it. By the time the two of them arrived home, unpacked the shopping and dangled a tea bag into a mug, that one fleeting touch would have been transformed into a kiss, a long lingering tongues and touching, eyes closed kiss, a stolen moment of raw passion that Sarah Colebrook imagined had gone unseen.

The other woman, blonde hair wetted down to the colour of damp straw, took a long pull on her cigarette. 'Reckon anyone else would want your Kevin, do ya?'

The first girl snorted, but before she could come up with something sharp the taxi drew up and the thought was lost in the effort of folding buggies and touting shopping and sleepy toddlers.

The rain hadn't reached quite as far as Barton, although there was a promise of it on the horizon behind the row of copper beech. Outside the vicarage Leo and Harry were making their way across the gravel to his jeep.

'Sexy little thing,' Leo said, rubbing a hand appreciatively over one wing of the 4 × 4.

Harry grinned as he slid his bag on to the passenger seat. 'Are we still talking about the jeep here?'

Leo laughed. 'You know you could stay a few more days if you wanted to, Harry. I mean, what's so pressing in town? There's plenty of room here, and you know you're always welcome. My housekeeper adores you, another few days and she'll have us on a double date with some of Barton's finest fillies. She told me this morning that in her opinion you just need a good woman to sort you out. Can't understand why a lovely young man like you hasn't been snapped up already.'

Harry looked around, tone a fraction less jovial. 'It took me years to finally get out of places like this, Leo, in fact it was a rectory just like this. Every time I come here it's like some hideous Freudian homecoming. No, what I need for peace of mind is the glint of plate glass, the rich bouquet of carbon monoxide and a decent balti house within spitting distance.' He embraced Leo and then climbed up into the driver's seat. 'Come and see me soon. I've got the report on St Barts and I promise I'll ring an inordinate number of influential people and pull lots of strings on your behalf, you know – the things I do best.' Harry patted the pocket of his Barbour jacket. 'I'd better be off. I'll ring to let you know that I've arrived back safe and sound.'

Harry took a cheese cutter cap from the glove compartment and pulled it on. Leo leant in through the open window and patted him solicitously on the arm. Harry checked the mirror.

'You do country squire very well,' said Leo with a smile. 'Don't leave it too long before you come down again.' He paused long enough to look back at the house to make sure they were not being overlooked or overheard. 'I miss you.'

Harry nodded and then added, 'I know, me too. Just don't blub,' with a wry grin. 'We want you back, Leo, this trip into the wilderness is all very well but –'

Leo held up a hand to silence him and then shook his head. 'Don't. Talk to you later.'

Harry shrugged, gunned the engine and drove slowly

across the gravel. It sounded like gunfire. As soon as the jeep was out of sight Leo sniffed a single tear back.

'And exactly what time do you call this?' snapped Chris, as Sarah eased open the kitchen door with her hip. She was struggling with a weighted plait of carrier bags in each hand and a giant box of cereal under one arm. Charlie was weaving in and out and around her like a spinning top.

'Sorry?' she said, looking up in surprise.

'You told me you'd be home at lunch time. You finish at twelve on a Monday. I rang the school to check. They said you'd left at twelve. I told you this morning that I'd be home early. Where the hell have you been?'

Sarah straightened up, stung by the edge in his voice. 'What?'

'I told you this morning that I'd be home early.'

Sarah made every effort to suppress the spark of indignation that flared in her belly. Not wanting to catch Chris's eye in case his petulance fanned the flames, she settled the shopping on to the floor, and pulled off her wet cardigan. Talking to Mac had unsettled something deep inside that she couldn't find a name for, and the way Chris was speaking to her was driving her harder and faster into an emotional place she barely recognised.

Chris stood by the hall door, hands on hips, expression closed and disapproving.

'There's no bread, nothing to eat in the fridge and the milk is off. And how come you didn't tell me Monica Carlisle had invited us all over for Sunday lunch? There's a message on the machine.' He managed to make it sound as if Monica had left them a mouldering dog turd.

Sarah looked heavenwards, making an effort to keep her tone light. 'For God's sake, Chris, you sound like one of the kids. There's loads of stuff in the pantry, beans, eggs

– there must be at least half a dozen loaves of bread in the freezer and the milkman put today's milk in the cool box on the doorstep. And lunch with Monica completely slipped my mind. It must be old age setting in.'

Across the kitchen Chris didn't move and he certainly didn't look amused or placated.

'So, where have you been then?' he repeated.

At Sarah's feet Charlie was rootling around in the top of one of the carriers to find a toffee yoghurt. He looked up at her as if he might be waiting to hear the answer too. Sarah hesitated, she was by nature a creature of compromise not conflict. It would be far easier to tell Chris some version of the truth, how she had been taken on a guided tour around the new arts centre by Leo Banning, and then had stopped for a coffee in town, but why on earth should she have to? And what gave Chris the right to stand there, wearing that expression, demanding to know? None of the thoughts that were passing through her mind were new or revelatory, it was just that today they seemed neon lit and seared into her retina.

Sarah took a deep breath. 'Why do you want to know, Chris?' Sensing the growing tension in the air Charlie grabbed a yoghurt and a spoon and made a break for the sitting room.

Caught off guard Chris coughed, 'Er . . . well, I was worried about you. You said you'd be back. You could have had an accident. Anything.'

Sarah lifted an eyebrow. 'Nice recovery,' she said with an icy snap. 'And what about all those days when you're not coming back for lunch and not home to worry about me, does it ever cross your mind then that I might have had an accident or is it only when you're hungry and bored?'

Scattered on the floor was the pile of wet dirty clothes, some had been clean and were still folded, others had obviously been worn. All of them were muddy. Amongst them was her favourite cream cotton sweater.

'Oh Chris,' she said.

He followed her gaze. 'That's it, change the bloody subject,' he growled. 'And anyway I don't know what you're blaming me for. It was that bloody cat of yours. He was asleep on top of the basket when I got in, there was stuff all over the floor.' He waved in the general direction of the laundry as if he had already recovered the whole basket full from the very jaws of damnation, dragging the kitchen singlehandedly back from the brink of chaos.

Sarah bent down to retrieve the sweater. Underneath it was a large dirty trainer, laces untied, soaking wet and larded with clay and gravel. Presumably because he had been caught out in an obvious lie – after all his clothes were under the clean things – Chris reddened and squared his shoulders.

Sarah could feel a headache closing in. Surely they were both bigger than this, bigger than these petty, picky, bitty peevish little things. She wanted to say that, to tell him not to be so silly, so bloody childish but before she could speak Chris continued, 'You really ought to have put them away, you know. I have told you that before. Leaving the basket there it was bound to get knocked over.' There was a fraction of a second's pause when Sarah felt her colour rising, and then Chris added as if to justify his remark, 'Of course I knew this sort of thing would happen if you went back out to work.' The voice of Neanderthal man echoed around the kitchen like a clarion call.

Sarah felt whatever it was shifting and stirring deep inside her. Did he know he had crossed over the wire into no-man's-land? Apparently not; 'It isn't my fault that you're so badly organised,' he added.

An angry voice snarled, 'No, of course not and that's

just it isn't it, Chris, nothing is ever your bloody fault, it's always someone else, the cat, the kids, me.'

Me? Sarah realised with a genuine shock that the voice and the venom were all hers. They bubbled up from somewhere old and angry and until that moment, completely overlooked.

Chris stepped back as if she had slapped him. 'What did you say?'

'You heard me,' the voice snapped. Sarah began to shake, and then clenched her fists, feeling as if she was fighting to retain control of some great raging angry animal that threatened to burst out and swallow them both whole. It was the most terrible feeling, struggling to hold in an anger she barely knew she had. The real problem was that even if she could hold it in, Sarah still couldn't shut it up.

'I've had just about enough,' growled the same furious bitter voice. 'You don't do anything to help, you moan constantly, you expect me to put up with whatever crap you dish out, however you behave. And I hate the fact that even after all these years, despite every scrap of evidence to the contrary you don't respect me and you don't trust me –'

There was an intense droplet of silence, cool and still and deep, and just long enough for Chris to consider saying something, for him to open his mouth, for him to inhale, but before he could speak the angry animal leant forward and snatched the breath right out of his lungs.

'You don't trust me, do you? It's like living with someone who thinks you're a thief. I hate the fact that your mind must be in a dark suspicious place half the time. All my life I've looked after you, Chris, you and your business, and your kids and your bloody half-done, just temporary until I get the time to fix it properly, house, and all that still isn't enough for you, is it? Well, tell me, is it?'

Chris's eyes had opened up like shop fronts, he was

reeling, hanging on the ropes, ashen and completely wrong footed. She sensed that he was afraid to say anything now, even though he was full of words, bright with justification and a sense of self-righteous indignation, full right up to the brim.

At last Sarah caught hold of the monster's throat, strangling the voice down to a whimper, although behind it she could feel a great tidal wave of fury, whipping its tail to and fro, eager to up the stakes and move in for the kill. And at that moment Sarah knew that if she didn't stop now she would blow Chris away, crush and destroy him on the rack of her hurt and anger and outrage. She took a deep breath, hoping to ease the tension in her shoulders, hoping to still the raging beast inside. Across the kitchen Chris was staring at her.

Impasse. For what seemed like a very long time Sarah and Chris eyed each other up like boxers waiting for an opening and at the same time each anxious to defend their vulnerabilities. The clock ticked. The fridge hummed. From the sitting room came the busy day-glo sounds of children's TV. On and on the seconds ground by turning into an eon. Sarah could hear the drumbeat of her pulse, her breath, in and out, and beneath it a muted feline growl of fury.

Finally Chris sniffed, then shrugged as if releasing himself from her grip, breaking the stranglehold.

'I'm going out,' he said, in a voice that could have levered manhole covers. 'No need to save me any supper. I don't know what time I'll be back.'

It was only when he got to the back door that either of them realised Sarah was still holding one of his trainers.

Chapter 9

'So, how's life been treating you then, Petal?' asked Tony Whelk. It was later that same afternoon. Jenny Beck had tucked the telephone up under her chin and was leaning forward to examine her eyebrows in the hall mirror. There were a few knotty stragglers that needed dealing with. She glanced around the things on top of the hall stand, opening drawers, moving ornaments, wondering where it was she'd last seen the tweezers.

'I wasn't expecting to see our Peter today,' continued Tony. 'He was lucky to catch me in to be perfectly honest. I've told him he can come round after school a couple of nights a week and earn himself a bit of pocket money if he likes. Stocking up the van, moving a few cases of tins. Defrosting the coolers. You know.'

Jenny had sent Peter round to his dad's from school at lunch time to ask for the money to buy new shoes, and if that worked then some trousers and possibly a decent mountain bike. Apparently Tony was planning to make him earn them.

'Peter told me you'd been having a bit of trouble with your washing machine,' said Tony.

'Like you give a shit,' Jenny murmured, not caring whether he heard or not, and wondering whether she ought to have her top lip waxed. There was very definitely a line of fuzz there in this light and it was important not to let yourself go. It was a thought that she had toyed with a lot over the last few days. Maybe she had let things slip a little bit. Not too much but it was a slippery downhill slope.

The pink tracksuit lying by the washing machine was a case in point; she mustn't get depressed and inadvertently let herself go. It happened all the time on day time TV.

'I know what my obligations to you are, Jenny,' Tony was saying, dragging her back from the mental trip to the beautician's above the hairdresser's in the high street; Mondays they had students in.

Tony was speaking in a voice she suspected was meant to engender respect and a deep sense of gratitude. 'Do you want me to come and take a little look at it? I wouldn't want to see you in a muddle, you ought to know that by now.'

Apparently leaving her with no money, a clapped out Ford Escort and a bitter sense of rejection didn't count as a muddle in Tony's book. She growled.

'And I think we're both agreed that there's no need for things to get nasty, is there now, Jenny? These things happen, and I bear you no malice at all. I'd like you to know that. None whatsoever. And I'm at least fifty percent to blame for whatever's happened between us. I'd be the first one to admit it.'

How very big of him, thought Jenny, bearing in mind it was Tony who had left her, Tony who had run away with the van, the classic Jag and a little bottle-blonde munchkin barely out of puberty. A bottle-blonde who, Jenny had been told by friends down at the pub, always referred to her in conversation as the old grey mare. Jenny snarled at her reflection.

On the far end of the line Tony was still talking. '. . . I told you right from the start. I'll always care about you and Peter. I'm a man, not a machine. I suppose I shall always worry about you, I can't switch it off just because life has moved on.'

Which was meant to mean what exactly? Her life was much as it always had been except now there was a lot less money coming in.

'So, getting back to the washing machine. Presently I'm really not in a position to shell out for a new one, Jen. Trade's a bit slow at the present. Summer lull, you know how it is. But if you can get by with the old one for a little bit longer, get it repaired, serviced, whatever it takes, then all well and good. I can probably see my way clear to paying the damage, but if the worst does come to the worst then I know this bloke who does reconditioned ones over at Fairgreen. I could give him a ring if you like, maybe he can do a deal, part exchange or something, you never know.'

Jenny shifted position so she could get a glimpse of her profile in the glass door. Part exchange my arse, she thought. She knew for a fact that Miss Weigh and Save had had a new pine kitchen fitted by that Country Living place over in Tower Street, because the woman who worked in there had told her so. Fitted kitchen, matching fascia door for the fridge, the whole nine yards.

Jenny sucked in her cheeks, and stood very straight making best advantage of her bust. Tony had to be mad to have left her for that girl. Those extra few pounds had really helped fill out the wrinkles, maybe dieting wasn't such a good idea after all.

'I bet he'd take a couple of those industrial fridges out of the garage if you ask him,' she said, with contrived casualness. 'They've got to be worth a few bob. And they're in the way here. I've had to switch them off, can't afford the electricity on the money you're giving me. And I can't get the car in with all them stuck in there. The age that car is it really needs to be inside at nights. Stop the body work deteriorating any more than it already has. The sill's shot on the driver's side.' She paused. 'I don't think it'll make it through the MOT, Tony. And you know that my solicitor advised me that I . . .'

She didn't need to complete the sentence to hear Tony's

hackles rise. 'You told me you wouldn't go back to see him again, said we could work this like adults.'

Jenny sniffed derisively. 'Adults, is it?'

Adults that barely paid any maintenance on the grounds that they were brassic and yet somehow could manage to take Miss Weigh and Save away for weekend breaks at expensive oak panelled hotels deep in the heart of the Cotswolds. Oh, Jenny knew all about the trips to the Cotswolds from the woman in the travel agent's in the precinct.

'Yeh, adults,' Tony's voice dropped to a purr. 'You know, she doesn't look after me like you used to, babe. Can't cook, can't keep a house like you do. Can't do a lot of things like you used to . . .' he let the implication hang in mid-air between them, hot and sticky and quite obviously still glowing white hot in his imagination. Maybe things weren't quite so rosy in the Weigh and Save garden after all.

'There's times I think that leaving you was the worst day's work I ever did, Petal. I hate to think of you stuck over there, all on your own, pining away. If I can ever do anything for you, anything at all . . .' his voice faded into a low throaty chuckle.

Jenny flushed scarlet, the words like an electric cattle prod straight to the heart. Arrogant bastard, how was it that he could still hurt her so much? She squared her shoulders; there was no way she was going to let Tony know that he had cut her right through to the marrow.

She took a breath, the air roaring in and out of her lungs like flame.

'Well, there yer go, Tone,' she said as lightly as she could manage. 'Times change. Like you said, life has to move on.' Worms turn. It seemed that the bush telegraph she had been so depending on to spread the news hadn't quite reached as far as Tony's little love nest yet.

'It's good of you to see it like that, Jen. I knew you'd come round to understand that it was for the best in the end.'

Jenny laughed without a shred of humour. 'For the best? You know, maybe you're right. I couldn't have put it better myself. It's nice to have my freedom to be honest.' She paused for effect. 'You aren't the only one with a bit of life left in them, you know.'

'Sorry, Petal?'

Jenny laughed again, more robustly this time, as if Tony had just missed the best punch line of the best gag ever.

'Trust me, matey, I'm way past pining. Waste of time and a real good woman.'

'Sorry?' he repeated.

'No, you're not, you heard me,' she said and this time the tone was as sharp and hard as a steel meat skewer.

At about the same time Chris was driving away from Sarah and their house, down through the village, out past the golf course, down towards the bypass. Wedged up under the dashboard was a clipboard on which were a couple of small wet weather jobs that would while away the rest of the afternoon if he really wanted. It wasn't as if Chris had nothing to do, there was absolutely no need to dwell on anything in particular, after all there were lots of things to occupy his mind. Lots of jobs, lots of . . .

A stray thought jumped out, it came up on his blindside and mugged him; Sarah was probably already on the phone, getting her side of the story over to Monica Carlisle. When they went over for lunch Monica would tut-tut him for being so petty and so very narrow minded. Not that he was but Monica could always manage to make him feel like that. Maybe he wouldn't go for lunch, maybe he'd stay at home and watch the TV, finish off the downstairs cloakroom, although he would need another bag of filler to do the holes around the pipes. He'd get Sarah to pick it up for him.

The windscreen wipers arced through the driving rain giving him a now-you-see-it, now-you-don't peepshow view of the world. The afternoon traffic was crawling inches at a time towards the bypass. This far back he couldn't make out what the hold up was. Even with the wipers full on it was impossible to see much beyond the tail lights of the car in front of him.

Maybe he ought to take a trip out to some of the nurseries, see if they'd had anything interesting in. He was looking for a centre piece for the gardens in the pedestrian precinct outside Fulsham bus station. Something red and delicate like a Japanese maple. Or . . .

Or maybe he could just drop in on Jenny Beck, see if she was okay, see if the washing machine hose had held. As he was passing, after all Jenny, better than anyone else, understood what he had to put up with at home, understood what sort of woman Sarah really was, staying out all night, completely barefaced and unrepentant.

Chris rummaged around in the back of his brain for an excuse, there had to be one in there somewhere that didn't come up all full of holes. Chris turned off the road to the bypass at the next junction, down a lane so narrow that in places the bushes on the verge brushed the sides of the van, still telling himself that it was because it would be quicker to go the back way. Cut across country; nip down through the village, up Gant's Lane, and miss all the traffic that way. Easy. It wasn't that it would also take him right past Jenny Beck's front door.

Back out on the main road, the rain finally called a halt and almost instantly the sun burst through. Steam spiralled up off the black top, like a sulphurous burst from somewhere demonic and dangerous that lurked just below the surface. The image wasn't lost on him.

Chris stole a glance in the rear-view mirror to see if he was being followed and then pushed the hair back off his face. Not bad for a bloke his age, good chin, good tan, great sweat shirt. He grinned back at his reflection. Very presentable.

Sarah tried very hard to re-establish some sense of equilibrium, while brow beating Charlie into changing out of his school uniform into shorts and a T-shirt before dialling Monica's number to say they would be coming over for Sunday lunch. It was a relief to get the machine. Finally Sarah sat at the kitchen table and re-read the flier Leo Banning had given her about a fundraiser at the arts centre. It had been in her cardigan pocket and was crumpled and damp and in places almost reduced to papier-mâché. The committee had arranged a party to be held while most of the building was still under wraps, a sneak preview in the empty newly plastered shell. She'd thought it might appeal to Chris, part of her wanting to offer him an olive branch.

Mind wandering, in a removed, abstracted way she watched the cat frisk the shopping bags. She was angry and confused and hurt and really had no idea what to do with the feelings. So they lingered and congealed into an enormous headache, which was as black and sticky and tenacious as tar on tennis shoes. Bloody sodding man.

Chris had made her so angry; Sarah straightened up, easing the kink out of her spine, feeling a great powerful surge rising up from somewhere low down in her belly. Maybe it was time she stopped hanging on to all this and being so nice – maybe it was time to let rip and let all the dark stuff go, once and for all. Maybe it was time to be angry.

On the floor the cat reversed smartly out of one of the carriers, dragging a pack of bacon wrapped in polythene with him. As Sarah stirred herself into action Henry dropped down a gear and made a wild lunge towards the back door, which, in an act of pure malice swung open, and before Sarah had the chance to speak, or call out, the cat vanished into the garden like a furry black rocket.

Oblivious to the theft the boys, Matthew and Jack, ambled in hot, noisy, damp from the rain, filling the kitchen with their voices, carrying bags and sports kits, laughing, and teasing and in desperate need of drinks and crisps, music and wall to wall TV.

'Hello, have a good day?' Sarah asked, realising that the headache had gone along with the bacon.

Matthew jerked the fridge door open and peered inside. 'Uh-huh, have we got any orange juice left?'

'Get us a yoghurt, will you?' said Jack, casually dropping his sweat shirt on to the pile of discards that Chris had left behind on the floor and that she hadn't yet had the time to rescue. His mind was elsewhere; he eased his school shoes off with his toes.

Sarah looked away but not before seeing a sharp little glimpse of the future.

'Oh, Chris. It's you,' Jenny sounded as if she was genuinely surprised to find him standing on her doorstep. Surprised but most definitely pleased. She was wearing a shiny turquoise blue bikini top, shorts, and was wielding a pair of secateurs.

Chris grinned. It was quite a fetching image. She had this little smear of something dark across one cheek and he was surprised that it was all he could do to stop himself leaning across and wiping it away, as an act of chivalry. Her hair was all mussed up like she'd just got out of bed. He swallowed hard, it wouldn't do to follow those thoughts home to roost, after all he was there to talk, to help her, to, to . . . and then he noticed the way a whole chain of little crystal beads of sweat were trickling down into the valley between her breasts. Large breasts, warm, warm . . .

'Do you know, you might be the very man I need,' Jenny said.

'Really,' Chris said hastily, swallowing hard. She wasn't his type, not really, too heavy, too . . . she moved closer so that he could smell her perfume. It was mingled with a hint of sweat and he was horrified to discover that his mouth was watering. Jenny waved the secateurs in his general direction.

Chris pulled a face and then comprehension dawned. 'Pruning? Oh right. Actually it's the wrong time of the year, really. You'd be better waiting until the autumn, when the weather cools off a bit. Sap's rising at the moment.' He reddened, pulling his T-shirt down, but thankfully Jenny seemed unaware of any double entendre.

She laughed. 'These? Oh no, I was out in the garage cutting the plugs off Tony's bleedin' fridges. I've had a little word with the scrap man and he's going to come round and collect them tomorrow, but to be honest I'm having a bit of a job. Can you give me a hand? It shouldn't take more than a few minutes.'

'Have you got a screwdriver? If not I think I've got one in the van somewhere.'

It was almost too easy. Before he could gather his thoughts Chris was in the front door, down the hall, out through the kitchen and into the garage before he really had any time to consider the consequences, and two minutes later found himself pressed into the tight dark, dusty space between two upright freezers, with a screwdriver in one hand and Jenny's secateurs in the other. Confined in the small space Jenny seemed oblivious to the effect she was having on him. Her perfume was making him feel dizzy.

'You know you're a real angel,' she was saying, bending

over to pull another plug out of the board. 'A proper knight in shining armour.' She was so close, so very close, and those shorts were so tight and then she stood up and just when Chris thought he could handle it, there was one of those strange moments when the whole of the world goes out of focus and it feels as if you're under water.

Their eyes met, their breathing synchronised and before he could stop himself Chris found himself leaning forward and kissing her. The kiss lasted probably no more than ten seconds, twenty at the most but it seemed to fill up the whole of eternity, maybe even longer and reach out into strange giggly excitable places in his head that he had almost forgotten existed. It was Jenny who pulled away first. Her eyes glittered like wet pebbles, uncannily bright in the gloom.

'Bloody hell,' she hissed, wiping her lips with the back of her hand. 'I wasn't expecting that.'

Chris struggled to suck in another breath. 'I'm so sorry,' he spluttered. 'I didn't mean to, I don't know what came over me.' Or at least that was what he was planning to say but by the time he got to, 'I don't know,' Jenny Beck was all over him like a rash and kissing him as hard and as frantically as she could, pinning him up against the side of one of the industrial sized coolers with a strength and vigour that was quite unnerving.

After a few more seconds Chris wriggled out of Jenny's grasp, gasping as he broke the surface and came up for air.

'Bugger,' he stammered. I . . . I . . . I'm sorry.'

Jenny reddened and swallowed hard. 'Maybe I had better go and put the kettle on,' she said, not quite meeting his eye. 'Cool down a bit.'

By the time she came back Chris had all the plugs off and had made up his mind that it would be safer for all concerned if he left and left quickly. This was far deeper water than he had planned for. Jenny Beck looked at the line of plugs set out on top of one of the chest freezers.

'You've been busy,' she murmured, 'do you want to come and have your tea indoors out of all this muck?'

Chris looked down at his wrist, a gesture that would have made considerably more sense if he had been wearing a watch. 'I think I ought to be getting off,' he said quickly.

Jenny nodded. 'It won't take a minute.'

And so Chris followed Jenny back indoors, into the kitchen and took a seat at the table. As she handed him a mug he saw the tear, just one great crystal droplet that rolled down over her cheek, softening the black smear and something about its progress made his heart ache.

'Thank you,' she murmured. 'You've got no idea how nice it is to have someone around to give me a hand. Just to know there is someone there. Oh Chris,' the last words were barely audible over a great wet rolling sob, and before he knew what he was doing Chris was back up on his feet, sliding his arms around Jenny Beck's ample waist and pulling her closer.

For the second time in no more than ten minutes he felt the soft burr of his sweat shirt catching on her suntanned skin, felt the pressure of her breasts hard against his chest, and smelt her perfume and suddenly he knew that it was too late. He should have run away while he still had the chance, gone home to Sarah before the trap snapped tight shut.

Jenny turned her face up towards him and as he kissed her again she made a peculiar, instinctive little animally moan that made every nerve ending in Chris's body glow white hot. It was so tempting just to dive in, to let go and let himself drown here.

'What the fuck do you think you're playing at with my missus, you two timing bastard?'

The voice snapped through Chris's thoughts like a bull whip, and what it said was so clichéd that for one wonderful moment Chris thought it might be his conscience finally waking up and dragging him back, kicking and screaming from the brink. Unfortunately it wasn't, it was Tony Beck aka Tony Whelk, standing in the open kitchen door, hands on hips and he was furious. More than furious.

'I was coming round to talk to you about *him*,' continued Tony, now addressing his remarks to Jenny. 'I was just going to drop by, have a few words about our Peter, see about the washing machine and then that loud mouth cow in the garage told me what's been going on between you two.' He jerked a thumb in Chris's direction. 'Exactly how long have you and him been having a thing? I need to know Jen. I deserve to know. How long have you been having an affair with Chris Colebrook?'

Chris looked at Tony in complete astonishment. 'What did you say?' he mumbled with a growing sense of unreality.

Tony shook his hand in apparent disgust. 'The bastard won't even stand up for you, Jenny, won't admit to it, even when he's caught red handed.' Tony swung round to face Chris. 'You know your sort disgust me, over here shaggin' another man's wife, creeping round behind my back when I'm at work. You bastard. I should kill you for interfering with my wife.'

Chris didn't feel it was a very opportune moment to point out that he was hardly creeping round and that Tony had already run away and left Jenny for someone else.

'Well?' Tony Whelk demanded, squaring his shoulders. 'What have you got to say for yourself?'

Chris took a deep breath, more of a hiatus than a necessity, trying very hard to work out what exactly he was going to say. Did he apologise, confess, get angry or just get out? For once Chris's instincts deserted him and instead of speaking he made an odd strangled grunt that for some reason appeared to infuriate Tony.

He guessed in an instant what Tony intended to do. He could see it in the other man's eyes. He watched Tony twist at the waist as if tightening a spring, saw him raise a fist, and then swing towards him with a great unruly haymaker of a punch, but seemed powerless or slower or something that felt like dreamlike disconnection, to resist or defend himself. It was years since he had fought anyone, and even then it had only ever been playground stuff. Tony Beck meanwhile was in earnest and as savage as a bull.

It seemed as if everything was happening in slow motion. At the very last instant Chris leant back to avoid the blow, miscalculated the degree of lean, and to his horror felt himself tumbling back over one of the kitchen stools.

Ridiculously, crazily, the person who saved him from crashing backwards headfirst on to the quarry tile floor was Tony Whelk. Tony grabbed him by the arm and pulling him into an upright position, off balance and out of kilter, tried another gangling shabby wayward punch that by some terrible stroke of ill luck caught Chris straight in the eye. And then Chris woke up and then it hurt and it was no longer abstract or unreal but explosive and painful and in a great furious rush he was suddenly angry. Very angry.

Instinctively he punched Tony back, and while still reeling felt a horrible bone crunching pain in his hand as his knuckles connected, saw a gout of blood from the other man's mouth and suddenly wanted nothing more than to rip the head off the crazy . . .

Jenny Beck leapt into the fray and caught hold of Chris's arm as Tony scuttled mewling across the kitchen, apparently suddenly aware that he had unleashed something potentially dark and dangerous.

'Leave 'im,' Jenny snapped, in a voice that resonated somewhere deep down in her chest.

Her voice drew Chris back from the brink but only just.

Seeing Tony Whelk retreating made something primal flare and burn bright in his belly. Awash with adrenaline and testosterone he stood his ground and made a noise that sounded not unlike a growl of triumph. Beside him, still holding on his arm Jenny Beck looked positively radiant.

Chapter 10

Mrs Vine, Leo Banning's housekeeper cleared away the remains of afternoon tea.

Leo had barely touched any of the sandwiches or the buttered scones she'd bought from the WI stall.

'Everything all right, Vicar?' she said, adjusting the heavy curtains in the big bay window so that the afternoon sun was forced to relinquish its gaudy hold on the peaceful old sitting room.

The change in light made Leo look up from his book, his expression unfocused and vague. 'I'm so sorry Mrs Vine, I was miles away. Did you say something?'

'Tea?'

Leo looked uncomfortable, like a little boy caught trying to hide cabbage under his cutlery. 'Looks lovely but I wasn't really very hungry, sorry. I'm sure it's this damned weather. It's very muggy, don't you think? Always affects my appetite.'

'Don't you worry. What do you fancy for supper? I had planned on doing a nice ham salad. New potatoes. Coleslaw. I've already cooked the beetroot, but if you'd rather have something a little lighter, something on toast p'raps. Sardines or a couple of nice poached eggs?'

Leo smiled up at her. He looked decidedly peaky but he always did after Harry or one of the others left. Sometimes Mrs Vine wondered how it was he could bear to be stuck out in the middle of nowhere, all on his own without a family, so far from the people who loved him just for himself.

Nice boy that Harry Fox, although he didn't fool Mrs Vine for a minute. Bent as a bucket of frogs, but you couldn't hold that against him, not in this day and age. He'd got such a nice way with him too, polite, very courteous, terrible shame that he was ... well, you know. She caught them sometimes out on the terrace having a good bitch – everyone needed to let their hair down now and again.

Shame about Harry. He'd have made some girl a lovely husband. She'd said that to the vicar after Harry had helped her find the raspberry netting out in the back shed for the gardener. No trouble at all, Harry had said, which is a very rare thing in a man, particularly after having caught the netting twice on the mower as he was pulling it out and spilling Growmore all over his brogues.

The vicar had smiled and said he'd pass the message on, although Mrs Vine had wanted to add, 'if he was the marrying kind, of course, which we both know he isn't' but she couldn't quite pluck up the nerve.

'. . . No, no,' Leo said, 'salad sounds splendid, Mrs V. It will have cooled down a little bit by then. I've got a couple of house calls to make later on so I shall have to liven up before then, shan't I?'

Mrs Vine nodded and headed off towards the cool stainless steel and white tiled confines of her inner sanctum. As if he had been dismissed Leo Banning's attention immediately dropped back to the open pages of the novel on his lap.

Back in the kitchen Mrs Vine was just about to make a start on the ironing when the house phone rang. Leo had had it installed for her as a surprise Christmas present so she could receive private calls. He was kind like that. Over the last couple of days the phone had rung itself senseless.

'Gina's Pantry,' hissed someone at the far end of the line. 'Absolutely shameless if you want my opinion.' Mrs Vine instantly recognised her sister's voice, there was no one else who could squeeze so many accusations and so much salacious thought into so few words.

Following her lead and dispensing with any of the social niceties, Mrs Vine said, 'So what about Gina's Pantry then?'

'The pair of them were in there today, this lunch time, your precious vicar and that fancy woman of his. No shame some people, bold as brass apparently. I've just been down to the school to pick the twinnies up and everyone is talking ten to the dozen about it. Bold as brass,' she repeated.

Mrs Vine was about to snap back an acidic denial but held her tongue. 'Are you sure?' she asked instead, in a tone approximating anxious concern.

'Are you saying I'm a liar? I tell you they were in there. Holding hands and everything the pair of them.' Her sister sniffed imperiously, implying that the ubiquitous 'they' would probably have had sex on the pavement if it hadn't been raining and they thought they could get away with it.

Mrs Vine sighed. 'Ah well,' she said, gathering her thoughts together. 'I really don't know what to say. Honestly, I don't.'

It had exactly the right effect. 'I don't suppose you can very well say much in your position but I think you ought to know what's going on, that's all. It's all out in the open now. Everybody's talking about it. No going back. I don't suppose you can tell me whether he brings her home or not can you? Only the girl from the dry cleaners asked me and I said more than likely but obviously you're not in a position to say, are you?'

There was an intense moment's silence in which Mrs Vine inwardly commemorated the point in time when lies become truth and supposition transmogrifies in to cold hard fact.

Her sister sighed. 'No, I thought not, the thing is there's

no going back now, is there? They've come out the pair of them.'

Mrs Vine took one last look at the elegant arrangement of discarded cream cheese and smoked salmon sandwiches that she had carried back from the sitting room. Oh no, they hadn't.

'And then he hit Tony, bang, right on the jaw,' Jenny Beck said, with an enthusiastic little whoop. She had plugged in the extension and was sitting at the kitchen table. Giggling, and miming, with the phone pressed tight to her ear, she was breathlessly feeding gossip into the bridge head of a vast network of intrigue, interest and wild exaggeration that fuelled – amongst others – the parishes of Barton, Hevedon and Harehill.

At the far end of the phone line the woman, a small grey haired creature, called Norma-from-the-pet-shop, said, 'Oh my God no, he didn't, did he? And what did your Tony do then?'

'Well, he was the one who struck the first blow so to speak – but you know what my Tony's like, when it comes down to it he's completely bloody useless. All wind and blather. He was out the back door like a shot the minute it looked like there was any chance Chris might be able to handle himself.' Jenny paused for effect. 'But Chris was really wonderful afterwards. I was ever so upset about the whole thing, I mean, you can just imagine. But he was really gentle with me, like some great big bear. Put his arms around me and held me up against his chest. Tight but still really gentle, you know? Well, I cried like a baby, I can tell you, Norma, I just couldn't help myself. And then he offered to make me a cup of tea but I said no, Chris, what I need is a drink, so he poured me a drink. I'd still got some brandy in the cupboard left over from Christmas I think it was, anyway, and then I got a bag of peas out of the freezer to put on his poor eye. You should see the state of it. He's going to have a real shiner tomorrow. God alone knows what his missus is going to say to him when he gets home.'

There was an infinitesimal pause.

'. . . But I thought she was carrying on with the vicar you said. You said his wife knew all about you and him?'

Discovery and truths glistened momentarily amongst the dust and fluff of lies and exaggeration.

'Well yeh, she does but I don't suppose she thought for one minute it would come to blows between Chris and our Tony, do you?' said Jenny quickly, moving fast, synapses firing like tracer bullets on a moonless night. 'I mean, her and Chris are very civilised reasonable people, whereas Tony's a complete bleeding philistine compared to them two.' She paused again, waiting for Norma to catch up.

'But I can tell you now, Norma, it was the sexiest thing in the world to see the pair of them set to over me. Like two gladiators slogging it out. God –'

Jenny paused again and let the image take life, edited by her imagination into a highly romanticised version of the brief and extremely ragged scuffle that had taken place in the kitchen. Something earthy and ancient made her stomach flutter with pure delight. The sensation was far too good to share with someone as ordinary Norma.

'Anyway, I'd better be going now. I sent Peter down the chippie on his bike, and he should be back any minute and I want to get some plates in the oven. Carry on as normal. I don't want to upset him, you know, about Tony and Chris and me. He's very sensitive about the whole thing at the moment. It's his age, you know how teenagers are, up one minute down the next. Although it's been a difficult time for all of us, really.'

Norma made a noise of understanding or possibly agreement and with the briefest of goodbyes hung up.

Jenny grinned. Peter was still over at Tony and Miss Weigh and Save's new house stacking shelves and sweeping out the stock room, but there was no need for Norma to know that. Jenny poured herself another brandy, topped it up with coke and then picked up her phone book and flicked through the dog-eared pages wondering who she ought to ring next.

At Hevedon Sarah, still feeling hurt and cross, made a point of not looking round when Chris arrived home and came upstairs into the box room that they used as an office. She had heard the back door close, heard him talking to the boys down in the sitting room, heard his footsteps cross the landing but struggled to keep her focus on the computer screen, where – in an interesting typeface and brief informative sentences – she was busy typing up her CV for her application for the job at the St Barts arts centre.

'I was wondering if you'd saved me any supper?' Chris asked in an uncharacteristically quiet voice.

'We haven't eaten yet, it's a bit early and no one was very hungry –' she said, talking to him over her shoulder.

'All right, okay.' He sounded tired and conciliatory and despite the fact that Sarah was still angry with him something about his tone made her turn.

'Oh my God, what on earth did you do to your eye?' Sarah had spoken and was up on her feet and standing in front of him before having time to consider what she was doing.

Chris reddened and winced away from her as she reached out towards his face. 'It'll be fine, no need to make a fuss.' He was still on the retreat. 'God, Sarah, you know, I feel such a bloody fool. There are some things in life that you really ought to know by the time you get to my age. Things that ought to be carved in stone in your brain.' He pulled a face while tentatively exploring the bruise. His knuckles appeared to be grazed and bloodied too.

Sarah looked at Chris more closely, trying to work out what the hell he was going on about. She looked him up and down for clues.

He had gone a peculiar colour and there was something about the way he was, the way he stood, the way he looked. It was hard to put a finger on what it was exactly but she sensed not just pain but something else, some underlying lack of ease that was making him twitchy and unsettled.

'Such as?' she said, on guard now, almost reluctant to feel her way forward.

Chris laughed. It sounded nervous and false. 'You know how you're always telling me to tidy things away?' He paused, watching her expression as if waiting to see if she would step through and follow the trail being laid down by the words. 'Should listen, shouldn't I? I was in the back of the van looking for my tape and slipped over on a spade, fell right over backwards and then the bloody door caught me, swung back and hit me smack in the eye.'

He mimed a ferocious impact.

'Wallop. God, and you know what? I've got such a headache now. I feel really odd. Brought me to my knees. I suppose I'm lucky it didn't knock me out, must have been a freak gust. To make it blow back like that. Caught the door.' He mimed the swing again.

Sarah looked him up and down. 'I'll go downstairs and get you a couple of paracetamol,' she said, not wholly convinced. 'Always leaves you a bit shaky that sort of thing, it's the shock, why don't you go and lie down for a little while? It would probably help.' The voice she used was cool and calm and totally neutral while underneath her mind was racing.

Chris looked relieved, as if he had got away with something. 'You know, that's a good idea, I think I will. Will you wake me up when supper's ready?'

Sarah watched Chris shuffle across towards their

bedroom. He was lying through his teeth. She would have staked her life on it.

Meanwhile over at her house Monica Carlisle settled back amongst the sea of pillows and cushions on the chaise longue and moaned softly.

'Harder, Mac, oh God yes that's it, it's wonderful, absolutely wonderful. Oh God. Yes there, there –'

Mac raised an eyebrow. 'You and your bloody feet,' he said, shifting position so that some of the weight was taken by a large mauve bolster.

They were in the conservatory and had been watching the storm and enjoying the pattern of the rain running down the thick, almost green, glass. The whole room was crammed with plants and climbers and bird's nest ferns, and was as humid and as oppressive as the tropics although Monica seemed perfectly comfortable there.

Mac pressed his thumbs hard down into the broad fleshy pad below her big toes, which made her purr in a rolling, throaty way, the noise rumbling up from somewhere way deep down inside her belly.

'I do hope that you gave Sarah my love when you saw her.'

Mac laughed. 'I would have preferred to have given her mine.' He ran a single finger lightly from heel to toe, triggering the grab reflex.

Monica shuddered and then kicked him. 'I'm amazed that you persuaded her to have coffee with you in the first place. I would have thought Sarah could see right through you.'

Mac grimaced.

'Oh, come on. Your intentions aren't exactly honourable. You are such a spoilt, self-indulgent little bastard, Mac.'

Unoffended he replied, 'And I suppose you're not? I just

think that Sarah is very, very – well there is something about her that is terribly appealing.'

Monica beaded him with one crow-black eye. 'She's married, she's naïve, she is my friend and she is most definitely off limits. Is that perfectly clear? The only reason you're interested in her is because she's not completely up her own arse like everyone else you know. You see her as a challenge. She is nice, she is normal, and I don't want you causing her any trouble, is that perfectly clear?' Monica paused and then settled herself back amongst the cushions. 'Your trouble is that you've got no scruples. I slept my way up the tree for money not mischief.'

'And that's something to be proud of, is it?'

She nudged him with her foot. 'We all need to believe that we're being true to ourselves. Now shut up and keep rubbing before I decide to evict you.'

Mac grinned and lifting her foot a little higher sucked her big toe into his mouth.

Over supper Chris Colebrook told the boys the story about how he got his black eye, except that in the retelling the whole episode seemed to have become much much bigger, and far more dramatic, embellished with sound effects and action replays, and Chris came back to it again and again as they were eating, as if polishing and refining it in his memory.

Sarah handed out plates, waiting for Chris to falter, waiting to pick up some clue about what was really going on, and yet at the same time was surprised at herself for doing so.

'So,' Chris said, the story finally drawing to a close. 'There we are then. Just have to be a bit more careful in the future, shan't I?'

No one had anything to add and an odd, uncomfortable silence settled on the people around the table. After a few seconds Charlie wriggled down from his stool to get some ice-cream and then the other boys helped clear the table before drifting back into the sitting room to watch TV. It all seemed a little anti-climactic and oddly stale.

'Any chance I could give Peter a ring and get a lift over later, only we've got this science project to finish off?' asked Jack from the kitchen door.

Sarah shrugged. 'I don't see why not,' she said casually.

To her astonishment Chris leapt to his feet. 'I'd rather you didn't ring.' He sounded irate. 'You spend far too much time over there with that boy. You want to get your own homework done and then get upstairs and tidy your bedroom. It's like the black hole of Calcutta up there. And it wouldn't hurt you to give your mother a hand. Pack the dishwasher. Tidy things away.'

Jack groaned but said nothing as Chris shifted his attention to Sarah. 'And I want to talk to you about this afternoon, you know, when you came home.' He looked uncomfortable. 'The thing is I wanted to say that I'm, I'm. I . . .' he stopped and looked away as something on the notice board behind her caught his eye.

'What's that?'

Sarah turned round. 'What's what?'

Chris walked round and unpinned a crumpled sheet of cream paper. 'Fundraising Evening at St Barts. Wine and cheese. An evening of musical entertainment with the Barton string quartet?'

Sarah nodded, while silently cursing whatever contrary demon it was that had made Chris spot Leo's invitation of all things amongst the jumble.

'It's on Thursday evening. I picked it up today while I was having a look around. What were you going to say about this afternoon?' Her attempt at staging a diversion didn't work.

'And I suppose you've already made up your mind that you're going to this haven't you?'

Sarah stared at him in genuine surprise. It seemed such an odd thing to say. 'I don't see why not. I'm going to apply for one of the jobs there – I've already told y . . .' she paused, the words drying in her throat. Was it Chris she'd told about Leo's suggestion or was it Mac? Sarah reddened. 'Anyway I thought that we could go together. It would make a nice change. And Leo Banning said the string quartet are absolutely wonderful.'

Chris sniffed, 'Well, he would, wouldn't he? It's not my sort of thing. Cheap white wine and the overpowering smell of mothballs from all those DJs. No, I'll tell you what, Sarah, I'll give it a miss and pick you up when all the preening and posing is over. Then you can have a drink, and this way I'll be sure that you get home afterwards.'

Sarah felt a raw red surge of indignation, and at the same time was aware that she couldn't work out whether what he had said was a joke or cheap dig. Chris's gaze didn't falter. The bruising around his eye was already changing from navy to a deep and dramatic purple and for just an instant as he turned away, looking smug, Sarah couldn't help but wonder if the conversation and all that outrage and indignation about the arts centre had been a diversion.

Before Sarah had any chance to regroup her thoughts, Chris took himself off to the polythene tunnel at the bottom of the garden with a can of lager out of the fridge, settled down amongst a pile of potato trays and stared fixedly into space.

Originally he had bought the tunnel to grow bedding plants in, but over time it had slowly filled up with the detritus of family and business life, bikes and boxes and bits of old machinery, things that had no other place to go.

Sheltered by next door's leylandii the polythene had gone green and brittle with age, and like a mantra, Chris's first thought as he stepped inside was always that it was high time he replaced it.

He had almost got to the point of apologising to Sarah for being such a complete bastard to her, but as the words formed in his head a little demonic voice had asked him why the hell should he. He'd got nothing to apologise for, had he? Not really. A washing machine hose, a couple of kisses, and a bit of misplaced lust, what was that in the great scheme of things?

And if Sarah had been kind and forgiving and understanding he might have told her how he really got the black eye.

Seeing the flier pinned on the notice board had been a pure stroke of luck. It had diverted him long enough to get a grip. He'd been a bit short with Sarah, that was true, but no more than she deserved for God's sake, after all she knew he was going to be in for lunch. He'd told her. There had certainly been no justification for her to fly off the handle like that.

And face it, it was Sarah who had stayed out all night. God alone knows what she had got up to. Even now, as the thought formed in Chris's head a louder more rational voice told him what he already knew – that Sarah had done absolutely nothing at all.

Although some vast internal self-justification engine was busily reworking Sarah's perfectly reasonable anger into a good reason why he had dropped in on Jenny Beck. Who was he kidding? Dropped in implied something casual whereas the truth was that he had deliberately driven over to see her not once but twice. Jenny Beck. The name stopped the rational thoughts from flowing. Jenny Beck who had been leaning against him crying, soft and warm and vulnerable. Jenny Beck leaning closer still to kiss him, Jenny Beck pressing herself against him with an explicit if silent request.

Chris got to his feet. It was just a passing thing, nothing of any weight or significance. He was making a mountain out of a molehill; maybe she had got a little bit of a crush on him but that was all it was and it would pass. He took a long pull on the can of lager. It was really high time he replaced the polythene on the greenhouse.

Chapter 11

'Chris is being really odd at the moment.' Sarah scooped the froth off her coffee with half a digestive. After he had gone out into the garden for a sulk she'd packed Charlie into the car and escaped for a little while. She'd left a note on the table for Chris. Not that it was likely to make a lot of difference. 'I keep wondering if it's some sort of mid-life crisis.'

She was sitting in Lisa's sitting room curled up on the sofa with her shoes off and Lisa's spaniel resting its head on her legs, a little of her concentration listening for Charlie who was playing in the garden.

'Male menopause, mid-life crisis, what do I know?' said Lisa, levering another biscuit out of the packet. 'There are days when I just think men are far too simple for their own good and then other times they're a complete bloody mystery. Look at me and Barry. I married a six foot sexy boy biker and I've ended up with a fat bald guy who saves jam jars to keep rawl plugs and nails in. Where's the sense in that? Barry's busy turning into his dad.' She paused. 'Like the ugly duckling in reverse. Do you think he's still pissed off about you staying out all night, or is there a chance he saw you with Mac in Gina's?'

Sarah reddened a bit. 'I hope not. I'm sure if he had he'd have said something. Wouldn't he?'

Lisa shrugged. 'Maybe he's trying to catch you out in a lie.'

Sarah shook her head, 'Nah, it would take a woman to come up with anything that complex. It's the black eye that's worrying me. And his knuckles are all bruised.' She paused and spread her fingers imagining the scuffs and bangs on Chris's hands. 'He told the boys that he did it trying to save himself from falling over in the van, but if I didn't know better I'd have said he hit someone.'

Lisa laughed. 'There's a first time for everything. It's not some irate husband, is it? You don't think there's any chance he's seeing the dreaded Jenny Whelk, do you?'

Sarah stared at Lisa for a moment. The thought hung for a few seconds spinning in the light like a dust mote. 'No, not Chris. I'd know, I'm sure of it. And Jenny isn't his type.'

Lisa lifted an eyebrow. 'You don't sound totally convinced.'

Sarah shook her head more emphatically this time. 'He's worried about money and work, and I'm not sure he is over my night out at Monica's. Just all the usual stuff and more besides.' Sarah slipped the digestive into her mouth a few seconds before it achieved melt down. 'I feel as if I've run out of steam.'

Lisa shrugged. 'God knows then, maybe he's turning into his dad too. Do you fancy some trifle?'

Sarah looked down at the coffee and biscuits and nodded. More comfort food sounded like an extremely good idea.

It was fairly quiet on Tuesday and Wednesday, and Thursday morning come to that. Everyone – or at least Sarah and Chris, were busy being careful and mindful of the other. In their house there was an awful lot of observation and rumination going on but not a great deal of comment which meant that things were tense but not unbearably so.

Chris's black eye slowly began to work its way through the colours of a half decent sunset, Sarah posted the job application to the arts centre and Charlie and the cat made themselves sick eating too much chocolate chip ice-cream. The weather was hot and the days which were overly blue seemed unnecessarily long.

By contrast, in her house at Harehill Jenny Beck had lots to say for herself and the stories about the fight in the kitchen had grown and grown until it was damned lucky that Tony and Chris had managed to escape without one of them being hospitalised, arrested or maimed for life.

Tony hadn't rung since making a hasty exit through the back door, although his solicitor had sent Jenny a very curt letter about the importance of her moral rectitude with regards the upbringing of their only child. It appeared that the embargo on any involvement with the legal profession had been lifted.

So, Thursday was really going quite well until the evening when Sarah was due to go to the fundraiser at St Barts.

'Seems to me it was a good thing you bought that dress. How much did you say it cost?' said Chris icily, eyeing Sarah up and down.

She'd just come downstairs and walked into the kitchen wearing the same outfit she'd worn for Monica's party and was carrying a shawl and an evening bag. Up until that moment Sarah had almost forgotten about the arc of tension between them. It had been easing, slowly over the last day or so, and she had believed things – whatever those things were – were on the mend and had felt increasingly good while getting ready. She'd been looking forward to an evening at the arts centre.

'It really suits you,' he said, scratching his backside. That was not what his expression said. Sarah stopped mid-stride, waiting, bracing herself for whatever was coming in the next volley. There was bound to be something else.

His gaze didn't falter. Sarah began to feel uncomfortable. She looked good in the dress. In fact Chris's words had already crossed her mind as she'd applied her makeup. The little black dress was extremely flattering and, with the weird alchemy of growing confidence and self-assuredness, the better Sarah thought she looked the truer it became. It was just that the tone of her thoughts was completely at odds with everything implied by Chris's voice. Even so, maybe there was still time to retrieve the good feelings.

'Chris, please don't do this, love. Why don't you go and have a shower and come with me? It doesn't start till eight and Matthew's already said he'll baby-sit Charlie if we want to go. We can get another ticket on the door.'

'We?'

Sarah felt a ragged edge of anger lift and begin to smoulder. 'For God's sake, Chris. Lisa is coming from school, and a few of the others. Anita, Gill, maybe Helen. I've already told you.'

He said nothing.

Sarah sighed. 'I'm not going to stand here trying to persuade you to come with me, but it would be nice if you did. End of conversation. All right?'

Chris shrugged and pulled a funny face that suggested he was sucking his teeth. He'd not long been in from work and was wearing a faded T-shirt and baggy jeans that hung in grimy folds around the knees and crotch. With the black eye added into the mix he certainly didn't look like the kind of man normally expected to be found listening to a string quartet.

There had been a time when he'd first swapped a series of uninspiring business suits for casual, rugged outdoor clothes more fitting a landscape gardener that she'd really fancied that nice bit of rough look. Designer stubble, a suntan and taut muscles had all added to a very sexy piratey look. Surely it couldn't have been that different from the way he looked now? What the hell had happened in the years between now and then that she'd missed?

'I've already told you it's not my sort of thing,' he said petulantly, snapping her thoughts back to the present. 'And anyway can't have me there showing you up now can we? The rough ill-mannered hoary handed son of the soil stuffing his face with canapés and farting in front of the assembled gentry.'

Sarah stared at him. 'What on earth are you on about now, Chris? It's black tie, you've got a dinner suit. You can walk upright.' Finally the anger caught light. 'If you don't want to come with me that's fine, but if you keep on like this I'm not going to want to go either. Or is that what you had in mind?'

He chose not to hear. 'That wasn't what you said this morning.'

Sarah looked heavenwards. Maybe half a dozen sentences over a cup of tea and a slice of toast and marmalade, said earlier in the day, which even as she'd spoken them Sarah knew would come back to haunt her. Why in God's name was it that Chris clung tight to the dross but could never remember the important things?

'All I said this morning was that if you were coming tonight I'd appreciate you driving so that I could have a drink. For a change, but if that pisses you off that much, Chris, then I'll drive. I don't want you to . . .' Sarah stopped, feeling her colour drop away, aware that she had inadvertently strayed a little too close to the edge and was about to say something else that would be noted down in the annals of history to resurface the next time they had a row – and lots of times after that.

Chris spotted it too and leant forward triumphantly. 'Don't want me to *what*?'

He smelt of sweat and grime and hadn't shaved. It wasn't sexy and nothing about the way he looked bore any resemblance to the pirate fantasies she had had a brief memory of. Under his chin was a ground-in oily smear of dirt that extended from jaw line to the curl of dark hair in the neck of his T-shirt. It looked as if it might have been there some time.

She said nothing.

'Don't want me to *what*, Sarah? Show you up in front of all your arty farty little friends? The vicar? The do-gooding bloody fundraising ladies of the committee. The fucking string quartet?'

Sarah took a step back astonished by how venomous Chris sounded. 'No, it isn't that at all. What the hell's gotten into you? I don't want you to get drunk, that's all,' she said, in as even and reasonable tone as she could muster.

He drew back his lips into something masquerading as a smile. 'Oh, so that's what all this is about, is it?'

Sarah straightened her shoulders, pulled her sleeves down, breaking eye contact in an effort to shake herself free of him. 'I don't want to have this conversation, Chris. If you don't want to come with me, that's fine. Do you think we can leave now?'

He looked up at the clock. 'You said we'd got plenty of time.'

'Yes, that was if you were coming with me, but if you're not then I'd like to get going. I told Lisa I'd meet her in the pub.'

Chris nodded. 'This shouldn't take long.' He pulled a rag from his back pocket and made a move towards the door.

'Where the hell are you going now?'

'Just want to check the oil and water in the van.'

'But I thought we'd take my car.'

'I said I'd drop some fencing panels off at Barry's on the way.'

'But Barry's house is in completely the opposite direction to the arts centre.'

It was like some anarchic game of tennis in which Chris, without a moment's hesitation, returned every shot, driving it past her with terrible instinctive animal cunning, that carried every ball a fraction out of her reach.

He picked up his jacket and opened the back door. 'It shouldn't take many minutes to get them loaded up. Give Matthew a shout, will you? He can give me a hand to shift them. Oh, and I should bring something to sit on if I were you, the seats in the trannie are absolutely filthy.'

It was a merciless rally. Sarah felt the last shreds of her composure and self-control ebbing away.

'Oh and by the way there's a hole in those tights.'

Game.

Sarah turned to go back upstairs. At the hall door she paused for a few moments to watch Chris's back while her mind filled slowly with the most terrible ice cold rage.

Since Monday evening Jenny Beck had told her story to as many people as would listen. It was old hat now. Since Tony had run away with the little blonde, Jenny usually went out on a Thursday with the girls, more often than not down to the pub, but occasionally tenpin bowling, the pictures or out for a Chinese meal.

Unfortunately in her attempts to gild the lily Jenny had given as many people as would listen the impression she and Chris had planned a hot night in, or maybe a romantic night out, and so was now stuck at home with nowhere to go.

Peter had cycled into town and the house seemed very quiet and very empty and there was nothing good on the television. She certainly didn't fancy cutting the lawn. Jenny looked at the phone, once, twice. What the hell? She picked up the receiver and dialled Chris Colebrook's number. Funny how up until last weekend she had always thought of it as Sarah's number.

'Hi, is your dad in?' Tone light and casual.

'Nah,' said Jack. 'He's just taken my mum to some do at the new arts centre in town. He said he wouldn't be very long though. Do you want me to get him to call you back?'

Jenny hesitated, wondering if she dare leave it to chance alone. She felt a bit odd ringing in the first place and some dark corner of her mind was still busy manufacturing all manner of excuses and lies in case Sarah had picked up the receiver.

'Do you want to leave a message?' pressed Jack.

She considered for a second or two longer. What if Chris didn't ring back, what if he was consumed with guilt and all manner of regret and remorse? What if he wasn't interested in her after all and he hadn't rung because he didn't know how to tell her. What if when he got home he'd confessed everything to Sarah? What if Jenny had imagined the whole thing. Did she dare risk it?

'Is Pete there?' asked Jack, breaking into her thoughts.

'No. He's gone into town on his bike.'

'Oh. Right.'

She could sense Jack's interest ebbing away. She had to act now before the moment was lost and Jack hung up. 'I'll tell Peter you rang when he gets in if you like. He shouldn't be very long. Could you ask your dad to ring me?'

'Yeh, sure thing,' said Jack. 'Bye,' and then he hung up.

Jenny stared at the phone. It was a chance that she would have to take. She just had to work out what she was going to tell Chris Colebrook she'd called for. Another leaky washing machine hose? Something else broken maybe? Jenny glanced around the kitchen considering the possibilities before settling down at the kitchen table to wait. Perhaps it was time to up the stakes a little.

*　　*　　*

153

In the newly painted foyer of St Barts Leo Banning smiled and kissed Sarah lightly on the cheek. 'Glad that you could make it tonight. Let me get you a drink. I've been singing your praises. Do you know Trevor Rosco? I'll introduce you, he's on the board of trustees . . .'

Sarah glanced into the main function room. It was already quite crowded. It was one of the few rooms of the old church that was close to completion. It had been plastered and painted off-white which seemed to emphasise the long elegant curves of the vaulted ceilings. Around the columns that supported the roof someone had wrapped great swathes of industrial polythene, tied with swags of ivy and woven lights in and out between the foliage so each one looked like a cross between a giant stick of rock and a mysterious cylindrical present waiting to be unveiled. It gave the whole place a wonderful impression of being a work in progress.

Thanks to Chris's plans to circumnavigate the globe before going to the arts centre Lisa and the others had arrived well ahead of her and were standing in a huddle over by the canapés, talking, laughing, drinking wine. They lifted their glasses in both greeting and a toast as they spotted her.

Sarah smiled, waved back, trying hard to release the twist of tension that was still tightened up inside her. She sipped the wine Leo gave her and took a long slow easing breath. It was a real relief to be away from Chris.

Over on a dais the string quartet were playing something by Vivaldi, or at least Sarah thought it might be Vivaldi. It must be wonderful to be able to play so well. The tune was lifting now, rising apparently effortlessly over the soft murmur of conversation, as sharp and clean as a flight of birds spiralling above the people. The sound made her shiver with pure pleasure.

'Oh and there's Carol Broadbent and her husband,' continued Leo, pointing into the crush, 'do you know them? She's a sculptor from near King's Lynn?'

Sarah shook her head and, glass in hand, allowed Leo to shepherd her around the room, pleased to find herself being introduced to the movers and shakers who were responsible for kick starting and sustaining the arts centre project. It took what seemed like an age to complete a grand tour of the crowded room. Finally returning to the starting point.

'And I think you've already met Adam Gregory, our projects manager? We like to think of him as the Eeyore to my Christopher Robin.'

Adam Gregory's expression did not change, there was not a flicker of recognition or warmth. 'Nice to see you again,' he said and although he extended his hand, everything about his demeanour belied the greeting.

Sarah wasn't sure what to say.

An elderly woman in evening dress beckoned Leo over.

'Will you excuse me for a few minutes?' he asked pleasantly.

Sarah thanked him.

Leo waved the words away. 'You might not be so grateful when you're working here,' he said with a grin. 'Back in a minute.'

Reluctantly Sarah turned her attention back to Adam, who had made no attempt to move on after their reintroduction. It seemed rude to hurry away and yet at the same time Sarah felt extremely uncomfortable.

'Did you manage to find the problem you were looking for on Monday?' she asked, wondering if it might be possible to find a conversation with him. There was an odd temptation to try and crack him, find words with slightly more weight than the social fluff of hello, how are you, what a lovely building, what a glorious evening, what an exciting project, that she had had with everyone else Leo had introduced her to, and see if she could make him smile, or at least react.

Adam nodded. 'Yes, that and half a dozen others. Here it's not finding problems that's the problem. Working on a building like this is always a challenge. You never know what you're going to turn up. It's a bit like playing architectural jack straws, disturb one thing and if you're not very careful the next sound you hear is the rest of it crashing in around your ears.'

Leo, who was standing no more than a yard away leant back into the conversation, pulling a face. 'Come on now, Adam. Optimism. Good cheer and optimism.'

'That was good cheer and optimism, Leo, you should catch me on a bad day,' Adam said, this time not quite able to disguise a wry grin.

Sarah smiled into the top of her glass; this show of saturnine stand-offishness was a game, and something about that made her warm to him. As she lifted her gaze, she realised Adam was looking at her, and for the first time she was aware of the humour hidden behind the apparently impassive expression.

'We wondered if you were ever going to get here,' said Lisa, sidling up to them, bearing a plate heaped with all kinds of small elegant edibles.

'Transport problems,' said Sarah, as casually as she could manage. Chris and the emotionally charged drive over to the arts centre were very slowly ebbing away.

'You should have given me a ring,' said Lisa. 'I was going to come over and say hello earlier but I didn't want to interrupt you on the royal progress.' She let her gaze sweep the room and then smiled in the general direction of Leo. 'Met all the nobs now then have you? There'll be no talking to you soon.' The last couple of sentences were in a poor imitation of a stage whisper.

Sarah grinned and stole a small prawn topped parcel off

her plate. 'I think you've met Leo. And this is Adam Gregory. This is Lisa Pearce. We work together at Whitefriars School.'

Lisa nodded and smiled in their direction but kept tight hold of her glass and buffet pickings. 'I can see why you'd want to work here though. Lovely acoustics, great light, brilliant food. Not sure that the school's cowboy bean hotpot and apple snow has quite the same cachet. We'll miss you –'

'I haven't got the job yet.' Sarah bit into the canapé. The crisp filo prawn parcel cracked like Italian glass; it was full of something smooth and creamy, seasoned with garlic and was delicious. 'Are there any more of these.'

Lisa nodded. 'Uh-huh. There is some truly spectacular finger food over there. Can't convince the rest of the gang to move away from it.'

As Sarah took another sip of wine, it occurred to her that she hadn't eaten all day. 'If you'll excuse me, Adam, I think I'll go and take a look. I'm famished.'

Walking across the room with Lisa she could already feel the wine playing hide and seek with good sense as it bubbled its way upwards through her bloodstream, giggling enthusiastically as it went. She really ought to eat something.

'Umm, very nice,' said Lisa in an undertone as they reached the table.

'What is?' Sarah was scanning the bowls and plates.

'Adam Gregory.'

Sarah laughed. 'Oh come on. I thought you meant the buffet.'

'No, I'm serious. He's gorgeous.'

Sarah picked up a plate. 'And my life isn't complicated enough already?'

'There's no harm at all in window shopping. Besides

flirting is such a nice way to spend the evening. Great for your self-esteem.'

'Then be my guest,' said Sarah, waving Lisa carte blanche.

Lisa's expression brightened. 'Well I'd be delighted to take you up on the offer but I don't think it's me he's interested in.'

'Did you say you were stuck for a lift home?' said Adam. It was a little while later; Sarah had found herself a space to stand that gave a clear view of the stage. He had been on his way to the buffet table and said it very casually, a throwaway line.

On the dais a very small woman with a huge voice had just sung something dark smoky blue and as deep as night that made Sarah feel tearful.

'I heard you mention you'd had a problem getting here,' Adam continued, 'Leo said that you lived at Hevedon. I'm over at Ash Ditton, so it's on my way.'

Sarah smiled. 'Thank you, but actually I've already got a lift home.'

He nodded. 'Fine. I didn't want you to be stuck.'

She watched him walking back towards Leo and the elderly woman. He moved easily, smiling at people as he crossed the room and looked very comfortable inside his own skin. Pity she had forgotten how to flirt. And it was nice of him to offer her a lift. By association the idea of a lift brought her squarely back to Chris.

From experience she expected that he would arrive late, or very early, certainly not at the time she'd told him. Either way he would end up angry or at best niggled. Maybe she ought to ring and tell him not to bother. It would be a relief not to have him waiting for her, and Lisa would run her home. Sarah couldn't quite bring herself to accept Adam Gregory's offer.

She turned back to Lisa who was still grazing through the buffet.

'See, I told you,' said Lisa, through a mouth full of smoked salmon. 'Most definitely interested.'

After the singer a man in a black velvet suit made a short and very witty speech about the glorious possibilities the centre could offer the community, and then Leo thanked everyone for coming. He was followed by a selection of poetry read by a local poet. Two percussionists and children from the local church. There was a short choral piece sung by what seemed to be most of the female guests and then more music from the string quartet. It was a real harvest festival of local talent.

Sarah began to relax. The wine helped but it wasn't just that. Leo Banning came up alongside her and refilled her glass.

'Quite amazing, isn't it?'

Sarah nodded and meant it.

'Jack said that you called earlier?' The voice at the end of the line was warm but very guarded.

Jenny Beck, smiling, allowed a little vibrato to flavour her reply. 'Hello Chris. I hope you didn't mind me ringing but, but . . .' she sniffed, a tiny crack opening up to spice the mix. 'I wanted to thank you for the other night. I was going to ring earlier in the week but I didn't really know what to say, and as I hadn't heard from you – I wasn't quite sure what to think. I wanted to say I'm so sorry, so sorry.' And then she sobbed a small sob, not much, nothing too hysterical, just a little hurt, a tiny bit needy. What man could possibly resist her?

Apparently not Chris Colebrook. In the seconds that followed she could almost feel him straining forward to comfort her down the phone.

'Oh Jenny, please don't cry,' he said softly. 'I didn't

really do anything. I'm sorry that I couldn't have done more. How are you anyway? I was worried in case your ex, your husband, Tony came back. I thought about ringing but I didn't want to make things any worse. You know. If he was there.'

Jenny waited until the silence became a little itchy before replying, 'To be honest, I don't think that anything could make it worse. But I don't want to bore you with my problems. I know you and Sarah have had your ups and downs, maybe you don't remember how hard things can be when you're on your own. All on your own.'

Pause.

It was a master stroke.

'Would you like me to come over?' he said, in a voice that barely crept above a whisper.

'I can't ask you to do that,' Jenny said. 'You've got Sarah and the boys to think about.' There was another pause, bottomless as a ravine that managed to imply the unplumbed depths of her isolation. She could hear Chris breathing, in fact the image was so vivid she could almost hear him thinking. 'Haven't you? Although it would be nice to talk to someone. Don't you think? Just to talk.'

'I can be over there in about half an hour,' Chris said.

'I'll put the kettle on or shall I open a bottle of wine?'

'I've got to drive.'

'Oh, one won't hurt you.'

'If you say so,' said Chris.

'Trust me,' said Jenny Beck and hung up.

She looked up at the kitchen clock; half an hour would give Jenny enough time to have a quick rub round with a flannel before Chris got there.

Chapter 12

At around the same time in Monica's conservatory Mac ground his cigarette butt into the stone floor.

'Why can't I come? I promise I'll behave myself. Best behaviour, cross my heart.' Outside the daylight was fading fast. Monica had lit clusters of creamy white candles in floor and wall sconces and now, as the darkness embraced the old house, the reflections of the flames added a peculiar through the looking glass dimension to the night sky.

'I didn't know you had a heart, Mac, and whatever you say or promise the answer is still no. I must have told you at least a dozen times. You're like some terrible evil child. You are not invited to lunch on Sunday – and that's an end to it. Finito, fin, the end, so don't keep on. All right? There is going to be me, Sarah, and that boring overbearing little man she married and the boys.' Monica counted them off on her fingers and then peered down through her bifocals, turning her attention back to the menu Fredo was proposing. Roast leg of lamb, baby new potatoes, Yorkshire pudding . . . she scanned down through the list of vegetables to dessert: summer pudding, strawberries and cream, or cheese. Simple but delicious.

It had been the arrival and reading of the menu that had triggered Mac off. He looked peevishly in her direction. 'Oh go on, be a sport. Please.'

'No. It's going to be nice civilised family Sunday lunch. There is no room for some arty little Lothario slithering around trying to jump my guests. And you know bloody well that it's only because Sarah isn't interested that you're chasing her. Nothing more attractive than being resisted. Now pour me another G and T and stop being such a complete and utter arsehole.'

Mac pouted. 'In that case, if I can't come I'll wander round the garden like some poor tormented soul, peering in at the windows, moaning pitifully, all pale and gaunt, rattling my chains.'

Monica lifted her glasses to look him over. 'They're forecasting storms and torrential rain for Sunday.'

Mac sniffed. 'I'll bring a brolly.'

At St Barts, Sarah had the sensation of being watched. The house lights had come up; everyone was looking pale and a little pinker around the eyes than when they arrived. On stage the string quartet were busily packing away their instruments and music stands. Some very mellow grown up jazz was playing softly over the PA and amongst those remaining there was a warm sense of a success, a good after-the-party feeling.

Some of the men had pulled off their bow ties and undone a button or two and at least one woman wandered by carrying her sandals by the straps. Over by the buffet table, Leo Banning, glass in hand was talking about a sponsorship scheme that the committee was busy setting up.

'It's a great way to buy into the St Barts venture, in fact the whole idea of art in the community. We're very committed to avoiding an ethos of elitism. You can buy in for as little as £500, you know,' he said, looking pointedly at Sarah, despite the remarks being for general consumption.

They were standing in a group with Adam Gregory, Lisa, one of the elderly women Leo had been talking to earlier, and a few other people, some were committee members, some hangers on. The conversation had already taken several turns around the circle and had only just settled back to St Barts and what was planned for its future.

The crowd in the hall had thinned down to those with a vested interest in the evening's success, the organisers, the performers and their respective retinues of family and friends. It was almost eleven, which though hardly the wee small hours was nearly an hour later than Sarah had arranged for Chris to come and pick her up. If he didn't show Lisa had already promised to run her home. But any sense of anxiety about where he might be was tempered with an odd sense of calm.

On other nights she would have been hovering around by the doors or standing out in the car park, looking nervously at her watch, following every set of lights as they approached, feeling increasingly tense, craning to see if it was Chris in the van, but for some reason tonight felt different, although she couldn't quite put her finger on why.

She'd gone outside just before ten to see if Chris was there and hung around until ten past before coming back inside and helping herself to another glass of wine. Deep inside some small steely part of her wanted very much not to feel intimidated. She was nearly forty for God's sake, surely she deserved some say in the way her life panned out – and if not now then when?

'. . . It'll give the investor guaranteed access to workshop space if that's what they want, or display space. There's plenty of slack in the system for all sorts of possibilities and packages. With a little luck I think we can find something for everybody.'

One of the elderly women nodded. 'We need to get a mix of time pledged and money invested so that no one who wants to be involved is excluded. We've had an awful lot of interest already.'

The other committee members who were there all nodded in unison, as if it had been choreographed.

'It should root the whole project firmly in the community.'

The way her family finances were balanced at the moment £500 a year might as well be five million. Sarah looked around again, scanning the faces, still with the sensation that she was being watched, and it was then that she spotted Chris lounging by one of the pillars. He was in the shadows, not quite far enough back to be accused of hiding but as good as.

Lisa looked at her watch. 'Shall we be off then?'

'I've just seen Chris.'

Lisa turned to try and pick him out amongst the crowd.

Sarah wondered how long he had been there watching them. He'd showered and smartened himself since the last time she'd seen him, although he was still casually dressed in an open neck shirt and cream chinos and had rolled his sleeves back to reveal muscular suntanned arms. He looked really good, kind of sexy and relaxed in contrast to the little groups of stuffed shirts in penguin suits and cocktail frocks. Sarah smiled and lifted a hand to attract his attention.

Maybe she had been too harsh after all, and then, just as she was berating herself for being such a shrew, Chris caught her eye and instantly his expression hardened up from benign open faced curiosity into a heavy-duty frown. It was the most horrible transformation, like a trap snapping shut. Sarah felt as if he had slapped her.

Reddening and uncomfortable she started to make a discreet retreat from the conversation, the last thing she wanted was for Chris to come over and join in, but Leo Banning had other ideas.

'You're not already going surely? I was hoping you'd stay and join us at the bar for a little celebratory drink.'

He looked around the faces for some sort of support. There were various murmurs of assent.

Sarah's colour deepened, she felt the heat rising in her face. 'I'd love to but I've got to go, my . . .' She hesitated over the word husband for a fraction too long and knew there was no way she could say it aloud without sounding angry, bitter or something much worse, '. . . my lift's just arrived.'

'Why not invite them to join us?'

Over my mouldering corpse, Sarah thought, shaking her head while still murmuring apologies, excuses and her farewells, desperate now to be gone. She backed quickly away towards the door. 'Thank you for a really good evening. I've had a great time.'

Leo smiled and leaning forward kissed her on both cheeks. 'My pleasure.'

Sarah felt like Cinderella. Behind him, head tipped on one side so that the others couldn't see her, Lisa grinned and mimed sticking her fingers down her throat. Social anarchy was never a thing constrained by age or sex.

Sarah suppressed a grin and turned away, almost crashing full tilt into Chris. His expression had now set rock solid. He caught hold of her elbow, implying that she had stumbled. The gesture was theatrical and over done.

'I thought you said you'd be outside waiting for me. I've sat in that bloody van for Christ knows how long. You told me to be here at ten o'clock,' he snapped.

Sarah adjusted her wrap, pulled her bag up on to her shoulder, taking a few moments to regain her composure. He was wearing the aftershave she'd bought him for Christmas. It smelt of sandalwood and citrus and something else a tone deeper that on other nights under different circumstances had made her mouth water and set her skin tingling.

'I was outside waiting for you at ten.' Her voice sounded flat and deliberately unprovocative. She wondered what to say next, which way to play it. The last thing she wanted was any kind of scene in front of Leo Banning and the other members of the committee, but she might as well not have spoken.

'And you reek of booze.'

She stared up at him. 'I'm sorry?'

'Oh, I'm sure you will be in the morning, you smell like a bloody brewery. And you were worried about me showing you up?' Chris snorted. There was no disguising the derision in his tone. Sarah trailed behind him hoping that no one was watching their progress, she felt like a naughty child being reprimanded. Outside parked on double yellow lines amongst the waiting B M W s and Volvos, the battered white Transit stood out like a lapdancer at an evangelists' jamboree. Chris jerked open the door and pulled away almost before Sarah had a chance to clamber aboard.

As they drove off there seemed to be a momentary pause in which Sarah weighed the possibilities, whether the best thing might be to laugh at Chris, attempt to defuse the tension or perhaps it might be better just to make a dignified but otherwise silent protest. Before she could set about doing any of them, Chris continued, 'You know I'm really beginning to worry about you.'

Which was strange, because that was exactly what Sarah had been thinking too.

So, it appeared that all the things that Jenny Beck had told Chris about Sarah were true after all. That was the only possible conclusion. Timely too – Jenny telling him about the rumours that were going round and then him seeing the pair of them together at the arts centre.

Jenny Beck had been keen to point out that Sarah having an affair with Leo was probably just a rumour, a nasty rumour that probably wasn't true, she'd made that very clear, but Chris could see now that she was only trying to protect his feelings. Situations like this always let you know who your real friends are.

And knowing about Leo and Sarah, even if it was with the benefit of hindsight, had made Chris feel better about going over to see Jenny in the first place:

Chris dropped Sarah off at the house; she hadn't said one single word during the drive home. Not that there was much she could say under the circumstances, after all he had seen the way she and that bloody vicar were carrying on.

Chris was making his way back to the house, walking very slowly across the gravel after parking the Transit over by the polythene greenhouse, contemplating the consequences of all the things he had heard and seen. Above him the sky was clear and crisp, the navy blanket of the night totally ravaged by a million silvery moth holes, not that Chris had many thoughts spare to notice.

The vicar had been all over Sarah like a rash, Chris had seen her laughing, seen the way the bastard looked at her. How could he have missed the signs for so long? Christ, she had started to dress differently, do her hair – it was a classic pattern, bloody hell the man had even rung her after that night she'd stayed over at Monica Carlisle's. Barefaced, bold as fucking brass, for a vicar he had the nerve of the devil.

And Chris already knew that that bag, Monica Carlisle, would lie through her eye teeth for Sarah, particularly if it meant cocking a snook at him. Oh yes, he could practically hear her now planning the whole bloody thing. In the dark fetid depths of Chris's imagination a handful of spiky paranoid little trolls were coming to life.

His expression turned from an unpleasant grimace into a snarl and then into a self-pitying pout. Sarah and the vicar. He sniffed. It was the sort of thing you read about in the Sunday papers. And that night Sarah had stayed away they could have been anywhere, Monica's house, a hotel, a motel, the vicarage, anywhere. How the hell could he work out what the truth was now?

And they'd been dancing together at the barn dance most of Saturday evening and even then he hadn't suspected anything, not a single thing. Just how naïve could a man be? The evidence was all there if you knew where to look.

Chris had assumed that Leo Banning was not particularly interested in women, not that he necessarily preferred men, it was just that up until talking to Jenny, Chris hadn't really considered Leo at all. He didn't know the man well – they had maybe spoken once or twice at school sports days and nodded in the street – and so he had taken it for granted that Leo, being a vicar, was someone who saw other people as a vocation, sheep to be tended, problems to be solved, rather than as, as . . . screwable. The word surfaced while Chris was busy trying to come up with some adjective to describe what he thought attractive women were that didn't make him sound like a Neanderthal. Too late now.

But the main thing, the worse thing, the thing that stung was that Sarah and Leo Banning had made a complete fool of him and it was this, far more than anything else, that was making Chris feel so angry and so hurt.

He straightened his shoulders and headed towards the back door, buoyed up and warmed through to the core by a sense of righteous indignation. As Chris turned the corner by the hedge he hesitated for a few moments; the bathroom light was still on. He waited, not altogether sure why and then after a few seconds it went off, and then the soft yellow glow of a lamp illuminated the window beside the bed. He stood very still, breathing very high and very shallow, aware of the sounds in the garden, the shush and flow of his heart beating, the velvet purr of blood coursing through his veins. A minute passed, perhaps a little more and then the light went out and there was darkness again.

For some reason Chris let out a great sigh of relief as if in the darkness his sins wouldn't be able to find him out. Chris blushed up a shade or two despite the fact that there was no one there in the garden to see him, no one but him and his conscience, which gave him a very pointed look.

Over at Harehill Jenny Beck rolled over on her bed and stared up at the ceiling. She had been lying there some time, thinking hard about the new possibilities that life had presented her with. Between the light fitting and the coving a very complex cobweb clung to the artex, a delicate shrine to stealth and spinning and the art of waiting and slovenliness. Time to clear that away. On the bed around her were a jumble of pillows, a tangle of sheets and clothes and an aura of satisfaction that was almost as tangible.

The bedroom windows were wide open, from outside came the soft rustle of warm summer wind through trees, moths danced a tango inside the lampshade, while a bird – some decadent party animal – picked out a rock and roll riff in the velvet soft darkness.

Jenny turned over on to her belly. Her son Peter had arrived home half an hour late, expecting a right earful, but she'd let him off, just this once because she had had other things to think about.

Her clothes still smelt of Chris Colebrook's body, or at least Jenny thought they might. She pulled the dress up to her face, breathing in hard to make sure. Yes, there it was: a subtle hint of his aftershave and a warm musky male scent of sweat and testosterone.

Chris had arrived with his hair still damp and curling into the curve of his neck. Under his tan was a hint of pink where his skin still glowed from the shower. He had stood under the back porch, smiling, quite obviously pleased to see her, pleased to be there but nervous; she could tell by the way he shuffled from foot to foot, hesitant to cross the threshold. Jenny had showered too and slipped into a soft cotton buttercup yellow sundress.

'I've opened a bottle of red,' she said, as if they were already in the middle of a conversation. 'I hope you like red. Good for your heart apparently.'

Between the phone call and Chris's arrival Jenny had been busy. She'd turned off the fluorescent strip light in the kitchen, packed all sorts of stray odds and ends into the dishwasher, sprayed with fly killer and Haze, and brought in a table lamp and lit some candles in the sitting room. She'd left the back door open, the outside light on and slapped a compilation tape of love songs into the midi-system. A quick spray of duty-free behind the ears and Jenny Beck felt ready for almost anything.

Chris still smiling nervously, looked her up and down and taking it as an invitation Jenny abandoned the bottle and glasses and slinked over to him, her face a mask of concern.

'Oh Chris, just look at your poor eye,' she said in a low hungry voice. 'Let me take a good look at it.'

Chris stared at her as if the words confused him, and then rather ruefully traced a finger around the corona of purple and yellow. On tiptoe – she was barefoot – Jenny Beck reached up and kissed the bruise as tenderly as if she was kissing a new born.

Chris gasped and made as if to step back.

She smiled and caught hold of his hand. 'You are so brave, Chris. I really don't know how to thank you.'

His expression, though still wary, softened a fraction. She knew then that she almost had him.

'It's hard for me here, all on my own. I don't think anyone realises just how hard it is.' A minuscule quiver. She bit her lip as if holding back girlish tears of bravery and gratitude. Chris lifted his arm a fraction – it could have been to scratch his nose, shake down his sleeve, any reason at all but without further encouragement Jenny stepped closer still and his instinctive reaction was to embrace her. As Jenny settled herself against Chris's broad chest she couldn't resist a smile of triumph. She wriggled closer, making tiny animal noises of pleasure and encouragement. He responded with an earthy groan that almost took her breath away.

Jenny looked up at him, all doe eyed and vulnerable, pressing her body against his in a subtle mixture of seduction and tenderness. She could see him weigh the pull of intellect and good sense against something older and less controllable, there was a moment's pause, where she could almost feel all rational thought being crushed by the leviathan of desire and, right on cue, Chris Colebrook leant forward and kissed her.

Jenny knew from experience that it was now just a question of keeping the flame alight under the blue touch paper until instinct caught hold. Her tongue slipped between her lips and delicately brushed his. Chris groaned again and stiffened, and then, when Jenny thought she might have to try something less subtle he suddenly surged forward and kissed her hard, almost recklessly as if there was nothing left to lose, her tentative tongue thrust aside by his.

Jenny squeaked and squirmed with a genuine sense of delight and surprise. God, he was a really great kisser. Sarah Colebrook was such a bloody fool. And as the thought passed through her head, Jenny let go too.

In that instant she forgot that it was she not Sarah who was the source of all the rumours about Leo Banning, Jenny who had told people that Sarah was having an affair. She forgot that it was she who – after overhearing a single telephone conversation – had set Sarah up with the vicar in the imagination of as many of her friends and acquaintances as she could persuade to listen. In that instant when

Jenny pressed herself closer to Chris she forgot it all, the lies, the gossip and the subterfuge and as she did, somewhere deep in her subconscious the myth hardened up like concrete and turned to truth.

So, a little while later, when she and Chris were kissing and touching and getting all hot and bothered, canoodling on the sofa in the sitting room, doing all those things that you never bother to do with your husband, it was no trouble at all for Jenny to tell him about Sarah and Leo, in an edited form of course because she was desperate to spare his feelings. No trouble at all as she poured them both a glass of wine to ease away his growing sense of guilt with lurid tales of how everyone else knew about what was going on between Sarah and Leo except him. And as she ran her fingers through the thick dark curly hair on his chest Jenny believed every word she said – well almost.

At the vicarage Leo Banning was sitting alone in his study, around him the old house groaned and mumbled arthritically as it settled down after the heat of the long summer day. With the hall door ajar he could hear the comforting heartbeat of the long case clock standing sentinel in the hall, ticking off the minutes of the night.

It had been a gift from his mother after he left theological college, the ceremonial passing of a family heirloom from one generation to the next, the gesture a mark of his passage into the serried ranks of maturity. He still missed her; her other gifts had been two cases of pink champagne, a frivolous amount of smoked salmon and the summer lease on a tiny villa in Greece.

How long ago had that been? The numbers he came up with seemed so utterly impossible that he left them where they fell.

Leo had been sitting looking at the phone for an awfully

long time. Thinking; thinking about old friends, old times, the unconnected things that drift to the surface in a mind loosened by a fraction too much brandy.

Harry would still be awake, no doubt about that. Probably be out with Pip and Brookie. Midnight and beyond was their natural territory.

Leo topped up the brandy glass with the last of the good cognac and swirled it around, letting the ice careen off the crystal. Harry would probably be at the club or maybe curled up on the sofa, not necessarily alone. And what could he say if he rang and caught Harry in? That he felt lonely? That he was desperate to reminisce with someone who knew all about him, and loved him still? That he missed him. That though time indeed was a healer grief left a silver white scar across your soul that never really went away.

He looked down at the amber coloured fluid where it clung to the sides of the glass. He had chosen this retreat into the wilderness, dragged on a hair shirt, he could hardly complain now that it felt exactly how he thought it might.

Not a good idea to drink so much really. It was making him maudlin, which would be a terrible shame after such a successful evening. Sarah Colebrook appeared in his mind unbidden. Nice woman, he wasn't altogether sure why it was that their paths hadn't crossed before. It would be good to have someone like her at St Barts, natural enthusiasm was a real joy to be around. And then he thought about Adam Gregory and the look that Adam Gregory had given Sarah Colebrook and for some reason it made him sad.

He stared down into the ice floe and the glisten of the alcohol and then stood the glass on the side table alongside the framed photo of Tim and Harry and Brookie and Pip, the one he had taken on a perfect summer's evening in Greece, God alone knows how many years ago. Leaving the glass and the phone untouched he went upstairs to bed.

Sarah dreamt that Mac danced her breathless around the grand hall at St Barts while Leo Banning and Adam Gregory clapped out the rhythm and looked on in amusement. The caller from the barn dance bawled out the steps and changes as Mac swung her around and around. It was good to see the caller again even if he had now got small goaty horns poking rather fetchingly from amongst his mop of thick black curls. He waved as she spun by.

Chris dreamt he was sitting at the kitchen table waiting for his dinner to be dished up. It was dark and gloomy and the food seemed to be taking an awfully long time to arrive. He couldn't quite remember who was supposed to be cooking it or what he was supposed to be having. He couldn't understand where Sarah was. Just when he was convinced he'd been forgotten, Jenny Beck appeared from nowhere and told him everything was going to be fine. Tony Whelk was bringing everyone fish and chips.

'Of course, you will have to pay,' said Jenny, shaking out a napkin and tying it tight around his throat with a big knot. As she leant a little closer he could smell the rich bloom of her perfume and sensed that she didn't just mean for the fish supper.

Monica Carlisle dreamt of sailing in the South of France, in a red sailed barque, while Mac – who had drunk so much that he couldn't make it back to the cottage and had slept on the chaise in the conservatory, snored and snuffled like a cheery little piglet and dreamt of nothing at all.

Leo Banning took a long time to get to sleep and when he did he dreamt of snow so white that it hurt his eyes, and crisp on the surface like the perfect meringue and so, so very very deep that it seemed impossible and destructive to cross over to the place where Tim was, Tim and Harry and the others. And by the time Leo finally did get there, sweating and exhausted and angry, Tim had gone. Not a sign of him anywhere.

Leo woke for a few seconds and stared unseeing into the darkness, sad but relieved that he'd been spared anything more graphic. It seemed that his mind was finally carpeting the bare boards of reality.

Adam Gregory dreamt of Sarah.

Chapter 13

Early on Friday morning Chris woke up in what felt like a good mood. It lasted for around fifteen seconds, which was how long it took him to roll on to his side, open his eyes and spot Sarah's little black frock hanging over the back of a chair by the bed. The dress was the key that unlocked the events of the night before and one by one they all came creeping out into the light. All he had thought, all he had seen, all he had suspected and all those things he felt guilty about came back to him in glorious Technicolor.

He looked across at Sarah, curled on her side facing away from him, her dark hair was fuzzed and folded against lightly suntanned skin, and for a few moments he watched her shoulders lift rhythmically, still deep asleep.

Something inside Chris was very hurt and very angry. He found it hard to piece all the elements together, not quite certain how he and Sarah had arrived at this peculiar, uncomfortable point in their lives.

There was a sense of unreality to the thoughts that scuttered like storm clouds through his mind. It felt as if he had woken up inside someone else's life. The alarm clock said that there was almost another half-hour to go before anyone needed to get up. Chris took a deep breath, there was just no way he was going to lie there and ruminate over all the ways of his life; he rolled out of bed. Not carefully, not gently but in a way that was meant to disturb Sarah, to wake her, to shake her out of the peaceful guilt-free place that she had found, but in a way that he could persuade himself was otherwise. It didn't work, Sarah snuffled, shuffled and then settled down again. For a few seconds Chris stood beside the bed and considered getting back under the duvet to give it another go.

The water in the shower was a fraction above lukewarm. He'd been meaning to fix the element for a while now or maybe it was the thermostat, but what with one thing and another he just hadn't had the time. Maybe, Chris thought, as he towelled himself dry, he would never get around to fixing it now, maybe it would stay broken forever. The idea did nothing at all to lift his mood.

Chris would probably have taken a perverse pleasure in knowing that the thing that finally woke Sarah was the sound of him revving the Transit up at the bottom of the garden, but by the time she was fully conscious Chris was already heading off down the lane and out through the village towards the bypass.

'. . . so, I was wondering if you might have something to contribute to the summer exhibition,' said a cultured but extremely insistent voice at the far end of the line.

It was barely eight o'clock and Sarah was trying to slice a banana onto Charlie's cereal, while preventing Jack from eating a bag full of fun-sized Mars Bars for breakfast and persuading Matthew that there was some point in going in to school to join in the study day that his form teacher had set up for their A level group. She also had the phone nipped precariously between shoulder and chin. Sarah couldn't believe whoever it was had rung at this time of the morning.

'I'm sorry, what did you say your name was again? Did we meet last night at the concert?'

'Yes, that's right. The Reverend Banning was kind enough to give me your telephone number. I wondered if I might put you down for what? Two or three pieces? What shall we say? Watercolour? Oil, mixed media? You just tell me and I'll jot it down – I've got my pad right here by the phone.'

Sarah pulled a face as the cat joined Charlie at the table and peered avariciously at the tidal reaches of his full cream milk. 'To be honest I'm not certain that I can be of any help really. Would you mind if I rang you back later?'

'Oh gosh no, not at all, I haven't caught you at a bad time, have I?' She sounded genuinely surprised. 'The thing is I'd really like to know what you're planning to put into the exhibition by Monday at the latest, that's when I've got to get the catalogue off to the printers, you see.' The woman would have done a great job driving a steamroller. 'Have you got my number?'

A name wouldn't have gone amiss either, thought Sarah, reaching across to grab a wax crayon out of the fruit bowl so she could scribble the information down on the back of a cornflakes packet. The sensible thing would be to say no, but it was extremely flattering to be asked and surely – as the mystery caller had pointed out a moment or two earlier – she could surely find something suitable amongst all the paintings she'd done over the years. She grinned; it made her sound like a real artist, a force to be reckoned with, someone with a body of work to be sorted through and selected from.

Were the paintings still on top of the cupboards in the spare room or had Chris finally put them out in the garden shed? While Sarah scribbled the digits she tried to remember exactly where she had stacked the boards and pads and portfolios that had accumulated over the years. Wherever they were they'd been there an awfully long time. She couldn't remember having painted anything other than a few extra ducks in the nursery since having Charlie. Mind wandering Sarah hung up, and turned her attention back to the on-going battleground of breakfast.

* * *

Chris was on site over at Norwich by half seven. He supervised the unloading of a trailer full of silver birch trees, watched the contractors set about laying a great lake of turf and then rang to check on the delivery of porous membrane he'd ordered. Outwardly Chris Colebrook appeared calm, his normal self. When the rest of the gang broke for breakfast he took his tea, clambered back into the van and rang Jenny Beck. It was just after nine – she didn't answer – and so he tried again at quarter past, half past and finally got through at a few minutes before ten by which time Chris was tense and unsettled, and had totally forgotten what it was he planned to say.

Jenny pre-empted him after the most basic pleasantries had been exchanged. 'I don't think we ought to see each other any more, Chris, do you? I mean it's not right.'

He could hear the little thrill of emotion in her voice. It made him shiver. 'We both know that it's not right, it doesn't matter how we feel about each other. I've seen things like this on daytime telly. I've got to tell you that I haven't felt like this since before our Peter was born . . .' she paused and sucked in a breath, obviously unable to go on in case she embarrassed them both. Even though it was deeply disturbing Chris couldn't help but smile.

'It isn't right, though, is it?' she said finally, after a few more seconds. 'Even if Sarah is, well, carrying on with the vicar and everything. I mean, we've got no real proof, have we?'

He realised that he quite liked the way Jenny said we.

'Could just be a malicious rumour or something, couldn't it? Has she said anything to you about it?' Jenny didn't wait for an answer. 'No, well then; two wrongs never did make a right.' There was another meaty little pause and then she said, 'I think I'd better go now.'

Chris struggled to find some space to speak. He wanted to tell Jenny that everything she had told him about Sarah was true, that he had seen the two of them at the arts centre – Sarah and the vicar – with his own eyes, but before he could say anything else or even protest she had hung up.

Chris stared down at the shiny black carapace of his mobile; Sarah had really misjudged Jenny Beck. She might be a bit eccentric, but she was a special kind of woman, maybe a little rough around the edges but there was a certain earthy attractiveness there, and she was obviously very moral. Not like Sarah. He visualised Jenny's face and as he did heard a little chain saw of obsession fire up somewhere deep inside his mind and carve an unhealthy slice off the side of reason.

'Chris?'

He jumped as one of the labourers banged on the side window of the van.

'Can you come and take a look at these trees?'

Chris tucked the phone back into his pocket and headed out across the site, head down, part of his mind turning in on itself. Jenny Beck. Sarah, Leo Banning; deep down in his mind their names and the faces turned around and around, a central core of betrayal and indignation, like a Tibetan prayer wheel.

Sunday:

'So,' said Sarah, waving her soup spoon like a baton, 'when I finally got up into the loft I found all this amazing stuff. I'd forgotten about a lot of it. I was up there most of the morning – there were two great big oils I can't even remember painting – a fenland landscape and a really nice nude, some interesting abstract stuff, pen and ink, water-colours. I'm sorry now that I didn't take better care of them. I'm surprised how much of it was passable – and some of it is quite good.' Sarah paused, her enthusiasm finally ebbing. She took a second or two to catch her breath. So far Sunday lunch at Monica's was not going very well at all. A root canal filling or a scale and polish would have been like light relief by contrast.

Sarah was sick of the sound of her own voice; she had been talking way too much, far too brightly, much too fast, in a single-handed attempt to lift the atmosphere above morose.

Chris had barely been civil all morning and hadn't improved after they arrived. The kids were edgy, Charlie was sulking. It felt like trying to push water up hill.

Across the table Monica Carlisle smiled. 'I don't know why you should be so surprised. I always thought you were very talented, Sarah. You ought to have gone to art school. When we first met it struck me as a terrible waste not to have done something bigger with it. I've still got the two little watercolours you painted for me as a birthday present. One of Holkham gap . . .'

'. . . Oh my God, and one of the harbour at Wells-next-the-sea? I'd forgotten all about those,' said Sarah with a genuine sense of delight. 'Where are they? Have you got them here?'

Monica nodded. 'Uh-huh, upstairs, in my dressing room. I'll show you after lunch if you like. Maybe the boys would like to go and have a look around the grounds, once we've eaten, explore – take a look at the stream?' She took another sip of her wine. 'This whole St Barts thing sounds great, particularly for somewhere out in the sticks like this, maybe I ought to ring up and have a word with them, see if there's anything I can do. Boys, please help yourself to more juice. Chris, how's your wine?'

At the far end of the table Chris winked. ''S fine, Monica, just fine.'

Sarah looked at him – she was on cranberry juice – and pulled a disapproving face, trying very hard to attract his attention. If Chris noticed her he gave absolutely no sign.

She couldn't work out what the hell he was playing at; maybe he was just tired.

On Friday he hadn't got home until nearly eight, had had his supper and a bath and then gone to sleep in the armchair in front of the TV. When she'd said something about him being busy Chris made some sharp aside about being behind schedule and her not being interested, so maybe that was it. It wouldn't be the first time he'd taken problems at work out on the rest of them. Also Chris had never liked Monica Carlisle very much, no, that was an understatement. Chris loathed her, but even so he was normally, if not warm and welcoming, then certainly civil.

This was out of character. He had accepted a small sherry when they arrived, and then a couple of the vodka martinis that Fredo mixed after Monica showed them around the house, and since they started lunch he'd been making light work of something white and glittering and quite obviously expensive that Monica was serving with the soup. Wine and soup were delicious and Chris was already a long way towards drunk – a very long way – and despite Monica's promise, Mac had joined them. He was sitting to Monica's left, opposite Sarah and was dressed in an old style white collarless evening shirt, open at the neck, sleeves rolled up, tucked into tight blue jeans. His sun-bleached hair was tied back to frame his even tanned features. To her astonishment seeing Mac again had made her salivate. Not a good sign.

Grinning now, sipping his wine he watched her with undisguised interest as she tried to encourage Chris back into the fold.

Catching her eye for an instant, Sarah saw Monica poke Mac with her fork and growl.

Sarah wasn't altogether sure whether she was annoyed or flattered by Mac's attention, whichever it was she didn't feel at all comfortable and Mac knew it. When she felt his foot slide up over her ankles it was all she could do to stop herself from leaping up and running out of the room. Her colour and discomfort intensified with every passing second.

'So Chris, how's business going? Sarah told me that you've expanded,' said Monica, trying very hard to shift everyone's attention to where Chris, at least in theory, commanded the head of the table.

He peered at them from over the rim of his glass and blinked. 'Oh yes, Monica, I'm on the up and up, me, or didn't my good lady tell you?' His voice was top heavy with sarcasm. 'No? Maybe it wasn't derogatory enough. Yes, I've got two vans now, two vans and some very good lads working for me. Good lads, Geordies mostly. Doing a new private nursing home over at Norwich at the moment, good pond, really good pond, we've got over there.'

He burped loudly and then pressed on with a flamboyant apology 'Sorry about that, better out than in, must have been something I ate, eh?' He giggled. 'Where was I, oh yes. Good pond, great pond – fucking enormous.' He spread his hands to encompass its girth.

There was a pause and beside Sarah, Charlie wriggled uneasily from side to side.

'Perhaps you'd like to tell Fredo we're ready for the main course,' said Monica to Mac, who didn't bother to get up but instead tipped back in his chair to jerk the bell pull.

'I could give you a quote for this place if you wanted,' continued Chris having finally found his voice. 'Lawns, hedges, borders, maintenance of the whole fucking shoot-ing match, should've brought my calculator. Tell you what, I'll even do you a discount as you're . . . well, whatever it is you are. Who have you got doing it for you at the minute? Not him, that's for certain.' He waved dismissively towards Mac. 'Now don't tell me, don't tell me. Rent-a-Spade from

Wisbech. Go on tell me that I'm wrong, go on, tell me.'

All eyes swung back to Monica.

There was a few seconds' pause, and then the dining room doors swung open to reveal Fredo pushing a trolley. Sarah wondered whether he had been waiting outside. Everyone's attention shifted again.

The lamb was as tender and pink as tissue. Chris shovelled it down, along with a bucket full of Syrah while continuing with his monologue about the landscape gardening industry, oblivious to the pained expressions on the other faces around the table.

'. . . and that lot over at Radleigh are no better, rip you off soon as look at you. Charged some pensioner fifty quid to prune three rose bushes. Fifty-bloody-quid, they should've been hung, no, hanging is too good for them. I'm serious.' He underlined his outrage with a dramatic stabbing gesture with his fork, hiccuped and then tried to drown the spasm with another glass of wine.

Dessert came: summer pudding, strawberries and cream and more wine. Sarah could hardly bear to look at Chris.

'So,' he said, through a big wet florid belch, '. . . me and Baz, that's Barry, Barry Pearce bought this enormous polythene greenhouse. He wanted to come in with me, as a partner, you know, but the timing was off. But it was a real bargain. So he said . . .' Chris paused again and refilled his glass, still with his gaze fixed on Monica. Everyone else around the table, with the possible exception of Mac was silent with undiluted embarrassment, although Sarah had considered that maybe Charlie just wanted a wee.

'What on earth is the matter with Dad?' Jack whispered, as he handed Sarah a dish of berries and a large jug of cream.

From across the table Mac grinned and lifted his glass in salute. 'Pissed out of his crust, kid. Out of his sodden God forsaken crust. Totally skewered.'

Sarah glared at Mac – everyone could see Chris was drunk, it was why the hell he was so bloody drunk that was the question that was bugging her. Aloud she said, 'Chris, love, don't you think you've had enough?'

He paused mid-sentence and then looked up at her as if, for a few moments, he had completely forgotten she existed. It was the most terrible, icy expression.

'No,' Chris said, and refilled his glass to the very brim. 'What was it you said a little while ago? I don't need you as my moral compass?' He sniffed then took a long pull on the glass, drinking it down to the lees. He had everyone's attention. 'Isn't that what you said, eh? But was it the truth, that's what I have to ask myself?' He paused, looked at his glass and with a growing sense of horror Sarah saw his colour drain, the muscles in his throat bunch, cheeks and shoulders lift in unison, and knew with absolute certainty that Chris was about to be sick.

His eyes bulged with sheer panic and his gaze moved back and forth in desperation around the faces at the table, around the elegant room, as if looking for an escape route and then finally, Chris pushed the chair away, was on his feet and with one mighty great retching bubbling sound was violently sick into the fireplace.

There was a tremendous, awe-inspiring moment of silence and almost as quickly it back filled with a general sense of astonishment, horror, the sounds of Chris retching and Mac laughing like a hyena.

Monica was the first on her feet. 'Why don't we all go and have our coffee and dessert in the conservatory. Boys, perhaps you'd like to bring the dishes through?'

On his hands and knees in the hearth Chris was heaving and coughing, spittle hanging from his chin in glittering ribbons, his complexion a rather fetching shade of eau de nil. Sarah stood up, clutching her napkin in a knot across her solar plexus, emotionally torn a dozen ways.

It was Matthew who caught hold of her arm and guided her away from Chris. 'Come on, Mum,' he said. 'Let's go into the conservatory and have some coffee.'

Chapter 14

At the vicarage in Barton, Leo Banning stood behind the carver and contemplated the vast, well polished expanse of walnut table in the dining room, before saying a prayer over his Sunday lunch.

After a few seconds of respectful silence, Mrs Vine said, 'Lovely sermon this morning, Vicar, very nice,' and then busied herself arranging the tureens within striking distance. 'Ye shall know them by their fruits; Matthew 7:16–20, one of my own particular favourites. Just a shame there weren't a few more people at church to hear it. Preaching's becoming a lost art, you know, like thatching and hedging and gas lamps. You'd think you could get a grant for that too, people seem to be able to get money for anything these days. Now, are you sure you wouldn't like me to dish up for you? It would be no trouble at all.' The words ran together in a long gaudy string with barely a whisper of breath between them.

Leo shook his head. 'Quite certain, thank you, Mrs Vine. It smells wonderful.'

She set a jug of water down alongside him. Condensation fogged the outside of the glass, ice chinking and jostling inside.

'I'm just glad that you've got your appetite back,' she said briskly, unable to hide the merest tic of a smile, and then folding a tea towel over her arm in the style of a maître d'. She stood back and waited until Leo was seated and had lifted the lid on the nearest tureen before heading back into the kitchen.

Piled inside the belly of the dish were enough baby carrots to feed a scout troop. Maybe the quantity was a hint that Mrs Vine would enjoy cooking for more than just the two of them. Perhaps it was time for Leo to consider inviting a few people round for Sunday lunch. It wasn't as if there was nobody he could ask; in his last parish the Sunday lunches had been famous. Leo lifted the second lid, inside were tiny new potatoes steamed in their skins, buttered and sprinkled with fresh parsley and nuggets of sea salt; Delia Smith had an awful lot to answer for.

With no encouragement at all a guest list began to take shape in an idle corner of his mind; there were a couple of people from the St Barts project that it would be interesting to meet up with socially, and then there was Adam Gregory, Sarah Colebrook and her husband, the verger and his wife . . . the list meandered on as he helped himself to Yorkshire puddings and gravy, working its way through various backwaters until he had come up with a round dozen.

The beef, a handsome slab of top rump, was as soft as butter. Maybe he would have a word with Mrs Vine to see how she felt about a little socialising. The possibilities grew into something more solid, more likely, and for a few moments the room, the house felt far too big for him. It would be good to have someone to share it with; his mind moved on, galloping past an acute pang of loneliness on a tight loop back to the idea of Sunday lunch.

To spare his feelings his imagination filled the empty chairs and for the briefest of moments he was surrounded by the ghosts of his likely guests, laughing and talking, drinking, passing the tureens backwards and forwards across the table until they came back to him.

'So, I want you to tell me honestly, is he always like this?' Mac dipped a half eaten strawberry back into the bowl of cream and then to his mouth.

Sarah was sitting on the terrace outside Monica's house, perched on a wooden sun lounger, under an enormous green sunshade. She was struggling with a sense of guilt and anger and embarrassment. Guilt because Monica had insisted she stay out in the sunshine while they – Fredo and Monica – went back inside to take care of Chris. And anger and embarrassment . . . well, those were too raw and too obvious and too close up to have to explain.

Mac leant across and topped up her glass of cranberry juice with a healthy measure of champagne. For once Sarah didn't argue. She'd really been looking forward to seeing Monica again, seeing the house, letting the boys wander round the gardens, relaxing over a long lazy lunch. A few fragments of the fantasy still clung on like burrs to torment her.

In the distance, picked out like colourful birds against a backdrop of lush green shrubs and dark trees, the boys were making their way down to explore the stream and the summerhouse. Matthew was striding ahead, Jack following behind, his body sloped at an acute angle, while between the two of them Charlie loped and skipped and hopped about like an over-enthusiastic Disney rabbit.

'It is so peaceful here.' Sarah tipped her face up towards the sun and took a long slow breath, thinking about the last time she had sat on this terrace at Monica's housewarming party. It seemed like months had passed since then. That night she had been filled with a sense of expectation, as if anything was possible. She had felt new and light, a stark contrast to how she was feeling now, weighed down by anger and responsibility and white hot fury that Chris could behave so badly and spoil such a potentially lovely day in such a glorious place. The early afternoon air was heavy with the scent of new mown grass and summer sun warming old bricks. A heat haze shimmied across the lawn.

Unfortunately Mac wasn't going to be fobbed off by any

attempts to distract him with small talk. 'Why the hell are you still married to him, Sarah? He is a total philistine.'

Sarah looked over her shoulder at Mac, annoyed that he had broken into her gentle observation of the boys; his voice dragging her back from the mellow middle distance. She was also surprised how full of tears she felt.

'Well,' he said, 'I'm right, aren't I? He is a total and utter prat.'

'Whatever you do, please don't be horrible about him, Mac, if you do I'll feel obligated to defend him and I really don't want to.'

Mac laughed, 'Defend him, you cannot be serious?'

Sarah nodded. 'Uh-huh. It's one of those terrible, instinctive, unfathomable woman things. I think it's got something to do with rooting for the underdog. It's perfectly all right for me to slag him off and complain, just don't agree with me. Don't tell me what an arsehole he's been today or how badly hard done by I am or I shall find myself having to deny it all. It's happened before. I do it all the time with my family. They've always hated Chris. Christmas used to be a nightmare until we decided to celebrate separately. I'd be in the kitchen with my parents telling them what a wonderful man he was – once you got to know him, "but you don't really know him, Mum, he's fine when he's on his own with me and the children, honestly. Family situations like this aren't his thing, you have to admit that these sort of days are hard work."' Sarah took a sip of the cranberry and champagne mix. 'I've done it for years and years – why should I have to apologise for him? And what a pig . . . I can't believe he was sick. What the hell is he playing at?'

Mac shrugged. 'Can I speak now?'

Sarah sighed, 'Okay if you really must. Even I don't think I can come up with an excuse for him this time. Have you any idea how angry I am, how mortified? How embarrassed? I should be inside offering to help clear up after him but I don't want to, who would? But why should Monica and Fredo have to do it? And, if he says anything I don't think I'll be able to control myself.' Sarah took another pull on her glass. 'Although chances are if I hit him really hard at the moment he wouldn't remember, would he?'

Mac filled up her drink, Sarah made as if to protest but Mac waved her hand away. 'I'll book you a cab or Fredo can drive you.'

Sarah sighed and then offered her glass up. 'Okay.'

As the bubbles circumnavigated the glass, Mac said, 'Why don't you come over on your own one day and I'll cook you lunch. You and me and a bottle of Chablis.'

'What?'

'No, I mean it. Come over to the cottage, let me take you for a long slow walk around all my special places. You take the next lane on the left after the one that leads to the main house. It's a different world. Say yes.'

Mac's invitation was unexpected, his tone intense. Sarah stared up at him but before she could fathom out a reply, Monica appeared through the French windows carrying a tray with cups on it. Behind her Fredo carried matching silver coffee pots. They were hardly on the terrace before Sarah was up on her feet. On top of everything else Mac's invitation had totally thrown her off balance.

'How is Chris? Is there anything I can do? I'm so sorry. I don't really know what to say.' She flapped.

Monica set the tray down. 'Then for Christ's sake don't say anything. It's not your fault and Chris will be fine. Fredo's put him to bed; let him sleep it off. Now, what do you want, black or white?'

'Where are the champagne truffles?' asked Mac, peering down at the tray.

*　　*　　*

Before dropping Peter off at his dad's Jenny Beck told him that she was planning to take a drive over to the Duck and Drake for Sunday lunch, maybe have chicken in a basket. The pub was right down on the river, the food was good, and often on a Sunday they had a band playing there, usually something bluesy and cool, outside on the sun deck if the weather was nice. It was the kind of place you might take someone you wanted to impress. Just the place a new lover might well take the new woman in his life.

Jenny told Peter three times so that he wouldn't forget, and although she didn't get out of the car when she got to the house she made sure Tony saw her waving regally from the driveway. Full make-up, big blow wave, low cut blouse and a lot of lipstick, she gave him the whole nine yards. Let him realise exactly what it was he was missing. Bastard.

There was no way she was really going to the pub on her own; the plan was to pick up a video from the garage, a microwave dinner from the freezer and spend whatever was left of the afternoon out on the patio sunbathing listening to the CD player and flicking through a magazine.

It was nearly eight by the time Tony brought him back home. Peter grunted hello, fished a can of coke out of the fridge, a packet of cheesy Wotsits out of the pantry and headed straight upstairs to his bedroom.

'Lover boy not about tonight then?' said Tony, peering nervously around the kitchen.

Jenny had lit candles, bathed and was dressed in a floaty little voile dress that left nothing much to the imagination. She could see she had Tony's undivided attention from the very second he rolled in through the back door.

'And what if he is, Tony, what exactly has it got to do with you?'

'You're still my wife you know, Jen,' he said, straightening up and squaring his shoulders.

Jenny snorted. 'Didn't stop you running off with that flighty little bitch now did it?'

Tony looked wounded. 'That was different, Petal, surely we can put that behind us now, water under the bridge, wild oats, mid-life crisis and all that. I thought that maybe we could still be friends.'

Jenny opened the fridge and poured herself a very generous rum and coke. 'Oh really, is that what this is about? Friends, eh? None of my other friends treat me the way you treat me, Tony. Are you telling me that you made a mistake now that you're living with her or do you just want to have your cake and eat it?' Her tone was neutral.

Not invited in, not asked to sit, not offered a drink, Tony shifted uncomfortably from foot to foot. 'What would you say if I said yes, Jen?'

She dropped a handful of ice into the tallglass, as it hit the coke it cracked and spat.

'Try me.'

Tony took another look around the kitchen almost as if he expected to find a sniper with his sights trained on him, hidden amongst the formica and brass knick-knacks.

'I'd rather not,' said Tony and backed very slowly out of the kitchen.

When she was sure he had gone Jenny Beck began to laugh. For the first time in the last few months she felt she was on top of the game and it really felt very good, very good indeed.

It was seven o'clock on Monday morning and Chris Colebrook was sitting at the breakfast table. He did not look well. 'Food poisoning,' he said with a shudder.

Sarah handed him another glass of water, slapped two paracetamol alongside it and then poured herself a mug of tea.

'Chris, it doesn't matter what you say, you were drunk, totally and utterly out of your skull. Wasted. I have never been so embarrassed in my entire life. And the idea that someone else had to clean the fireplace out. I'm horrified. Monica was amazing about it. I hope you're going to ring up and apologise?'

He looked up at her, eyelids clenched, he looked like an extremely bad tempered lizard. 'I most certainly am not, I think it was something she put in the hors d'oeuvre. That pâté tasted bloody strange. You know, you're damned lucky I didn't end up in casualty.'

Sarah looked him up and down, wondering whether he might have overheard her plan to hit him.

Lisa was replenishing the coffee machine when Sarah rolled into school. The smell of newly filtered Blue Mountain seeped down the corridors like an invitation to linger. For a few minutes it dulled the usual institutional perfume; mornings at Whitefriars ran on pure caffeine.

Sarah glanced at her watch. Plan Monday involved the design and making of a Viking long boat and then laying down the first stages of a papier-mâché relief map of East Anglia.

The open-plan staff room was relatively empty, most of the teachers had already made their way to the classrooms to give themselves pole position on the day. Whitefriars was a busy, clever, bright school. A few support staff lingered, using the photocopier, picking up resources; there was always something to do. The room had an air of quiet industry.

Lisa handed her a mug. 'You look rough, here. I've got to go back to the office, you can tell me all about it at break. Oh, and before I forget there was a call for you on the answer machine when I got in.'

Sarah looked up. 'For me?'

'Uh-huh, sounded important.' Lisa peeled a Post-It note off the ring binder she had picked up.

'Number doesn't mean anything to me, did they say who it was? Damn, I didn't ring *that* woman about my paintings. Did I tell you that the committee at the arts centre want me to put something in their summer exhibition?'

At the door now, Lisa shook her head. 'No, anyway this was a man.'

'Was it Leo Banning? I'm waiting to hear whether I've made the short list.'

Lisa, in the corridor, carried on shaking her head. 'Didn't sound like him either; said they'd like you to ring asap. I'm on my way back to the office if you want to use the phone before school starts.'

Sarah took another look at her watch. 'I'm pillaging and plundering with the Vikings after assembly.'

Lisa pulled a face. 'If you don't ring now you know it'll gnaw away at you all morning.'

Sarah took a swig of coffee. 'Am I that transparent?'

'I'm afraid so.'

It was Mac. He picked up the receiver on the second ring as if he had been sitting waiting by the phone for her call.

'Lunch at mine today.' It wasn't so much an invitation as a government directive. 'I've got champagne in the cooler, salad, stunning dessert.'

Sarah laughed, 'You've got a nerve ringing here. I thought it was something important.'

'But it is. I'm really hurt now.'

'You've got skin like a rhino. Look I've got to go, I'm at work.'

'What about lunch.'

'Not today, I'm afraid not, no.'

'You are way too repressed for your own good, Sarah.

You know that you want to. I'll be expecting you at one. Don't be late.'

Before Sarah could reply Mac had hung up. Part of her was outraged at the nerve of the man, unfortunately it didn't quite out vote the other bit which was flattered and curious and a bit giggly. She was a big girl now, she could take care of herself. What harm would it do to have lunch with him?

Lisa had settled herself behind her computer. 'So, who was it?'

'Sorry?'

Lisa grinned. 'Well it wasn't one of the women from the arts centre, was it? You've gone all red.'

'I have not,' said Sarah indignantly.

'Please yourself,' said Lisa, the grin lingered, and with it an air of expectation. She was obviously waiting for Sarah to spill the beans.

Sarah shook her head, uncertain why she felt defensive or quite where to start. It wasn't until she began to speak that she'd got any idea what she was going to say. 'It was nothing very important really, just someone about the position at St Barts. I'll ring later when I get home.'

Lisa looked at her long and hard and then shrugged. 'If you say so.'

Without meeting Lisa's eyes again – they both knew, the lie was obvious enough – Sarah thanked her for the use of the phone and headed off to get ready for the first lesson.

The morning wasn't easy; it was hard to keep her mind under control. There was no fooling herself, Mac fancied her; which sounded clumsy and immature spoken aloud, but whatever you wanted to call it she could see the attraction and desire in his eyes. The way his body moved when she was near him. Although she kept trying to convince herself it was just a trick of the light, going to his cottage for lunch was not a good idea. Not a good idea at all.

Sarah went out to the store to find some more paint. Wasn't it true that she felt the same way about Mac? Maybe not enough to jump into bed with him but enough to make her fantasise about it, to feel flattered by his attention. The morning was not getting any easier. She avoided Lisa and spent the run up to lunch time laying down great gouts of papier-mâché to build the relief map of East Anglia and SE England in preparation for some Viking raids.

It would be totally crazy to go to lunch. He was a terrible flirt, beautiful to look at and had the morals of an alley cat. She didn't know anything about him. He could be an axe murderer or a serial rapist, certainly nothing he'd done so far would convince anyone he was a sober trustworthy pillar of the community. It was playing with fire. As if life wasn't confusing enough already.

All of which convoluted ramblings brought Sarah's thoughts round to Chris. She was still smarting about the way he had behaved over the last few days. Getting drunk at Monica's was the last straw, and although she tried hard to ignore the voice whispering that if she went to see Mac it would serve Chris right, ultimately this tiny tit for tat, childish thing was the featherweight on the scales that tipped the balance in favour of accepting his invitation.

All the way there in the car Sarah told herself that she could turn round and go home if she wanted to. At any time. It was easy, no problem; even when she pulled into the single track lane a few hundred yards beyond the main driveway to Monica's house. In places the trees had grown together overhead to make a tunnel. It would be easy, simple to go home, there would be no loss of face at all.

Sarah dropped the Golf into second to creep around the potholes, and then first, driving at little more than walking pace now. There was bound to be a gateway up ahead where she could turn round if she changed her mind. As the car crept forward a foot at a time she planned what she would do when she arrived home, how embarrassed and silly she would feel, while all the time edging closer and closer to journey's end.

And then she saw it. Mac's cottage stood on the edge of a lake fed by the stream that they had followed down to the summerhouse. She stopped the car in the mouth of the long lane and stared. The road was margined by trees and tall rambling hedges. It was one of those perfect still early summer days. Sunlight clamoured for attention, dappling the grass and compacted bare earth that made up the roadway and the sky seemed impossibly blue and way way above the ground. Here and there wild flowers burst through the grass verges and tumbled into the ruts that marked the path.

Sarah was enchanted by the place even before she got out of the car and knew instinctively that it was another bad sign. She had been married nearly twenty years a voice reminded her, okay so they hadn't always been easy, and things weren't presently at their best, but it was a big slice of time to gamble on lunch and the attentions of a snake like Mac.

Ahead of her, settled down amongst a summer landscape the cottage lay in wait. It had a low pantiled roof with two tiny dormer windows set into it. She could imagine the ceiling of the bedroom sloping above a big brass bed and had to stop herself from taking the image any further. It would make a lot more sense to go home, just turn around and go home. She hadn't done anything to be ashamed of yet and changing her mind certainly wasn't a hanging offence.

From where she was sitting Sarah could see that the top half of the door was open, it looked like an ink-black eye and it seemed to be staring right at her. In her imagination the interior was cool and inviting. She dragged her mind kicking and screaming back to reality. There was still plenty of time to leave, still time to acknowledge that this was a silly mistake.

Sarah checked her reflection in the rear-view mirror, fluffed her hair up a bit and then wondered whether she ought to put on some lipstick or maybe a little kohl on her eyes, not too much, maybe something to lift the just-left-work look. She popped a Polo into her mouth, crunched it into pieces, still considering the possibilities. As she had slipped the car into reverse, Mac appeared in the doorway. He was wearing an open necked shirt, a soft cream that emphasised his tan and he looked divine. Even then Sarah could have waved and driven off, in fact doing so would probably have made him chase her all the harder. But she didn't. Instead Sarah picked up her handbag, got out of the car and locked it.

It felt as if she was moving in slow motion through air as dense as treacle. She could feel him watching her, watching her every step of the way, unable to hide the amusement and desire in his eyes. Sarah swallowed hard, trying to hold down the frantic rhythm of her rising pulse. It wasn't going to be so easy to leave now.

Chapter 15

Jenny Beck remembered now why it was she had never bothered playing hard to get. It was boring and difficult to keep up for any length of time. Chris Colebrook had rung first thing on Monday morning – not that she'd answered the phone, just turned the machine up a little louder to hear how keen or desperate he was to keep on talking and reasons for him to drop by later and see her. All very gratifying but what if he got disheartened and gave up? The whole point of playing the chase-me, chase-me games was to make them show their hand, and then run away so fast that they overreached themselves and fell head over heels. But what if – despite appearances, Chris didn't really want to play or didn't know that those were the rules? What if he came to his senses and decided that she wasn't worth the effort after all?

Jenny pulled the clean sheets out of the washing machine and headed off outside to the linen line. She could always think better when she was busy. What if, in the space and silence left behind while she was playing hard to get, Chris found out that the rumours about Sarah and Leo Banning were not true, just lies and fluff. And in the worst case scenario – which kept coming back to haunt her – what if Chris and Sarah turned up together at the house and demanded to know what the hell she thought she was playing at? Jenny sniffed, slung the sheet over the line and jerked it straight. She'd tell them that she had no idea what they were on about, no idea at all. The phone rang. Jenny resisted the temptation to go in and answer it. Playing hard to get was really not all it was cracked up to be.

Later that morning, upstairs, Jenny flicked the feather duster around her bedroom and wound in the long cobwebs that garlanded the ceiling. It had been a hectic morning so far. She'd sorted out all the clothes that had been heaped up on the chair in her bedroom, and on the floor, and on top of the tallboy, changed the sheets, hoovered under the bed and was now almost ready for – for – the thought caught her out. Ready for what?

She stood very still, feather duster in hand and felt her way around the edge of the idea. There was no getting away from it, she was getting the bedroom ready for Chris Colebrook. Scrubbing the dust and talcum powder and odd bits of make-up off the dressing table, binning a snow storm of dirty tissues, arranging those little bowls of pot-pourri and candles on the bedside table was all for his benefit. Which was daft, what man was ever overcome with lust at the sight of a few dried leaves in a dish? Not her Tony that was for certain.

'What the bloody hell is all that about, then?' he would have asked if he was there now. 'Salad, is it?' Making fun of her. He told her once that he liked his sex like he liked his food, straightforward, plenty of it and no mucking about with any of that bloody fancy nonsense. Well bugger him. Jenny poured another few of drops of oil on to the rose petals. When she felt their love life had gone a little stale she'd sent off for one of those books out the back of a magazine.

Tony had quite enjoyed the pictures but said that sort of thing was all very well for people who had the time to bugger about with baby oil and handcuffs, but not for ordinary normal people like him and Jenny, surely after all these years she knew what he liked. All this stuff in books was just a put-up job.

He had turned the book sideways to get a better idea of

who was doing what to who. 'I reckon,' he'd said, 'that the bloke who came up with this one is laughing himself silly at the idea people are going to give it a go. I mean can you imagine anything more bloody daft?'

Jenny hadn't said anything, and then he'd turned the book over and looked at the price.

Tony really couldn't see what all the fuss was about. His idea of a good sex life was something quick and easy on a Friday night with the lights out after he'd had a pint at the Hogshead, on his way home from the long delivery round out to the airbase, and very occasionally on a Saturday if it was a special occasion.

Things were different now apparently, he was up to it all ways, up against the fridge, in the bath with lots of bubbles, outside on the car rug that he and Miss Weigh and Save kept in the Jag in case of accidents. Jenny knew it was true because Pat in the butcher's had told her, and Pat's first cousin was Miss Weigh and Save's best friend.

All those years wasted when they could have been trying out a few of those things in the book; anyway Tony had gone now and it was good riddance to bad rubbish. But what if Chris was the same? What if he thought potpourri and candles were all window dressing, all air and no substance. There was just no telling.

Maybe she wasn't cut out to be a mistress after all. How the hell Miss Weigh and Save managed it Jenny could only guess at. According to Pat in the butcher's, until she'd met Tony she'd still been living at home with her mum and dad and sharing a bedroom with her sister.

Chris called at ten and then again at eleven, each message sounding slightly more desperate than the last. It didn't matter how hard he tried to maintain an air of cool detachment she could hear the growing frustration in his voice and it made her feel good. Jenny hurried downstairs to listen.

'I know you said that we shouldn't see each other, and I understand that. Obviously. And I respect what you're trying to tell me. I was just hoping maybe you might ring or that I could ring you. Occasionally. Just for a chat, you know, friends. I'm worried about you. Not that I don't think you're capable of sorting things out for yourself, no I don't mean that at all. I was worried that's all.'

She could hear him squirming. Worried about her, eh? Jenny smiled and pulled a packet of prawn cocktail crisps out of the cupboard. She needed a little comfort food to help keep her strength up and sustain the whole hard-to-get game plan. While she ate Jenny rewound the tape and listened to the message again. And again.

'I'm glad you decided to come.' Mac's eyes were as dark and as unsettling as a summer storm. Sarah smiled, trying to hang on to some shred of composure, despite the fact that the air was arcing with an abstract electric rush that they both knew was desire. He stepped towards her and instinctively Sarah stepped back. A rabbit to his fox, dove to his hawk. She knew without a shadow of doubt that accepting his invitation and driving to the cottage had been a bad move, maybe even a very bad move. He grinned as if he could read her mind.

'What's the matter, Sarah? I'm not going to bite, honest. Well, not unless you insist. I was just going to take your coat.'

Sarah had draped a cardigan around her shoulders. The idea of him being that close made her shiver, and then he was, and as he touched her shoulders she shivered again and then he leant forward ever so slightly and brushed the back of her neck with his lips. The warmth of his breath, the smell of his body against hers made Sarah leap across the kitchen as if she had been scalded.

'You're jumpy,' Mac purred. 'Relax.'

Sarah swung around to face him, well aware that he was playing her like a fish and that if she didn't take control soon she really was going to be in real trouble. The kind of trouble where reason and logic lost out to something older and more compelling. What surprised her too was how much she longed to be desired, how glorious it was to feel wanted in the most uncomplicated, instinctive ways, and oddly enough it was this that gave her the strength to face up to Mac. If she was going to be desired she would prefer it was by somebody she liked and got on with.

'Actually I can't stay very long at all.' She deliberately kept the tone bright and crisp, eyes moving around the interior of the kitchen. 'Nice place you've got here,' she said, grinning.

And he had. The walls of the kitchen were washed cream, the furniture made up of a jumble sale of oddments; above them was a wooden airer hung with a selection of white shirts and thick navy blue towels and bunches of herbs drying. Along one wall was a battered Welsh dresser displaying unmatched plates, cups, bowls and jugs. A large scrub-top table dominated the centre of the room and on it stood an ice bucket packed with sunflowers. Arranged around the table were half a dozen mongrel chairs, carvers and café chairs, a ladder back and stools. In the fireplace was a dusty black range, hung with more towels and an assortment of kitchen tools. Every flat surface had something on it, a hat, a basket full of pebbles or cones, there were trays and bowls, buckets and jugs, an amazing mass of objects reflecting Mac's butterfly mind, some of the things seemed sensible and logical, some were otherwise and those otherwise things, a stuffed fish in a glass cabinet decorated with paste jewels, a jam jar full of what looked like glass eyes, a lady's ostrich feather fan propped up against a curled white china cat, drew the eye and the mind closer. The overall effect was lovely, and intriguing and inviting;

it felt as if this room had evolved over years and years and at the same time was complete and had been that way forever.

'Let me pour you a glass of wine and then I'll show you round.'

Sarah was about to protest and then realised that was exactly what Mac was expecting her to do. It seemed important not only to foil whatever plans he had but to leave with some sense of victory.

'Okay,' said Sarah, 'what's for lunch?'

'Hungry?' Mac managed to imbue the word with a heavy erotic emphasis, as he uncorked the bottle. Under normal circumstances the tone would have made Sarah laugh. Now she felt it was another gambit, another opening move.

'I've been at work all morning.'

'Oh of course, I forgot.' He poured the wine. It contrived to sound a rich sensual thing. 'I thought we'd eat outside. I've got an awning up out there, and a table overlooking the lake. Great view.' He paused to see if he had her attention. 'I've made a salad, tiger prawns, French bread. Fresh fruit, yoghurt and honey to follow. Do you approve so far?'

'So far sounds good.'

He handed her a glass.

'Let me take you on the Cook's tour first and then we'll eat.' He held out a hand in invitation. Show no fear, whispered a tiny voice in her head. Sarah closed her fingers around his.

'Where do we start then?'

Mac laughed. 'God, you're good.'

Sarah stood her wine down on the kitchen table. 'And I intend to stay that way.'

Too late. Instead of leading her outside as she had imagined Mac pulled her into his arms and kissed her hard. Sarah was absolutely stunned. Gasping, and furious that she hadn't seen it coming, at the same time Sarah was astonished by the way he made her feel. His lips were soft and yet invasive. The sensation of his arms around her lit something nameless and unnerving that she had completely forgotten about. It would be so easy to let go, so easy to blame him for whatever happened next in the delectable erotic silky mist that filled her mind. Sarah struggled to catch her breath and then, fists clenched against Mac's chest she pushed him away.

'I didn't realise that you were going to play dirty,' she gasped.

Mac pulled a face. 'Whatever works.'

In the half light of the kitchen she could see him more clearly now, he was a predator, sensual and dangerous, and hypnotically attractive, used to getting what he wanted, when he wanted, though she suspected he probably didn't have to try very hard.

'It won't work with me, Mac.'

He looked sceptical.

'I know what you're thinking. But just because Chris is being a complete arsehole at the moment doesn't mean I'm looking around for someone to take his place.'

He aped hurt. 'Come on, Sarah, don't be angry with me. A little fun never hurt anyone.'

Her expression didn't change. 'This isn't fun.'

'Isn't it?' he continued, a slightly more conniving wheedling tone underpinning the words.

'This isn't about having fun, Mac. It's about trying to take something that isn't yours.'

'Oh picky, picky, picky, you can't tell me that you're happy with that philistine.'

Sarah looked him up and down; the spite in his voice surprised her. He was long and rangy with an arrogance that was at once both incredibly sexy and completely infuriating. The mother in her was tempted to slap him for being such a cocky little sod. Instead, she said in a low even voice, 'That's got nothing to do with you or this. I really think I ought to go now.' She made a show of picking up her bag, taking the cardigan from where he had hung it, generally announcing her departure.

As a game of brinksmanship it worked. As she got to the door, Mac held up his hands in a gesture of surrender. 'Okay, okay. Pax, Exesis. Look, just stay and have some lunch with me. I've prepared it specially and I promise not to jump you, and I'd like to show you the house and the parkland.' A flicker of mischief returned to his eyes. 'I thought we'd walk down by the lake for a bit and then return, hot and terribly exhausted, and then before we eat I'd show you round the cottage. Starting with the master bedroom.'

In spite of herself Sarah laughed and in that moment they both knew she would stay.

Mac picked up the wine glass and handed it back to her. 'You might as well bring this with you. I intend to make every effort to seduce you. Consider this an opening salvo in what may prove to be a long and bloody battle. Like range finding. I've always loved a challenge.'

He led the way back out into the sunlight, and as they crossed the threshold the energy between them changed back to light, jokey and warm as quickly as if someone had thrown a switch.

Hunting around for neutral ground Sarah told Mac about the musical evening at St Barts, and while they walked he fished for gossip and intrigue and led her along the lake's edge, over a bridge where the water narrowed and down through a dozen little inlets, each one a perfect place to stop and stare at the scenery. Nearly every break in the trees or reeds framed either the cottage or Monica's house, making it look like some glorious impressionist oil painting. Sarah was suitably impressed and delighted, but carried on talking, just in case her silence might be taken as an invitation. By the time they had got back to the cottage she was tired of the sound of her own voice.

'I'd really like to invest in St Barts,' she said. 'It would give me access to a shared workshop space. I'd be part of the whole set-up from the start. First generation member.'

Across the river a heron stood like a statue, beady eyes fixed on the water.

'Why don't you then?'

Sarah smiled and rubbed her thumb and first two fingers together. 'I couldn't justify taking that much money out of the family kitty, and certainly not on an annual basis, even if we could find it in the first place.'

Mac grimaced. 'Five hundred pounds is a drop in the ocean.'

'Maybe from where you're standing, but it isn't only that, it's the materials to do the space any justice. Paints, paper, canvas or oil board – none of those things are cheap.'

'What about the job you've applied for there, won't that get you what you want?'

Mac was busy decanting covered dishes from a large tray and refusing to be helped.

'I don't know and I'm not certain whether I'll get the position anyway. I'd have to give up the job at Whitefriars. It fits in so well with Charlie and the other boys at the moment, and working at the arts centre would be different from going in and having access to a workshop, developing my own voice. Really I'd like to be in the position to do both. Seeing the canvases I've got stacked up in the loft I keep thinking maybe this is the time to start doing it for real. This might be my last chance.'

She looked across at him, having assumed that small talk of things domestic would have glazed him over, but instead Mac's expression suggested he was ruminating over her dilemma. Once the tray was empty he loped back up the slope to the kitchen.

There was no denying he was very beautiful. What would it be like to be in love with someone like Mac? He was a liar and a cheat, Sarah knew those things without any evidence, with a man like Mac you would never know where he was or what he was doing. He was fickle and flirtatious and as free as a bird; a brightly coloured tropical bird totally unsuited to captivity. He would break her heart, particularly as Sarah knew that part of her appeal, if not all of it, was that she hadn't succumbed to his charm and had no intention of doing so. Had she?

He reappeared carrying more wine, linen napkins and a basket of French bread. Lunch, as promised, was wonderful. They sat either side of an old kitchen table, its dark brown varnish peeling away to reveal the wood beneath, set on a grass terrace that abutted a jetty, the whole area shaded by a makeshift canvas canopy. Closer to the water's edge Mac had unrolled an eiderdown, and scattered it with ticking bolsters and a heap of pillows. A novel was set face down on the cover, alongside a discarded wine glass, a mug and a pair of sunglasses; it was no wonder Mac wanted to spend time there. A few feet away water lapped at the lake side, the silky black surface broken only by the occasional fish rising.

Sarah refilled her glass with iced water, careful not to appear too content, or too at ease. Nearby, ducks squabbled for crusts in the reeds, while the sun beat down and birds in the lake side trees added the incidental music for the long, uncompromising, idle days of summer.

There are only so many idyllic moments a body can handle in a lifetime and as Sarah felt her shoulders ease and then began to feel drowsy a warning bell went off inside her head, so loud that it made her jump.

She looked at her watch, making the gesture large and obvious. 'I'm sorry Mac, but I've really got to go.'

He pulled a face. 'But we haven't had dessert yet. I was going to prove my undying devotion by peeling grapes for you.'

But Sarah was already on her feet. 'Sorry,' she said, smiling and kissing the end of her fingertip touched it to his forehead. 'Thank you for a lovely lunch, Mac. There's no need to see me to the car.'

He pouted, looking for all the world like Charlie on a bad morning. 'But I've bought strawberries and everything.'

Still smiling, Sarah shook her head and headed up the bank.

'Call me,' he shouted after her. 'If you don't call me, then I'll call you.'

Sarah half turned, about to rebuff him but guessed that it was just a tactic to delay her leaving a little longer, the first sentence in a line of attack that might persuade her to stay and if she stayed then there was a chance Mac still might win.

It felt good to be back in her car. Sarah opened all the windows, slipped a tape into the machine and headed home, congratulating herself on the way she had handled Mac. Or was that part of his plan too? Let her escape this time, lull her into a false sense of security? Would she go if he asked her over again? Sarah caught sight of her reflection in the rear-view mirror. It was amazing how a little attention did wonders for the appearance.

'You're home early,' Sarah said.

Chris was the last person she expected to see when she pushed open the back door and the words were part statement, part surprise and part greeting. He was sitting at the kitchen table a newspaper spread out in front of him and was apparently staring blankly into space. His focus tightened and his expression – which had been neutral – hardened up.

'I can't bloody win, can I?' he said, with an unpleasant edge in his voice. 'Friday and Saturday you complain that I'm in late. Today I'm home at a half decent time and you're at it again, there's no pleasing you, is there?'

Sarah winced. 'That wasn't what I meant at all, Chris. I wondered if you were okay, that's all.' What she was thinking but was reluctant to say aloud was that he probably still felt rough from getting drunk on Sunday. Lunch with Mac had flattered her ego and lifted her spirits. Maybe this was the moment to hold out an olive branch.

'Do you want to talk, Chris? Things are so tense between us at the moment I hate it. Everything I say and do seems to wind you up. What's the matter?'

He stared at her as if she was totally mad. 'What's the matter? Sometimes I just don't believe you, Sarah, I really don't. I would have thought it was bloody obvious what the matter was,' he said, shaking his head.

Sarah stared at him, wondering what it was she had missed. Something obvious, obviously. Was he still mad at her for having stayed out all night, it couldn't be that could it? She took a breath to ask him.

It was then the phone rang. It was Monica. Sarah began to suggest she call her back later when Monica interrupted. 'No don't go, this will only take a minute, we can talk more later – but I've just spoken to Mac; how about if I paid for your first year's studio fees at the new arts centre.'

Sarah laughed nervously. 'It's a really kind thought, Monica, but I couldn't possibly . . .' she was speaking fast to cover her surprise and a peculiar sense of embarrassment.

'Whoa, hang on a minute,' continued Monica. 'I told you yesterday that I'd like to get involved in the whole arts centre thing. This way I can kill two birds with one stone. You get your studio space and I get involved and am seen as an all round good egg and before you go all Oliver Twist on me, darling, let's get this into some sort of proportion – I wouldn't think twice about paying five hundred quid for a pair of shoes.'

Sarah reddened. 'Put that way . . .'

'Put that way you have to say yes. And anyway I'm not stupid, I'm investing in what may very well be a saleable commodity. Do you think you could get your vicar to give me a ring? In my new role as philanthropist and patron of the arts I'm rather hoping to be courted by the great and the good.'

Sarah laughed. 'Of course. I don't know what to say Monica.'

'Say yes then, but only to me. You're playing with fire saying yes to anything that little bastard Mac suggests.'

Sarah felt her colour rising again.

'Anyway, talk soon,' Monica said in conclusion. 'Got to go, my masseuse has just arrived and you know how impatient these new age hippies get. Her name is Gudrun De Vine, I'm sure she made it up, and she is absolutely desperate to get to grips with my aura, as if life isn't complicated enough as it is.' Monica laughed. It was throaty and rich, stained dark brown by an excess of life.

As she put the phone down Sarah was suddenly very conscious that Chris was sitting at the table watching her. She smiled, anxious that the olive branch didn't wilt before she had the chance to cut it from the tree.

'That was Monica, she's offered to sponsor a workshop space for me at the new arts centre this year. I'm just going to ring Leo Banning, you know, the vicar,' she said, with a broad smile, wanting to cheer him up, wanting to share her good fortune, wanting to lift his mood. She knew she sounded excited and hoped it might be infectious.

As Sarah keyed in the number Chris got very slowly to his feet, as if standing was an enormous effort, and headed slowly into the sitting room. It was a good job Sarah couldn't see the expression on his face.

Chapter 16

Chris hadn't intended to stand and listen to Sarah's conversation with Leo Banning, but he did. He listened to every sentence and every peal of laughter, every joke, every single damned word. It made him feel sick to the pit of his stomach. Not that there was anything overt or flirtatious in the things Sarah was saying or the way she was saying them, far from it, she sounded bright and chirpy and rattled on about the arts centre, her job application, and bloody Monica Carlisle and some sort of sponsorship scheme. But then again Sarah didn't know that Chris already knew about her. Her and Leo Banning.

A little part of him had admired the sheer audacity of ringing her lover when she knew he was in the house. Was it audacity or had Sarah simply reached the point where she didn't care whether Chris knew or not? Or was it that she was over confident, assuming that he, Chris, wouldn't find out about her sordid little affair. Chris gritted his teeth. A bead of sweat trickled down the side of his face.

He found himself craning forwards so that he didn't miss anything. It was a worrying turn of events. So worrying that after a few seconds he checked himself all over for signs of paranoia, and fortunately found none, just well-founded suspicion and doubt, riddling his consciousness like leprosy. And anyway wasn't paranoia when you thought everyone was out to get you and that everyone was lying, he already had the proof that Sarah was lying. Jenny Beck had told him so.

Suspicion began to gain its own momentum. Like acid

rain it trickled down his spine to mix with the other dark and unpleasant things that he felt in his belly until he was so angry that he didn't know if he could contain himself. The fury and the hurt was like a great whirling wind, and in an instant Chris Colebrook understood what people meant by murderous rage, and it shocked him that he could feel it too. What he felt crawling around inside his skin was wild and raw and quite terrifying. White hot, he burnt in the hall with no one to see him, and knew then that things couldn't go on as they were. Something had to give. Wrenching himself away from the closing moments of Sarah's conversation Chris marched out of the front door and then in a great arc around the outside of the house to the back garden, down the path and into the polythene greenhouse.

His mood swung backwards and forwards like a rag in the wind. By the time he sat down amongst the debris Chris could barely remember his own name. One thing though, for a few minutes the chain saw that had been buzzing around in his head with Jenny Beck's name on it stopped. When his mind formed the name, his mood changed again. Jenny Beck. She would understand. He pulled his mobile out of his pocket and punched in the number, although when she didn't answer and the machine cut in, he was very tempted to throw the bloody thing away.

Sarah rang off and then glanced at the kitchen clock. Charlie would be out of school in a few minutes; she needed to be gone, unless of course Chris had already left to pick him up. Through the window she could see the van and the Golf still standing side by side.

Picking up her bag and keys, she headed for the door. Leo had reminded her about finding something for the exhibition – not that she had forgotten – and had promised to ring Monica as soon as he could and to make a fuss of her. Sarah grinned. Those two might be very good for each other. Things were really coming together.

Not bothering to lock the door as Chris was about, Sarah called goodbye into the shadows and the silence and hurried across the gravel, her mind was on other things. She smiled. A workshop space, her paintings in an exhibition, things to look forward to, even the lunch with Mac had helped brighten her mood. Driving down to the school she began to hum. The traffic was light until she got to School Road, where it looked as if the whole population of the town was busy looking for a parking space. Sarah slipped under the lee of a Volvo, locked up and headed for the playground, still wondering what to put in the exhibition; whatever it was she'd need to get it framed. Maybe Chris would give her a hand to bring some of the paintings down out of the loft when she got back so that she could get a better look. She smiled and let the busy thoughts fill her head.

Monday night was darts and dommies down at the Lamb, with refreshments at halftime and a raffle for big prizes. It said so on the canary yellow flier pinned to the notice board in Jenny Beck's kitchen. She looked into the yard. Peter should be home from school soon; and then she'd have a bath and get ready. Take her time, shave her legs, pluck her eyebrows, show everyone she had a good reason to make the effort.

Going out in the week was different from weekends. Weekends you were supposed to be with a bloke if you'd got one, but weekdays it was all right to go out with your mates. In fact, if you didn't, people accused you of shifting loyalties and being fickle and disloyal.

'Never see her now that she's with that bloke, dropped us like a hot potato.'

'Not a word, not a phone call, nothing, the nights I used

to sit listening to her on the phone when her husband cleared off and now she won't give me the time of bloody day. I'm pleased for her, don't think that, but I'm hurt –'

Jenny had heard it all before over a lot of red wine when she wasn't driving and endless diet cokes when she was; there was a hard core of about six women, friends of a sort, all of them divorced or separated, all the wrong side of thirty-five – and that was a very diplomatic estimate – who rang each other up for a gossip, met up for coffee and shopping every so often and shared the round of nights out. If the truth was told Jenny had been very glad to find her way into the group.

The faces might change as the girls moved on, matched up or drifted back. It was a slow spiral of changing faces as one by one they were snatched away by Mr Right or more often, Mr This'll-do-till-something-better-comes-along, or worst of all, Mr I'm-tired-and-something-has-got-to-be-better-than-nothing. They drifted back with broken hearts or having broken one, or with a sense of having a lucky escape, or sometimes they just came back older and wiser. Sometimes when they sat at their usual table by the jukebox in the Lamb Jenny thought they looked like old soldiers scarred by the rigours of battle, but still desperate to be chosen for the next skirmish. Which brought Jenny back to Miss Weigh and Save, with her perky little boobs and that silly girly little laugh, who called her the old grey mare. Jenny leant forward and parting her hair, took a good look in the mirror. There was time enough to put a colour on, something warm and sexy like autumn maple or maybe toffee apple, she'd a couple in the bathroom cabinet. Not that she was very grey, no there was just an odd one here and there but it never hurt to give Mother Nature a little hand now and then.

Peter slouched up to the kitchen door, a rucksack almost as big as he was slung between narrow shoulders. As he acknowledged her through the glass Jenny caught a glimpse of the man he would grow into. He favoured her family with only the slightest hint here and there of his dad, which was a good thing.

After school Sarah took Charlie into town to get a new pair of plimsolls, then headed home. The older boys were in when she arrived and busy grazing their way through the contents of the fridge and the larder.

'Okay?' she asked as Charlie headed upstairs to get changed out of his school clothes.

Matt was manhandling an enormous bowl of cereal towards the sitting room, Jack had a family-sized bag of crisps under one arm and was pouring himself a glass of juice. 'Uh-huh,' said Matt, 'it was like the *Marie Celeste* here when we got back. Door unlocked, no one about. We thought you'd been abducted by aliens.'

Sarah plugged in the kettle. 'Your dad's about somewhere.'

Matthew looked heavenwards.

'And what is that supposed to mean exactly?' asked Sarah.

'He's been in a foul mood for days.'

'Yeh, what's up with him?' asked Jack.

Sarah considered for an instant. It was difficult to tell. 'Don't worry, I'm sure it's not you. Probably something to do with work,' she said dismissively, wondering whether to go outside and track Chris down. Maybe he'd like a cup of tea. Maybe it would help his mood. She looked at the kettle not altogether sure she wanted to go and find out. Matthew was right, she wasn't certain what sort of mood Chris was in and couldn't bear the thought of any more aggravation. 'Could one of you help me get some stuff down out of the loft? It's only a few paintings and things, nothing very heavy.'

Matt nodded. 'Sure, can I just eat this first?'

His tone was easy and light and he seemed happy to oblige. Sarah, mind made up, dropped a single tea bag into a mug. 'Absolutely. What do you fancy for supper?'

At that moment the back door swung open and Chris walked in. Sarah wondered if somehow she had managed to summon him up like some dark wraith. He looked Sarah up and down as if he wanted to say something and then spotted the boys. Caught out, he said, with the greatest effort, 'I'm going to go and get some petrol.'

Sarah painted on a pleasant smile. 'Oh right, did you want a tea before you go?' she said, lifting the mug while maintaining the lightness in her voice.

Chris shook his head and was gone. Odd how everyone sighed with relief the moment the door closed behind him.

While he was in the greenhouse Chris had planned to come in and confront Sarah with the things that he suspected. Unfortunately he hadn't factored the boys into the equation, so seeing them all together in the kitchen had thrown him, totally. He needed a little time to rethink, to regroup.

Burdetts Garage was on the Old London Road. It wasn't that far out of the way, and although it had no frills, fading paint and forecourt attendants who always looked as if they had either been recently released into the community or were on parole, cheap diesel was cheap diesel. He filled the Transit up to the brim, the night watchman in his brain monitoring the progress of the dials on the pump, while the rest of his mind was engaged in chasing Sarah round the kitchen.

In his imagination he shouted all the things he wanted to say, pinning her down verbally and asking her lots of very difficult questions, staying put, watching her face for clues until she answered every single one. Oh, yes. He would have been so good and got to the bottom of this if only the kids hadn't been home.

The pump clicked as the fuel flooded back into the nozzle, once, twice. It took a trainer full of diesel to attract his attention. Swearing under his breath Chris holstered the fuel pipe, wiped himself down with a paper towel from the dispenser on the pump and headed in to the cash desk. The woman behind the counter smiled warmly. Although he was a regular at Burdetts he could never remember her being this pleased to see him before.

'Pump three, is it?'

Chris nodded

'So, how are you doing?' she purred.

He looked at her. 'Sorry?'

She looked him up and down and then winked. 'You know you're a real dark horse.'

Chris reddened and glanced over his shoulder in case she had mistaken him for someone else or he was intercepting a conversation not intended for his ears. Behind him the shop was as empty as the tomb. The woman rang the fuel through on the till.

'So, be seeing you down the Lamb tonight, then, will we?'

Chris pulled a face. 'I'm sorry, I'm not with you.'

She giggled. 'No, pity about that, but then again I didn't know you were on the market. I would never have guessed to be perfectly honest. You just don't look the type.'

Nervously Chris pulled out his cheque book and wallet. She had to be on some sort of medication. 'I'm not on the market,' he said slowly, in case she needed to lip-read.

'Well, no, I know, not now, but then. Don't worry, I've got a stamp for the top.'

Chris smiled but generally kept his expression quite neutral and unprovocative, wondering as he did about the wisdom of letting someone delusional loose on God knows how many thousand litres of flammable liquid.

The woman took his bank card, smiling like a crazed

piranha. He was tempted to forget the card and back out while he still could, but she hadn't finished with him yet. 'To be honest I'm surprised about you, really.'

Caught like a rabbit in the headlights Chris stood very still, and unable to stop himself, wanting to find out what the hell she was on about, couldn't resist asking, 'Surprised about what exactly?'

'Well, I wouldn't have thought Jenny Beck was your type at all. Not really, not that she isn't nice and everything, but . . .'

Chris didn't hear the rest of the sentence. He felt his colour draining and comprehension dawned so hard that it felt like she had punched him in the solar plexus. Jenny Beck. So that was what this was about. Bloody hell. He was sweating hard before his mind had time to process any of the implications.

He hadn't for one instant considered that Jenny might say anything to anybody else. It was as if the things they had done existed inside a bubble, a closed space totally unrelated to any other part of Chris's life, or her life. Their lives. Bloody hell. Bloody sodding hell. Struggling for breath he snatched his bank card off the counter together with the receipt she offered him. What if anyone else found out, what if Sarah found out?

'But then again it takes all sorts,' she was saying philosophically.

'You aren't supposed to know,' Chris muttered lamely, because he couldn't think of anything else to say, as if that would make any difference at all.

The woman's smile broadened. 'You know, I always had you down as a gentleman. Discreet, protective. I really like that in a man.'

Chris looked the woman up and down. The state of her, he thought unkindly, maybe having a pulse might have been the deciding factor. What he needed to do was speak to Jenny and fast. Maybe he ought to call round on the way home but as Chris turned towards the door he realised that if his boys were home Jenny's son, Peter, would be too. Ring? He'd got the mobile clipped to his belt but had already made half a dozen fruitless calls in the greenhouse before he left. Finally he turned back to his inquisitor.

'What did you say about going to the Lamb?'

He had her full attention now. 'It's darts and dommies tonight. I thought Jenny would have told you. It's always a good laugh, though to be honest I'm more of a karaoke woman meself.' She took a great lung full of air and before Chris could protest or make a break for it, she lifted her hands to shoulder height, snapped her fingers and broke into the brain melting chorus of *'I will survive'*. Very slowly, so as not to startle her, Chris began to back away down the gangway between the shelves and display units.

Seeing his discomfort the woman stopped and said, 'That's my favourite one. Me and Jenny usually sing it together, that or something by Celine Dion. So, will we see you down the Lamb tonight then?'

Chris crouched behind the cover of a neutral smile hoping she wouldn't read anything into his expression. He'd try ringing Jenny again. He might just drive by to see if he could see her in the garden, but whatever else he did Chris decided there and then that he would have to look for another place to buy cheap diesel.

Leo Banning had been expecting the telephone call from the bishop's palace for some time. He was surprised it had been so long in coming, really, after the article in the papers. The summons, disguised as an invitation to come in and discuss minor administrative matters normally dealt with by other people, had followed almost immediately after he had spoken to Sarah Colebrook.

In public the Bishop of West Anglia wore an air of Christian humility and had spoken at length about the role of bishop as servant of the wider community. From the pulpit and from the front pages of any rag that would publish him, Bishop Fulbright proclaimed that he stood for old-fashioned family values and if that was what was seen as being controversial these days then let it be so. Let it be so, he could stand the heat, and planned to stay in the kitchen for as long as it took to put things back on an even keel. The remark always raised a polite round of laughter and occasionally applause. Not, he assured the media, that he didn't welcome healthy debate and Fulbright could certainly be relied upon to provide a quote for every situation.

Since Leo had been vicar at Barton he'd read them all, and those he missed had been sent by friends: there was Fulbright on Europe, Fulbright on the young princes, Fulbright on the Irish peace talks.

Leo closed his eyes for a moment, and nipped the bridge of his nose; he'd got a headache coming on and felt tired and isolated.

Bishop Augustus Fulbright was a tall well set man with mellow blue eyes, and a trim of grey hair edging out a large bald pate. He looked like the archetypal benign aging cleric, while at the same time contriving to look good in photos. At Christmas Fulbright sent half Christendom and many provinces of Mammon, personal cards of himself, photographed with his wife, her eyes demurely lowered in the presence of the great man. Leo could see the last one as clearly as if it was in front of him now; the phalanx of angelic grandchildren gathered around the tree, sitting at the bishop's feet looking up with a mixture of reverence and affection. Sod it.

But Leo hadn't been fooled for an instant; Fulbright's eyes were as hard as glass marbles and, despite a feeble attempt at a warm smile, the man had a tiny draw-string mouth that appeared to have no lips whatsoever.

Everything about the way he moved, the way he spoke – even down to his forked tongue – made Leo think of something reptilian. Fulbright's conversations would often begin with the words, 'I speak, I feel, for the silent majority . . .' Not silent enough in Leo's opinion.

He looked down at the newspaper article on his desk that Fulbright had written recently about modern family life and his plans to purge the negative forces from within his own diocese. Which for Fulbright was quite subtle, once upon a time he would have called the devil a devil. Someone had obviously pointed out that his case was better served by a nod towards the mores of political correctness, and so the whole thing was carefully couched to draw a thin but not totally opaque veil over his homophobia, his racism and his misogyny.

At first Leo had believed that Fulbright's supporting him to take on the living at Barton had been an act of philanthropy. He had been teetering on the edge of the abyss and had seen the hand reaching out to him as an act of Christian kindness, and been prepared to accept it as such. Now Leo wondered if it wasn't more likely an act of contrived malice. Had Fulbright brought Leo into the fold just to drive him out? And would he jump or wait for the push, perhaps Fulbright would offer to send him on retreat, to pray for heterosexual tendencies and the good grace to go quietly.

Startled out of his thoughts by a noise close by, Leo looked up. Mrs Vine was framed in the doorway of his office. 'Tea?' she asked pleasantly.

He smiled. 'Wonderful idea.'

The condemned man ate a hearty breakfast, thought Leo ruefully and sighed to try and shake off the tension in his shoulders. It wasn't as if the invitation to the palace was unexpected. He glanced down at the other notes on his desk. Alongside other parish business was Sarah Colebrook's name and beside it Monica Carlisle's address and phone number.

'Mrs Vine, do you know anything about Monica Carlisle? She lives at The Orchards.' His housekeeper was a fount of information and with a little gentle persuasion could be delightfully indiscreet.

The woman looked heavenward as if seeking inspiration. 'Name doesn't ring a bell. I know where you mean though. Carlisle, you said?'

'That's right. Sarah Colebrook rang to say that Monica Carlisle is interested in becoming involved in the arts centre. Looking to invest, which is excellent news.'

Mrs Vine's face brightened visibly. 'Did you say Sarah Colebrook?'

Leo nodded. 'You must know Sarah, she works at Whitefriars school, something to do with the art department. In fact I'm rather hoping she'll come and work as part of the team at St Barts once we're up and running.'

'Oh,' said Mrs Vine, unpacking the tray on to the sideboard. 'That could be handy for you.'

Leo was puzzled. 'Handy.'

Did Mrs Vine redden or was it his imagination?

'What I meant to say was – was . . .' She was quite obviously struggling for the right words, though Leo had no idea why. Finally Mrs Vine said, 'She's used to dealing with kiddies, isn't she? She'll be good, you know, patient with people.'

Leo wondered if there was something Mrs Vine knew about Sarah Colebrook that she wasn't letting on. So he pushed a little harder; it would help take his mind off Fulbright and the prospect of his inquisition.

'Do you know Sarah Colebrook well?'

'No,' said Mrs Vine, 'no, not at all really . . .' She paused for a millisecond as if considering her options and then said, 'Only what people say, you know.'

'And what do they say?'

Mrs Vine's face brightened up to the colour of raw beef steak. She swallowed hard. 'Only that, that –' He could see her fighting with her conscience or whatever else it was that held the words in check, and was now full of curiosity.

The words finally breached the banks of her discretion and poured out in a great torrent. 'I don't think, to be perfectly honest, that she's very happily married. Well, that's what I've heard anyway. Not that I know for certain but I have heard a rumour that her husband is seeing someone else. You know, seriously, not just some sort of mad fling. And it came from someone very reliable although you know how I feel about gossip.'

'What a pity,' he said, getting to his feet to inspect the contents of the tea tray. 'She is a really charming young woman,' he sighed, 'but there's an awful lot of it about.'

He caught Mrs Vine looking at him with an odd expression on her face and wondered what else she knew and whether it was worth pursuing. On the tray were tiny home-made scones topped with prawns on a bed of something creamy. 'You know you spoil me, Mrs Vine.'

She looked away, self-conscious and blushing. 'Someone has to.'

'Look, I'll hold the ladder and then you pass me the pictures down. They're over by the big blue trunk. You can't miss them, Matthew. They're wrapped in a striped sheet.' There was a pause, the sounds of muffled footsteps and things being moved. 'Can you see them?' Sarah was standing on the landing, looking up into the gloom beyond the loft hatch. The bulb had burnt out in the attic, and so periodically a torch beam cut through the darkness like a lighthouse beacon.

'I've got them, but I can't hold the torch and carry the

pictures as well. This place is booby trapped, the planks keep tipping up.'

'Dad hasn't got around to nailing them down yet. Just be careful and don't put your foot through the ceiling. What about if Jack comes up and holds the torch for you?'

She had barely finished the sentence before Jack was scuttling up the ladder, climbing and adventure-envy getting the better of him. Beside her, Charlie was hopping from foot to foot, more than a little disgruntled at being told that he had to stay on terra firma.

'I wouldn't break anything and I wouldn't put my foot through the ceiling. I wouldn't. I wouldn't,' he squeaked.

Sarah smiled. 'Okay, once the boys have got the paintings down maybe you can go up, but just for a little while, and you must do what Jack and Matthew say. Now stand back and don't get in the way, all right?'

He grinned and nodded, reversing into the doorway to his bedroom, not still, but far less frantic now that he knew he would have his turn.

Above them a bundle appeared in the opening.

'It's really heavy,' warned Matthew, as Sarah scrambled up the first few rungs to take the pictures from him. She coughed as the cloth fell forward. The paintings were bulkier than she'd expected and covered with a thick rime of dust despite her having already taken a look under the dustsheet. She sneezed violently and struggled with the weight. Jack was right.

None of them had heard the back door close or Chris climbing the stairs.

'What the bloody hell are you up to?' Chris snapped. It took Sarah all her time not to fall. 'Why didn't you ask me to do that. Here –' He caught hold of the cloth covered bundle, almost snatching it out of her hands. Instantly she was furious. He was talking to her as if she was a child.

It was all she could do to stop herself from climbing down off the ladder and punching him.

'We were doing just fine,' she said in as even a tone as she could manage.

Charlie was alongside now. 'Can I go up now? Please, can I?'

'No, you can't,' barked Chris, standing the paintings up against the wall. 'It's too dangerous.' He turned his attention to the two older boys. 'And you two, stop pratting about and get down here now.'

Sarah stared at Chris. He was looking up at the loft hatch, hands on his hips, face white and set. Matthew and Jack dropped down on to the ladder like monkeys.

'If you've got so much time on your hands you can get the back yard cleared up and mow the lawn,' he said in a tone guaranteed to infuriate. He turned to Sarah. 'You should have asked me rather than let them up there.'

Sarah didn't point out that she already had, instead she defended the boys. 'They weren't pratting about. I asked them to get the paintings down for me.'

Chris didn't looked convinced 'The yard needs sorting out and they're always up here on that bloody computer or parked in front of the TV, it won't hurt them to do a bit of real work for change.' Of them all Charlie looked the most outraged.

'How long before supper, only I thought I'd nip over and see Barry tonight,' said Chris, pulling off his T-shirt and heading for the bathroom.

Sarah didn't reply. In under a minute he had undermined her authority, contradicted her instructions, upset all the boys and lit a rage in her belly that burnt like fire. Not bad going.

Chapter 17

Jenny Beck settled back in the bath and closed her eyes. She'd put a country-and-western tape in the machine, from across the landing came the sounds of Peter playing on the computer, and beyond that the rest of house was still and quiet and smelt of fish and chips.

A strand of damp hair clung to her cheek, another wrapped itself around her neck like seaweed. She'd just finished rinsing it off after adding the colour – nothing too dramatic, something to give her a lift and cover those odd grey hairs. At the moment it was the colour of red wine, shiny and damp. Jenny stretched; she was wearing Dead Sea mud face pack that her sister-in-law had given her for Christmas and the water, presently pale blue and bubbly was something out of a bottle she'd bought at Pound Stretcher. It smelt a bit like fruit gums but seemed all right. But the majority of Jenny's thoughts were occupied with images of Chris Colebrook and the things she planned to tell the girls down at the Lamb. There was quite a list already, but now she was relaxed her mind had moved away from cold hard facts and the little exaggerations based around them to pick up rather larger, more interesting fantasy strands.

She wriggled down in the bath until only her shoulders, head and knees broke the surface, and followed the yellow brick road; actually Mrs Jenny Colebrook had a really nice ring to it. Jenny let the combination roll around her mind; that would certainly show Tony Whelk. It was a long time since she'd played Mr and Mrs with anyone else, that little

229

game where you imagined what your name would sound like tied to your boyfriend's. That and all those fancy scribbles in the back of a school rough book to practise your new signature. That idea took her back years and made her feel young and giggly which was a great improvement on what she had been feeling a few weeks earlier, which had also involved a bath, a bath and a lot of pills, the outcome a whole lot less attractive.

This is Chris, my boyfriend. Boyfriend. This is Chris Colebrook, my fiancé, that sounded even better. Jenny spread her fingers, eyes still closed, imagining the way an engagement ring would look. She could imagine the expression on the faces of her friends, of strangers, of Tony-bloody-sodding-Whelk.

Chris Colebrook's voice had filled up the tape on the answer machine. It felt good to be wanted.

The phone rang; she ignored it, concentrating instead on the fantasy Chris Colebrook. They'd have a nice house, maybe one of those Victorian carrstone cottages on the lane that backed on to the common. One of the ones with nice bay windows and fancy fret work round the roof. She'd always liked them. The one on the end had a cedar wood summerhouse, painted yellow inside, and a dove coop. Now that would be nice, not that she knew anything about doves but you could always get a book out of the library. Messy though, and doves probably attracted vermin. Perhaps they'd board the holes up and keep it as a feature. Jenny had always wanted a house with a feature.

The phone rang again and she heard Peter's footsteps going downstairs. She swore under her breath. She ought to have told him to leave it too. There was the sound of mumbling from the hall that registered over the soft twang of steel guitars and the harmonica of something by Willie Nelson.

'Mum?'

'Uh-huh.' She didn't really want to move too far from the fantasy.

'It was that woman from the garage on the phone, Elaine. I told her you were in the bath.'

Elaine was one of the women that Jenny had anticipated showing the engagement ring to, one of the women who would congratulate her while spitting nails.

'Good boy. Did she leave a message?'

'Nah, just said she'd see you down the Lamb later.'

'Okay. If it rings again leave it.'

'Leave it?'

'You heard me.'

'But what if it's important?'

'Then they'll leave a message. I'm not in the mood to talk to anyone at the moment. It's me nerves.'

She heard Peter pad back to his bedroom and closed her eyes a little tighter, picking up the threads of fantasy where she'd left off. Elaine from the garage was her matron of honour now, walking behind Jenny up the aisle between the shelves in the forecourt shop, carrying her train and what looked like it might be a port and lemon.

Chris Colebrook was soaking in the bath too, he had used all the hot water and locked the bathroom door. Sarah knew those things because there was no water to wash up with and when she'd gone upstairs to give Chris some clean towels she couldn't get in.

Downstairs, the kitchen door was open, the cat curled up on Matthew's discarded sweat shirt in a puddle of sunshine and Sarah stood at the stove waiting for supper to cook. She was watching the boys without really seeing them. They had had bad patches before but she had always known why – this time he was distant and closed off in a way that didn't add up. Okay, so she was angry, and she was hurt, but underneath it all Sarah was worried.

It felt as if all the things she knew and trusted were slipping between her fingers like dry sand and she felt powerless to do anything about it.

Out in the back yard Matthew and Jack were clearing up. There had been some swearing but it had eased off; stacking this and that, pallets and barrels and tubs and all manner of debris that had needed sorting out for months. Matthew was taking bags of compost round to the green-house on the big barrow, Jack was sorting out piles of fencing posts. To deflect the clash that was brewing Sarah had bribed them a tenner each. After doing the yard they were going to cut and edge the lawn too, and not tell Chris that she was going to pay them. Charlie was in charge of ice-cream, encouragement, drink distribution and riding shotgun on the barrow.

It would have almost felt like fun and some kind of positive step if it wasn't for Chris's mood, which hung over Sarah and the boys like a dank wet fog.

Sarah fried off the chopped peppers, garlic and mush-rooms and scooped them into the sauce that was bubbling away on the stove. What she really wanted to do was sort through the paintings on the landing, choose which to put into the exhibition, and then open a bottle of wine to have with supper, but there was no way she could do it now. She'd wait until Chris went to Barry's.

'Why don't you come and stay with me for a few days?' asked Harry Fox. 'Plead ill health. Have a holiday, a sabbatical. It would be good to see you. I'll get us tickets for a musical – *Cats*, or *Les Mis*? We could go to dinner at Guido's. Just say when, Leo. Norfolk isn't the dark side of the moon, darling. You told me that when you moved down there – under two hours on the train. So when are you coming up?'

Leo Banning tucked the phone up under his chin and topped up his brandy and soda. 'I've got responsibilities here, Harry, and even if I could come I'd only have to face Fulbright as soon as I came back. No, I'll be fine. I'm just ringing to moan, fret, hear a friendly voice. Worry out loud.'

There was a weighty pause.

'But,' said Harry carefully.

'But what?'

'There hasn't been anyone since Tim, has there? No one serious anyway.'

'No one at all, serious or not, but that doesn't make any difference as far as Fulbright's concerned, celibacy is almost as bad. His plan is fairly simple, the way I read it, he believes in summary execution, which he believes we should be grateful for. He is putting us out of our misery, after all.'

'You speak for yourself, I've met this super guy, barman at Louie's. Six foot, blond, dances like a dream.'

Leo laughed. 'Has he got a name?'

'Yes, I'm just not sure what it is, but I promise you, I intend to find out.'

The phone rang at Sarah's house just before eight. It was Lisa. She got straight to the point.

'I was wondering if you could pick me up on your way to school tomorrow from Burdetts Garage? Only I've got to drop my car off for a service and an MOT and Barry's got to be in Cambridge by nine.'

'Sure, not a problem.' While they arranged the time and buffed up the details, Sarah hunted around to find the right words. 'Actually I'm glad you rang, Lisa. I'm really worried about Chris at the moment, I don't suppose you've noticed anything odd about him. Or has he said anything to you?' There was a tight little pause. Lisa's phone was in the hall near the sitting room, maybe Chris was within earshot. 'Is he there at the moment? Can you talk?'

There was another odd little silence, and then Lisa said, 'No, you're all right. He's not here, Sarah. I haven't seen Chris for ages – not since he dropped some fencing stuff off for Barry last week.'

There was another pause while Sarah considered the things that she knew, and the things that she'd been told and then said very slowly, 'Oh, that's odd too. Chris told me he was coming over to see Barry tonight. Is he outside with Barry?'

'No, Barry's flaked out in the lounge watching the tennis; but I shouldn't worry, maybe he just hasn't got here yet.'

Sarah turned the possibilities over in her mind. Chris had had his supper and left for Barry's house which was maybe fifteen minutes' drive away at the most. He had been gone, what? She looked up at the clock – forty minutes probably a little longer.

Maybe he'd stopped off on the way to price up a new job, fill up with fuel, something. Maybe he'd fancied a pint or a walk or . . . one by one the thoughts ebbed away until she was left with a few nuggets of truth. He had barely spoken while they'd eaten, hadn't said anything to the boys about the state of the yard, he'd shaved and smelt nice, and dressed casually but with care, although Sarah had chosen not to think too much about it until now. Now, when she knew for certain that he wasn't at Barry's.

Sarah began to tremble but didn't quite know why. She wasn't certain whether it was anger or fear or trepidation. Maybe it was time she went and sorted out the paintings on the landing, carry the ones she needed to get framed out to the car, and then Charlie ought to be getting ready for bed. There was the washing up to do, sports kits to sort out, all sorts of things hurried into the front of her mind, forming a cordon to keep her away from the scene of the crime or was it an accident? What the hell was Chris playing at, and more to the point who was he playing with?

Chris Colebrook parked in the lay-by down by the playing field for a long time before finally driving to the Lamb. It was early evening and the sun was playing hide and seek between the leaves of the poplars that fringed the field. A man and his dog and a couple of families with young children wandered across the daisy strewn grass, quite obviously glad to be out, delighted to be alive. The cricket pitch had recently had a crew cut and new lines painted on. It was a perfect summer evening although Chris wasn't really registering any of it.

He was thinking, thinking about going home and talking to Sarah. Thinking about driving over to Harehill to catch Jenny before she went out and finally thinking about going over to see Barry and asking his advice about the whole Sarah and Jenny situation. He wanted the chance to talk about things, aloud, see how they sounded out in the open. Although even as the thoughts formed Chris knew that when it came to the moment when Barry popped the ring pull and said, 'So, what's eating you, mate?' he would throw the opportunity away.

There was no way he'd be able to say anything, despite Barry being the closest thing Chris had to a best friend. There was the heart of the problem; Lisa was one of Sarah's best friends, Barry was her husband. It didn't take a Nobel prize winner to work out what the dilemma was there.

How many times had he curled up in bed beside Sarah and she had said things that began, 'I'm not really supposed to say anything about this, but . . .' And how many times had he lay there listening, all ears? Then there were other nights when the situation had been reversed and he had confided in Sarah, hoping that by sharing whatever it was that was bugging him it would somehow make the problem go away. Often, because Sarah was the kind of woman she was, it worked. She had this real knack for finding subtle ways to influence things, ease the burden, or find ways to set things right or just make him feel better. But he could hardly talk to her about Jenny Beck and no matter how many times he rehearsed it in his head there was no way he could tell Barry about her either.

It appeared that the only choice left was to nip down to the Lamb and sort things out, face to face, before it went any further. He'd have his say and then go home, older and wiser and hopefully relieved that he'd got away with it.

Chris puffed out a few breaths to help ease the tension in his gut. No use denying it, he felt sick, imagining the rumours rolling out from that bloody woman at the garage, the words as acrid and destructive as mustard gas, great boiling poisonous yellow clouds spiralling through his life. Unless the wind changed it could easily destroy everything he had, everything that he had worked for, everything that he wanted.

The car park at the Lamb was full, early birds boxed in back to back by late comers. Chris parked in the street. He checked his hair in the mirror, straightened his collar, locked up and strode across the pub yard like a western gunslinger. It was only when he got to the door that his confidence wavered. From inside he could hear the cluck and babble of female laughter, braying out over the sound of the jukebox, glasses clinking and someone on a PA system calling the dart scores. It was too much. There was part of him that had been expecting an almost empty bar, just him and Jenny and a handful of dusty old darts players and all the time and all the words in the world to set things straight.

He hesitated, hand resting on the door handle. He had worked out a speech while sitting in the lay-by, something kind and gentle and sensitive, all about bad timing and how he really didn't want to hurt her.

'Going in are y'mate?' said a gruff voice behind him. Chris jumped and stepped aside, quickly gathering his wits back into an untidy heap.

'Er actually no, I'm not. I wasn't planning to go in, well, not to stay. No, no not really,' he said, knowing that he was talking too much and making no sense.

The tall rangy youth and his female, tattooed, gum-chewing companion looked him up and down.

Chris reddened. 'Actually I'm looking for someone. Jenny Beck? I don't suppose you know her, do you?'

The boy pulled a face, his moist lips framed by the first coarse hairs of a trainee moustache, pouting like the suckers on an octopus. 'Nah, don't reckon so, name doesn't ring a bell, but if you don't wanna go in you can always nip into the offie and look through the hatch. I used to do that all the time when I was a kid coming in here to look for me mum.'

Chris smiled and thanked him for his advice. The little glass hatch, just inside the pub doorway, was closed. He tapped on it and waited patiently to be served.

'Yeh,' said the barmaid. 'What d'ya want?' She was obviously used to dealing with children. He recognised her face from somewhere which didn't help.

'Crisps,' Chris said, using the opportunity to look around the faces on the far side of the bar.

'Right, so what flavour, d'ya want? We've got plain, smokey bacon, cheese and onion, salt and vinegar, Quavers and cheesy Wotsits.' She counted them off on her fingers, obviously well used to being asked to recite the full running order. She was small and blonde, with an expression that suggested she had no patience with time wasters.

His mind went blank and it was at that moment Jenny Beck walked past on her way to the ladies' toilet, deep in conversation with two female friends. Their eyes met and before he knew what was happening Jenny was scuttling over to say hello – and when he saw the look on her face, Chris felt himself losing the grip on his master plan. He was also aware that the barmaid's interest had increased considerably.

'Plain,' said Chris quickly, handing her the money, hoping she'd shut the hatch. She didn't. Jenny Beck slipped her arm through his and leaning forward on tiptoe kissed him on the cheek. He was stunned. She giggled, looking as self-conscious as a teenager, blushing furiously, eyes twinkling like Christmas lights.

Chris groaned under his breath. She was quite obviously delighted to see him.

'Hello, Chris, what on earth are you doing here?' she asked, fluffing up her hair and generally preening.

'Well, er – er.' He scrambled around looking for something to say and was finally left with the truth, 'Actually, I came to see you.'

Jenny Beck giggled again and he winced as he realised how that sounded. The two other women, who had been hanging back, now excused themselves, although he suspected that the instant the toilet door closed they would be falling over themselves to talk about what they'd just seen and heard. Things were going from bad to worse to bloody nigh on impossible. He should have stuck to calling her, calling by, calling it quits and hoping everything would blow over, anything had got to be better than this.

Jenny moved a little closer. 'My mate down at the garage told me she'd seen you today. I didn't think for a minute that you'd come down here. Do you fancy a drink?' She nodded towards the bar door.

Chris shifted his weight, feeling increasingly uneasy. 'I wouldn't say no to a beer,' he said, after a pause. It sounded ungallant. 'Just a half. I'll get them, what are you drinking? Is there anywhere we could talk?'

Jenny's smile broadened. 'We could go in the lounge if you'd like, or what about outside in the beer garden? I'll have a diet coke; driving, you know.'

He'd seen the beer garden on the way in, a strip of fenced tarmac set with dusty flowers in half barrels, mulched with fag ends, half a dozen bench tables and a rusty swing. The lounge wasn't a lot better and for reasons best known to themselves Jenny's friends kept drifting in and out to ask her things. He felt as if he was on show.

Chris perched on the edge of the bench seat, sipped the trim of froth from the top of his second half and embarked upon the conversation he'd planned in the lay-by.

'I do understand that, well, the thing is . . .' this was not going quite as smoothly as he had imagined. 'I'm really worried that Sarah might find out about what's been going on. I didn't think that you'd tell anybody about, about . . .' the words dried in his throat. How best to describe a snog and a bit of a grope in inoffensive, sensitive terms? Chris was particularly careful not to say 'us'. Us would have implied something altogether bigger than he wanted to contemplate.

'You mean about us?' said Jenny breathlessly, moving even closer.

Chris blushed; it was out and said despite all his best efforts.

'Yes, yes that,' he stammered. 'That is it exactly.'

Jenny paused for a few seconds as if considering her reply. To pass the time she prodded the slice of lemon and the gaggle of ice cubes down in her coke. 'Even though you know that she's seeing someone else?'

Chris coloured. 'I've got no proof that Sarah's seeing Leo Banning, only the things that you've told me, and to be perfectly honest . . .'

Jenny cut him off short. 'You know, Chris, I was the

239

last one to know that Tony was carrying on with that little cow from Weigh and Save. The last one, and I'll tell you now Chris, I felt such a fool. No one said a word about him and her and they were out and about together all over the place. Pub up the road from us, that new Thai restaurant in town, out arm in arm, hand in hand and what did I know? Zilch, zero, nothing – zip; didn't want to hurt me everyone said afterwards.' She mimed zipping her lips. 'But trust me it couldn't have hurt any more than it did.'

Chris stared at her. 'Are you saying that's what's going on with Sarah and Leo Banning?'

'I'm not saying anything but you think on it, Chris, think on it.'

One of Jenny's friends shimmied over, gaze firmly fixed on Chris.

'Hello Jenny, I just wanted to know if you pair wanted any raffle tickets?'

Jenny looked across at him expectantly.

'Er, yes, yes I'll have a ticket,' he blustered anxious to crack the tension, 'how much are they?'

'50p a strip or three for a pound.'

Chris rootled round in his pockets for some change, but even so he caught the look that passed between the two women and groaned inwardly.

Once Charlie was in bed and the boys had finished working outside Sarah settled down in the sitting room to watch TV for the evening. There had to be some perfectly reasonable explanation for why Chris had lied to her. Who was she trying to kid? Sarah flicked through the TV channels again, unseeing, unhearing, the centre of her soul ripping itself to shreds as she considered every possibility, every option; none of it came up looking good.

Lisa rang again at half past nine. 'Chris hasn't shown up yet.'

'No, he's not here either. I'm trying not to jump to conclusions – although I haven't quite worked out exactly what the conclusions are yet.' It seemed as if she was listening to herself speak from the bottom of a pit.

'Are you all right? Do you want me to come round?'

'No, I'm fine,' said Sarah, struggling to paste a cheery voice on over the cracks. 'He's probably gone to price a job up and got caught up with some garden buff. It wouldn't be the first time.'

Lisa sniffed. 'You don't sound convinced.'

'I'm not,' her voice faltered and threatened to break, 'but what else am I supposed to do? I'm going quietly nuts here, but I'll be buggered if I'm going to drive round town like some demented bunny boiler looking for his sodding van. He's been like a bear with a sore head for days. I can't do anything right, he's snappy as hell with the boys. Everytime he's come in over the last few days it's like this great heavy cloud settles on everyone – I'm on edge waiting for him to snap at me or one of the kids.'

'Work? Money? Mid-life crisis?' suggested Lisa.

'I don't know any more.'

'If he shows up I'll get him to give you a ring, and if not see you in the morning. I'm sure he's fine – but.'

'But what?'

'If you need anything, you know I'm here.'

'Thanks, Lisa. If I need help to pull him out from under some rampant blonde you'll be the first one I call.' She laughed. Lisa didn't join in, which didn't strike Sarah as odd until after she had hung up.

It was a long slow evening. Just as Sarah was thinking about going to bed, she heard the van pull into the yard and without thinking jumped to her feet. She stood in the gloom uncertain whether to hurry out to meet Chris or scurry upstairs to avoid him.

In the end she loitered in the hallway, feeling uncomfortable and self-conscious and uneasy in her own home, not certain where to begin or what to say. Chris appeared not to notice her as he shut and locked the door.

'So, how was your evening,' she said in a low even voice.

He spun round in surprise, looking hunted. 'Fine, fine. I didn't see you there, I didn't think that you'd still be up.'

'I was about to go up to bed. How was Barry?' she said, setting the trap and waiting for him to fall in. But perhaps it was too obvious and too soon. Chris looked at her intently as if seeing Sarah for the first time.

'Actually I didn't go to Barry's in the end,' he said with care. 'I'd got a couple of customers to chase up, and that guy who was going to supply paving slabs on the way to Emneth. Remember him? Bit of a fly boy – anyway, it's taken all bloody evening to sort it out, I'm completely and utterly knackered.' He yawned theatrically and turned towards the stairs.

Sarah nodded, although every molecule in her body told her that he was lying. 'You smell of beer, did you call in at the pub?'

'What is this, twenty questions? I don't know what's got into you, Sarah. No.' He was emphatic, drawing an angry line under the words. 'I didn't go to the pub, the slab guy, Eric, offered me a can of lager, couldn't very well say no, could I?'

'No, I suppose not. I only asked.'

And then the phone rang. Sarah hurried past Chris into the kitchen in case it was Lisa.

'Hello,' said a female voice over the muted babble of many more, 'is Chris Colebrook there?'

Before Sarah could say yes or no, the woman continued, 'Only he forgot to pick up his raffle prize tonight.'

'I'm sorry, who is this?' A flare went off inside her mind illuminating every word Chris had said since he arrived home.

'It's Jez – the barmaid from down the Lamb? If you'd like to tell Chris he can drop by any time and pick it up, only he rushed off after we'd drawn the tombola. Good job his telephone number was on the back of the ticket.'

'Oh, okay,' said Sarah, unable to find anything else to say. She felt as if someone had hit her in the stomach, and while she reeled and fought for breath, her mind scurried round offering up this new piece of information into the jigsaw. It didn't fit which ever way she turned it.

'Thanks. Thank you,' Sarah managed before she hung up. She sounded flat and defeated and when she turned around Chris was hanging on her every word while trying to appear disinterested.

'Who was that?'

'It was a wrong number, I think, some woman,' Sarah said, amazed how easily the words rolled off her tongue.

'What, at this time of night?' said Chris, 'you'd think people would be more careful. I'm knackered – I'll see you when you come up.' He made his way back into the hall, although Sarah suspected he knew that she was lying too.

And why had she lied? Sarah went around switching off the lights, and checking that everywhere was locked up. Was she afraid of what Chris might tell her? She could hear him in the bathroom. All the years they'd been together it had never occurred to her that he might be so unhappy that he'd go looking for someone else. She felt a hot rush of panic as the words formed clearly in the front of her mind. She knew with a terrible sense of certainty that was what this was about, Chris had found someone else. She swallowed hard as a wave of nausea rolled up behind the heat.

Chapter 18

'I think there's a possibility that Chris might be having an affair.' Sarah said the words very slowly and very precisely in a quiet voice. She looked across at Lisa, waiting for her to deny it and tell her not to be such an idiot.

It was a little before half past eight the next morning and they were sitting on the forecourt outside Burdetts garage. Sarah had arranged with Matthew to take Charlie into school on the bus so that she could pick Lisa up and have this conversation, although now that the words were out in the open, she wished there was some way she could claw them back. They sounded ridiculous and yet scratched across the quick of her soul like wire wool.

There was a freeze frame moment in which Sarah waited for Lisa to say something jokey, counter with a flippant throwaway line, instead she went very pale.

'I didn't want to say anything,' Lisa began. 'To be honest I didn't really know where to begin.'

Sarah shivered.

'. . . but there have been a few stories going about, I thought they were rumours – and then I was talking to the woman in the garage while I was waiting for you just now and she said – she asked me if I knew you, and then she said . . . she said.'

'For Christ's sake Lisa, don't bottle out, what the hell did she say?' Sarah hissed in desperation, looking over towards the forecourt shop wondering if the woman inside was still watching them. 'Please. Tell me what it was she said.'

Lisa took a deep breath. 'She told me that Chris is carrying on with one of her friends. Her best friend she said, Jenny Beck. You know, Peter's mum? From Harehill?'

Sarah's first reaction was to think it was a mistake, ridiculous, far too ridiculous to be anything other than funny. She was almost as surprised as Lisa to hear the peal of laughter. 'You have got to be kidding, not Jenny Beck? For God's sake the woman is barking mad. Surely to God Chris wouldn't . . . not . . .' Sarah stopped, choking on the words, the certainty that the woman in the garage had made a mistake, the surety trickling away as all sorts of images formed on the screen inside her head. The edge of the earth began to crumble.

Jenny Beck had been at their house when Sarah had stayed out all night, Jenny Beck had supported Chris and believed in him and stood up against her. There had been a few hours when Sarah had been the enemy and Jenny Beck had been Chris's only ally. Was that enough, was that all it took? Was what she and Chris had created so fragile after all these years, so vulnerable that it could be shaken down by Jenny Beck, a few glasses of scotch and a single act of stupidity?

'I don't believe it. Not Jenny Beck.' Her voice crackled with emotion.

Lisa touched her arm. 'Look, I don't know. Let's go to school, I'll make you some coffee. Or do you want to go home? You could ring in sick or something. I can get a cab.'

'No, I don't want to go home. I need time to think about this, and I can't think if there's any chance I might run into Chris.' She looked at Lisa trying to find some part of the answer in her friend's face. 'Jenny Beck, are you sure?'

Lisa nodded. 'That's what she said, it sounds crazy to me too, but apparently it's common knowledge. He was down the pub with her last night. The Lamb? It's out in the open, Sarah. I'm so sorry.'

'It's not your fault; thank you for telling me.' Sarah gunned the engine and pulled out into the morning traffic, heart beating out a tango, after shocks of pain rolling through her, wondering what Lisa would have done if she hadn't brought the subject up. Would Lisa have mentioned it at all?

'And there's something else.'

Sarah glanced across at her. 'Sorry?'

Lisa chewed her lip, reluctant to speak. 'She told me you'd got someone else too.'

Sarah gasped. 'Someone else?'

'I was as surprised as you are, and then I wondered if it was maybe that Mac guy. I mean, I know you didn't do anything but people can make a mountain out of a molehill, and you said yourself he was gorgeous and – you did stay out all night and you don't know who saw you with him.'

Sarah slumped forward as if all the air had been sucked out of her lungs. 'Bloody hell. I don't believe this is happening.'

Lisa shook her head. They drove in silence to White-friars.

When Sarah got to the school gates she stared at the colourful outcrops of mothers. She wondered how many of the women already knew about Chris and Jenny Beck, and thought they knew something about her and how long they'd known. She was very careful not to look directly at any of them. Humiliation, shock and glowing anger were a horribly volatile mix.

The rest of Tuesday morning was a total blur. It was as if there was a fire wall between her real stream of thoughts and the rest of her life. Her body functioned and answered and talked and even laughed, it did all the things expected of her, while deep inside she was turning the idea of an affair between Jenny Beck and Chris over and over in her mind like fingers working worry beads. As a base note to every other thought she had a horrible sense of unreality – this just couldn't be happening.

Lisa came to find her at break time. Sarah was setting up the tables and equipment for a potato printing session with the reception class. Reception was probably the best place to be. It was the front line. The infants were messy, intense, anarchic and had to be watched like pickpockets, and yet at the same time were truly wonderful to be with as they discovered the magic of colour and the tactile pleasures of thickened gloopy poster paint.

Sarah poured half a cup full of pillar box red paint into a print tray and wondered if Lisa had come to check that she was all right, and prayed that she didn't ask.

'Message for you.'

Sarah wiped her hands, changing her supplication to a prayer that the message wasn't from Chris.

'Monica Carlisle rang to ask if there was any chance that you could meet her at the arts centre this lunch time, about one, if that's okay. And could you ring to confirm? She said you'd probably get the machine but that she'd still get the message.'

Sarah nodded, followed her back to the office and left a message after the tone as instructed. Lisa looked up from her computer.

'I'm really sorry. If you need to talk – or if I can do anything, anything at all, you only have to ask, Sarah, you know that.'

Sarah smiled, surprised at how vulnerable and shaky she felt. Had the situations been reversed she would have said the same things and meant them just as sincerely. What a shame it wasn't that way round.

'Thanks, Lisa. I don't know what I want at the moment, or even what I'm feeling.'

She sloped off back to the infant room. It would be good to have a really valid reason not to go home at lunch time, although maybe she wouldn't say anything about Chris and Jenny Beck to Monica.

Monica was a friend but not close, not intimate, and she was too sharp, too life hardened to confide in about things like this, or then again maybe she was the perfect confidante. Someone who had seen it all before and would throw the situation into perspective without batting an eyelid. Strange though how very quickly and strongly Sarah's rogue mind had already bound Chris and Jenny's names together.

On site in the newly constructed gardens on the outskirts of Norwich, Chris Colebrook watched the subcontractors finish laying the last of the turf around the pond, watched the leaves of the silver birch that he had planted by the newly installed benches, twist and glitter in the soft breeze like a shoal of tiny fish moving against the current, and wondered what the hell he was playing at and how he had got this far without really making any kind of conscious decision.

There was no way he wanted any sort of relationship with Jenny Beck. He wanted his life back, he wanted Sarah. He had always wanted Sarah.

Okay, so things were a bit rough between them at the moment but nothing that couldn't be put right if he came clean and . . . the thought wedged somewhere in the arid recesses of his mind and refused to budge, so he swung it around and came in from another direction. There was nothing that couldn't be aired and talked about with the possible exception of what he'd been up to with Jenny Beck. Wasn't that what his mind was having trouble with? But even that wasn't so bad, not really.

Whatever else she was, Sarah was reasonable and kind and understanding. Even if he told her about Jenny she might be angry, she would most certainly be hurt, maybe even outraged, but he also knew that she wouldn't condemn him if he made a clean breast of things. Okay, she would probably drag it up over and over again like a rank mouldering corpse every time they had a row, but she wouldn't see the damage as irreparable.

Unlike him, said his conscience. Chris winced. He knew very well that if the situation was reversed he could never let Sarah forget, never, ever and worse still he could never forgive her. He hadn't forgiven her yet for staying out all night. So was that what this was about, sauce for the goose, sauce for the gander? Did he really think Sarah was having an affair with the vicar? The answer, going on what he knew about his wife – stripped bare of all the supposition and rumour fed to him by Jenny – was no, and he knew it. It just suited him to believe the worst as a salve to his own conscience.

His mobile rang. Chris peered down at the screen and his stomach contracted sharply.

'Chris Colebrook, how can I help you?' He used his formal office voice hoping it might protect him.

There was an intense little giggle that crackled and spat as the signal broke up and then, 'Hi, Chris, it's Jenny. I wondered if you fancied coming over for lunch. You said last night that you might be in the area today and I thought you'd like a little something.'

Chris reddened and then looked over his shoulder in case anyone could see or hear him. The only thing he was aware of, hunkered down in the back of the van, was what remained of his conscience.

'Er, well, actually I'm in Norwich at the moment.'

'Oh.'

He could sense her disappointment.

'But I'm more or less finished here, I'm famished.' What was he saying? 'Lunch sounds great. I can be there in about an hour, how's that?'

What the hell was he doing?

He was going to talk to her, that was what. He was going to sit her down at the kitchen table and finish the speech he had planned to make the night before. When he was done, there would be no more ambiguity, everything would be sorted out and then he would go home to Sarah, and after a few tears and a lot of humble pie life would get back to normal. Simple. He even had a sense of relief.

'And just who are you trying to kid?' mumbled his conscience from the back of the van.

Okay, so he had kissed Jenny Beck in the pub car park, and okay, so there was no way anyone could have mistaken it for the kind of kiss you'd give your maiden aunt and true one or two of her friends had been there to witness the event. But – but . . .

'But what?' asked his conscience.

But he hadn't accepted her invitation to go home for coffee, and when she curled herself around him like an octopus on heat he had smiled gently and peeled her right off again. And he had left before closing time and he knew for certain that, despite appearances, he'd got the balls to put everything straight.

His conscience mumbled something dark and uncomplimentary, but Chris couldn't quite make out the words over the sound of the engine revving.

'Well, I must say I'm extremely impressed. It's going to be wonderful when it's finished,' said Monica Carlisle enthusiastically. 'One would have to be very short-sighted not to see the potential in a place like this. Presumably you're thinking theatre as well as everything else?'

The acoustics in the newly plastered performance space at St Barts were good and so although she spoke quite quietly, her voice rolled around the hall, as crisp and sharp as it left her lips.

Leo nodded. 'Absolutely. I've got a friend currently looking at the possibilities.'

Monica was certainly up for the part of Lady Bountiful. She was carrying a delicate gold lorgnette and wearing the most amazing shot silk coat dress in iridescent sea green that Sarah had ever seen. It glittered under the house lights like some exotic liquid.

It was half past one and Sarah was trailing along behind the grand tour, this time just a maid of honour in the wake of the great and good. Monica was being shown around by Leo Banning and the lady chairperson of the Friends committee, together with a representative of some arts trust. They had managed to rustle up an impressive entourage at such short notice. Monica must have promised them a great deal, but then again as a very wealthy unknown quantity they obviously felt obligated to make a tremendous fuss of her.

As the group turned back towards the foyer Sarah saw Adam Gregory standing at the frontier where the arts centre turned back into a building site still. He watched the procession pass and then grinned and lifted a hand in acknowledgement.

She followed suit and slowed so that their paths crossed. 'You're here almost as much as I am these days.'

Sarah indicated the worthies. 'Take no notice, this was a royal summons. I'm here in my capacity as trainee minion.'

He laughed. 'Great career move.'

Ahead of them the main party were still on their progress, deep in conversation, bandying projections and figures and endless possibilities, while heading towards the office and the promise of coffee and expensive chocolate biscuits.

'So, are you needed for any more fawning or have you got time to come and look at something amazing?'

Sarah looked at the backs ahead of her. 'Realistically, I

don't think anyone's going to miss me. And I'm bored and my feet hurt; so far it's been a totally shitty day.'

He handed her a hard hat. 'In that case it can only get better, come and take a look at what we found while we were clearing away a load of construction debris. Museum services are coming down later to take an official look. But until then –' he pulled aside the curtain of industrial polythene like a magician. '– it's all ours.'

Intrigued Sarah stepped through and followed him down a spiral staircase into what had once been some sort of crypt. The ceiling was quite low, and made up of a series of stone arches, now strung rather incongruously with industrial lighting and thick black cables.

'Mind your step,' Adam said, as they neared the bottom. It was a tight turn and the treads suddenly narrowed; her concentration was broken by his warning. Sarah stumbled. He caught tight hold of her arm. The touch of his fingers was warm and strong and for some reason it made her feel good, that was the only word for it. For an instant she looked across at him and their eyes met and Sarah was stunned to realise that there was an unexpected needle-sharp spark of connection between them.

It was an odd and unnerving sensation and made something contract deep in her belly. Sarah realised with a flutter that she was attracted to him. She liked this man and wanted to know more about him. It came as a real surprise, in fact so surprising that Sarah froze.

'Are you okay? Not afraid of the dark or anything?' he asked, still holding her.

Sarah reddened and snatched her arm away, afraid that he might have sensed the thoughts that had passed unexpectedly through her head.

'No, no I'm fine,' she stammered. 'Really.'

'It's not much further now.'

They rounded the last corner.

'I hope when you see it you don't think I've got you down here under false pretences.' Adam switched on a torch, and they made their way through a small cellar which was more or less cut in half by two great pillars that looked as if they had sprouted like trees and grown up through the flagstone floor.

Set in the wall opposite the door, amongst course after course of stone blocks and stained flaking plaster was a fragment of what appeared to be a carved panel. Framing one edge was a complex braid of ivy and behind it, peeping out, was a woman's face caught in profile, one hand lifted to her cheek. The whole thing no more than perhaps a foot square.

Sarah gasped in amazement. 'Oh wow, it's fabulous,' she whispered on a long outward breath. 'Where did it come from? What's it doing down here?'

Adam was standing at her shoulder, pointing the torch beam. 'No idea, really. The guy who came to take a quick look yesterday said it's probably Roman, robbed from somewhere else. A temple or maybe a villa. It was fairly common practice – dressing stone is expensive and down here who was going to see it? Look, there's some more of it.' He pointed out another smaller piece, this time no bigger than a saucer where life-sized fingers appeared to be pressed against the stone face searching for a way out.

For some reason the image made Sarah feel sad and a wave of tears prickled up behind her eyes, making her blink furiously.

Beside her, Adam was saying, 'Maybe one of the original stonemasons saw it and thought it too beautiful to discard or put in the other way round. These two pieces have been hidden away down here for donkey's years. We might even turn some more up yet. This part of the crypt was used for storage not interments and by the time we got in here it had been back filled with rubble and rubbish for the best part of a century.'

Sarah leant forward eager to touch the main panel and then thought better of it, 'Is it all right?' she asked, trying to control the emotion in her voice.

Adam nodded. 'I don't see why not.' He stepped aside.

Under Sarah's fingertips the stone felt as cold and smooth as glass. The quality of the carving was breathtakingly beautiful. It would be hard to render the features so perfectly and so finely in pen and ink let alone in a medium as unwieldy as stone. To her surprise she felt the tears press even harder.

Adam looked at her with a puzzled expression and then, as if in slow motion, as she straightened up he opened his arms.

The tears trickled out on to her cheeks. Without thinking and without hesitation she stepped towards him. It was that simple. It was an act of kindness, one human for another, sensing pain and need, nothing sexual, not even fuelled by desire but the need for comfort for something that she couldn't even put into words. Adam Gregory felt warm and strong and smelt of soap and sunshine.

To her horror instead of pulling away, apologising and blowing her nose on the crush of tissues that lay mangled in the bottom of her handbag, Sarah found herself sobbing uncontrollably, great big snotty shoulder heaving sobs that racked through her like shards of broken glass. And to her great relief Adam held her tighter still. How strange to be here in the dark with someone she barely knew crying for reasons she barely understood.

After a few minutes he said, 'That is the last time I show you any Roman carvings.'

Sarah laughed through the last of the tears, pleased that there was no light in the cellar other than the torch. 'History. Gets me every time,' she snuffled, rubbing across her face with the back of her hand, extricating herself reluctantly from his embrace.

'Do you want a drink?'

Sarah rootled around in her bag for the tissues. 'What I could really do with is somewhere to wash my face and a couple of paracetamol. My head feels as if it's about to explode. I'm so sorry.' Her voice quavered again as she apologised. 'I didn't mean to . . .' she stopped, and bit her lip to stop the tears resurfacing. 'I'm not normally like this.'

He shrugged. 'Happens to me all the time.' He grinned. 'The ladies' toilets in the foyer were finished weeks ago and I've got paracetamol in my office. C'mon.' He caught hold of her hand. 'Is there anything else I can do?'

And this time when their fingers touched it was about desire not sympathy and she stepped closer again and he kissed her. It was gentle and unfamiliar and made the hairs on the back of her neck lift. Over in seconds they parted and stood in the dark, a breath apart and Sarah's heart began to thump and she chewed her lips and wondered if she had done a terrible thing.

'All right?' he said quietly.

Sarah shook her head. 'Not really. I probably owe you an explanation but don't think I can face it. Everything is in bits at the moment. I wouldn't know where to begin.'

Adam looked down at his watch. 'Then don't. I'm on my lunch hour now, how about I show you around. There is this fantastic little place I've found sheltered from the wind, a perfect sun trap Not many people know it's there.'

Sarah looked up at him, still dabbing at her face. 'How bad do I look?'

He smiled at her in the gloom, as if genuinely sizing her up. 'Bloody terrible,' he said after a few seconds, 'but nothing that a good wash won't put straight.'

For one moment she wondered if Adam was going to

kiss her again and when he didn't, Sarah realised that amongst all the other emotions the most powerful was disappointment.

Over at Harehill Jenny Beck checked the dressing table mirror and then drew the bedroom curtains closed so that the room was thrown into an array of soft shadows. Making love in the daylight was one thing but there was no need to throw a spotlight on the whole affair. She pulled her shoulders back and looked at her reflection critically. She'd only had one child – and that was years ago – whereas Sarah had had three. Okay, Sarah might be a few years younger but three kids had to have taken its toll on a body. She must remember not to lie on her side and keep her hands behind her head whenever possible.

Jenny was wearing a little button through shift dress – no trouble at all to get that off – and underneath was the cream lace bra and knickers set she'd bought from Littlewoods in the sale to put away for her next holiday with Tony. Tony. She jiggled her bra down and then flicked her hair back off her face; hot toffee apple along with the hint of tan looked good and the bits where the grey had been most obvious looked as if the sun had bleached them.

She could give that little bitch from Weigh and Save a run for her money – and there were men, real men who appreciated maturity and strength in a woman. That's what Elaine from the garage had said. Women with experience who ripened like good wine, getting better with the years.

Jenny sniffed and lit a joss stick on the dressing table before looking round to check that everything was okay. Clean bedspread and sheets, a scattering of cushions. She wriggled and adjusted her straps – maybe the bra was just a little bit tight.

Although of course there was always a chance that Chris would want to have her downstairs, up against the sink unit, or over the end of the kitchen table. The idea made Jenny shiver with a little frisson of anticipation. Rita from the Co-op reckoned her old man – who must be sixty if he was a day – often biked home from work and dragged her into the cupboard under the stairs for a quickie. He couldn't always get it up these days since all that prostrate trouble he'd had but the thought was still there.

A table ender. When Jenny closed her eyes she could almost feel the cool press of wood against her back and the warm, sweaty bang, bang, bang of flesh on flesh.

She shivered and started to salivate. There were two chicken sandwiches already in the fridge, nicely garnished with side salad and a bit of tomato. Wine was maybe taking it a bit far for weekday lunch time but she had got a bottle of white chilling just in case, and two cans of lager and a jug of orange juice. Jenny Beck was ready for almost anything.

Chapter 19

'I wondered where you'd crept off to,' said Monica conspiratorially as she met Sarah on her way back to Adam Gregory's office. Sarah had been away just long enough to wash her face, re-apply sufficient make-up to give her a natural look and add a quick ssssst of perfume into her newly brushed hair. She still felt shaky.

As Monica spoke, Adam appeared at the door carrying two mugs of tea. Monica didn't miss a beat, she looked him up and down and smiled. 'Ah, now I can see why you wanted to give the main party the elbow.' And then to Adam. 'Hi, I'm Monica Carlisle.'

Before Sarah could think of anything to say, Adam grinned, completely unfazed by her frank appraisal of him. 'Adam Gregory, project manager. Excuse me if I don't shake hands. You must be the bigwig. Tired of all that adulation?'

'Good God no, you can never have too much attention, but I've got another appointment in a while. This is a great place. I'm glad Sarah told me about it. I'm looking forward to adding a little anarchy into the mix. Anyway I'm afraid I have to be off, I've made my apologies. Do you fancy coming to the pub?'

The invitation was directed as much to Adam as Sarah.

He indicated the shadowy interior with a mug. 'We were going to take a little sun.'

Monica arched one perfectly plucked eyebrow, her attention shifting back to Sarah. 'It's always the quiet ones you've got to watch.'

'I could always make more tea,' he said.

Monica laughed and then waved the lorgnette in a gesture of dismissal. 'How kind, thanks but no thanks, at my age the sun leaves me looking like a toasted granary loaf. And besides I'm getting far too old to keep playing gooseberry for Sarah.'

Sarah reddened. 'But you wouldn't be.'

Monica laughed. 'No? And where have you been looking? Can you ring when you get home? I'd like to talk about this sponsorship thing.'

And with that Monica was gone, leaving behind the whisper of an expensive perfume.

'Tea?' suggested Adam, and without another word Sarah followed him back through the sheets of polythene. She may have managed to wash away a lot of the puffiness and the smears of dust from the crypt, but not the strange little electric buzz that arced around inside her. Every time she looked at Adam it crackled between them, like that Van de Graaff machine at school where you wound up the handle, building the current inside a sphere until a great blue flash leapt across and made your hair stand on end. Without thinking Sarah ran her hand back over her head just in case it really was that obvious, and at the same time wondered what they would talk about now, beginning to feel horribly self-conscious and awkward.

He turned back to ensure she was following. 'How are you with heights?'

Sarah blushed. 'Do they make me cry, is that what you're saying?'

He laughed. 'No – should I have?'

Sarah shook her head. 'No, I'm fine – ish.'

They went in under another arch and this time climbed up a spiral staircase set behind a panelled wall. At the top was a wooden door set with iron straps that opened on to a flat roof between steeply leaded valleys. After the gloom of the interior, stepping out into the brilliant afternoon sunlight came as a real surprise. Sarah blinked, blinded by the glare and then, as her eyes adjusted realised that from where they were standing she could see for miles in every direction, out over the town, over the little town square, the roof tops picked out in faded orange pantiles and sharp grey slate. Beyond that, where the houses thinned the land dropped away sharply to the river, in the middle distance were a scattering of villages and then the fen beyond, an expanse of rich flat land, its stark lines softened by summer mist.

She had had no idea that St Barts commanded such a vantage point and for a few seconds was totally mesmerised by what she could see. And then she was aware of Adam standing behind her and turned around. He had balanced the mugs on a ledge and was busy pulling two folding chairs out from behind a parapet.

'You should have tables and umbrellas up here. It would be a great place for a roof top café.'

'You don't know how close to the truth you are,' he said, indicating a chair. 'When we first did a survey that was one of the proposals the team came up with. In the end the cost of re-enforcing the roof was just too much – although it does mean that we are amongst a select few.'

She sat alongside him – despite her fears he felt remarkably easy to be with. From the pocket of a battered Barbour he produced half a packet of chocolate digestives, before folding the coat into a cushion. Sarah laughed.

'What a man.'

He grinned and offered her the packet. 'Well, you missed out on the tour's posh biscuits, seems like the very least I can do under the circumstances.'

Sarah sat in the sunshine for about an hour, out there on the roof with Adam Gregory. They talked about her paintings, his job, the conversion work on the church, the

Roman carvings, the roof, the view, fundraising and what sort of events might take place at St Barts once it was up and running. They did not talk about the fact that he had kissed her.

'I've been invited to put something into the summer exhibition too.'

'Really?' Sarah said, realising how rude it sounded the instant the word was out.

Adam grinned again and she was struck by how much the expression suited him. 'Thanks for the compliment, although the derision is probably justified. It's part of the committee's non-elitist ethic, all the guys who work here have been asked if they'd like to contribute something. Once they stopped buggering about and taking the mick, it was amazing what they came up with. Two of the brickies have contributed a mosaic. I'm hoping to persuade the powers-that-be to have it installed in the foyer.'

'And what are you going to put in?'

'I'm not sure I want to tell you now.'

Sarah blushed. 'I'm sorry.'

'Good. It's a little pen and ink drawing with a watercolour wash that I did last summer while I was in Barcelona. I've just got to get it framed –'

The thought lit a similar one in Sarah's head. 'Oh God, yes. I meant to bring mine in today and drop them off at the art shop. Bugger.' She glanced at her watch wondering whether there was time to nip home and pick the paintings up.

'I know this chap who does it from home. He's very reasonable, I could give you his number if you like,' Adam said. 'He's got a workshop at Magdalen St Joseph. Do you know where I mean?'

She said yes, she did know and yes, she would be interested and finished the dregs of her tea, hoping that he wouldn't notice in case that meant that they would have to go downstairs again and step back into the real world.

During the moments of silence – silence that was remarkably easy to bear – she examined the way the crisscross pattern of lines around Adam's eyes emphasised the humour in his voice and the way his thick greying hair curled into the curve of his neck and how strong and beautiful his hands were. It was so easy and so very tempting, this funny little electric crush.

Adam showed her back downstairs at a little before half past two. Sarah drove home feeling warm and sunny. It was only as she reached the junction that led back into the village that the make-shift dam her mind had built finally breached with a tumultuous crack.

She braked hard. What the hell was going on? How could she manage to forget what she knew? Wasn't she in danger of doing exactly what she was being accused of and in that silly euphoric rush, forgetting what it seemed that everyone else knew. Graphic images of Jenny Beck and Chris poured through her mind like flood water, boiling and rolling, layered with debris and dirt and all manner of flotsam and jetsam. By the time she drove into the lane leading to her house Sarah felt physically sick.

Chris Colebrook realised that it was an ambush the instant he set foot into Jenny's kitchen. He sensed that he was in big trouble. Very big trouble. The blinds were at half-mast, giving the room a indolent sleepy look and the air was heavy with the scent of incense.

Jenny had opened the door wearing a long black shift dress that clung to her ample frame like wet kelp, revealing every curve and yet at the same time managing to look like some kind of exotic gift wrapping. She smelt of something spicy and warm, and although Chris had no idea what the perfume was called he suspected the subtitle was sex in the afternoon.

'You got here real quick,' she said, eyes dark, pupils glittering in the half light.

'Not a lot of traffic on the A47 today, busier past Swaffham obviously,' he bumbled, attempting to block whatever seductive glamour it was that was trying so very hard to ensnare him.

'Anyone would think you were keen to get over here to see me.' Jenny didn't seem to be moving her lips as she spoke and was now standing within a foot of him, so close that as Chris focused on her face she had an extra eye in the middle of her forehead. 'Wouldn't they?'

'Wouldn't they what?' he whimpered as she moved closer still. Any words that he said after that were no more than a crackling white noise, an undecipherable soundtrack, unconnected to the events unfolding before him.

Jenny moaned softly and leant against him, pressing her lips to his neck, running her fingers through his hair, pushing him hard up against the sink unit.

Chris was about to protest when he felt the heat of her body and the heaviness of her breasts through his T-shirt. The words dried in his throat, burnt off by the sheer radiance of her desire. He swallowed hard as she made a soft almost inaudible little sob of pleasure in her throat. It made Chris gasp for breath as if he was drowning.

His conscience, which had reluctantly followed him in from the van, tried very hard to resist, struggling to be heard over the roar of Jenny's libido. It even threatened to walk out if things didn't stop right there, but before there was any chance to save him, it was mugged, bound and gagged by a whole tribe of earthy little trolls who had prised open the trap door to a deep, dark blood-red chasm slung low in his belly. They were as ugly as nuns, appeared to have huge dangling genitals and – from what Chris could make out as Jenny Beck's fingers closed around the belt buckle on his jeans – all the moral fibre of tinned fruit. His conscience whimpered once and then surrendered, which was all the encouragement Jenny Beck needed.

What happened next was not pretty but was hellishly effective. Jenny Beck pulled Chris's trousers down around his knees and while she was doing that and undoing his shirt and touching him in all kinds of interesting and very compelling ways, his hands – which appeared to have staged a mutiny and were now under the direct control of the tinned fruit trolls, were off on an eager reconnaissance mission of the more intriguing bits of Jenny Beck's ample and extremely compliant body.

She seemed delighted by the turn of events and giggled and groaned and thrust forward, encouraging him to seek out exactly what it was he wanted, wherever it might be hidden.

Chris groaned and closed his eyes, beginning to feel as if the real Chris Colebrook was barricaded somewhere, trapped inside a small dark room high up in the front of his skull, along with his conscience, while the whole of the rest of his body went awol.

Jenny must have planned this moment for days; there was a packet of condoms in the cutlery drawer tucked in alongside the potato masher and a thing for crushing garlic into worms. She had those out in no time at all and having ripped the packet open with her teeth grabbed tight hold of his manhood with all the skill and finesse of a dog catcher. It was pointless and potentially dangerous to resist.

'Well, well, well,' she murmured.

Chris did not feel well at all.

Meanwhile back at the house Sarah poured herself a glass of cranberry and raspberry juice straight from the fridge, then sat very quietly in the kitchen enjoying the coolness and the calmness, aware that this was most likely the eye of the storm.

She glanced up at the clock; Matthew ought to be leaving the library any minute now to go and pick Charlie up from school. Sarah closed her eyes, and resting her elbow on the table, settled her head on thumb and forefinger trying very hard to outsmart the headache that threatened to engulf her.

What was she going to say to Chris when he arrived home? Was there any point in asking him outright what he was up to with Jenny Beck? Demand the truth or pretend nothing had happened? Was it possible that the whole thing was just the product of the cottage industry gossip factory. Had they, the ubiquitous they of myth and legend, bored and looking for a way to pass a long slow afternoon, invented the whole thing. It made some sense, after all Sarah wasn't seeing anybody – or at least not in any way that would give rise to the rip tide of rumours.

She nipped the bridge of her nose feeling another wave of nausea coming on. Whitefriars school was ablaze with gossip. There was that woman in the garage, no doubt telling anyone who'd listen about Chris and Jenny and the mystery man she was supposed to be seeing.

Sarah wondered if Lisa might be able to find out who it was she was supposed to be sleeping with – it would be nice to know. Sarah fumbled around in her pockets for a tissue and came up with a folded scrap of paper on which Adam Gregory had written the telephone number of the picture framer. And what did she think she was doing with Adam Gregory? Sarah groaned.

At least she could do something positive with what remained of the afternoon. Ring up and arrange to take the paintings over – maybe when Charlie and Matthew got back from school. She had been flattered and excited, but now in comparison with the rest of the things that were happening in her life, the idea of putting something in the exhibition seemed like small potatoes.

The phone rang.

'And who exactly is the mystery man?' purred Monica the instant Sarah said hello.

'No mystery, just an acquaintance, a friend, a nice man.'

'Oh no, not nice, please don't say nice, darling. Not nice, not okay, say gorgeous, gorgeous is fine. Gorgeous with those naughty eyes and a lovely crackly dangerous edge to him. I'm almost envious.'

Sarah hadn't got the time or the energy. 'Monica, do you think Chris is having an affair?'

'Are you serious? You are serious, aren't you? God, let me think –' there were a few seconds' silence and then Monica said, 'Under normal circumstances I'd say no, but he is the type who might get tricked and led. I bet it said that on his school reports. "Christopher Colebrook is a nice boy but easily led."'

Sarah sighed. 'Would you mind if I rang you back later?'

'Of course not. Do you need to talk?'

'At the moment I've got no idea.'

'Well, whatever you need,' Monica said in a gentle, remarkably level voice. 'I'm here. Just ring, and if you need a bolt hole, a place to stay there's another cottage on the estate. It's empty if you ever need it.'

Sarah was about to protest that she was nowhere near needing a place to run to, but the words refused to come.

'Think about it,' said Monica before she hung up.

Taking her drink, Sarah went upstairs to look at the paintings. Her brain desperately needed the diversion. Pulling off the covers she stared at the first canvas. Her thoughts were so convoluted and inward looking that it took a while before the images registered, and then, despite everything, she found it impossible not to smile.

The first one was a picture painted while she was pregnant with Charlie, when the smell of linseed oil had made her mouth water with anticipation. It was a view from the French windows in the sitting room, looking out over their garden. The picture was frost bright; they hadn't lived in the house that long then, not a year, so that Sarah hadn't known how the seasons would move through the garden, or how the light would change as the year turned. The brush strokes were bold and confident, catching an energy, maybe the hormonal rush of pregnancy, that gave the painting a real vibrancy. Sarah ran a finger over the rough swirls and ridges of paint; it felt like another life.

The crab apple tree, which Sarah had always thought probably outdated the house, framed part of the image, a bent gnarled body that held the edge and defined the borders. Beneath its arthritic branches the earth was flecked with spring flowers, daffodils and crocuses, and in the foreground wooden tubs raw with scarlet tulips and the promise of the year to come.

The soil, cracked by hard frost was so dark and so rich that you could almost smell the loam, the abundance and fecundity just below the surface that had echoed almost exactly the sensation she had of being pregnant with Charlie.

Sarah swallowed hard, feeling a great pain and the promise of tears wash through her, remembering the long chilling afternoons when she had been working on the painting, interspersed with memories of Chris stepping up behind her, his strong arms circling her fast vanishing waist to support the bump who, knowing Chris was there, settled and pressed forward as if eager for his touch.

Finally, Sarah lost the battle against her anger and grief and the tears ran hot and plump down over her face, exploding on to the stair carpet like small wet mortars. Bastard, how could he think about ruining what they had built for someone like Jenny Beck. Okay, so their relationship wasn't perfect, there were chips and bangs and scuff marks all around the edges but what could you expect after twenty years? There were things that she would change but wasn't that the nature of every relationship? Some days she wanted to run away and never see Chris again and then there were other days when she loved him so much she thought her heart would burst.

How could he throw so much away, how could he – and why did she believe the rumours about him, knowing that the ones about her were untrue. All her thoughts abruptly disintegrated and were replaced by a pain, so volatile and all consuming that for one awful moment Sarah clung to the banister thinking the sheer force of it might knock her over.

After a few minutes, when the worst had ebbed away, Sarah went into the bathroom and washed her face, empty, but well aware that the cistern would soon fill again.

It was almost time for the boys to get home. While waiting for them to arrive she picked three paintings for the exhibition – the view out over the garden, one of the cat stretched out like a fur stole in the sunlight on a wall, and a still life of bread and fruit on an oval dish that she remembered setting up in the kitchen when Matthew and Jack were small. Tucked into a folder at the back of the canvas were their efforts. She could visualise them working alongside her at the kitchen table with crayons and chalk, the smell of pencil shavings and crayola, and wondered how they would feel if she had theirs framed too, and hung their work together at the exhibition, a triptych of artistic endeavour.

Last of all, as she heard the bus draw away from the end of the lane Sarah called the framer and arranged to drop everything off at his house later in the day; and at the back of those thoughts and those actions were the other thunderous things, the big things, the things that still threatened to sweep her away if she didn't run fast enough.

As she went downstairs to greet the boys Sarah checked the clock, wondering what time Chris would be home.

'I've really got to go,' murmured Chris, amazed that he was still speaking in the voice he came in with. Jenny Beck was curled up alongside him, naked as the day she was born, one heavy arm draped around his chest, one leg raised to pin him down to the mattress. Her skin was dappled by shadows as the bedroom curtains moved in the wind. It made her look almost serpentine. He tried to ease out from under the weight of her body but their skin was sandwiched together by prickles of sweat. She gave no signs of letting him go, so he very gently rolled her away, and as he did so realised that she was asleep.

Around them the bed was a sordid tangle of sheets and clothes, wet patches and tissues, there could be no mistaking what had taken place there, there and downstairs in the kitchen up against the sink.

The first time it had been over and done with in no time at all, although Jenny Beck had smiled as he fought to maintain some control, as if that was exactly what she had planned. She looked almost triumphant as he shivered and juddered and then apologised.

He could imagine her telling her friends all the sordid details, that woman at the pub and the one in the garage, how he had been so turned on, so eager to get at her that he couldn't wait, couldn't hold back. Even though it wasn't true. Although, he thought with a wry smile, twice in one afternoon wasn't bad for someone his age. Not bad at all.

But unfortunately, as his conscience, which had wriggled free, pointed out, he had driven over to Jenny's to sort the situation out once and for all, not get himself laid, so on that count he'd failed.

A leg over, that was the last thing Chris had wanted, or anticipated. Well, maybe not the last thing, but Jenny had taken him by surprise. He had been about to launch into the carefully prepared speech about how lovely she was, but how much he loved and valued his relationship with Sarah, despite all the nasty rumours about the vicar. He could hardly tell Jenny that now, could he?

Beside him, she rolled over on to her back and began to snore and snuffle. Where she had been resting her head on him there appeared to be a little puddle of drool. Which for some reason made his mind drift back to the climb up the stairs, and the way she had kissed him so hard that he had been worried she might consume him whole, there was that, and then the sweaty press of her body against his.

Chris groaned, feeling an unexpected stirring in his groin. The second time had been bloody good, despite everything, and now it looked as if there was a distinct possibility of a third if he wasn't very careful. Clutching one of the damp sheets to his belly, Chris rolled very carefully over the side of the bed, landing clumsily on all fours. Looking back, the mattress resembled a relief map of passion, highs and lows marked out with pillows, a twisted towel and the rolled back duvet. As quietly as he could, Chris crawled towards the open bedroom door, rescuing his clothes as he went, desperately trying not to disturb Jenny. Not more than an hour earlier, carried along by some unlikely mating madness he had made her shriek out with sheer delight, which thinking about it now, maybe hadn't been the most sensible approach to take.

On the landing, he struggled into his jeans and pulled on his T-shirt, all the while very careful not to look back into the shadowy bedroom in case Jenny saw him and he was inadvertently trapped for ever. Carrying the one sock he could find and trainers, Chris made his way downstairs and out through the back door. In the garden the sun was so bright it made him flinch.

* * *

'If I may speak frankly, I'm very disappointed in you, Leo, saddened at this recent turn of events. I've invited you here so that we could discuss the matter before the press gets hold of it.' Bishop Fulbright paused. 'I had thought that you of all people would be above such things.'

Leo Banning looked dispassionately at Fulbright, who was standing in front of the large picture window of his first floor office at the bishop's palace framed by sunlight so bright that he looked as if he was radiating godliness.

It was impossible to look at him for more than a few seconds without blinking or screwing your eyes up. Leo was not intimidated, knowing that Fulbright had chosen the position for effect. The drama was everything, staging the key.

'I'm sorry,' he began, meaning that he had no idea what the bishop was talking about, but the great man held up his hand to silence him.

'No, no, please, let me finish. In the last two weeks I have had numerous calls from concerned individuals, tattletales by another name I know, but unfortunately we have to take them seriously and show that their concerns are being addressed. How I hate that bloody expression. Addressed, issues, sharing.' He paused giving time for a little sigh of resignation before continuing, 'The church had problems enough without another double page spread in the *News of the World*.'

Now Leo was confused, Harry had been down to stay a couple of times but only briefly and they had been discreet. Harry was a friend rather than a lover. 'I'm not altogether certain what you're talking about,' Leo began again.

'Oh really,' Fulbright's tone was harder now and his expression less benign, 'I want to talk to you about your duty as a servant to the community. A principle, I'm sure you're aware that I take very seriously.'

'You've lost me completely.'

Fulbright beaded him with those ice floe blue eyes. His humour was not improving.

'Don't insult me by hiding behind some show of innocence, Leo. I thought you would have the decency to make a clean breast of it. I got you here to hear what you have to say about this blasted affair with Sarah Colebrook.'

There was a pause in which Leo didn't know whether to laugh aloud or throttle that daft old bugger.

'My affair with Sarah Colebrook? Are you mad?' he finally snorted. The words were out before he could stop himself

Across the room Fulbright didn't appear to be in the least offended.

'There's no need to look so stunned, Leo. I'm afraid, despite your best efforts to the contrary it appears your secret's out. I need to hear what you have to say for yourself.' As he spoke the bishop pressed his fingertips together and adopted an attitude of intense, benign concentration. Leo suppressed a grin as Fulbright continued. 'I am by no means unsympathetic. Perhaps in a more progressive diocese, a more progressive area, your affair might go unnoticed but country people still take the commandments very seriously.' He smiled thinly. 'At least when it comes to other people.'

Leo arranged his face into an impassive mask. 'Have you spoken to anyone else about this?'

Fulbright stared at him. 'And if I have? As it happens I've discussed the matter with several people, Rory Woodlen, for one, he just laughed and told me he thought it highly unlikely. I have to admire the man for standing up for you. You have a great many very loyal friends Leo.'

Leo looked Augustus up and down and then shook his head, slowly wondering at the man who shepherded the flock. Rory Woodlen was as bent as a box of frogs.

He caught Fulbright's eye and said quietly, 'I can assure

you, your grace, that I am not engaged in an affair with Mrs Colebrook, have never had an affair with her and have no intention of beginning one. What I have done is suggest that she apply for a position at the new arts centre, where I truly believe she will be a boon to the project. She is a very pleasant and capable woman and that is as far as my interest extends.'

Fulbright was the first to look away.

'I have your word on this?' he asked.

Leo nodded, 'Absolutely,' he was going to add that he was prepared to swear on a stack of bibles but didn't think Fulbright would see the joke.

At which point Rory Woodlen came into the room bearing a tray of tea. Leo couldn't help but notice that the bishop's private secretary had taken to buffing his fingernails to a high shine. They exchanged glances if not greetings. At the door, certain that Bishop Fulbright couldn't see him, Rory turned and winked.

As if the matter was now closed Fulbright indicated the tea. 'How is St Barts coming along by the way, I've been meaning to ring your father.'

Leo smiled; he knew very well that one of the reasons he had got the position at Barton was because Fulbright and his father had been up at Cambridge together. Although Leo wasn't altogether certain how hard his father had pulled that particular string or whether it was just another pennyweight on the scales. After all, his record had been exemplary until Tim had died, when he had teetered on the very edge, wracked by all manner of doubts, pushed to the brink by the sense of pain and loss, and the terrible irony of a lover lost not to Aids but to common or garden flu, something that everyone took for granted as part of the long slow haul of winter.

Chapter 20

When Leo arrived home he was surprised to find Harry's little black jeep parked up under the shade of the laurels in the drive, although he was considerably less surprised to find Mrs Vine plying him with Earl Grey and Viennese whirls in the sitting room. Before Leo could say anything Harry leapt to his feet.

'Well, if the mountain won't come to Mohammed, you know – Mrs Vine was just telling me that you're both making plans to take the Barton social scene by storm. Sunday lunches for the local nobs, afternoon tea for the well connected and the upwardly mobile. I suppose I'll have to book to come and visit you from now on?'

Harry embraced him warmly.

Over by the sideboard Mrs Vine, teapot in hand, blushed furiously. Leo grinned, delighted to see him, pleased that Harry had had the foresight to warn him Mrs Vine was still in the room, and touched too that Harry had driven from London in what he had quite reasonably assumed was to be Leo's hour of need. Leo realised that he ought to have known better. It had been Harry who had been there last time too.

Still blushing, Mrs Vine vanished into the bowels of the vicarage to make a fresh brew.

'And?' said Harry, once the door was safely closed.

Leo sighed. 'I don't know whether to laugh, cry or swear.'

Harry took a big bite out of one of the cakes. 'I'd go with profanity every time; something short, ugly and Anglo-Saxon. What I really want to know is if I've got to smuggle you out in the back of the jeep, crouched under a greasy old tarpaulin, flashbulbs going off all around, world weary hacks pressed up against the windscreen, begging for my story.' He played out the whole thing full on, to some imaginary audience.

Leo settled himself in the armchair on the other side of the hearth. 'Fulbright thinks I'm having an affair with Sarah Colebrook. You know, the woman you met at the barbecue? Charming, she is. He's had several phone calls apparently.'

Harry's eyes widened as he choked, and then snorted, peppering the genuine Georgian fire surround with small moist crumbs of cake. 'You're joking?'

Leo shook his head and then laughed. It was a tiny tight laugh that had been threatening all the way home from his audience with Bishop Fulbright. Close behind the first laugh was another, pushing its way forward, eager to be out, and behind that one, another, until by the time Mrs Vine reappeared carrying the refreshed tea tray she was confronted by the unexpected sight of the two normally sedate middle-aged men convulsed with fits of the giggles, red faced, racked and desperate for breath, tears rolling down their faces.

She set the tray down and with a show of mock disapproval shook her head. 'I just don't know what I'm going to do with the two of you. Whatever would Bishop Fulbright say if he could see you now?' Which for some reason made them laugh all the harder.

Mrs Vine folded her face into neutral and made her way back towards the kitchen, relieved that Harry was there. Despite the proposed plans for Sunday lunch, the vicar had been looking very drawn and tired over the last few days. Nothing better than a bit of like-minded company to cheer a body up.

* * *

At the house over in Hevedon, Sarah set the kitchen table. One, two, three, four, five. She counted aloud marking off the places for the people she loved most in the world, or had done; for the people she knew best in the world, or had done. Cutlery and glasses, thick cotton napkins faded from bright orange to the colour of sharp sand by countless trips through the washing machine, a bowl of fruit in the centre. It all looked very inviting. Not dissimilar in style to one of the paintings she had taken to the framer's.

When all this was over it might be a good time to start painting again. Sarah wondered where the thought had surfaced from, but not before imagining the sensual pleasure of drawing a broad bristle brush across a new canvas, and the bite and glide of working a palette knife through thick paint, almost carving the image out from the base clay. How was it she'd forgotten just how much painting fed her soul; she wasn't sure whether it was the smell of onions or the thought of painting that made her salivate, and as fast as it appeared the thought ebbed and faded away.

Outside, on the patio, that backed right up to the open door, Charlie was flapping around in the paddling pool, pouring water from a jug into a bowl, and then through a colander, while trying hard to entice the cat to come and play. From upstairs came the driving heartbeat of bass from Matt's stereo and downstairs in the sitting room Jack was watching television. Outwardly everywhere and everything seemed so very normal. She glanced at the clock, wondering how much longer Chris was going to be and whether she would wait for him, whether serving supper would constitute some grave act of betrayal.

Sarah was stirring the pasta sauce when the van rolled in over the gravel, and almost instantly she felt something snap shut inside her. The sensation was followed by a great rush of heat and air as if she was caught outside in the back draught.

Through the window Sarah watched Chris walking briskly across the yard. She screwed up her eyes, searching for some sign, some symptom that would tell her everything she needed to know, but saw nothing.

'Dad, Dad, look at me. Watch. Look.' Sarah heard the bubbling rumbling tumbling rush of water pouring.

'Great,' said Chris. 'Mind you don't slip over, Charlie. I should get out and get dry if Mum's got tea ready.

'Hi. Smells good, how long before we eat?' he continued, stepping in through the back door, dropping his jacket on to the work top, pulling open the fridge, taking out a can of coke and popping the ring pull.

Sarah stared at him. The sensation of watching someone so intently, someone who had been part of her life for so long and yet having the feeling that despite everything she didn't know him at all, was horribly unsettling.

Across the kitchen he back heeled the fridge door closed and picked the free paper up off the top. Sarah wondered if not looking at her, not catching her eye was part of his plan.

'We were just waiting for you,' she said, careful with the tone. 'Did you have a good day?' Should she say something now? Ask him what was going on, look deep into his eyes to see if she could see any trace of Jenny Beck reflected there. What form would the evidence take? Why couldn't she see it on his face?

'Not bad. Bloody hot out though,' not taking his eyes off the paper, 'I think I'll nip upstairs and have a quick shower, if you don't mind. I'm sweating like a pig.'

Sarah shrugged. 'Sounds fine, there are clean towels in the bedroom,' aware that she didn't say our bedroom, and at the same time wondering how long they could sustain a marriage, any kind of relationship that existed purely on the surface, barely dipping down through into the top layer, the present, the now, too afraid of what may be lurking deep down in darker water. Sarah shivered and scurried the pasta out of the packet and into the pan.

Chris reappeared as she was draining it. The boys took their places around the table and Sarah dished up. It felt like the last supper.

As they ate – Sarah knew that the sauce was good but in her mouth it tasted like liquid sawdust – she told Chris about taking the paintings to be framed. He told her about the turf and trees in Norwich and then they all settled back while Charlie described, with much embroidery and hand waving, the high adventure of going to school on the bus with Matthew.

Across the table, Jack mopped the remains of the rich tomato sauce up with a wedge of French bread and waited for a break in the conversation. 'Is it okay if I go over to see Peter after tea?'

'No,' Sarah and Chris snapped in unison, and in that instant when their eyes met across the table, Sarah felt that she knew the truth and so did Chris, and that if they spoke then, got up from the table and walked outside into the sunshine and said all those things that needed to be said, then maybe there was still a chance that they might claw their way back from the raggedy edge.

Instead Chris broke the eye contact almost instantly, raised his voice and said, 'You'd be a lot better off upstairs getting on with your bloody homework instead of clearing off to see your friends all the time. You spend far too much time gadding about doing bugger all. And you can wipe that smile off your face, Matt, you're no better. You're both bone bloody idle.'

For a moment everyone stared at him. It seemed a pretty outrageous accusation to make to the two boys, who had spent almost all of the previous evening clearing, tidying and sorting out Chris's extended chaos around the yard, and who did more to help around the house than their accuser, whose favourite post-work position was on the sofa in front of the TV with the remote control cradled in his lap. Sarah felt outraged on the boys' behalf but it seemed that that particular truth had been lost along with all the others. And so nobody said anything.

'Got any ice-cream?' said Chris, pushing his plate away and getting up from the table, 'only I thought I'd just go and catch the news.'

Sarah took another look at the clock; the news was long gone but she couldn't find the fuel to argue about that either.

At the door he turned. 'Oh, I'm going to nip round to Barry's and drop off some cleats for those fencing panels in a little while. It shouldn't take very long. All right?'

No, all wrong, Sarah hadn't got the stomach for much more of this. The boys stayed around the table while she went to the freezer, operating on automatic pilot scooping vanilla ice-cream into bowls. She had never really been jealous in her life; it wasn't in her nature, and never been possessive either, so what was this terrible thing that clung to her back, gnawing and scratching and biting at her flesh? Sarah struggled to catch a glimpse of it and realised with a start that what she felt was the most terrible cold hard anger.

How could Chris be such a complete idiot? Was he seriously putting his family on the other side of the scale and weighing them against whatever it was Jenny Beck was offering. Or was she not supposed to care or notice. Sarah squeezed raspberry sauce all over the ice-cream; it looked like the aftermath of a massacre.

'I think we really have to talk,' Sarah said, standing the bowl on the little table by the sofa where Chris liked to arrange his personal effects within reach: the TV remote control, a mug, a can, an origami-ed newspaper, a plastic tub of peanuts, half a tube of Pringles; the contents may change as the year turned but the concept didn't. Here were all the things that kept Chris happy, while ensuring he didn't have to move too far. God forbid that anyone should screw with the shrine to indolence.

He looked up at her wearing an expression altogether too empty, and much, much too bland to be real.

'I was watching that,' he said, waving her aside even though she wasn't blocking the screen.

'Crown green bowls?'

'Uh-huh. It's a damned good game, once you get into it; takes a lot of skill, you ought to watch.' He threw a cupped handful of peanuts into his open mouth.

Sarah sighed, looking for the way in. 'I was talking to Lisa this morning.'

Casually Chris picked up the bowl of ice-cream and stirred sauce through the edge where it had melted. 'Did she get the car done?'

'Chris, I want to talk to you about Jenny Beck.'

Now she had his full attention, if only for a fraction of a fraction of a millisecond, and in his face she saw a flash of terror before the door slammed shut.

'Jenny Beck?' he said, with what sounded like a forced lightness.

Sarah nodded, wondering if he would pretend not to know who Jenny was. He pulled a face, a hapless innocent, bottom lip out kind of face that probably worked when he was a little boy and considerably cuter than he was now.

'What about her?'

She took a deep breath, catching hold of her courage. 'There's a rumour that you are having an affair with her, Chris.' How else could she possibly say it without wasting words and energy? What was there to gain by taking the long way through the woods? Sarah wanted him wrong footed, not with time enough and clues enough to construct solid answers to build into his defensive wall.

'Jenny Beck? Oh yeh right, and I suppose Lisa told you that, did she?' He sounded angry, verging on outraged. 'For Christ's sake Sarah, what do you take me for?'

What indeed? She looked at him, stretched out on the sofa, barefoot, dressed in baggy sweat pants and a buckle-bottomed T-shirt as if seeing him with new and critical eyes. His reaction was too big, too overdrawn to be convincing, and although she dearly wanted to catch hold of every word and believe that every one of them was true, some world weary part of her knew, some terrible old part without hope or illusion understood that Chris was lying through his eye teeth. Worse still Chris wasn't lying to protect her or spare her any pain, but to save himself.

Sarah took another deep breath, not knowing where to go next with the conversation but Chris's eyes had already moved back to the television screen – apparently he had dismissed her, their audience was over, although under one eye she could see a little tic, like fingers tapping nervously on a table top.

'Is that all you've got to say?' she asked.

Sarah looked down at him. 'Chris. I need you to tell me this isn't true, that you aren't screwing Jenny Beck. That this is, this is – oh, I don't know, stupid, crazy, impossible. Please talk to me Chris.' Her voice shook with emotion. 'I'm angry, I'm hurt, I'm afraid and I need you to tell me the truth.'

'The truth? Christ is that all?' He was ridiculously dismissive, and then, as if suddenly finding the inspiration continued, 'People probably saw me talking to Jenny at the barbecue the other night which – I'd like to point out – wouldn't have happened if you hadn't spent all night out at bloody Monica Carlisle's. You know what people are like around here. Add two and two together and before you know it they've come up with some story or other. I'm amazed that you listen to crap like that, Sarah. No, really. I am surprised, someone of your intelligence.'

Sarah was trembling and felt sick. He had barely finished the sentence before being ensnared by the glamour of the astro-turf and middle-aged men in white cheese-cutter caps calling the ends. Sarah turned away in total disgust.

So, it was her fault after all. Of course, she ought to have guessed. Walking back into the kitchen Sarah was so furious that she imagined every step catching light, leaving her exit, her terrible hurt and fury, burnt into the carpet forever.

Not more than half an hour later Chris was parked up in the lay-by just outside Hevedon, sweat rising on his forehead and top lip like a line of glistening bugle beads. He seemed to have spent a lot of time there over the last few days.

Shit, he thumped the dashboard in frustration, finally boiling over with an acute attack of guilt, tension and adrenaline. Deep in his belly, Sarah's pasta sauce ignited a fusillade of indigestion.

She knew exactly what was going on, there was no way Sarah had been fooled. He had seen it in her face, heard it in her voice. Why hadn't he confessed, thrown himself on her mercy, fronted it out and told her that he knew he'd made a terrible mistake, told her that he knew that they could work it out. Couldn't they? Alone with his thoughts, Chris felt more like Jenny Beck's lunch than her lover.

Although, Sarah had no real evidence, she didn't know for certain that anything had happened between him and Jenny, rationalised the part of his brain that planned to be a lawyer when it grew up. Chris back-handed the sweat away. For a few minutes, stripped of all self-pity and all self-delusion, he knew that Jenny Beck was about as benign as a praying mantis.

Sticky, dangerous and ultimately self-seeking, she would eat him alive for her own purposes, with no regrets, no remorse, not so much as a backward glance at the chaos she left trailing in her wake. Chris sniffed. Shit. What the hell was he going to do now?

In the lane a car slowed as it passed him in the lay-by, the driver staring up at the van, and for one awful moment Chris thought that the man, a small elderly man wearing a straw trilby, knew as well. Was there anyone left, in the entire world, that didn't know that he had screwed Jenny Beck?

Chris puffed a little and opened the window right down to the rubber. Calm down, take a deep breath, don't panic. He did have a plan, not much of a plan – it was much the same plan as he had had all the way through – but everyone had to start somewhere.

He would stay away from Jenny, not answer the phone, or his mobile, not return any calls she made, not drop in, not drop by, not go to the pub or the garage – Christ, he should have told Sarah not to go to Burdetts any more, he'd need to spin some yarn about the fuel there being, what? Watered? Weaker? Full of insects and unspecified unpleasantness that would eat the heart out of her Golf with barely a second thought? And if all that failed, then when he wasn't at work Chris planned to hide out in the polythene greenhouse at the bottom of the garden.

'Mum. Phone.'

At Harehill Jenny Beck's eyes snapped open and she sat up with a start, galvanised by the urgency in Peter's voice. Where the hell was she? What time was it? And why was she stark naked on her bed in the middle of what appeared to be the afternoon? Was she ill? Was it flu?

As fast as the panic surfaced it receded, pushed away by the arrival of her memory, and then it *all* came back to her, as warm and pleasant as a bowl full of steamed treacle sponge and custard.

Jenny purred, rolled over on to her belly and then eased herself off the bed, feline now, picking up her robe from the floor as she made her way downstairs, every movement, every gesture a study in eroticism.

Let him wait, let him beg, let him be so desperate to get some more of her that he felt like crawling down the telephone wire to get at her. Jenny smiled, pushing her fingers back through a tangle of hair and took a moment or two to check her appearance in the mirror on the landing. Hot toffee apple. Jenny felt like Sharon Stone as she sauntered down the stairs and picked up the receiver.

'Hallo.' Her voice was a degree or two over-heated and still husky from sleep.

'Oh hi there,' said something bright and breezy, 'my name is Belinda, and I was wondering if we could have a few minutes of your time. We're doing a promotion in your area for replacement windows and conservatories and we're looking for suitable . . .'

Jenny dropped the phone back on to the hook.

'Peter?'

'Uh-huh?' He swung in around the door frame, arms as long as an orang-utan, still dressed in a mishmash of school uniform and PE kit. Jenny pulled her handbag out from under the hall stand.

'Nip down the chippie and get me scampi and chips will you, there's a love.'

He pulled a face. 'But we had chips for tea last night.'

She eased a tenner out of her purse. 'You can have a kebab if the van's there.' Over the years she found nothing was quite as persuasive as bribery.

'And a can of drink?'

Once Peter was gone she put the kettle on and settled down to wait for the phone to ring.

Chris took a few seconds to compose himself before ringing Barry's front doorbell. Lisa answered it on the second ring and judging from the expression on her face she knew all there was to know about his current situation and a lot more besides.

On other days Lisa would have waved him inside without a second thought, pleased to see him, but today he saw the doubt on her face. She held the door close to her body so they talked around a wedge of open space.

'Barry's round the back,' she said flatly, not quite catching his eye. 'Gate's unlocked.'

So much for innocent until proven guilty.

'Right, thanks. And how are you?'

Lisa shrugged. 'So so, and yourself?'

'Fine.' He stuffed his hands in his pockets, a stranger with someone he'd known for the best part of fifteen years, divided by what they both knew but didn't dare mention.

Anxious to be away, he said, 'Okay, well I'll just nip round and see Barry then.' He lifted the hessian sack he was carrying like a trophy and shook it. 'I brought some cleats for that fencing.'

Lisa had got the door shut before he had turned around. Chris shivered, she had made him feel like a leper.

Round the back, Barry was busy brushing dry mix over an interesting combination of paving slabs and cobbles that edged the new driveway. He looked up at the sound of Chris's arrival.

'Well, bugger me, if it isn't Don Juan himself. I'm surprised you can fit me in between all that gardening and getting your leg over.'

Chris flushed crimson. 'Bastard. It isn't like that. Here, I brought you these.'

Barry set the broom up against the wall and taking the cleats nodded his thanks. 'Don't tell me, Jenny Beck is a really amazing woman.'

Chris groaned. 'Amazing doesn't get anywhere near it. What the fuck am I going to do, Barry? This is getting way out of hand.'

Barry picked a can of beer up from the rockery and took a chug on it. 'Multivitamins, plenty of pasta and avoid red meat, you're going to need to keep your strength up now. Rumour has it you're a complete animal.' He rolled his eyes skyward. 'You know, this Jenny Beck is totally wasted selling fish or whatever it is she does, she ought to be in PR. She's done a real number on you, Chris, my boy. Everyone is talking about it; Chris Colebrook, superstud. Maybe I should get her to do something for me.'

Chris slumped down on to a pile of gravel. 'Oh, for Christ's sake. I don't know what to do. She is a piranha.'

Barry peeled another can of beer off the pack and dropped it into Chris's lap. 'That's women for yer, mate. Have you thought about writing your memoirs?'

Chris groaned. 'What the fuck am I going to do, Barry?'

Barry hunkered down alongside him. 'You want my honest opinion?'

Chris waited.

'Grow up.'

Which would have been a very worthwhile piece of advice had Barry not belched and squashed the beer can flat on his forehead immediately afterwards.

Chapter 21

Sarah and Charlie took the cat for a walk round the block after supper, although it couldn't shift the headache that had taken up residence somewhere deep in the front of her skull. As Sarah walked, her brain chased its own tail around and around and around, while springing backwards and forwards over Chris and then Jenny, pawing and digging until she thought her head would explode from the sheer effort of holding so many thoughts in the air at once.

But that was inside, on the outside Sarah, Charlie and the cat appeared to be taking a leisurely evening stroll, meandering along the narrow sunlit summer lanes, down past the dried out pond and then out through the tail end of woodland that bordered their cottage. Ahead of her, Charlie skipped and hopped and sang, solar powered, while the cat schmoozed along behind them both, wearing an imperious expression, tail up. Sarah walked with her arms folded across her waist, defensive, holding the thoughts and the pain and the indignation and the very last remnants of energy close up to her.

The sun was slowly going down, the light softening when they wandered back into the yard. Charlie had a new stick, the cat was hungry. Chris wasn't home, which was a relief, although the phone started ringing the instant Sarah walked in through the back door. If it hadn't been that the sound drilled through her skull like a jack hammer she would have let it ring on until the machine cut in or whoever was calling got bored.

'I wonder if I could speak to Sarah Colebrook, please?'

'Speaking.'

'This is Elizabeth Tomblin, general secretary of the St Barts Trust? I'm not sure if you remember me but we met at the fundraiser last week? I'm delighted to tell you that you've made the short list for the position of assistant at the arts centre.'

Sarah smiled, surprised. 'Oh God, that's wonderful.' She hadn't expected to hear so soon, and wasn't sure – although Leo Banning had said she would be ideal for the job – whether the selection committee would feel the same.

'I hoped you'd be pleased. Although I appreciate that it's terribly short notice but we wondered if you could possibly come for an interview this Friday? We're looking for four part-timers at this stage; I have to say your CV was extremely impressive. What we're hoping is to take on some of the staff prior to opening, to help co-ordinate and arrange various projects, that sort of thing. The summer exhibition of course but there are several other terribly exciting things in the pipeline. Now, Friday, time wise . . .'

Sarah rootled a diary out of her handbag. It felt as if her life was swinging through a great arc, a lantern blown by storm winds. Any jubilation at making the St Barts short list was tempered by a memory, recently rediscovered, of Chris talking to Jenny Beck at the barbecue, standing much too close to each other for casual acquaintances, mirror images of drunken excess. The image did nothing at all for her headache.

After reading for a while to Charlie and having a long soak in the bath Sarah went to bed, leaving the older boys up and the phone off. Despite everything she was asleep in a few minutes, unconsciousness taking her away, the tension ebbing out of her neck and shoulders as she drifted slowly across a midnight blue ocean.

* * *

In Leo's garden at Barton the twilight was as soft and fragrant as antique velvet. Mrs Vine had left for home after making the coffee. Dinner had been magnificent, and now Leo Banning and Harry Fox sat side by side on one of the low walls that edged the terrace. They sipped Pimm's under the stars, silent, but completely at ease in each other's company. It seemed like an eternity before Harry said, 'It's time for you to come back in from the cold, Leo. Come back to town. We all miss you.'

Leo stretched. 'Don't think I'm not tempted, but truly, I love it here.' He was almost as surprised by the words as Harry.

'Tea dances and jumble sales? Come on, you never were that sort of priest, Leo. Where's the fiery zealot we all know and love; out to change the world, determined to make a difference?'

Leo shrugged. 'I didn't say I understood it.'

'You used to be a real crusader; incensed by injustice, outraged by prejudice, because you can't see it out here in the backwoods doesn't mean that it's gone, cured.'

'Maybe I'm getting old.'

'What about Fulbright?'

Leo shrugged. 'He told me today that he's up for retirement in eighteen months. I may hang on and see who follows. I've found a real sense of place here, I never gave myself time to grieve after Tim died – there was always so much to do, all the fundraising for the hospice, the drop-in centre and the night shelter, besides parish business.' He smiled wryly and took another swig of Pimm's. 'That and leaping tall buildings in a single bound. I'd assumed I was excused grief on the grounds that I knew what it was and had seen it so many times before. I had far too much to do, and by filling every waking hour, I thought maybe it would pass me by. Well, it didn't, and out here I've finally found the time and a place to say my goodbyes.' He took another pull on his glass. 'I'm not surprised about the breakdown when I look back, I just wonder that it didn't happen sooner. And there is a lot of work that needs doing out here. It's just more subtle.'

'And you've got the arts centre.'

Leo grinned. 'Tim would have loved it.'

'He would have taken the highest piss.'

'And loved it.'

Harry conceded with a nod of the head. Both of them knew that Leo could never have had what he had with Tim in Barton but it didn't matter now.

Ironically it was death that made it possible to breathe life into the fantasy that he and Tim could have lived happily ever after in the vicarage cosied up under the watchful eye of Mrs Vine.

Leo shivered as if cold fingers had tracked up his spine.

'Chilly?'

Leo nodded.

'Shall we go in now?'

Leo Banning grinned. 'No, I think I'm just fine out here in the cold.'

When Chris got back home from Barry's only Matthew was still awake, curled up in an armchair in the sitting room eating cereal and watching TV. Not that it was particularly late.

'Where's Mum?'

Matthew switched off the video. 'She said she thought she'd got a migraine coming on.'

'Right, well you want to get to bed, too. School tomorrow.'

Matthew didn't bother arguing.

Chris had a thirst. On the way through to the kitchen, he spotted the answering machine blinking in the gloom, noticed the phone was switched off and pressed play. For the first time in a long time he was really interested by what might be on it and stood by, watching the spools slowly turning.

'Hello Chris,' said a female voice over the muted babble of other voices. The hairs on Chris's neck prickled. He glanced over his shoulder, worried who might be within earshot and turned the volume down to something barely above a whisper, wondering what time the call had come in. It took him a few seconds to register that it wasn't Jenny Beck speaking.

'This is Jez, the barmaid from down the Lamb? You forgot to pick up your raffle prize the other night. At the darts on Monday. Anyway I just rang to say you can drop by any time and pick it up. Good thing your telephone number was on the back of the ticket. I wasn't sure that you got the last message, only it's perishable –'

There was nothing else on the tape. Chris wiped it. On the landing he hesitated outside the bedroom door long enough to feel awkward, debating whether Sarah might still be awake, whether she was lying there waiting for him and whether she really did have a migraine.

Matt passed him on the landing, grunting a good night. Still Chris hesitated, hand resting on the door handle. If he didn't go to bed with Sarah, if he went to sleep in the spare room or downstairs on the couch was that tantamount to an admission of guilt? Or was telling Matthew that she had a migraine a veiled suggestion that he sleep elsewhere. Christ. Women.

Chris turned on his heel and went back downstairs. He'd watch a bit of telly and then make up his mind. It wasn't late. Maybe he'd have a drink. Barry had offered him another beer but Chris couldn't afford to lose his licence and had gone on to coffee instead. Lisa had made it grudgingly, not that she had said anything, just looked at him as if he was an axe murderer while he imagined the coffee tasted different; bitter and lukewarm.

There was a film on 4, something with Elstree vampires and squealing half naked girls, running around a fantasy glass fibre castle in floaty, practically transparent nighties. Worth watching, he decided, in a cult, B movie kind of way. Chris poured a tot of Bell's and eased down on to the sofa.

There was a blonde girl – quite obviously not the heroine but a make-weight who was going to get bitten or staked fairly early on, who had the most bizarre jiggly little breasts he had ever clapped eyes on, worth watching for those alone. He fluffed up a comforting surround of cushions, switched off the lights and turned up the volume.

Which was exactly where Sarah found him several hours later when she had woken up to find his side of the bed empty and went downstairs to investigate. Headache gone, she felt a mix of worry and annoyance.

Even so, she was relieved to find him at full stretch on the sofa, glass and bottle on the floor beside him, sound asleep, snoring softly, with his hands stuffed down the front of his tracksuit bottom, presumably cradling that part of his anatomy that he loved the most. Like a comforter. Sarah sighed and went back upstairs. On the TV screen, a man in a cloak was busy biting a girl with enormous breasts. For some reason it seemed a fitting back drop to her thoughts as she headed to the peace and calm and solitude of her bed.

Over at Harehill Jenny Beck slept with the phone beside her bed and dreamt that she had moved into the cottage at Hevedon with Chris and was busy redecorating the kitchen. Peter was handing round fish and chips for everyone while outside in the darkness Sarah pawed at the windows along with Tony Whelk and a man from the Co-op who had short changed her once.

Sarah dreamt that she was at St Barts, sipping a glass of white wine at the summer exhibition along with Monica, Leo Banning, and Adam Gregory. Everyone seemed very pleased to see her, although she had the feeling something important was missing. It took her a while to work out that it was Chris.

Downstairs spread eagled, on the sofa, Chris dreamt of vampires in short nighties, one of whom looked remarkably like Jenny Beck, although he didn't hang about long enough to see if that was actually the case. Running away seemed a far better idea.

Over at Barton, all alone in his king-sized bed, Leo Banning dreamt that he was walking through the garden with Harry and Tim. He couldn't remember a time when he had felt so at ease, so at peace with himself and his life. Sitting under one of the old apple trees he watched the other two head back towards the house and turned his face to the sun, but not before murmuring a silent prayer of thanks.

Over at The Orchards, under the pleated canopy of her four-poster bed, after taking her sleeping tablets, Monica Carlisle fell over the precipice of sleep into a dark moist dreamless place, that made her head ache and her mouth dry.

And in the gardener's cottage, Mac would probably have conjured up some sensual dream time delight, if he hadn't been screwing the arse off the teenage girl from the village who Monica employed to do a bit of cleaning and pack the dishwasher.

Mac could never remember her name, but she was young and ripe, in the way that only teenage girls ever are, with a body that was pleasantly plump now although it held the promise of some serious fat later. She had a very slight cast in one eye which gave her an artful animally expression that really excited him.

Her clothes and hair inevitably smelt of frying but that didn't perturb Mac unduly as they usually began their evening with a shower, or sometimes a swim in the lake. What she lacked in finesse and style the girl more than made up for with sheer enthusiasm and staying power. When she spent the night, she told her mum that Monica needed her to wait at table, and usually left at around five to go and do her paper round.

Mac lay back on the bed, watching the stars through the open bedroom window as the girl slowly worked her way down over his chest. She was particularly talented with her tongue and lips, pressing kisses to the dark V of hair between his nipples, and then working very slowly down over his belly . . . Mac shivered and imagined for an instant that it was Sarah Colebrook. In the instant before the girl took his mind off such matters he decided that he really ought to give Sarah a ring some time soon.

And in his newly renovated cottage, Adam Gregory lay alone in his bed, staring up at the ceiling thinking about Sarah Colebrook too, thinking of ways he could see her again without it looking too obvious and whether he could reasonably ask her out to lunch.

From outside came the sounds of the night, an owl, the soft caress of wind moving through the trees heavy with leaves. He had been thinking about Sarah a lot recently, and wondered why she had cried, and as the idea grew, his mind conjured the tentative press of her lips against his, the delicate smell of her perfume and the way her body felt against him. How very good it had felt to kiss her and hold her in his arms.

Chris was up and gone by the time Sarah got up the next morning. He left a note on the kitchen table, weighed down by the remains of a mug of cold tea:

Sarah – shouldn't be late tonight.
love, Chris.
xx
ps: Don't use Burdetts garage for fuel,
Barry told me that cheap stuff they're buying
in doesn't do your engine any good.

Nor your marriage, Sarah thought ruefully, as she crumpled the note and dropped it into the bin. Even the word love scrawled beside his name gnawed at her. Just how much love did he think it might take?

Wednesdays she didn't go into school. Another half an hour and it would be time to get the boys up but meanwhile Sarah collected the laundry bin from upstairs and began to sort the dirty clothes. When she opened the lid there was an odd smell. It was floral, with an undertone of something musky. She picked up her shirt and sniffed, no. Charlie's pyjamas? Matthew's sweat shirt? No. Rolled up alongside a damp towel was the T-shirt Chris had been wearing when he came in from work the night before. She held it to her face and took a deep breath. Alongside the familiar odour of his body was the smell of perfume. A perfume that she didn't recognise. Sarah sniffed again, wondering if there was any real point in visiting Jenny Beck.

'Under the circumstances I think it's time we moved on, don't you?'

Jenny Beck stared at Tony Whelk as if he was the devil himself.

'I don't know what you mean,' she said. It was later the same morning at around the time Sarah was hanging out Chris's newly laundered T-shirt.

Tony looked heavenwards. 'Don't give me that, woman, everyone is talking about you and that bloody gardener bloke. In the garage, up the shop. Although to be perfectly honest I'm glad you've found someone, Jen. No, really. You're a good woman, I've always said that, and I wouldn't want you to be on your own and he seems like a decent enough chap. What I'm saying, Jenny, is that I want to get this divorce thing sorted out, over and done with once and for all, as soon as we can, really.'

Jenny stared at him across the kitchen table, feeling the colour drain out of her face. This was not what she'd got planned at all. She had wanted revenge yes, and for Tony to be jealous, and okay a little fun along the way, but then she wanted Tony to come to his senses and see what it was he was missing.

'. . . so we can move on. We've got plans,' he was saying.

Jenny caught hold of the back of the chair. The we he was talking about was not him and her.

'Plans?' she said in a low voice.

Tony nodded. 'Come on, Petal. Don't make it sound as if you don't know what I'm talking about.'

She blinked, trying to clear her head. 'But I thought . . .' was all she managed, through the pain and disappointment.

'You thought what?'

Jenny stared at him, trying hard to find the words to explain herself. It felt as if her tongue was too big for her mouth. 'I thought that you wanted to come home.' Her voice sounded reedy and pathetic. 'The other day when you were here – you said she wasn't, well, that you weren't happy. I thought you'd get it out of your system, change your mind, come home, Tony. I thought that's what you meant. Chris Colebrook is nothing, just a flash in the pan, a bit of company, nothing important.'

Tony looked her up and down, rubbing his jaw where Chris had hit him. 'Pity about that, seems like a nice chap to me. And as for not being happy with Linda, you know as well as I do that these things take time. Me and Linda haven't been together that long. It takes a bit of time to settle down to each other's little ways. The thing is she wants to start a family, Jen. And you can see her point, she's only young.'

Jenny swallowed hard, feeling the world open up in front of her; a family? Miss Weigh and Save was only young, that's what he'd said. The inference was that Jenny was no longer young, no longer wanted those things.

'But you've already got a family,' she said unevenly. 'You've got me and Peter.'

Tony straightened his tie. 'Now come on, you know what I mean, Jen. I'm going to talk to my solicitor this morning and try and get the ball rolling. I've got a very fair settlement on the table, Petal. Very fair bearing in mind as how you've already gone out and got yourself someone else.'

'But I haven't,' she began.

Tony must have seen the madness in her eyes because he was already backing very slowly towards the door. 'I'll sort it out, don't you worry, Petal,' was the last thing he said as he closed the door behind him.

When he was gone Jenny picked up the phone and rang Chris Colebrook's mobile, squealing with frustration when she got his answering service again.

The next few days were very strange. Chris spent a lot of time either at work or in the greenhouse and ran a mile every time the phone rang. He and Sarah spoke but they didn't really talk and he skirted around her as if she was an unexploded bomb.

Sarah felt as if she was living inside someone else's life, a life that didn't altogether fit and that, with the best will in the world, she didn't want to grow into.

Jenny Beck willed the phone to ring.

*   *   *

'So how did it go?' Sarah was sailing out of the interview at St Barts on Friday morning with an enormous smile on her face. The voice snagged her sleeve and she swung round to unhook it.

Adam Gregory was standing in the shadows cradling a mug. There was a smell of varnish and paint in the air, and a sense that things were almost ready to be unveiled, but it wasn't that that made something tighten and then back flip in her stomach.

She grinned, and grabbed hold of her composure, convincing herself that she was way too old for a crush. 'Not another tea break, surely?'

'Uh-huh,' he said, raising the mug in salute. 'Care to join me? I've just made a pot.'

She paused weighing the possibilities. Why not. There were so many dark, heavy and hurting things inside her head that it would be nice to step out of the gloom into the sunshine.

'So how did it go?' he asked, opening his office door for her.

Sarah couldn't keep the delight out of her voice or off her face. 'They've offered me the job. It sounds more or less perfect. Few more hours a week than I'm doing now, better money, and the chance to develop my own work. Charlie can come along during the school holidays and join in with the activities.' Her grin broadened out a few degrees. 'In some ways it couldn't be better.' And in lots of others it couldn't be much worse.

'Congratulations, not that I'm surprised really. They would have been mad not to take you on. I saw the paintings you're putting into the exhibition when I dropped my watercolour off at the framer's. You've got real talent there. Now it's official that you're on the staff maybe I ought to buy you your own mug.'

Sarah took the cup he offered. 'How long before the

conversion is complete?' she asked, eager to change the subject, glancing up into the vaulted ceiling above his desk. Adam Gregory must have one of the most spectacular office ceilings in the known world. What she really wanted to ask him was how much longer he would be around, but it sounded much too forward.

'The main project will be completed pretty soon. Under a fortnight.'

Did the disappointment show on her face?

'But that's just the first phase. You're going to have to put up with me for a bit longer yet. Once we've handed over the first phase we're straight into phase two – converting the lady chapel and far end of the transept into self-contained craft workshops and then there's going to be a restaurant. He took a sip of tea. 'Conservative estimate is another year.'

Sarah looked away, not wanting to examine too closely why it was that knowing Adam would be around for another year made her even happier. 'We need a good restaurant round here,' she said conversationally.

'Have you got any plans for lunch?'

Sarah looked up. 'Sorry? That wasn't a hint.'

He waved the words away. 'No, I know that, I was going to nip over to pick up my painting from the framer's. I wondered if you fancied coming along for the ride? We could maybe grab a sandwich on the way?'

Sarah coloured; it was incredibly tempting but that didn't make it right. 'I'd love to but I'm afraid I've already promised to go into school to tell them how I got on.'

He shrugged. 'Another time, then?'

'That would be nice.' It occurred to her that once she started work at the arts centre they would be seeing each other every day and for some reason the thought gave her a real lift.

This was dangerous territory.

Sarah caught his eye and was aware of that little electric burr arcing between them, sharp and blue and compelling. Sarah stood her cup on the edge of his desk, she had drunk less than half. 'I really think I'd better be going.'

Their eyes met again and she shivered, and turned towards the door, wishing that he would call her back, and yet at the same time terrified that he might.

So, that was Friday, Sarah sailed through the interview at St Barts, went into school to tell them the good news and officially handed in her notice at Whitefriars, her leaving coinciding with the beginning of the summer holidays. She planned to spend whatever spare time she had helping to co-ordinate the arrangements for the summer exhibition and setting up a summer holiday arts scheme for under twelves. And when she wasn't doing that Sarah watched Chris, and tried not to encourage the nasty crush she was developing on Adam Gregory.

There were eighteen messages on the mobile phone when Chris finally switched it back on. Not that many of them were actual words. Some were just a breath or two, others tiny tight squeaks of frustration and then when he was considering wiping all of them off, there was one from a woman who wanted her patio de-algaed and a hawthorn hedge pruned back to make way for a pergola, and after a few more squeaks and sighs, two from a man who wanted to know if Chris could recommend a good tree surgeon.

Chris was driving several miles out of his way every day to avoid Jenny's house at Harehill, going by a circuitous route, skirting the perimeter of some imagined emotional exclusion zone. No longer just lying by omission he was living his whole life by omission. He wasn't talking to Sarah, wasn't answering the phone at home, was ignoring the children and when one of the subbies called his name on site it was all he could do to stop himself from running and hiding in the van.

'They're all the same,' said the woman from the garage, topping up Jenny's gin and bitter lemon with the dregs of the bottle. 'Love you and leave you.'

Jenny sniffed. 'I thought that Chris was different.'

'We all always think they're different,' said Nita, from the chippie, shaking up her bag of pork scratchings so that she could get at the little salty fragments wedged in the crease at the bottom.

It was a while since their single, glorious, afternoon of passion, and Jenny was past the sobbing stage and had reached the affronted, hurt, humiliated slightly paler, slightly thinner and interesting stage of recovery. That Chris hadn't rung after the event had cored her down to the quick; that Tony hadn't been driven mad with jealousy and rushed back home had – strangely – hurt far less.

A little unsteadily Jenny headed off towards the toilets. From behind the bar, Jez, the barmaid, beckoned her over. 'Eh, Jenny, that bloke you were in here with, Chris? He still hasn't been round to pick up his raffle prize so I've stuck it in the freezer.'

Jenny stared at her. 'Done what?'

'When you were in here with him the other week he won a fresh cockerel. Well, it was fresh then, it's frozen now, I've rung him a couple of times but he hasn't been round to fetch it yet. D'you want to take it for him?'

Jenny thought for a minute, a plan formulating, fuelled by an excess of Gordon's gin.

'Yeh, yeh all right,' she said, 'can you keep it in the freezer until I go home?'

Jez looked heavenward. 'I'm hardly going to get it out and leave it on one of the tables, am I? Just don't forget it. The boss is getting a bit arsy about the space it's taking up. Reckons if he leaves it in there much longer she's gonna charge him storage.'

Chapter 22

'So,' Sarah mumbled, thinking aloud, working a finger down the list pinned to the notice board, letting the programme of activities for the day form and re-form in her head. 'Pick up glasses from the off-licence, green napkins, floating candles, iron dress.'

Charlie stood beside her, thumb in mouth, looking up in awe, enthralled by the unfolding litany. 'Iron dress, like armour?'

Sarah smiled down at him. 'Like crease free.'

It was very early on a Thursday morning just over a fortnight since Chris had spent the afternoon in bed with Jenny Beck and the morning after Jenny had picked up the frozen cockerel from the Lamb. It was also the morning of the private view for St Barts first summer exhibition; Sarah was excited, pleased and anxious but mostly preoccupied.

Charlie, already dressed in his school uniform, grey shorts and white polo shirt, saw it as his role to murmur the responses. 'Glasses, napkins, cangles, dress,' he whispered.

Matthew was still upstairs in the shower, God alone knew where Jack was, although Sarah really hoped that he was up, there was no time for a tussle this morning. She was due in school early to help organise the costumes for the year five assembly; Noah's ark – the PVA coating on tusks and an emergency pair of antlers were still drying on top of the fridge. Sarah cast a fond glance in their direction, knowing she would miss the wildlife and the childish sense of joyous expectation once she moved permanently to St Barts. At the moment life was a mad balancing act, and not only at work.

Across the kitchen, Chris was hunched over the breakfast table reading the paper. He was looking quiet, but then again over the last couple of weeks he had spent a lot of time looking quiet when it was quite obvious to Sarah that just below the surface he was raging and roaring, though she was loath to disturb the illusion of calm.

When he didn't think she was looking Chris wore a hunted uneasy look, and at other times – when he wasn't snapping or snarling at everyone – was closed off and totally unreachable. Sarah wasn't certain that she wanted to try and pick the lock that would open him up, afraid of what she might find lurking inside.

'What time do you think you'll be home?' she asked.

Over the last couple of weeks Chris had been arriving home later and later, as if shutting down the time they had together alone to an absolute minimum. At first she had wondered whether he was going to see Jenny, but he arrived home dirty and exhausted, as if he was trying to purge the things that were eating away at him through sheer hard work.

'Maybe seven, perhaps a bit later.'

'The preview starts at seven thirty.'

He watched her lips moving as if the words had got absolutely nothing to do with him.

'The preview?' she repeated. 'At the arts centre? New job, the thing that has consumed my every waking thought for the last fortnight?'

He nodded and finished the last of his tea. 'The preview?'

'At the arts centre. You said that you were going to be there.'

Chris seemed to spring in a single disconcerting bound from complete indifference to sharp annoyance. 'Did I say that I wouldn't be there? Did I say that? I'll be there, I might be a little late that's all. What's happening with the kids?'

Sarah flinched, resisting the temptation to snap back at him. It was too early in the morning and she had too much to do to risk pitching into a full-scale row that would rub everyone's fur up the wrong way.

'I'm taking Matthew over to see his girlfriend, Jack's going to bike over to Phillip's after school and I'm taking Charlie with me, although I suggested Matthew could come to the exhibition if he likes. The committee's invited the high school's art students.'

Chris nodded; this was acceptable, apparently she had his seal of approval.

'And what time do you think this thing'll finish? Only I've got to be on site by six tomorrow morning, they're bringing the timber for the pergola.'

'Not late, ten, half past at the latest.'

Chris folded the paper and got to his feet. 'Bit late for Charlie on a school night, isn't it?'

'I thought maybe you could bring him home with you. I didn't think you'd want to stay there all night.'

'Oh right, so you want me to come, don't want me to stay, just put in an appearance, take Charlie off your hands and then bugger off home. Very nice.'

Sarah felt a fist tighten up inside her solar plexus. 'No,' she began evenly, 'that wasn't what I meant at all.' But she could see his expression close like a door before she could say anything else. There was no way they could go on like this. Whatever it was between them was drawn as taut as a bow string.

'It's all right, it doesn't matter,' she said, turning away, making every effort to keep her tone neutral. 'Get there when you can. I'll sort something out for Charlie.'

Charlie pulled a face. 'But I don't want to be sorted out.'

Once upon a time Chris would have grinned and

launched himself into the void, make the effort, offered his help despite his earlier words, backtrack, but they both knew that something had radically changed.

He picked up his jacket and the keys to the van. 'See you later, then. I'll try and get there as early as I can.' He made no effort to sound sincere.

Sarah nodded, not trusting herself to speak. She'd ring Lisa or her mum. Up at the table now, Charlie was busy driving a small blue truck through a puddle of milk. As Chris left he lifted a hand in farewell and made a revving engine noise.

'Is it all right if Jack and Phil come round after school?'

Jenny Beck looked up from her mug of tea in surprise. 'What?'

Jenny hadn't seen hide nor hair of Jack Colebrook since Sarah had stayed out all night.

Peter carried on spreading Marmite on to his toast. 'I meant to ask last night. Only Jack's staying over at Phil's, cos his mum's going out, and I thought they could come here, you know, after school, play on the Playstation and stuff. Don't mind, do you?'

Jenny shook her head, tucking the information away in a quiet corner of her mind. 'Did you say Jack's mum's going out?' she asked a few minutes later, casually, handing him a mug of tea.

'Uh-huh, she's got this new job, there's an exhibition on tonight or something.'

So Sarah was going to be out, and outside in the garage, lurking in the back of Tony Whelk's last remaining industrial freezer was a frozen cockerel with Chris Colebrook's name on it. Jenny smiled. She felt Part B of the plan coming on.

It wouldn't take very much to find out where Sarah was going to be, and for how long. Jenny waited until Peter had left for school and then picked up the phone. Three phone calls and less than half an hour later and she knew everything, except of course whether Chris was going to be going to the St Barts' summer exhibition private view with Sarah. She sucked her bottom lip and weighed up the possibilities; the only real option was a stakeout.

Jenny slid the cool box out from under the kitchen sink and then went to see if she had any of the ice packs already frozen; it would be a waste to let the chicken go off.

Sarah took one last walk around the exhibition, admiring the overall effect of the paintings, the lighting and the various pieces of sculpture arranged around the newly completed hall. Although she didn't officially begin work at St Barts until the tail end of July, Sarah had really enjoyed giving a hand to get the summer show up and running.

They had continued the work in progress motif with industrial polythene and ivy as a back drop to a wide range of visual arts – there were paintings, drawings, sculpture, ceramics, an amazing selection of pieces that reflected a range of local talent.

Sarah's work hung in an alcove near the door, in the bay adjacent to the contributions made by the construction workers, staff and members of the committee. As the pictures had gone up she was surprised how eager she was to see what Adam Gregory's work would look like, and now, walking back down the hall she found herself seeking it out amongst the rest.

It was quite small, a long thin panel, drawn in pen and ink on heavy laid paper. The paper had been cropped to deliberately echo the buildings in the picture, tall narrow houses with peeling shutters and flower-filled balconies, either side of an alley, the sunlit centre garlanded by row after row of washing. Perspective drew the eye down into cooler shadows of the narrow cobbled street. Although the buildings themselves had been executed with an almost architectural precision, what made the picture exciting was the use of colour, colour that somehow managed to suggest the sunlight and heat in the faded old plaster work and the smell of geraniums mixed with the soft perfume of soap and sheets drying in a warm wind.

'Looking good.'

Sarah turned round to smile at Leo Banning who was watching her progress through the large double doors that opened up into a glazed atrium.

'It certainly is,' she said. 'And all this from the locals. It's incredible really.'

'Anything I can help with?'

She shook her head. 'I don't think so, I've said I'll pick up a couple of spare boxes of glasses from the off-licence on the way home but other than that I think everything is more or less under control. Or at least that's what I've been told to say.'

He chuckled and put his hands in his jacket pockets. 'You're settling in here all right?'

Sarah nodded, aware that he was hanging back, dithering as if there was something else he wanted to say. She lifted her eyebrows and smiled. 'And?'

Leo pulled a face and lowered his voice. 'I need to talk to you, Sarah, although I'm not altogether sure where to start or whether this is the place, really. There have been some rumours.' His voice dropped away. Leo looked as uncomfortable as she had ever seen him, and felt herself redden furiously, wondering what on earth he had heard and worse still what he might believe, but before she could say anything Leo continued. 'This is terribly difficult. I'd just like to point out that my interest in you is purely paternal. Patronly rather than – well, you know – anything else.'

Sarah blinked, bemused. 'I'm sorry? I'm not with you, Leo.'

Leo waved a hand around, a gesture which he obviously hoped would explain everything, and then he said, 'Apparently there have been several calls to the bishop's office about our relationship.' He shifted his weight, and ran a finger around inside his collar. 'I've got no wish to compromise your position here, Sarah. You should know you're here through your own merit, not my influence. I wasn't going to say anything at all, but this morning Adam – Adam Gregory and I were speaking and ... Well, under normal circumstances I think it is a mistake to give gossip any validity by repeating it but as it might have an effect on your new position, I just wanted to ensure that you were all right about it.'

He was scarlet, Sarah was really none the wiser, and then slowly like the tide rising Sarah caught a glimpse of what Leo was trying to tell her.

'There have been calls to the bishop about you and me? About us?' She tried hard not to sound incredulous in case she offended him.

Leo's focus sharpened. 'You hadn't heard about it? Oh, good God, I'm so sorry. I'd assumed that you knew.' He held up his hands again, this time in a gesture of apology. 'I'm sorry, I don't know what to say now.'

She heard Leo hastily retreat behind a wall of embarrassment and waved the words away, while painting on something approximating a smile. 'I've heard lots of things on the grapevine. Up until now I had no idea who I was supposed to be having an affair with.' She laughed; it wasn't any more convincing than the smile.

His eyes widened and then he said, 'I'm not sure what to say.'

'I don't think there is anything you can say really. I'm very grateful for your concern, Leo, although I'm not sure what we can do about this. I would have thought the wisest move would be to carry on exactly as we are now.' She paused to see if he had any other suggestions and was relieved when he said nothing. 'I've got to go now, I'll see you tonight.'

Still Leo didn't move. Sarah looked at him and was horrified to feel her eyes filling up with tears. Leo's expression conveyed more sympathy than Sarah could handle.

'My first instinct,' he said in a low, even voice, 'is to put my arm around your shoulders, but under the circumstance I think perhaps that's a little unwise.'

Sarah felt a single tear roll out on to her cheek. 'Things are a real mess at the moment,' she said. Just beneath the surface she could sense a great raw sliver of emotion she'd barely been aware of. 'I'm grateful that you told me.'

'I'm sorry to make things more complicated. If you need to talk –' he left the invitation open.

Sarah saw him relax a little, far more comfortable in the role of shepherd than adulterer.

'Thank you.'

Leo smiled.

One thing Sarah did think about as she hurried back out into the foyer was that Leo had been talking about her to Adam Gregory. She couldn't help wondering what they had said, and also if either of them had heard the other end of the rumour. Thinking about Chris made her glance up at the clock.

Lisa had promised to pick Charlie up from school and so now all Sarah had to do was go home, collect the glasses, then take a long leisurely fragrant bath, take ages with her hair and make-up and iron her dress.

At the main doors Sarah stretched. Making a conscious effort to dissipate the tension in her belly, she stepped out into the sunshine and tried hard to focus on the next few hours, shifting the emphasis away from Leo's revelation. After a few seconds, Sarah smiled and shook her head, fancy anyone thinking she'd be interested in Leo; she had always assumed that he was either gay or celibate, or possibly both.

Over at Harehill Jenny Beck had had her shower and was planning what to wear with care too. She'd trawled through the wardrobe looking for something comfortable, not too obvious for out and about, but with a subtle hint of sexual promise. Something with a zip down the front would be good. At the back of the cupboard, hanging under an evening dress she found just the thing she was looking for.

Jenny planned to get to the end of the lane that led to Chris's house by around half past six; plenty of time yet.

Jack had already arrived at her house and while handing out the ice-cream and Coca-Cola Jenny had managed to bend the conversation through a hundred and eighty degree loop to find out what time dads – Jack's dad in particular – were likely to get home. Late these days apparently.

Jenny loosened the belt of her bathrobe and added a little perfume, behind her ears, behind her knees and in the warm valley between her breasts before slithering into the zipper dress. She checked the mirror, and undid the zip another inch, deciding that on balance a little bit more cleavage was fine now that she had the figure for it.

At Hevedon Matthew got home half an hour or so after Sarah. They shared a glass of juice in the kitchen which seemed very civilised. It felt as if it had been a long time since Sarah had had time alone with her eldest son. He offered to throw something in the microwave for them both while she went and had her bath.

'Can I have the car keys to stick my bag and stuff in the boot, Mum?'

Sarah was halfway across the landing, wrapped in a freshly laundered bath sheet that she'd hidden in the bottom of the airing cupboard for that exact purpose.

'Sure, love. The keys are on the hook, just be careful, there are glasses in there.'

And then she slipped down into the deep bubbly-blue water and closed her eyes. So, she was supposed to be having it off with Leo Banning. Sarah grinned and shook her head in disbelief, wondering who the hell had thought that one up, and she then let the warm water ease away the last of the aches and the tension. Something sensible told her the gossip would blow over given a little time, anyone who knew Leo or come to that Sarah, would surely realise that they just weren't the type.

At the arts centre the first of the workshop areas were almost ready for hand over; Adam had taken her on a whistle stop tour of the space she'd be working in through the summer, and as the water soothed away everything but the memory, Sarah imagined her paintings stacked up against the wall of the workshop, and the tantalising smell of linseed oil and turps, and shivered.

Oddly enough in her imagination Adam Gregory was watching her from the doorway, cradling a mug of tea. She decided not to edit him out; it gave her a good feeling to know that he was around.

Chris Colebrook missed meeting Sarah at the cottage by no more than ten minutes Jenny estimated. She had seen Sarah drive out towards the main road with her eldest boy in the front seat at just after half past six and some part of her knew that it wouldn't be long before Chris put in an appearance. She tore the silver foil off a packet of extra strong mints. Nothing worse than bad breath.

Right on cue the van swung in off the bypass. Chris Colebrook barely slowed before he pulled into the driveway. He looked preoccupied and tense, poor little lamb.

In the arts centre car park Sarah popped the boot open and swore under her breath; Matthew had taken care with the flat packs of glasses all right. It appeared that to make room for his rucksack and guitar he had taken them out. She checked the back seat – they weren't there either. Where the hell had he put them?

In the front porch apparently; after she'd finished speaking to Matthew on the phone Sarah rang home. Chris wasn't there so she left a message on the machine asking him to bring the glasses with him when he came in.

'Damn, look I'm sorry, I've got to go, there's the phone,' said Chris. The sound of the beep and then Sarah's voice recognisable but incomprehensible headed out towards the back door.

Chris had just got out of the shower and pulled on tracksuit bottoms and a T-shirt to answer the door, and discovered Jenny Beck standing there done up to the nines.

For some reason best known to herself Jenny was carrying a large tartan cool box. She stood in the open doorway, framed by the early evening sunlight. She smelt of perfume and the soft heat of a hungry body.

He started to back away as some little thing, that whatever-it-was that had both warned and ensnared him last time around, tingled and glowed low down in his belly.

Jenny looked up at him with dark hooded eyes and stepped into the kitchen.

Chris fought the temptation to whimper.

'I brought you your raffle prize,' she murmured, sliding the cold box across the floor. 'I thought you might have been round to see me. I've missed you.'

'I've not been well,' he said in a tiny voice, still backing away, but it was far too little, much too late. Jenny was after him like a cat on a gerbil; he felt the table top hit him squarely in the buttocks, stumbled backwards, trying to regain his equilibrium, but by then she was on him and he was powerless to resist. Somewhere close by his conscience groaned and covered its eyes.

'Oh Chris,' she said, wriggling and giggling and rubbing herself up against him. 'We can't do it here, someone might see us. Not here, oh no – can't we go upstairs?'

He had no idea what she was talking about until, opening his eyes, he saw that by some strange quirk of fate he had one hand halfway up her thigh while the other appeared to be busy unzipping her dress. Surely they couldn't be his hands?

Deep inside his head, the tinned fruit trolls appeared to have stormed the Bastille and taken control again, while making obscene little lip smacking noises. And then he was kissing her, could feel her tongue rammed halfway down his throat, and the press of her not inconsiderable breasts against his chest and then – before he knew it – they were both halfway upstairs, shedding their clothes as they went.

Although some part of him was aware of everything, every little decision and its consequences, Chris decided not to listen to its increasingly high-pitched, anxious voice and instead followed the instinctive homespun lusty wisdom of the tinned fruit trolls, whose needs were altogether more obvious.

'Sarah. Hi.'

Adam Gregory slipped his hands around her waist and held her lightly, pressing a kiss to each cheek, which instantly flamed blood red, despite the fact that his touch and the kiss were meant to be filial rather than erotic.

'You look fantastic,' he said, pulling away a little to admire her. 'Great dress.'

Sarah's colour intensified. He looked pretty tasty himself in faded Levis and a grey T-shirt. She was wearing a soft long cotton shift dress in rich terracotta that clung to every curve and made the most of her tan and big blue eyes. It could have been made for her, although it wasn't; she'd bought it from Barnado's for £3.50 earlier in the week. No need for Adam to know that though.

'Glad you like it.'

'Do you want another drink?' He indicated her wine glass, with its half-inch of orange juice in the bottom.

Sarah shook her head. 'No, I'm fine. Actually I'm just on my way out, I left some glasses at my place; it looks like we're going to be needing them later.' She paused, wondering whether she ought to wait for Chris to show up – would he be offended and angry if she went home to collect them after asking him to do it, one more insult implying that he was incapable? Then again if he wasn't home and hadn't got the message; a few more people drifted in through the doors. Their arrival helped Sarah make a definite decision to nip home. At least then she could relax and enjoy the evening.

Adam took her glass anyway.

'I won't be very long.'

He grinned. 'No worries. I'll have it ready for you when you get back.'

He made her feel good. Dangerous ground, whispered a voice in her head.

'I was wondering if we could have that lunch some time? If you'd like to –'

Sarah stopped dead. His turn to go red now; the words had sounded clumsier than she knew he meant. The dangerous ground was far, far closer than she had imagined. Formulating her reply with the utmost care, aware that she sounded like a cliché, Sarah said, 'I'd really like to Adam but I don't think I can at the moment. I'm sorry.'

He looked embarrassed. 'I shouldn't have asked. Sorry.' He was backing away physically and emotionally.

Sarah reached out and touched his hand. 'No, no I'm glad you asked me. If things were different then I'd say yes in a second. Really.' She paused, feeling her way forward into the warm uncharted space between them. 'Really . . .' she repeated, her voice fading, she let her eyes drift off into the middle distance; this was the moment when she should say she was happily married, that she loved Chris and that there was no way she would ever go out with Adam, ever, but the words dried in Sarah's throat and she blushed. 'I've got to go.'

The main hall was already quite full and there were small pockets of conversation in the foyer, with other people gathered around the bar and the buffet table, laughing and talking. More people wandered into the exhibition area, sipping wine, and slowly ambled around the gallery space admiring the images. Sarah looked back over her shoulder to see if she could still see Adam and wondered why seeing him and hearing his voice had become so important to her.

'Yum yum.'

Sarah spun round to be confronted by Mac and Monica walking towards her, arm in arm.

'Not off already surely,' said Mac, eyeing her with all the tact of a stock breeder. 'The evening has barely started.'

'Stop it, Mac,' Sarah snapped. 'I'm not playing, I'm at work.'

He grinned. 'And very nice you look too. I may have to sign up for one of your courses. I wondered when you'd like to come over to lunch again. How about tomorrow. I've missed you, you know. Maybe we can begin again where we left off?'

If he was trying to make her feel uncomfortable it was working.

Monica glared at Mac and then prodded him with her

lorgnette. 'Sorry, darling, I forgot to bring his leash. It looks good – what's the wine like?'

'Fine. Look I've got to go, but I'll be back in a few minutes.'

'Oh, but surely you don't have to go yet, do you?'

Mac stepped forward to block her exit and as he did ran his tongue over her shoulder. Annoyed, Sarah pushed him away, resisting the temptation to slap his handsome smug face.

She could see Adam now, over by one of the pillars, looking at her and also Leo heading in their direction. Mac was so close that she could feel his breath on her skin. It felt as if she was being trapped in a pincer movement.

And then she heard another voice, something young and giggly with a little country burr. 'I didn't know you were going to be here, Mac. You never said nothing about it the other night.'

To her amazement Mac froze. She practically saw his hackles rise.

A teenage girl, maybe seventeen or eighteen at the most, sidled up to him. She was wearing a tiny little halter top with shoestring straps and trousers so tight it looked as if they had been sprayed on. Every toenail and every fingernail was painted a different colour glitter polish. Her hair looked as if it had been cut with a hacksaw and was clipped back from her face with lots of little glitter strewn butterflies.

Mac did not look happy, whereas the girl looked as if she had just stumbled across the holy grail. She rubbed up against him like a plump little heifer, hands flat on the front of his midnight blue velvet jacket, and then leant over and whispered something in his ear. He shivered. She was chewing gum and her nails were gnawed down to the quick.

Sarah was astonished to see Mac's colour drain.

'Er hello,' he said, all his bluster gone.

The girl grinned and then ran her tongue around the top of his ear. Mac whimpered.

Trailing behind, in the wake of the first girl were half a dozen other giggling jiggling ripe little munchkins, who crowded around him. Mac rolled his eyes like a terrified horse and waved frantically to Monica and Sarah as they fairly swamped him.

Monica winked and motioned Sarah away. 'Leave him be. I rather think our cocky little stud has finally met his match. She's not sophisticated enough to be taken in by any of his stupid little games.'

The girl had settled her head on Mac's shoulder now.

'They make a lovely couple don't they?' Monica said.

Sarah grinned and slipped away, through the crowd and out into the car park.

There were still people arriving, accompanied by a buzz of conversation. Outside summer hung in the air like perfume and the evening sun touched everything with gold highlights. Music tracked her across the asphalt, the soft strains of a jazz standard, and for a few moments Sarah stood and breathed deeply. She had a sense of real delight; maybe there was a god, maybe everything was going to be all right after all.

The drive back home through the countryside to Hevedon continued the upward trend, the landscape conspiring to make her smile. She began to think about Chris, wondering whether their paths would cross en route. Thinking about him made her think that it was time they sorted this thing out, all this had gone on for too long. Whatever it was that had happened – it was poisoning the pair of them.

He looked so unhappy and she felt the same. She loved Chris too much to let this glitch strangle and tangle and destroy the two of them. The thought helped lift some dark energy in her soul, and lever the idea of Adam Gregory out of her consciousness, so that when she drove into their yard Sarah was light as air. Maybe it was time to just let everything go and start again.

Chris's van was parked in the yard. The back door to the cottage was open. Inside Chris's shirt was slung on the kitchen table. There was a trainer and a damp towel on the hall floor. Sarah smiled wryly as she picked them up and then shook her head. God, that man really was a slob.

The boxes of wine glasses stood in the front porch where Matt said he'd left them and Sarah was about to call to let Chris know she was there when she heard a noise, an odd noise that made every hair on the back of her neck stand on end.

Sarah waited in the hall with one hand on the bannister, one foot on the first step, frozen stiff, every molecule of her body charged and wired and glowing with some terrible surety. And then she heard it again; an appalling throaty giggle right on the very edge of audible, and in that instant Sarah knew everything.

She knew that Chris was upstairs in their room, in their bed screwing Jenny Beck. She knew that the rumours were all true. And worst of all she knew, without any shadow of a doubt, that even if there was a way back from this place she no longer had the energy or the inclination to try and find it.

The realisation dragged a sob up from her belly that she forced back down again. It felt as if everything she knew, everything she trusted had been destroyed by that one tiny noise.

As her gaze, fuelled by adrenaline, scanned the stairs she saw a single sandal – a sandal that didn't belong to her – and further along the landing its twin. Close by was a bundle of cloth that Sarah suspected was underwear, and a dress and a pair of tracksuit bottoms. As she examined the evidence her feet began propelling her upstairs without any conscious decision on her part.

One, two, three, up and up, across the landing towards their bedroom, the giggly noise and a whole chorus of others getting louder and louder, more defined, less excusable or defendable, pulling her closer like magnets. There was no mistaking their meaning and then she got to the open doorway. Sarah stood there for no more than a heartbeat or possibly two before she had seen everything she needed to see.

The face she recognised was there, the one Chris wore when he was making love to her, something vague and unfocused, slightly slack around the jaw, as if every single brain cell was busy elsewhere seeking out sensation not logic, and it was this expression that disturbed her far more than the sweating heaving butcher's shop of naked limbs tangled and bent, that blank open face, switched off to everything but the pursuit of pleasure. Pleasure with Jenny Beck.

Neither Chris nor Jenny were aware that she stood there watching them. Unseeing, unthinking, Sarah turned back and walked very slowly across the landing, downstairs, one, two, three, picked up the glasses from the front porch, got into the car and drove back to St Barts.

Adam Gregory was waiting for her in the foyer with a glass of orange juice and that lazy easy smile that suited him so well.

'Okay?' he asked. The sound of his voice broke the spell. His expression registered concern but it was when he touched her arm that Sarah started to shake, shake so hard that she didn't think she would ever be able to stop.

Chapter 23

'So, where do you want this to go, and what the fuck is in it?' gasped Mac, struggling in through the back door carrying an enormous cardboard carton on his shoulders. He appeared to be buckling at the knees.

Sarah, no make-up, hair tied up in a scarf, sleeves rolled up on an old shirt, glanced at the label. 'Books and games, boys' bedroom, first right at the top of the stairs. It does say it's heavy.'

Mac groaned, 'Whoever wrote that is a master of understatement, I thought the boys were going to be here to help with all the moving.'

Sarah, who was busy lining the kitchen cupboards with paper, smiled indulgently. 'They have been, unlike some people I could mention. They've just gone back to the other house to get the last few bits and pieces. Bikes, that sort of thing.'

Right on cue there was the sound of a van pulling up outside in the drive, sides scraping along the hawthorn and elderberry bushes that lined the driveway. Sarah pushed aside the kitchen curtain. Seconds after the engine died Monica and the boys tumbled out of the hire van. Charlie came following up the rear carrying a blue plastic spade, a teddy bear and a policeman's helmet.

'Here come the cavalry.'

'Thank Christ for that,' groaned Mac. 'Do you want me to put the kettle on?'

'You've only carried two boxes in,' she said incredulously.

'Two very heavy boxes,' Mac protested, slumping down at the table in the centre of the room. 'And anyway I can't be very long. I've got a previous engagement.'

Sarah lifted an eyebrow. 'Date with Lolita?'

Mac sniffed. 'Do I detect the slightest whisker of envy there? It could have been you, you know, Sarah. Besides I'm totally enamoured with her and all her earthy little ways.'

Sarah sliced off another square of wallpaper from the roll and smoothed it on to the shelf. 'And her nose ring and Gameboy?'

Mac growled, as Monica pushed open the kitchen door. She was carrying a picnic hamper.

Mac grinned. 'Ah, at last, Lady Bountiful.'

Monica eyed him up and down. 'Hands off. It's not for you,' and then turned her attention to Sarah. 'How's it going? Do you think you're going to be all right here. I've had the chimneys swept and the roof sorted out and I'll get my man to come over and trim back the hedges. It's a tiny bit Briar Rose round the back – it might be a bit draughty, it's been a while since anyone lived here.'

Sarah cast her eyes around the mellow lines of the kitchen, a twin to Mac's on the other side of the lake.

'It's lovely, it's perfect. I don't know what I'd have done without you Monica.'

Monica laughed. 'You won't be saying that when the wind is blowing down the chimneys and the windows rattling out of their frames.'

The majority of unpacking and work in the kitchen was finished; the walls had been painted cream, there was a bright rug on the flag stone floor, a housewarming present from Lisa, the cupboards were filling, and a ragtag and bobtail collection of furniture Sarah had bought from the Salvation Army shop in Lynn arranged around the room. It looked homely and inviting in an unfamiliar way. The rest of the cottage was much the same.

Sarah hadn't wanted to take anything from the house in Hevedon; just the boys' things and her personal possessions, the paintings from the landing, clothes, books. Odd how little there was she wanted despite having chosen every stick of furniture, every picture, every yard of fabric. It seemed so little to show for all those years of being together, barely a van load when it came to it.

The oddments of furniture had vanished into Monica's cottage as if they had been made for it.

Sarah pushed the back door to, despite it being the tail end of a bright sunny day she could already feel the year turning. Matthew and Jack started to crocodile the last few things upstairs into their new bedroom under the eaves, bed linen, books, tapes, CDs, an angle poise lamp, the things that would give them a sense – eventually – of being at home.

Sarah filled the kettle. 'Did you see Chris while you were there?'

'Uh-huh, he wanted you to know that he's sorry, and that he doesn't blame you for leaving.'

Sarah nodded, not catching her eye, and went on a hunt for the teapot. The things she felt about Chris weren't for public consumption, at least not yet.

It was nearly ten by the time Sarah finally pulled off her headscarf and rubbed her hair back into life. Her back ached; she felt dirty and tired and ready for bed. In the kitchen she saved herself the remnants of Monica's picnic supper and opened a bottle of wine she had thoughtfully included to go with it.

Matt had lit the Rayburn to burn off the evening chill, and now as the day died it creaked and ticked as it settled in the fireplace. Henry, the cat, had taken up residence on the rug in front of the hearth and looked for all the world as if he had been there forever.

Gazing around the room, despite the air of disconnection and displacement, Sarah knew that she would be all right. The cottage didn't feel like home yet but it would; the question was what would she feel like by the time that had happened.

It was only a matter of weeks since she'd found Chris in bed with Jenny Beck. Other women might have forgiven him, and realistically, up until the moment it had happened Sarah had always thought she would have been amongst them. She was almost as surprised as Chris when she told him she was moving out. He had been devastated, begged and pleaded, told her Jenny Beck was a brainstorm, no more than a flash in the pan.

Watching him wriggle, listening to him whine and wail and justify himself, Sarah knew all those things – finally – were true, but also knew that she didn't have the energy or the desire left to sort it out, to be forgiving or under-standing or even angry – she was tired of it all. Tired of being wrong, tired of being judged, tired of having to sort life out, tired really, of being married.

From upstairs Sarah could hear the soft thump, thump, thump of music from Matt and Jack's room. In the little back bedroom Charlie had fallen asleep almost before his head had touched the pillow. He was exhausted by the move and the undercurrent of emotion – and in that he wasn't alone. Sarah didn't feel that much different. She pulled a chair up close to the Rayburn and prised open the doors. Inside the coals grabbed a breath of air and glowed cherry red. Sarah sighed, letting the tiredness claim her.

Half a glass into the wine she heard a car pull up outside; at least it wasn't the van. Maybe it was Monica coming back to check on her; the last thing Sarah wanted was to come face to face with Chris tonight, tonight or any night. Stretching she headed for the door.

'Hello?' said a familiar voice, almost before she had chance to open it.

'Adam?'

He laughed. 'Don't sound so surprised, I'm sorry it's so late but I've just been to a meeting and was passing. I thought I'd drop off your housewarming present. Am I disturbing you?'

'Not at all. Mind your step,' she said. Stacked up outside the door was a pile of cardboard boxes and balls of rolled newspaper, debris from the move.

Adam eyed the boxes ruefully. 'Moving is such a pain in the arse. I was serious about my offer to give you a hand, you know.'

Sarah beckoned him inside, horribly aware that she looked as if she'd been grubbing around up chimneys all day. 'Thanks, it was really appreciated, but it would have put me in a difficult position.'

He nodded. 'I know, that's why I didn't push it, but the offer was genuine.'

He followed her back into the kitchen that Sarah already knew was going to be the heart of the house. The lights were low, the open stove gave off a whisper of heat and on the table were the remains of supper on a dish covered with cling film.

'Would you like some tea, coffee? Or a glass of wine?' She indicated the bottle.

'Wine would be great. Are you sure I'm not disturbing you?' He looked around, as if trying to gauge whether he was truly welcome.

Sarah shook her head. 'No, not at all. It's really nice to see you. Bit chaotic at the moment I'm afraid. I've only got tumblers.'

'That will be just fine.' He looked around. There was a little burr of discomfort as they felt their way forward, the conversation couched in social niceties and clichés as they looked at each other in the lamp light. 'Nice place, great setting too. It's really cosy and homely already.'

She motioned Adam to sit and handed him the glass. Silence took over and intensified, punctuated by the stove ticking and clicking, and briefly their fingertips touched. It was like brushing a live wire. Sarah looked at Adam again and saw with a shiver that he had felt it too; whatever it was, it was most definitely still there, alive and as dangerous and compelling as ever – as if she hadn't known. Seeing him standing in the doorway had made her stomach flutter and her pulse change gear.

'I thought you might like this for your new home,' he said very evenly, handing her a long flat parcel. Sarah recognised the shape immediately.

'Oh Adam,' she said, unwrapping the pen and ink from the summer exhibition. 'Thank you – but I can't.'

He reddened. 'Please, I'd really like you to have it. And when you're settled, I mean, God, this is really difficult to say without sounding crass – I was wondering, could we go out, do something, you know, if you'd like to.'

Sarah propped the picture up against the wall, trying very hard not to meet his eye.

'I've got just the place for this in the sitting room.'

He was on his feet now not more than a yard away from her.

'Have I offended you?'

'No, not at all, I'm flattered. But it may take a while for me to answer. I'm not sure how long to be honest. I don't want to make any promises that I can't keep, Adam. I'm not sure exactly what I am or who I am and although part of me is scared another part of me is looking forward to finding out.'

Adam Gregory smiled, his expression warm and humorous in the soft lamp light. 'I can wait,' he said, and easing closer, kissed her gently. It was a kiss that promised much but demanded nothing.

Sarah pulled away, feeling hot and flustered.

'You want to share my supper?' she asked, trying to subvert the wave of desire that rolled up through her.

Adam grinned and settled himself back at the table. 'I thought you'd never ask.'

Just Desserts

Sue Welfare

Katherine Bourne has been a member of that endangered species, the full-time housewife, for over twenty years, but things have finally turned sour. When she disembowels her delicious home-grown tomatoes, she dreams of murdering her husband. Why can't Harry have an affair with a younger woman and just leave, like normal men?

But Harry has no intention of giving up his home comforts; he's been sampling forbidden fruit for a long while. Glamorous banker Carol accompanies him on weekend trips and business beanos, but she too is beginning to find that the pleasure's growing stale.

So who's fooling who? Harry, happy in his illusion that he's a sex god and that all his women love him really? Katherine and Carol, unlikely partners in Harry's parallel lives?

Against a background of succulent suppers, cosy Cambridge cafés and the unexpected joys of unexplored freedom, the women decide that revenge is a dish best eaten cold. And discover the perfect recipe . . .

ISBN 0 00 649993 7